NO SUN
UNDER THE MOUNTAIN

NEF HOUSE PUBLISHING

NO SUN
UNDER THE MOUNTAIN

DEAD AGAIN: BOOK ONE

BRUCE JAMISON

CHAPTER 1

Magic is neither good nor evil. It is a force of nature that can be used as a tool or a weapon. Flames can roast a boar large enough to feed an entire village. That same fire can burn down the mightiest forest. Water can quench a drowning man's thirst as it pulls him below its surface. As with nature, magic exists to be used and controlled. That was what the Scholars from the Citadel taught the Acolytes on their monthly visits to the Bastion.

Such arrogance . . . Jacoby's thoughts distilled into palpable resentment for the lecturers. He'd seen the destructive force of a tornado, but he'd never seen one turn an entire nation into a graveyard. Countless souls in this damned mountain existed in an undead hell, and to call that evil magic nothing more than a tool was beyond disrespectful to their memory.

But who was he to turn up his nose at the use of magic? Jacoby had spent decades perfecting his own spells and Abilities. He couldn't be mad at the Scholars' ignorance, either. They taught his Acolytes much like they would teach other academics, focusing on ambiguous theory and leaving out practical application. What made them think reading a few books gave them a proper understanding of the nature of magic? They had never set foot in the world's largest crypt, the ossuary Jacoby knew better than the rooms in his own home.

Two young Acolytes trotted quickly just a few paces in front of him. Usually, there would be a third, but only eleven had passed the final trial of the Bastion a week earlier. The other teams of four, three Junior Acolytes and a Master Instructor each, had entered the underground city from different locations. Jacoby and his two students would follow the standard plan for the soldiers' first time through and would rally later that day at the large ramp on the far end of the cavern before proceeding down to the second level.

Skid and Flash kept up the quick pace, their heads on a swivel and their weapons ready. Those weren't their real names, of course, but the nicknames they had earned during their training that would stick with them for a few years until they were promoted.

They had been selected from among the ranks of ordinary soldiers based on their performance and put through months of rigorous training before earning the title: Acolyte. They were still normal humans, but the years of training that were to follow would turn them into the elite fighting force that protected the nation of Ikrit.

Their armor clinked softly, and the pad of their boots on the sand thumped along with their synchronized steps. The young men were far too loud, Jacoby thought with a smile. He couldn't fault the soldiers for their inexperience with the heavy training gear, but after a few lessons learned the hard way, they would take more time to cinch up their armor and soften their steps.

Skid was tall and thin, a fair-skinned boy from one of the poorer districts of Ikrit City. He was scrappy, but his Strength was low; he hadn't put on enough muscle to have much force behind his attacks, and he could easily be thrown off-balance due to his high center of gravity. Luckily for him, his Mobility and Perception were high enough to compensate, and he could often outmaneuver stronger foes. He earned the name "Skid" after one of the morning mountain runs when he slipped down a rocky incline and lost a considerable amount of skin from his hands and knees.

Flash was a few inches shorter than Skid but had him outweighed by at least thirty pounds. The long-haired farmhand with sun-darkened skin was from a prosperous rural district outside Ikrit City. His life of heavy labor and a good food supply had grown him into a solid wall of a teenager. Unfortunately, he used his brawn instead of his brain to handle most situations. That was how he got his nickname–he had set himself ablaze one night trying to start a fire. He'd gotten so focused on banging his axe against his flint and producing as many sparks as he could that he didn't notice that the pine needles around him, and subsequently his pants, had caught fire.

The two young men were so different that they began their training hating each other. Insults would fly, and the exchange would end with Flash pummeling Skid, but not before the lanky youth had bloodied the nose or blackened an eye of his heavier opponent.

The Instructors thought both would drop out from their inability to get along. After all, working as a cohesive unit to defeat the stronger monsters in the lower caverns was paramount. If they didn't work together, they would die separately, as Jacoby liked to tell them. Strangely, something clicked between them one day, and they instantly became close friends. Skid's cunning and speed perfectly complemented Flash's clout and stamina, propelling them to the top of the class.

They both wore the red tunics of the Ikritian army on top of their heavy platemail. Large white shields, each crossed by a sword and scroll, emblazoned their backs. The shield signified the mission of the Bastion: to train the advanced soldiers, known as Acolytes, in defense of the Ikritian empire. The sword symbolized power, and the scroll represented knowledge, the two cornerstones of Acolyte training.

The crest of the Ikritian empire was sewn on their right shoulders in the form of three overlapping circles. The circle on top looked like a ring of fire and represented the military. The circle on the bottom left was in the shape of a barley wreath that stood for the empire's prosperous farmland, and the final circle on the bottom right was a series of interlocking hands which stood for the nation's inhabitants. The triangle in the middle of the overlapping circles contained a single, smaller circle representing their leader, Lord Stavros, who protected their nation from the dangers of the mountain they had just entered and the threats of the foreign nations that sought to destroy them. The Acolytes were the Great Lord's premier weapon, but like any tool of war, they required a certain amount of forging and sharpening to reach their potential.

The platemail the Acolytes wore under their tunics, as well as their helmets and heavy boots, was more for training than for defense, as the weight made it difficult to move quickly. Jacoby focused on their bulky armor and activated one of his Drift Amulet's enchantments, ensuring the Junior Acolytes hadn't accidentally left out any heavy plates.

Assess

Item: Acolyte Platemail (Uncommon)
Description: Armor, Heavy Plate. Standard training armor for Junior

Acolytes (Physical Resistance 4, STR -2, MOB -3, STR and MOB advancement +20%). Hardness 10, Structure 40/40

Good, Jacoby thought with a pleasant smile. The structure would have been reduced had they removed pieces of the plate or had it been damaged. The heavy armor would slow them down, but the Strength and Mobility they'd gain from training with it would be substantial.

Jacoby didn't bother to identify the rest of their ensemble, as he could clearly see it. Both soldiers carried the large kite shields and had their swords drawn, eagerly anticipating their first battle. Blades were less effective against skeletons than the wooden or metal clubs that were typically used to clear out the city streets, but in the end, they were training to fight humans, so they'd left the clubs behind. Strapped to the thick leather belts at their waists, they carried small packs of rations and water as well as two healing crystals each.

Each Acolyte wore their Drift Amulet on a metal chain around their neck. The Drift Amulets were the precious treasures of the Ikritian Empire, created from highly refined flow crystals. The oval charms were blue on the right half and red on the left, displaying the current mental and physical state of the Acolytes. The crystals also displayed a transparent 1 for each soldier, showing they had not gained any Soul Essence toward their next Tier. Jacoby knew that would change in a few seconds as they rounded the next corner and encountered their first set of enemies, but he wasn't about to let his trainees in on that secret.

Jacoby's raiment was quite different from that of the Junior Acolytes. He wore the same tunic, but the bottom fringe had interlocking circles to represent his rank of Master Instructor. Skid and Flash's tunics only had one small stripe for Junior

Acolyte on the bottom. He also had no shield or helmet and wore enchanted chainmail underneath his tunic. His magic-absorbing short sword was still in its sheath at his left hip, and the leather bandolier around his chest had about twenty slots filled with various colored crystals, each containing different powerful spells. Finally, the Drift Amulet around his neck displayed the number **32**. The number was mostly transparent except for the bottom quarter, which was black, indicating that he had only absorbed a relatively small amount of soul energy since achieving his latest Tier. He activated his Drift Amulet's second divinity enchantment with minimal mental effort.

Status

Translucent glyphs and numerals appeared at the periphery of his vision, showing a description of his Status as numerical values. They didn't obscure his sight, and the information they provided was crystal clear, allowing him to simultaneously focus on the glyphs and the Acolytes in front of him. At the top of his vision, the number **32** was inscribed in an oval, almost as though carved from physical stone. A red bar extended to the circle's left and a blue bar to the right, mimicking the information displayed on the Amulet around his neck.

Name: Jacoby Karanos

Race: Human

Tier: 32

Health: 384/384

Vitus: 412/412

Attributes:

STR: 42

MOB: 29

FOR: 63

ACU: 62
PER: 31
RES: 36

No glyphs or numerals showed on his right. That area would notify him of any Status changes or effects such as Tier gains, inflictions from enemy Abilities, or boosts gained from spells in the heat of combat. Three boxes rested at the bottom of his view to allow him to review or modify his Status if he focused on them. They were labeled *Abilities, Damage Resistances,* and *Active Effects.* He had a few minutes before the action would start for his students, so he mentally selected the *Resistances* box.

Physical: 12
    Slashing +2
    Piercing -1
Environmental: 4
    Cold +2
    Lightning -1
    Heat -1
    Poison +2
Magical: 5
    Mental +1

Derived from his Attributes and magical Abilities and bolstered by his equipment, Resistances showed how much damage of certain types he could withstand before losing points of Health. The minor enchantments from the Drift Amulet would have seemed simple to the untrained eye, but the advantage that came from understanding one's own body and mind, as well as the surrounding world, was immense.

Dismiss

The display faded. It wouldn't distract him, and some Acolytes left it in their vision at all times, but Jacoby preferred a clear field of view instead of the jumbled information provided by the Drift Amulet.

He kept a second Amulet tucked inside his left boot. The Amulet was special to him because his children had set it in silver and engraved his name on the back as a gift for his birthday several years earlier. He felt it was far safer inside the leather bindings of his greaves than dangling about his neck. Also, keeping a second Drift Amulet on his person was a technique given to him by the Bastion's leader, Commander Cirilo, when Jacoby first became an instructor. It seemed odd when he'd heard the advice, but on several occasions, he had to give it to a first-time Junior Acolyte who lost theirs.

Skid and Flash would hopefully reach Tier **5** today and receive the accompanying boost to their Attributes—Strength, Mobility, and Fortitude for their bodies, and Acumen, Perception, and Resolve for their minds. After that, the Tiers would become exponentially harder to achieve, requiring more Soul Essence from stronger foes. Jacoby had been training Junior Acolytes for over twenty years and wanted to reach Tier **35** before hanging up his sword. Before he reached those heights, there would be several more years of battling through weak skeletons with new Acolytes.

Tier **32** was respectable but not legendary. His grandfather had reached **39**, and his father was one of only five warriors to ever break into the forties. Sadly, both had been slaughtered on the lower levels, each on separate expeditions nearly ten years apart but in the same location. Neither of their parties had survived, so both teams were still down there. They could be considered enemies now, as the deadly magic of the mountain would have resurrected their bodies and poisoned their minds so that they would attack any Acolyte who ventured close.

Jacoby had never been down far enough to look for his father or grandfather, though he had seen the horrors of resurrection magic hundreds of times. The bodies of vanquished foes would slowly reform and pull themselves back together. It usually took a few days, but the abominations were technically immortal. No amount of muscle or magic could stop them from coming back. As the only silver lining, the curse provided an endless source of training and Soul Essence for Acolytes, and he was more than happy to be their guide through the massive underground caverns.

Massive didn't even begin to describe it. The location was a city-state built inside an entire mountain range over thousands of years. The once-prosperous nation of Jallfoss had spent a few millennia excavating stone and precious metals from deep within the mountain and using that stone to build their cities and castles on the cliffs high above. They harnessed lava from deep within the earth to power their machines and uncovered entire ecosystems in hidden caverns. They even had farms, mostly of mushrooms and lichen, that could feed their vast population. Tens of thousands of humans, elves, dwarves, gnomes, orcs, and several less-common races once called the underground world their home.

Sadly, Jallfoss's industrial progress had been their downfall. One hundred years earlier, the miners searching for the precious flow crystals dug too deep and released a being of pure evil. The Necromancer, as the Ikritians referred to it, killed all the mountain's inhabitants and cursed them with eternal undead resurrection.

Jallfoss's Empress at the time, Lady Destria, gave her life to banish the Necromancer back to the depths of the mountain, but his evil curse remained. The Ikritian army tried to rescue Jallfoss, but the spell was too powerful, and the rescuers were either killed or pushed back by endless waves of skeletons. Hundreds of Ikritian soldiers would die at the hands of the undead in the century that followed.

Jacoby shook his head. The thought of his father and grandfather dying against those endless waves of undead would forever haunt his mind. Even though he hadn't seen their deaths with his own eyes, he knew how terrible they must have been.

Ten years ago, under the order of Lord Stavros, Jacoby had led a stealth group of elite warriors to the highest castle to dispel the curse. Jacoby lost nearly a dozen of his closest friends on the month-long expedition, and all he found was the ghost of the dead Empress who couldn't be bothered to even acknowledge their presence.

Coming out of his thoughts, Jacoby led the two Acolytes into the seventh-largest cavern of the entire mountain, which was once a bustling city of merchants, food vendors, entertainment venues, and even a gladiator coliseum. The large circular chasm was every bit of three miles wide with about fifty pillars, each a few hundred feet in diameter, holding up the three-hundred-foot ceiling. The underground city stayed almost as bright as a cloudy day thanks to the engineering of a famous dwarf who discovered how to pipe in sunlight to the two dozen or so house-sized globes embedded in the rock ceiling. Jacoby couldn't remember the dwarf's name, probably because dwarven names were gibberish to the human ear, but he remembered hearing that he was the same engineer who created the nearly indestructible automatons below. The metal and stone monstrosities were fueled by fire and a century of neglected maintenance made them unpredictable and extremely dangerous. Even though Jacoby had passed his second

Threshold in both Fortitude and Acumen, he wouldn't want to face a dwarven construct without an army of Senior Acolytes at his back. Skid and Flash had many years of training ahead of them before they would be strong enough to face monsters like that.

They entered through one of only three tunnels to the dead nation. All three went to the ground-level metropolis, so they would have to cross the city if they wanted to get to the vast, curving ramps that made up the entire back wall of the cavern to go up or down to the next cities.

The team of soldiers was nearly at the end of the half-mile passage that led to one of the housing districts. The thirty-foot tunnel had a smooth stone floor covered by about an inch of sand. The walls were streaked with veins of different minerals but were otherwise featureless, save for the occasional empty metal sconce.

Jacoby made out the first few buildings a hundred yards from the tunnel's exit. Most of the structures of the central city followed a similar theme: flat, square walls made from large sandstone blocks with flat wooden roofs. The former residents were not worried about rain, but surprisingly, the structures would lead one to believe that there was also little fear of a rock dislodging from the tall ceiling above and crushing anything below. Jacoby assumed that after a few thousand years, the engineers had solved the problem, or perhaps every rock that could have fallen already had.

The trio continued their brisk jog, nearing the end of the tunnel. Jacoby could almost feel their excitement when the young Acolytes saw their first enemies. Their pace quickened, and their bodies lowered like two hunting wolves stalking their prey. Jacoby had witnessed the scene play out before him dozens of times, and his students' first kills always brought him deep joy and satisfaction. Up ahead, he saw the skeletal forms of the two tunnel guards looming at their eternal post.

The skeletons stood hunched over at awkward angles, staring blankly ahead. They looked like frail, dead tree branches waiting for the slightest breeze to send them tumbling to the ground. The guards wore no armor and had no weapons. The Bastion's Acolytes had long ago stripped anything the undead could use as weapons from the first few levels and stored them in the coliseum to reduce the risk of accidents while maintaining the amount of Soul Essence available.

Jacoby was past the point where one of the skeletons could hurt him. A Fortitude of **63** gave him substantial bonuses to Physical and Elemental Damage Resistance, and enough Health to weather the current cavern's weaker threats. If that wasn't enough, his chainmail was woven with enchanted flow crystals and would stop most non-magical attacks. Only magical weapons and the powerful beasts far above and below could do him harm.

The Acolytes, on the other hand, had absorbed no Soul Essence and were as vulnerable as any average human. Even the slightest nick from a sword could pierce an artery and lead to a fatal hemorrhage without the quick application of a healing crystal or equivalent spell.

The skeletal guards noticed the approaching Acolytes and charged. Jacoby never got used to their unnatural movements. There was no hesitation and no consideration; no plan of attack, just impulse-driven violence. Their bodies straightened, and their arms were raised, reaching toward the young men with icy, dead fingers. Evil magic took the place of muscle to propel rot and bone forward. Their mouths opened, shouting silent screams of murder and hate.

The undead guards had taken only a few steps before

the two Acolytes crashed into them. With mighty downward swings, Skid and Flash crashed through their adversaries, nearly cleaving them in half. As they had been taught, a downward strike from the shoulder, through the spine, and out the ribs did the most damage. Heaps of bones toppled to the ground, rolling just slightly in the sand before coming to a stop.

After months of training at the Bastion, their increased physical Attributes allowed them to slice though the skeletons like scythes through bernelli stalks during the fall harvest. Both soldiers halted in front of their vanquished foes. Skid brought his hand up to his head, still holding his sword, and rubbed his forehead just above his right eye. Flash was taking the event a little harder. His sword fell to the floor, and he dropped to a knee.

Jacoby knew the feeling his students were experiencing would only last a fleeting moment, but the raw hate and rage that came with their first Soul Essence absorption would linger in their minds for years. "It gets easier," Jacoby said, slowing to a walk.

"You weren't lying, sir. The kill was a breeze, but the vileness of its soul was overwhelming," Skid said, turning to face his mentor.

"It . . . it . . . it wanted to tear the flesh from my face. It wanted to devour me," Flash stuttered as he picked up his sword and returned to his feet.

"Yes. It did," Jacoby explained. "Experiencing the final emotions of our fallen enemies is the price we pay to absorb their life force. If you weren't convinced, you should now have no question about the evil of the Necromancer's curse. Speaking of Essence . . ." Jacoby tilted his forehead slightly forward and looked at Skid's neckline. Skid's eyes widened as he reached for his Drift Amulet and lifted it to his face.

Flash grabbed Skid's hands and pulled them down so he could look at the object. "How much did you get?" he asked excitedly.

"Look at your own, dummy. They should be the same," Skid answered, pushing the stocky warrior back.

Flash opened his mouth in a beaming smile like a child who had just realized it was his birthday. He fumbled with his Amulet and focused his eyes as he held it up. "The **1** is half-full!" Flash exclaimed. "It's half-full already!"

A few feet away from the celebrating warrior, skeletal hands emerged from the darkness between two buildings. The hands flashed with a translucent blue flame, and a skeleton lunged from the alley at the unsuspecting Acolyte.

CHAPTER 2

op! Pop! The flames surrounding the skeleton's hands disappeared in flashes of blue light and sharp, loud explosions. The blue flames instantly reappeared around the undead hands and just as quickly vanished in another *Pop! Pop!*

A very un-warrior-like squeak emerged from Flash's mouth as he jumped backward, only to stumble over the pile of bones behind him. He tumbled backward, lashing out with his sword, but his grip failed him, and the weapon flew from his fingertips. His blade clattered harmlessly against a building wall near where the undead mage had emerged.

The blue, flaming fingers reached down to the prone soldier. The skeleton's mouth wrenched open like a snake dislodging its jaw to devour larger prey. Flash saw his own death in the hollow black eyes as he kicked his legs wildly, flailing in a futile attempt to push back his mindless attacker.

The blue flames flickered and died as severed skeletal hands dropped to the sandy ground. Having just dismembered the only apparent weapons from the undead creature, Skid used the momentum from his cleave to spin behind his opponent and slash with enough might to sever the spine in two. Like the other skeletons, this one immediately collapsed, crashing directly on top of the flailing Acolyte. Flash released another squeal, even less masculine than the first, as he struggled to push away the lifeless bones and regain his footing.

He jerked his head from side to side, frantically searching for more hidden enemies. Finally, his eyes came to rest on his compatriot who had just saved his life. Skid held his sword and shield low, staring blankly at the sand as he recovered from his second Soul Essence exchange.

"Ha, ha, ha, ahh lad! I hope the other three teams don't come running, expecting to save a beautiful princess after hearing a squeal like that." Jacoby laughed at Flash as the boy's face turned red in embarrassment.

"I th . . . thought you said there were only basic skeletons on this level. That was a magic user. I could have died!" Flash shouted in defense before he recovered his composure and added the obligatory, "Sir."

"Oh, that's just Blue. He's harmless," Jacoby said, still with a slight chuckle in his voice. "He must have been a mage, but they have no Vitus when they regenerate. The flames and pops were failed spells. Unlike most others, he does wander a bit, so you never know where he'll show up."

Flash lowered his head and furrowed his eyebrows, mentally kicking himself for the apparent lack of bravery.

"Don't worry. There are only two dangerous skeletons on this level. We're not going near the first, and we'll fight the second as a group." Then Jacoby added with a teasing smile, "We'll all be there to protect you, won't we, Skid?"

Skid looked up, regaining his thoughts, and summoning a grin. "The second time was a bit easier." He reached to his neck and lifted his Drift Amulet where he could see. The **1** was now entirely black and slowly pulsing. "Now what?" he asked, looking to his mentor for guidance.

"The Soul Essence is already in you. The Amulet just acts as a conduit to channel the energy into your body. You must understand that it's only showing the wearer's current Status. All you need to do to gain the next Tier is relax and let the energy diffuse through your body. Clear your mind and drop any mental blocks."

Skid did as he was instructed, tilting his head back slightly and drawing in a deep breath. He felt clean, warm energy spread over his skin, like an ocean wave lapping on a beach. The little fatigue he had from the run through the tunnel and the brief battles instantly retreated. He felt strong. He looked down to see the **1** on his soul crystal flash and disappear before being replaced with a transparent **2**.

Jacoby focused on Skid and activated his Amulet's divinity enchantment.

Assess

Name: Skid
Race: Human
Tier: 2
Health: 22/22
Merq: 12/12
Attributes:
    STR: 11
    MOB: 12
    FOR: 8
    ACU: 12
    PER: 8
    RES: 9

The heavy armor had done the trick. Skid had gained two points in Strength and one in Mobility, as well as a single point in Acumen. The Amulet's Ability displayed the boy's moniker, though if Jacoby chose, he could have it show his full name and a much more detailed description of his Status, but he'd already gathered the information needed to see Skid's Tier advance.

"Now," Jacoby said, turning to Flash, "push him as hard as you can."

Flash looked at Skid questioningly, who returned a slight nod, telling him it was fine. He walked over to his fellow warrior, planted both hands firmly on his chest, and shoved with all his might. Flash expected his partner to fly backward after that much effort, even wearing heavy armor. Instead, Skid took one step back, planted his foot, and refused to move another inch.

Now it was Skid's turn. He shoved against the chest plate of the shorter, heavier warrior. Usually, pushing the larger soldier would have been like hitting a brick wall, but Flash had to take three whole steps backward before regaining his footing.

"He's stronger than me," Flash exclaimed, "which means that when I gain a Tier, I'll be unstoppable!" The two warriors clasped each other's forearms as they both laughed and congratulated themselves on their first victory.

Flash pointed to Skid's Drift Amulet. "Can you use your Merq yet?"

"I don't think so, but I'll try," Skid replied, balling his fists and scrunching his face as he tried to concentrate.

"*Merq.*" Jacoby said the word with a chuckle. Every generation seemed to come up with a different word for it. He liked this one more than most because it annoyed the Scholars who wanted the Acolytes to refer to it as the "mental endurance and resiliency quotient." The Junior Acolytes had taken the phrase and shortened it to *Merq.*

Long before the Drift Amulets existed, the few mages of the world who could direct the flow of magic called it *Vitus*. Most people thought that mages had a pool of magic inside them that they could utilize on a whim, but in truth, they only channeled that magic in a process called *flow*.

Vitus, or Merq, represented how much magic you could channel before your mind was too fatigued to operate. Before the Drift Amulets, a mage had to become conscious of his or her Abilities to gauge how much Vitus they had left. Now, they could simply look at the blue section of their Drift Amulets or focus on their visual display to get a good measure.

Likewise, the red section of the Amulets represented the physical state of one's body. The difference, however, was that if your Vitus dropped to zero, it would just leave you mentally exhausted. If your Health dropped to zero, you were dead. The Scholars had taught Skid and Flash the theory behind of the magic of the Drift Amulets. Now it was time for them to learn the item's application through firsthand experience, which meant fighting hundreds of undead on their way to the far side of the city.

"No time to waste, boys," Jacoby said, drawing his sword as he walked past the two Junior Acolytes. "We're just getting started. Let's practice by clearing this row of houses before we move any further."

The two set off at a sprint, completely passing the first door on their left. Jacoby chuckled to himself and shook his head. Those two had so much to learn, but at least their abundance of enthusiasm made up for their lack of knowledge and experience.

I might as well clear a few houses while I let the boys have some fun, he thought as he approached the entrance to the house the Acolytes had just run past. He knew two skeletons were inside because he had killed them several times before. The door had long ago fallen off its rusted metal hinges and lay broken on the ground. The two soldiers running in front of the door would have alerted the waiting skeletons, but only for a moment. The things operated on line of sight alone, and once they could no longer see something, they would lose interest and go about their busy day of not moving and staring a hole into whatever was in front of them.

Jacoby walked calmly through the stone doorway. The wooden ceiling had caved in slightly more than he had remembered, and the ladder that once led up through an opening had collapsed entirely and lay broken against the left wall. The room was about twenty feet wide and twice as deep with smooth sandstone walls. The back wall was covered in dark scorch marks that had faded over the century. The only objects in the room were an old stone hearth, broken dwarven plumbing, some rotting wooden furniture, and two angry-looking skeletons.

"Morning, gents! Glad to see you're well," Jacoby greeted as the two skeletons charged forward. The taller one on the left was always the fastest, so he dispatched it first. He grabbed its outstretched right wrist with his left hand and simultaneously booted it square in the chest. It hit the wall at enough of an angle that it rolled and slid more than impacted. That one had always been resilient and would take a second hit to kill.

He cocked his arm and launched his enchanted sword with a backhand throw at the second skeleton. The blade pierced its skull and was buried clean to the hilt. His assailant dropped to its knees and face-planted with a crunch as the sword drove further through its head, coming to rest with the blade sticking straight up in the air. Jacoby let the wave of hatred wash over him as he absorbed the minuscule amount of Soul Essence.

The first skeleton had recovered from the blow and

launched itself at him once again. Jacoby stepped to his right to avoid the rush and raised his fist high in the air to crush the skeleton's spine as it lunged past. That was his intent, had his equipment cooperated.

As he stepped to his right, two lower buckles on his boot gave way and snapped. His foot caught the stone floor, but his momentum forced his body to continue, rolling his ankle and making him stumble. A flash on his right side indicated that his Drift Amulet had a notification to show him, but he ignored it, knowing that it was little more than a notice for a sprained ankle.

He hadn't moved out of the way fast enough, and the skeleton barreled into him, latching on with its remaining appendages and spinning him to his left. As he twisted, the monster snapped its jaws, aiming at the flesh of his unprotected throat. Jacoby jerked his head back, throwing himself further off-balance. He had prevented the skeleton from getting a windpipe snack, but instead, the skull clamped down on his Drift Amulet, ripping it from his neck.

The skeleton flailed again, increasing the momentum of the spin. With his rolled ankle, Jacoby could no longer keep his balance and fell straight forward, crushing both skeletons beneath his weight. He had the awareness to realize that the first skeleton had not yet expired and was craning its neck to try and bite his ear. He still held its arm in his left hand, so he jammed the broken wristbone in the creature's mouth. More notifications flashed into view, but he ignored them as well.

He pushed away from the ground with his right arm to get enough space so he could bring an elbow down on his adversary's skull and crush it. As he planted his hand, it slipped out from under him, causing him to crash down on the bones once again.

"How is the stone slippery?" he wondered as he looked down to his right. The growing pool of blood he saw answered his question, and he finally allowed the notifications to display.

Status Effects:
>   **Injury: Ankle Sprain (Minor): MOB -10%, STR -5%**
>   **Injury: Bleeding (Severe): STR -10%, FOR -20%, RES, -20%**
>   **Injury: Nerve Damage (Severe): STR -50%, MOB -50%, FOR -50%**

The bleeding wasn't good, but the last notification shocked him. He'd never seen nerve damage in his Status before. *No skeleton bones could possibly pierce my armor or even my skin. It would have to be magic—*

For the first time in many years, Jacoby felt fear. His own sword had gone right through his torso, and he would soon bleed to death if he didn't cast a healing spell or activate a healing crystal. He tried to bring his legs underneath him so he could get away from the sword and the relentless skeleton, but his legs wouldn't respond for some reason. The blade must have severed the nerves in his back and left him half-paralyzed.

Jacoby's situation was bad, but he knew a healing spell should buy him enough time to kill the skeleton and call for help. He focused his magic reserves into a single point, visualizing warm golden light pouring from his core, and directed that energy to the sword wound. He expected to feel warmth and a bit of pain as his body stitched itself back together, but he only heard a loud *pop!* from the wound.

His display had manifested into view when the first notification appeared, but he had been ignoring it. Now he saw that his red health bar was less than a third full, and his blue Vitus bar was at zero. The sword had completely drained his magic and caused his healing spell to fail.

Status

Health: 112/384

Vitus: 0/412

Status Effect:

Injury: Blood Loss (Severe): STR -10%, PER -30%, FOR -30%

His vision started to blur, and he was losing the feeling in his fingers. His Acolytes were too far away. His only hope was to activate a healing crystal. Jacoby reached with his right hand to his bandolier, hoping to pick the right crystal, but the skeleton wrenched its leg and clamped down, pinning his arm to his side, and driving the sword further into his gut.

He'd lost the Strength to hang onto the bone in the skeleton's mouth. He could no longer see, and his body had gone cold. What a fitting way to die, battling in the dungeon he had spent his whole life exploring. In his final moments, he regretted not finding his father and grandfather. He would neither make it to the Source Crystal nor destroy the Necromancer and break the curse.

CHAPTER 3

"**N**o time to waste, boys. We're just getting started. Let's practice by clearing this row of houses before we move any further." The skeleton heard the words, but they were lost in the fog of its mind. It could have happened that very moment, it could have happened years ago, or never at all. There was no way to tell.

It saw the reddish-brown sandstone that made up the floor and walls of the room in which it resided. It saw the building across the sandy street through the stone doorway. It could also see the skeleton to its left, standing motionless and surrounded by a faint, green aura. It looked similar to colors diffusing from a tea bag when it was first dropped into hot water, lingering and insubstantial, like the slightest breeze would disperse them through the room.

"How can I see without eyes and hear without ears?" was a question the skeleton would never ask itself. It didn't even realize that it was a skeleton, let alone that it lacked any semblance of sensory organs. No thoughts existed in its mind, only the slightest awareness of the world around it. It just waited, not caring what it was waiting for.

"Henry!" A woman's cry pierced the blank mind of the skeleton like a spider's fangs pumping venom into a fat, juicy beetle. The shout was accompanied by a whirlwind of sensations both foreign and familiar. As quickly as the thoughts and feelings came, they dissolved back into the nothingness of its mind, leaving no trace of their existence in the skeleton's memory. It was empty again, but only for a moment.

A burst of red aura filled its vision as two humans sprinted in front of the open doorway. The aura of the intruders was more tangible than the green mist encircling its quiet friend. The humans seemed like the end of a torch, surrounded by a glowing blaze bright enough to draw the skeleton's full attention. The red aura saturated the undead creature with hate and the uncontrollable desire to destroy the trespassers.

Its neck bones creaked as its head turned to focus on the targets, but they were gone as quickly as they had appeared. The feeling of hate and malice faded from its awareness, and the fog of its blank mind returned, halting the attack before it had a chance to start.

It didn't notice the aura of the third human until his body came into view through the stone entrance, but at that moment, it permeated the entire room. The red blaze radiated from his body in waves filling every corner of its vision. The creature didn't possess the logic to derive the ratio of aura size to potential strength. If it had, the information would have given the skeleton pause. Instead, its mind filled with hate once again as it prepared to welcome the guest into its home with all the hospitality of a starving piranha.

"Morning, gents! Glad to see you're well," the human roared, flashing his teeth in a confident smile. The skeleton didn't return his greeting. It wasn't the slightest bit happy to see him.

There was no hesitation in the attack, not a moment spent planning or analyzing, just bones flying toward their target's throat, trying to catch up to the malicious intent. The skeleton lunged forward and cleared the distance between itself and the intruder in a few quick steps.

The human turned his eyes toward the attacker and booted the skeleton in the chest, sending it flying in the direction from which it had just charged. The skeleton didn't notice its arm was still in the human's hand as it impacted the wall and spun twice before skidding to a stop on the ground.

A cracked sternum and a missing arm didn't stop the creature from returning to its feet. Bone fragments chipped and fell to the floor as the creature returned to its full height. It saw the aura of its fellow skeleton suck into its body and vanish, like watching someone blow smoke from a pipe in reverse. The other skeleton dropped to its knees and fell forward, the blade of a sword protruding two feet from the back of its head.

The skeleton didn't acknowledge the death of its friend. It only lunged forward again with the same vigor and intent of the first attack. Just a few feet from impact, the human shifted a foot to the skeleton's left, almost enough to avoid the attack. Almost.

The two collided and spun through the room. The skeleton tried to bite the face of the intruder but only managed to get a mouth full of the pendant around the man's neck. The skeleton thrashed with its remaining limbs until the human fell to the ground, crushing both the attacking skeleton and its lifeless partner under the weight of his body and armor.

The skeleton's remaining hand had become stuck under the human's body, but its legs and skull were still free to attack. The human jammed the skeleton's own wristbone in its mouth as it tried to bite and kick. The soldier tried to push away, but he eventually collapsed, letting the bone drop to the floor. The skeleton continued thrashing and gnawing until the red aura of the trespasser faded away.

—

The burning rage, fueled by the representation of the human's Essence, quickly faded, only to be replaced by the first real emotion that the skeleton had felt in over a hundred years: a deep, hollow regret. It saw images of the human's lineage slain by monsters in the catacombs below. It also witnessed a scene of a gigantic crystal jutting from the floor of an open cavern, glimmering with all the colors imaginable, reflected from a light source that seemed to originate within the shining geode itself. These weren't memories the human had experienced but rather things he had mentally created and latched onto. The images faded, but the feeling lingered for a few moments longer. Then the skeleton was aware.

"Henry!" A woman's cry rippled through the skeleton's bones like a rock being thrown into a calm mountain lake and jolted its entire being into the present moment. The decaying wooden rafters above and the surrounding brown-red sandstone walls slowly came into focus. Words, numbers, and flashing glyphs appeared at the edges of its vision, but it was too overwhelmed with fresh sensations to focus on them.

The skeleton moved its head as it tried to make sense of the environment. It was startled to find a man lying on top of its body, pinning it to the ground. The man had short, sandy-blond hair with a small bald spot at the crown. What first appeared to be freckles turned into tiny flecks of blood spattered on the man's head.

The skeleton tried to push the man off but only managed

to adjust his body to the side. It saw what looked to be claw marks on the man's face, as well as chunks of flesh torn from below his left eye. Maybe from a scavenging animal of some sort? *No*, the skeleton thought, the blood hadn't clotted, and there were no signs of animals in the vicinity.

The man wore a red tunic covering expensive chainmail. A double-edged blade protruded from the man's back, and he appeared to be lying in a pile of human bones. That was when the skeleton noticed those bones were its own body.

The creature panicked and let out a cry more like a scared beast than a human. It shifted back and forth, eventually rolling the dead body to the side and scooting its mangled bones from underneath. The sword protruding through the man's back was lodged in the skeleton's ribs and pulled from the man's gut with a sickening slurp.

With the sword still embedded in its chest, the skeleton lifted itself to a sitting position, but its legs were too mangled to allow it to stand. It scanned the stone room and tried to make sense of the mess. When the skeleton turned its head, a loud jingle resonated through its skull. It reached up to its mouth, pausing to examine its trembling bony fingers. A few molars and one sharp incisor fell to the floor when it pulled out the Drift Amulet. As the Amulet moved around in the light, it saw that the right half was clear and the left half had just a tiny sliver of crimson that came up to the bottom of a black, flashing **1**.

A translucent glyph in the shape of an eye appeared over the sword. The skeleton focused on the glyph, not sure why it could look like it was carved from stone but not obstruct his sight. As if responding to his focus, the glyph flashed, then faded, quickly replaced by words that described the item in its skeletal hand.

Item: Drift Amulet (Epic)

Description: Accessory (Enchanted). Ikritian item crafted from a rare flow crystal

Abilities:

> **Essence Siphon III. Transfer Soul Essence of defeated enemies to advance the user's Tier**
>
> **Assess I. Display basic information about items and beings. This Ability scales with use and Tier**

The words faded from its view. The **1** disappeared and was replaced with a translucent **2**, which quickly filled with black and began flashing. Then, in the same way, a **3** replaced the **2** and filled about three-quarters of the way up with black.

The skeleton's bones vibrated and creaked as they ground against each other. It watched in amazement as its body repaired itself and the bones shifted into what looked like the original positions. There was a shaking hand and wristbone on the ground that belonged on the creature's right arm. It leaned over slightly and touched its hanging upper arm bone to the forearm on the floor. The elbow snapped together and fused into a moveable joint. The skeleton sensed pressure as the bones mended together, though, surprisingly, no pain or other sensations accompanied the reconstruction.

Fingers clinched and flexed as the skeleton tested the function of the reunited hand before turning its attention back to the pendant. It marveled at the jewel, watching as the left filled with a brilliant crimson. "Alright, this thing is useful," the skeleton said out loud, surprising itself as the unfamiliar voice resonated in its head.

The shock from the unexpected sound sent a wave of

exhilarating energy through its body, and the numerals and glyphs at the far edges of its vision flashed and came into sharp focus. So many new sights and sensations were bombarding the skeleton that its mind spun in muddled confusion.

One thing at a time. Just breathe.

The mental pep talk calmed the skeleton's frayed nerves, though it chose to ignore the fact that its rib cage rose and fell without lungs or an accompanied airflow.

Focus . . . you. Whatever your . . . my name is.

It swiped its hand through the air, trying to push away the letters and numbers, but the skeleton couldn't interact with them. The information at the top of his vision resembled what he saw in the Amulet: a circle that looked like it was etched in stone contained a nearly full **3** with a red bar extending from the left. There was a definite connection between the jewel in its hand and the strange messages before its eyes, but that did little to explain why he was a living skeleton.

The characters on the left clearly described him, but there was a series of three letters followed by numbers that didn't make sense. With a little mental effort, the letters expanded into full words.

Name: Unknown
Race: Skeleton
Tier: 3
Health: 36/36
Unknown: 0/15
Attributes:
  Strength: 12
  Mobility: 14
  Fortitude: 10
  Acumen: 10

Perception: 12

Resolve: 14

Without a frame of reference, the numbers meant little, and the skeleton had no idea what to do with them. More glyphs flashed to its right, and it addressed them in the same way it had the left side. The skeleton nearly jumped back as words appeared in front of its face.

Human Killed, Soul Essence Claimed, +2 Tiers:
STR +2, MOB +2, FOR +2, ACU +1, PER +1, RES +2

Status Effects:

    Soul Anchor: +2 Health/Hour

    Skeletal Body: STR -20%, FOR -20%, Damage Resistance: Physical -1 (Bludgeoning -2), Environmental +1, Poison: Immune

Item Ability Discovered: Status I (Drift Amulet). Display basic information about the user. This Ability scales with use and Tier

That's not doing anything for me. The skeleton knew the thought wasn't entirely true. It had been given a wealth of information, but the implication of those words was that it could gain some sort of power from killing humans, and also that it truly was a skeleton. With the same mental steps it used to select the glyphs, it dismissed the information from its view.

I'll figure that out later.

It looked down at the sword lodged in its ribs and jerked it side to side until the blade came free. It examined the sword, quickly recognizing that it was of exceptional quality. The double-edged blade narrowed after the hilt, then smoothly flared out before coming to a sharp point. The cross guard had a multi-faceted gem embedded in the center sparkling with hints of gold and purple in a swirling green cloud. It showed signs of heavy use, but its owner, perhaps the dead man on the floor, had kept it in good repair. The blade was heavy, if not a bit short, but it was well-balanced and felt good in the skeleton's grip.

Another glyph displayed to the right. With a snort of growing annoyance at the continued barrage of notifications, the skeleton selected the glyph.

Assess

Item: Short Sword (Epic)

Description: Weapon (Enchanted). Ikritian xiphos crafted with an extremely rare flow crystal (Legendary)

Epic and *Legendary* told him little more than that the weapon was of higher-than-normal quality, but the indication that the weapon was enchanted made him slightly uneasy. While trying to discern the meaning of the words in relation to the blade, he noticed a blue bar had begun extending from the circle at the top of his vision.

He looked at the pendant in his hand and saw that the right side was quickly filling from the bottom with a blue color, like heated mercury expanding in a thermometer.

Item Ability Discovered: Drain V (Short Sword). Unknown Effect

The skeleton brought itself to its feet. Still examining the sword and Amulet, wracking its brain for any clues to what was going on, all it could remember before waking up under the dead human was feeling that man's regret and the sound of a woman's cry, yelling, "Henry."

"Apparently, I'm a skeleton named Henry," he said to the room, hoping for but not expecting a response, "and I can read dead people's minds. What the hell is going on?" The reply he got was a pad of footsteps and clank of armor coming from just outside the doorway, joined by the voices of two men.

"Maybe Jacoby got tired and went in here to rest," one of the men's voices said.

"He's probably taking a nap," the second replied.

Oh, good, Henry thought. *Maybe these two can explain what's going on.*

The notion of a friendly conversation fizzled from the realm of possibility as the two men stormed into the room with their bright red auras filling Henry's vision. He didn't know these men, but something deep in the animal part of his mind welled up and forced itself to the front of his consciousness. These men were intruders and had to die. Nothing in the world would matter until he ended their lives.

Status Effect: Enraged (Severe)

"Sir, we're both Tier **3**, and Skid gained an Ability . . ." The color from the face of the front man drained as his eyes took in the skeleton and the body of his fallen instructor.

He's barely a man, Henry thought as he looked at the first intruder. His mind seemed to move in slow motion as he took in every detail of the soldier. He wore the same tunic as the dead man on the floor, but the platemail underneath was bulky and didn't fit him well, limiting his mobility. His broad shoulders indicated the youth was robust, but the shaky way he lifted his sword and shield and the unconfident steps of his advance betrayed his inexperience. Henry had no conscious memory of ever being in a sword fight, but his instincts led his attention to every open kill spot on the youth's body—and there were many.

The man drew his sword across his torso, preparing for a heavy backhand attack that would easily cut Henry in two, but in that instant, he exposed an open shoulder. Henry sprang to his left, planted his foot, and drove forward before his opponent could unleash his strike. Henry's blade entered the man's right armpit and exited the left side of his neck, spraying blood and gore into the eyes of the taller soldier behind him. As he removed the blade, he felt a jolt of energy from the hilt spread through his bones. Henry only had an instant to notice it, but the blue bar at the top of his vision had extended all the way to the right.

The boy was dead before his knees hit the ground. His dying thought entered Henry's mind: he was confused as to how a skeleton could move like that. The boy didn't even know he had been killed. The other soldier, however, appeared to have much better battle sense.

Even though his companion's spray of blood temporarily blinded him, he knew where Henry was moving. He slashed the sword erratically to his right while rubbing his eyes on the tunic cloth near his shoulder. From the first swing of his blade, Henry could predict where the attacks would go, so he chose to switch the direction of his movement. Frail bones protested the abrupt shift, and Henry's skeletal body lagged behind his mind, but the overwhelming urge to kill forced the attack nonetheless.

He circled to his right and leapt past the falling body of the first soldier, barely missing the toppling mass as the body dropped forward and its red aura dissipated. He jumped into the air and planted his right foot in the wall, compressing his leg and gathering momentum before springing back into the flailing boy's shield. The impact caught the man off-guard and sent him stumbling into the far wall. Henry was on him in an instant, smashing the shield into bits with two quick swings.

The soldier retaliated with a sideways swipe of his sword that missed Henry as he dodged backward, though the attack was close enough to have cut him, if he had skin.

The man's eyes flashed with anger, and his lips curled into a snarl. "Die, undead scum!" the boy shouted. He gripped his sword in both hands and raised it above his head. The red aura from his body flashed brighter, swirling around him like a fiery tornado. "Mighty Cleave!" He stepped forward to drop a crushing blow down on his opponent.

Fool, Henry thought. He bent his knees and dug his boney toes into the stone floor. The world seemed to slow and his awareness shifted to his own mind. Where one would expect thoughts and memories, only an empty expanse of near-tangible nothingness made up his thoughts, like he'd shoved his head in swamp water at midnight and tried to see the bottom. The harder he focused, the murkier his swampy mind became, but he knew something was just beyond.

Henry pressed his consciousness forward, wading through the nothingness but failing to make much progress.

This is my mind, Henry realized. *Even if there's nothing here, I still control it.* Instead of trying to pull his way forward, Henry focused his will and forced his mind behind him. Somehow, the nothing around him managed to churn. It swirled and blew past him, almost taking him with it, but with another forcing of will, Henry held strong.

Flashes of white lightning lit his surroundings, and Henry burst through the murk. Before him, a blue cloud billowed. There was no perspective on its size; it seemed large enough to fill his mind, yet small enough to be able to fit in the palm of his hand. Arcs of electricity flickered over the cloud's surface, giving it a deep and gray-blue tint.

Even though Henry could clearly see the cloud, he knew he was looking at something deep inside his mind, something that existed at the core of his being. Henry pulled on the cloud. It resisted at first, but then multiple arcs of lightning shot from its surface, filling him with its power. The surge forced Henry back through the empty expanse of his mind and into the red sandstone room. The angry soldier before him brought down his sword with all his might.

Energy thrummed through Henry's body like adrenaline surging through veins that didn't exist. He allowed that force to expend all at once as he shot forward with a lightning-fast thrust.

He landed his attack just a split second before the soldier delivered his blow. Still, the expulsion of energy in his body sent him forward with enough power and speed to lift the soldier off the ground. The blade entered through his mouth, out the back of his skull, and through his metal helmet with only the smallest amount of resistance before embedding into the stone behind him. Henry heard the snap of bones and tendons separating in his neck as the impaled head pulled the rest of the body with it. The boy's sword fell to the floor, and his limbs jerked sporadically as his last few synapses fired before his aura whisked away.

A wave of anger rushed through Henry's mind. The boy's last thought had been the intent to destroy him with a brutal chop, which was apparently the Ability the other soldier had boasted about. It seemed Henry also had a powerful fighting technique. The thrust that had secured Henry's victory felt intuitive but still unnatural at the same time. He mentally searched his body, trying to find the source of that energy, but the cloud had dissipated, like tipping back a bottle of whiskey just to see the last drops fall.

Status Effect: Enraged Removed

Flashing glyphs tried to grab his attention but failed to distract him from the torrent of emotion. Instead, he reached up to the dead soldier to retrieve his sword in case any more trespassers barged into the room. He grabbed the hilt and pulled, releasing the corpse from the wall. The instant he touched his fingers to the hilt, he felt another jolt of energy like the one he felt after killing the first soldier.

He looked down at the Amulet still in his left hand and saw that the right portion was transparent again but quickly filling back to blue. The **3** had turned completely black and was flashing.

This Amulet is much more than a fancy piece of jewelry, Henry thought as he rolled the token over with his fingers. He relaxed and let his rib cage expand, only partially aware that the action failed to pull in a breath. He focused on the **3** as it disappeared and was replaced by a translucent **4**. His bones creaked and hardened, and he felt the well of magical energy inside him grow more extensive. More glyphs flashed, begging for his attention, but he pushed them away. Reading was the last thing he wanted to do at that moment.

He searched his mind for some clue to explain what was happening. *How are this strange Amulet and sword making me stronger when I kill humans? What was that rage that overcame me when I saw their red auras? And why the hell am I a skeleton?* No answers came. His memory was a blank fog, and the harder he tried to concentrate, the more it seemed to dissipate and slip through his grasp. The woman's voice calling his name was the closest thing to a memory he could feel. That, along with the final thoughts of the three dead soldiers, was all his mind could muster. Desperation from the woman's cry, anger from the tall youth, confusion from the other, and regret from the old warrior on the floor.

The regret he felt from the first soldier meant Henry had killed him too.

"The marks on his face and his other wounds were from me. We were fighting," Henry said aloud, more of a question than a statement. The soldiers were his enemies, but he didn't know why.

"The only things I know for sure are that I'm a skeleton named Henry who kills humans," he said to the empty room, "and I'm damn good at it."

CHAPTER 4

Henry needed answers, and the dead soldiers on the floor were unlikely to provide them. He surveyed the bloody room and looked out through the open doorway. He saw a sandy street in the dim light with blocky, red sandstone buildings on the other side. *I must be in a city, maybe around dawn or dusk*, he thought. He needed to venture outside but had no idea how dangerous it could be.

"Apologies, gents, but I need your gear more than you," Henry said to the dead men. He began stripping off their armor and sorting their belongings.

Scattered around the old soldier were skeleton bones that didn't belong to Henry. A green mist formed around the pile as he examined them. It resembled the red aura from the soldiers that drove him to violence but was much more faint, and it didn't seem to evoke a reaction from his subconscious. A quick movement grabbed his attention as one of the bones skidded a few inches across the floor and connected to the end of another, forming a joint. A glyph appeared over the bones, similar to the identify glyph, but the eye squinted a bit more, like it was evaluating the bones.

Not understanding what the Attributes and their corresponding numbers meant frustrated Henry. He forced his will
into the Amulet, almost demanding it provide him a better
explanation. The Amulet resisted for a moment, but then, to
Henry's surprise, it gave in and the information before his eyes
expanded.

Assess

Name: Unknown
Race: Skeleton
Health: Low
Magic: None
Attributes:
    Strength - STR: 4
    Mobility - MOB: 5
    Fortitude - FOR: 4
    Acumen - ACU: 0
    Perception - PER: 12
    Resolve - RES: 0

Each Attribute was a physical or mental characteristic,
though the associated numbers meant little to Henry. "I have
too many of my own problems to try and figure out yours," he
said to the moving bones, "but it looks like you're sorting yourself out just fine." It could have been his imagination, but as he
worked, the green aura spread to the three dead men as well.

The heavy platemail of the younger soldiers was too bulky
to allow him full Mobility, so Henry elected to don the chainmail of the older warrior. The description offered by the
Amulet's Assess Ability gave little more insight than it had for
the blade, but he could tell the chain was of much higher quality than the plate, even with sword holes in the front and back.

Over the chain, he draped the red tunic of the taller youth, as it had the least amount of blood of the three, then secured it with a leather belt and two of the leather pouches.

Henry examined the waterskins, pieces of dried meat, and packs of mixed nuts but discarded them when he decided that a skeleton lacking a stomach did not need snacks. He did, however, elect to keep the four red crystals that he identified as flow crystals from the young soldiers as well as a few daggers, strips of leather, flint and steel, and other essential fieldcraft items.

Around the necks of each of the boys, Henry found pendants that matched the one he pulled from his mouth. The two pendants were clear with transparent 1s on them, but when Henry removed the necklaces, he noticed that they filled with red and blue, and the clear 1s changed to 4s. He stored the two pendants safely in his pack and tied his own firmly inside his rib cage with a few leather strips. The act of reaching inside his own body to affix an accessory felt unnatural, but he quickly dismissed the reservation and decided to take advantage of his skeletal existence any way he could.

He took the taller soldier's leather boots and bracers, but he had to stuff both with strips from the tunics to make them fit properly. He did the same with the helmet from the shorter boy to keep it secure to his skull without rattling. The other two blades from the young soldiers looked dull and chipped, so he decided to leave them, but he did pick up the one unbroken shield and steadied it in his left grip.

He fastened the older warrior's scabbard on his belt and cleaned the blood from the enchanted sword before sheathing it. Though his mind lacked any hint of his past, his bones felt very familiar with weaponry, almost like the blade was an extension of his own body. That subconscious knowledge had aided him greatly in the fight, and he wondered what other hidden expertise lay buried in his foggy mind.

He raised his shield, drew his sword, and mimed a series of slashes, thrusts, and shield bashes against an imaginary enemy. The shield and short sword combination felt familiar and comfortable to him, like he had practiced with it thousands of times, but the mind fog still blocked any recollection of *how* he knew to use either. He wanted to say it was muscle memory but didn't feel he could credit the few stringy tendons on his bones with such knowledge.

Finally, he strapped the leather bandolier holding a dozen or so variously colored crystals tightly around his torso. Each crystal swirled with different colors of magic. One was purple and looked like it held a lightning storm. Another was orange with a small burning flame. Some were red or blue with tiny spinning clouds inside them, just like the four he had stored in his belt pouches. Even if he'd had his memory, Henry felt he would have known next to nothing about magic. Still, he recognized that the items would be valuable one way or another.

Assess

Item: Flow Crystal (Uncommon)

Description: Consumable (Enchanted). Unknown magical properties

Consume an unknown magical item? Not today, Drift Amulet. He carefully replaced the Shard, wary of its nonspecific description.

He had no mirror to review his ensemble, but he hoped the tunic, shield, and helmet would disguise his skeletal frame long enough to give him a few seconds of advantage against any enemies he might encounter. A pulsing glyph in his periphery forced his focus away from his equipment.

The glyphs were persistent. He'd dismissed them several times, but every few minutes they would reappear in his vision. Their cries for attention made him want to ignore them out of principle, but eventually he gave in.

Human Killed x2, Soul Essence Claimed, +1 Tier:
STR +1, MOB +1, FOR +1, ACU +2, PER +1

Ability Discovered: Thrust I. Harness magical energy to power bursts of strength and speed

He'd suspected the blue cloud in his core was a store of magical energy, and the Ability's description seemed to confirm it. Though he had to admit, having a magical lightning storm inside him was even more unsettling than strapping magical crystals to his chest. Curiosity replaced his unease as he observed the effects of his Tier increase.

Status

Name: Henry
Race: Skeleton
Tier: 4
Health: 33/33
Magic: 24/24
Attributes:
    STR: 16
    MOB: 15
    FOR: 13
    ACU: 12
    PER: 13
    RES: 14

He was stronger. Everything had increased except his Resolve, but he wasn't sure how that differed from Fortitude. That was a question for later, and he was eager to leave the tiny dwelling.

One last look around the room revealed that his skeleton companion was indeed reforming itself at a glacial pace. Several bones rattled and repositioned themselves into the beginnings of a whole skeleton. The green mist around the bones had grown into a faint swirling aura, and more auras were clearly forming around the bloody soldiers. "You four get along until I come back, or I'll bust your heads open again," Henry said to the corpses. He wasn't sure how effective his threat of violence would be to something ambiguously dead, but at least he had set the expectation.

He stepped cautiously through the stone doorframe, listening for any sound that would indicate the presence of more soldiers. Once sure the street was clear, he stepped into the open. Based on the ambient light, he expected the sun to be either rising or setting, but instead, he found a sky made of stone and filled with a dozen or so orbs illuminating the entire cavern. The two-story stone houses lining either side of the street prevented him from getting a good layout of his surroundings, but it seemed to stretch on for miles. Above the roofline of the stone buildings, he saw several massive pillars holding up the cavern's ceiling, and he could just make out the top of a large building about a mile away.

To his left, the sandy street curved, allowing the houses to obstruct his view. To his right, he found the entrance to a tunnel that disappeared into the dark. It was large enough to fit four, maybe five wagons side by side. At the mouth of the tunnel lay three distinct piles of bones. The first two looked like his companion from inside the stone hut. The bones slowly clinked together, and their green auras swirled like lazy rain clouds.

The third green aura towered over the other two. At nearly five feet tall, it blazed like someone had thrown dry brush on a bonfire. The pile of bones on the ground had reformed entirely, and Henry saw the creature pick itself off the ground and stand to its full height. Although the green aura looked like a raging fire, it was completely translucent. Henry could easily see the skeleton inside the aura and make out the stones of the tunnel wall behind it.

The creature stood motionless, its countenance unwavering as it stared at the sand, eyes black from the shadows its skull cast. Its jaw hung loose in a deathly smile. Henry took a few cautious steps toward the looming ghoul. He had strapped his gear and armor down to quiet them as much as he could, but his bones were less cooperative. His knee joint creaked with a grind that was loud enough to break the silence and alert the other skeleton.

Its head snapped in his direction, taking him in with an ominous stare. Henry paused for a second, but when it didn't react any further, he continued to approach within a few feet.

"Hey, buddy. Any idea what's going on here? It looks like those soldiers got to you and your friends, but don't worry, I took care of them."

His new friend didn't respond, so Henry took another step forward. Then he had an idea. "I wonder if those weird necklaces work on you too?" he said. He dug through his pouch and procured one of the Amulets and a few leather straps. He cautiously tied it around the skeleton's neck and stepped back. A transparent **1** appeared on the clear jewel, then the left half filled with red.

Assess

Name: Unknown
Race: Skeleton
Health: Full
Magic: None
Attributes:
> **STR: 7**
> **MOB: 6**
> **FOR: 7**
> **ACU: 0**
> **PER: 20**
> **RES: 0**

"Just like I thought," Henry said, "you're at full Health, but you've killed no humans, and you have no Magic."

As if in response to his statement, the skeleton's head shifted slightly, and its gaze pointed to Henry's chest. It lifted a skeletal hand and touched the leather strap on his chest.

"Is this what you want, buddy?" Henry asked, pulling a blue crystal from its leather holster and placing it in the skeleton's hand. The creature closed its grip around the crystal, and Henry noticed a blue shimmer spread from its hand across its arm bones and through the rest of its body. The shimmer faded as quickly as it appeared, and the clear half of the Amulet around the skeleton's neck filled with blue.

Its hand opened, and the crystal dropped to the ground, clear now instead of blue. Once again, the skeleton lifted a bony hand toward Henry, but this time, it seemed to reach for the sword at his side. He Assessed the weapon again, noting that the information available to him had grown, and the sword now had a name.

Item: Akşam Xiphos (Epic)

Description: Weapon (Enchanted). Contains Drift Crystal (Legendary). Hardness 30, Structure 100/100

Ability: Drain V. Absorb magical energy from an enemy

While Henry parsed the new information, a glyph flashed in his view. Finally, he was starting to understand what each of the glyphs meant. This one had three chevrons and indicated something about an Ability. He allowed the glyph's message to replace the sword's information.

Item Ability Discovered: Assess II (Drift Amulet). Display more advanced information about items and beings. This Ability scales with use and Tier

His Drift Amulet's Assess Ability advanced, allowing him to gain more information from the item's description.

Apparently, the more I struggle with the Amulet, the more information it allows me access, Henry thought. If he could increase the Amulet's Ability, maybe he could do the same with Thrust.

As he worked through the Amulet's display, the skeleton's hand inched forward, almost demanding to be given Henry's blade.

"So, you're a fan of magic, huh? It's not that I don't trust you, but I think I'll hang on to this for now," Henry said, taking a step back. The skeleton lowered its hand but kept its gaze fixed on Henry.

"It looks like there's a tall building near the middle of this place," Henry continued, still keeping a cautious eye on the skeleton. "I'm going to check it out and see if I can get a better view. I'll let you know if I find anything."

Henry turned to walk away, intending to leave his new friend in peace, but the skeleton followed.

"Or you can come with me," Henry said, suppressing a chuckle and continuing to walk. "That's fine too, but we have to be careful, buddy. There are probably more humans around here."

The skeleton shambled along behind him at a slow but acceptable pace.

CHAPTER 5

Henry and his cryptic companion slowly made their way to the center of the town. Their progress was primarily quiet except for the occasional creak of a bone. Henry knew he would need to fix that problem if he wanted any hope of avoiding detection. He was also unsure about letting the other skeleton follow him, but the creature seemed harmless and only interested in Henry's magic items. He wasn't about to give up his gear and didn't have the heart to cut down his new friend. Letting the magic-hungry skeleton follow him was the best option he could come up with.

Streets and alleys twisted around the red stone houses in a confusing pattern, but Henry would occasionally catch a glimpse of the tall building and reorient himself. The building towered above the rest by several stories at least and seemed to curve around into a full circle. The distant walls of the structure were a series of lighter-colored stacked arches and darker stones that set the building apart from the rest. Henry continued toward the city center with his shambling companion trailing closely behind.

One thing was evident to Henry: he wasn't alone. He found

dozens, if not hundreds, of skeletons just in the short distance he walked. The fleshless guardians of the dead city filled the streets and most of the houses.

Except for Henry and the skeleton following him, none of the others moved. They all stood rigid with their blank stares. A few had tattered garments clinging to their bones, but most were naked in their green auras. Each aura was unique to its skeleton. Some swirled around like small dust devils, some pulsed, and some just hung lazily around their owners' bones. All were translucent, but the strength of the green varied from almost invisible to very dark. None of them, however, matched the intensity of the skeleton that followed him.

"I'm not sure what's special about you, buddy," Henry said to his companion walking closely behind him, "but in a city filled with skeletons, you're the most unique."

The two continued, leaving the housing district and walking through areas that may have been markets. The streets widened a bit and burnt wooden remains lined the storefronts. Henry walked through the stone threshold of what looked like a smithy, pushing past a wooden door barely clinging to its hinges. Broken containers and rusted tools were scattered around a stone forge, but little else remained.

Thin stretches of black and green mold grew along the stone walls, partially obscuring a strange mark. A circle of deformed stone, just a bit wider than his xiphos was long, looked like it had melted into the wall. Soot, dust, and mold had covered the mark over many years. Henry felt an intense heat would have been necessary to create such a warped pattern. The scorch mark was too far away from the forge to have been caused by it, and he'd seen several other instances of the blemish in other buildings throughout the city.

"I think there was a mark like this in the house where I started," he said to his skeletal follower, "but I was too scatterbrained to pay it any attention." The skeleton only stared blankly at Henry. "Yeah, good point, buddy. No brains for me to begin with."

They found a few burned-out buildings with charred and crumbling wooden ceilings, most of which had long since collapsed. He hoped to find some weapons or maybe something that could give him an explanation of what happened here, but everything was either broken or rusted beyond use.

"I guess skeletons aren't much for keeping their businesses stocked." Henry chuckled and eyed the other skeleton as though he expected a response, but its stoic gaze left the quip unappreciated.

A few hundred yards past the smithy, the lane opened into a circular courtyard with a statue of a human in the middle maybe twenty feet tall. The figure wore long robes, like those of a scholar, and it held an open book that it examined intently.

As Henry studied the statue from afar, two skeletons sprinted into the courtyard from a building on the left, their arms outstretched and mouths agape. Henry stepped to his right and dropped to a knee, taking cover behind a broken wooden table that lay on its side. The other skeleton didn't take the tactical hint and just stood in the middle of the street, uninterested in the two running skeletons in front of it. Henry grabbed its arm and pulled it behind him, then peered up in time to see the two disappear behind a building on the other side of the courtyard.

Crack! Crack! The sound of thunder tore through the quiet city, and flashes of blue light filled the courtyard and lit up the scholar statue. Bones tumbled from where the two skeletons disappeared and clinked across the ground. A skull bounced over the cobblestones, discarding its jaw and rolling to a stop with its eyes facing Henry.

Men's voices echoed from the right side of the courtyard, but Henry was too far away to make out what they were saying. He lowered his head so he could just barely see over the broken table.

A tall human man with short, black hair carrying a large hammer walked out into the courtyard. He wore the red tunic of the soldiers that Henry had battled earlier draped over heavy platemail. He hoisted the massive hammer and rested it over his shoulder. He looked like a lumberjack surveying a tree he had just felled.

Three men followed closely behind, all with identical red tunics. Each carried a wooden shield and a drawn sword. The man with the hammer said something, and the other three began laughing, but Henry wasn't paying attention to their words. He could focus on nothing but the four soldiers' blazing auras. Rage filled his mind, and every piece of his body cried out a request to murder the men and extinguish the offensive red blazes. Henry reached for his sword and began standing, readying his charge.

What am I doing? he thought. *If I attack four soldiers in the open, they'll surround me, and I'll be dead in an instant. That's if I even get the chance to attack before that hammer crushes me.* With every ounce of willpower he had, Henry forced his head behind the crumbling wood and collected his thoughts. Absent the red auras in his direct view, the overpowering urge to murder quickly dissipated. A glyph flashed and he tried to dismiss it, but the icon disregarded his attempt.

Status Effect: Enraged

Status Effect Subdued: Enraged Dismissed (RES +1)

"Think, Henry," he said to himself, "you can't fight them all at once, especially in the open. You have to figure out how to separate them before . . ."

A streak of blue fire and bone interrupted his train of thought. While fighting his internal battle of will, he had forgotten about his skeletal cohort. Apparently, his friend couldn't restrain himself as easily as Henry. The skeleton was running down the street before Henry had a chance to realize what was happening. The dullard was launching a direct assault on the humans.

Henry cursed under his breath. There was no way he'd be able to stop him before the soldiers noticed, leaving only seconds to act before losing any possibility of surprise.

He dashed between two buildings and made a hard left down a narrow alley, piecing together a plan in his mind. Henry was much faster than the other skeleton, but there was no time to spare if he wanted to make up for the head start. His boots pounded against the stone slabs of the alley floor as he propelled himself over rubble and under hanging beams of splintered wood. He could only hope the soldiers were distracted enough to allow Henry to launch a surprise attack from behind.

Henry approached what he thought was the location from which the soldiers emerged. The smoking scorch marks on the wall and fresh footprints confirmed his assumption. He slowed his pace just enough to minimize the noise he was making to a suitable level and steadied his mind in preparation for the mental assault of the red auras.

Luckily, the soldiers' backs were turned to him, and they focused all their attention on the skeleton charging them from the front. Red filled Henry's vision, but he suppressed the welling rage enough to keep focused on his strategy. If he only attacked one, the other three would overwhelm him, so he planned to slice the legs of the three soldiers in quick succession, maiming them and rendering them immobile. If he could face their leader one-on-one, he might have a chance of winning, or so he hoped.

The three soldiers raised their shields in anticipation of a magical attack from the blue flames. "Relax, boys," the man with the hammer boomed to the others, "this one is harmless. He only thinks he's a mage." He lifted the hammer over his head, casually preparing a mighty blow to crush the charging skeleton. Fingers of electricity arced around the weapon's head as if the hammer itself anticipated the kill.

Henry sliced the back of the first soldier's knees. It would take the boy nearly a second to react, giving Henry just enough time to strike at the next and hopefully the third.

The man with the hammer erupted in blue flames. A ten-foot blue ball of destruction completely engulfed him. Though Henry couldn't feel the intense heat on his exposed bones, the drop in his Health made him slightly grateful he had no skin to experience the searing pain that should have accompanied the damage. He lifted his shield to protect himself from the brunt of the blast. The middle soldier jumped back to avoid the wave of fire, putting him directly in Henry's path. Henry knew he couldn't avoid a collision, so he lowered his shoulder and drove all his weight into the man's ribs as the fire's rumble filled the courtyard.

The two tumbled to the ground in a mass of flesh, bone, and metal, but Henry was able to use his head to hold the man's arm away from his body long enough to slip his sword into the exposed rib cage. Henry knew he had punctured the man's heart and lungs when he heard a satisfying gurgle from the man's throat. He twisted the sword for good measure as he pulled it out, then looked up to locate the remaining soldier.

The leader dropped his hammer and crumpled to the ground. His screams were muffled and garbled enough to let Henry know they were his death throes. The other skeleton stood over the burning soldier with his outstretched arms continuing to blast waves of blue flame into the writhing body.

A quick glance revealed Henry's third foe. Just ten feet away, he saw the man's shocked expression below a wobbly helmet. His wide eyes and boyish cheeks betrayed the soldier's youth and lack of battle experience. He held his sword and shield low as though he had forgotten their presence, and his face went pale as he locked eyes with Henry.

He expected the boy to turn and run, but instead, his open mouth curled into a snarl. He raised his sword and charged, roaring a wordless battle cry. Henry had no idea if the young soldier had ever been in a battle, but the man rallied his courage like a true war veteran.

The red aura rushing toward Henry flushed out most of the respect he would have had for the boy's bravado, though there was at least a small piece of his psyche that regretted killing someone who had the potential to be a great warrior.

Henry rolled off the soldier below him, avoiding a sword slash by just a few inches. He planted his boots and cocked his sword close to his side, feeling a well of energy spread through his body. He launched forward, propelled by magical energy, and aimed for the center of the platemail covering the soldier's chest.

The boy raised his shield just in time to absorb the brunt of the attack. The shield splintered apart as Henry launched his assault, but the block managed to deflect the thrust just enough to avoid a fatal blow. Henry's sword punched through the armor on the man's shoulder and sank into the flesh and bone below.

The soldier winced in pain and tried to slice Henry with a wild swing, but Henry ducked under the blow and pivoted behind the exposed back of his adversary. Only a few centimeters of open space existed between the top of the soldier's platemail and the bottom of his helmet, but that was all Henry needed. His instincts guided the tip of his blade through the small opening between the vertebrae of the soldier's neck, severing bone, muscle, and nerves.

The soldier crumpled to the ground, and Henry knew the man had died instantly. A flood of sadness replaced the aura-induced rage in Henry's mind as the dying soldier's thoughts penetrated his consciousness. The three younger soldiers were close friends and had a large amount of admiration for their hammer-wielding leader. His dying thought was realizing he would never see them again.

From behind him, Henry heard the woosh of flames and pain-filled screams. He turned and saw his skeletal follower near the two soldiers Henry had felled earlier. The skeleton was reaching out to both men and roasting them with its deadly blue fire. Within seconds, their red auras winked from existence.

Henry stood quietly, not moving a bone. If this skeleton's waking experience was anything like his, it would be a shock at the very least, and Henry wanted to give him time to absorb it. He was also wary of accidentally soliciting the wrath of those blue flames.

The seconds crept by as Henry waited patiently. Slowly, the fire around the skeleton's hands dissipated. Its head turned to each of the dead bodies on the ground, and then it looked up at Henry. Its jaw opened, and a voice came from the skeleton, though the words didn't immediately register in his head. He was too focused on the unnatural communication emanating from the creature, and he found himself wondering if he looked the same when he talked: a skull with a loosely hanging jaw and voice coming from no discernable location.

Assess

Name: Unknown

Race: Skeleton

Tier: 4

Health: Full

Magic: Full

Attributes:

> **STR: 8**
>
> **MOB: 8**
>
> **FOR: 9**
>
> **ACU: 24**
>
> **PER: 22**
>
> **RES: 18**

"I request an explanation, skeleton," his newly conscious friend demanded. "This feels like no dream." His voice croaked, but his crisp diction led Henry to believe he came from either nobility or academia.

"I will do my best to provide one, but you may find it lacking," Henry replied, then added for emphasis, "*skeleton*."

The undead mage cocked his head slightly as though he hadn't actually expected Henry to respond, then looked down at his hands and body. "This is rather peculiar," he said after a moment of examining himself. "Very well, proceed with your lacking account."

Without muscles, skin, and eyes, it was nearly impossible to read the other skeleton's facial expressions, but he seemed to accept the situation. Henry did his best to explain the little he had discovered in his short time being alive. "I came into this world a few hours ago, just like you, battling for my life and doing everything in my power to snuff out the red auras of these soldiers."

"That would explain the rage I felt and why I chose to kill these men," the skeleton said, "but why is yours green, and why does it not invoke the same response from me?"

It was Henry's turn to examine his body. He looked all over himself but couldn't locate his own aura. "Not sure," he said. "I guess we aren't able to see our own. Yours is the largest aura I've seen yet. It looks like a billowing tempest preparing to unleash its fury."

"Yours is crystalline in nature," the skeleton returned, "it clings to your body like a beetle's carapace."

Henry wanted to ask more questions about his own aura but decided instead to continue his account. He told the skeleton about fighting the soldiers and finding the skeleton reforming himself in the street. When he got to the part about tying the Amulet inside his rib cage, the skeleton reached inside the cavity and fished it out, holding it up to his face and examining it closely.

"It has something to do with us being alive, if that's what we can call it," Henry said. "I have a feeling I would still be illiterate in magical jewelry speak even with all of my memory intact."

"It appears to have two functions," the skeleton began, not removing his gaze from the crystal. "The first is a powerful divinity enchantment that scales to the user's power. The Amulet displays the physical and magical Status of one's body, but this visualization is truly remarkable." The mage swiped his hand through the air as he analyzed the various glyphs. "To understand one's body and the surrounding world in such a quantified way is a blessing beyond measure."

"Maybe, but the glyphs are annoying while I'm trying to fight, even though the red and blue can be helpful."

"The glyphs provide an abundance of information, young warrior. You would be wise to observe them." Henry considered the advice as the mage continued. "The red is obviously a proportion of your Health, and the blue is your Vitus."

"Vitus," Henry said, mulling the strange word over in his mind. "That must be the energy I used to quicken my attacks and what you used to create the blue fire."

The skeleton chuckled and nodded his head, the first semblance of emotion he had displayed. "Magic is much more than battle tricks, but yes, you are correct. Vitus is your resistance to the fatigue associated with channeling magic."

"I think our magic, er, Vitus, will regenerate slowly, but if you kill enough humans, the Amulet will restore it instantly. This sword also seems to steal it," Henry said, lifting the magical blade. "Or you can use a blue crystal. I gave one to you, and I think that's how you were able to use magic to kill the leader of these soldiers, even before you woke up."

"The forces of magic flow like water through all corners of the universe. We use objects to channel that flow and direct it to our desired outcome," the skeleton said. "You have my gratitude for restoring me."

"Happy to help," Henry replied. "The other skeletons aren't much for conversation. It would have eventually gotten lonely. But jokes aside, you mentioned a second function of the Amulet?"

"Yes, it seems to be able to channel one's essence to another being upon death, as well as their last few thoughts and emotions. That is an overly simple explanation, and the mechanics of the spell involved are a mystery to me." The skeleton returned the Amulet to the inside of his rib cage. While tying it securely, he asked, "I remember more of these men than I do of myself, which is nothing at all. I am well-versed in magic, but I cannot locate the source of this knowledge. Is the experience similar for you?"

Henry nodded his head. "Almost. I know how to use a sword, or almost any weapon for that matter, but regarding actual memories, I can recall scarcely more than my own name."

"And that would be . . . ?"

"Henry," he replied. "I can hear a woman's voice saying my name, but her words are a cry of desperation. The harder I try to remember, the foggier it becomes. That's really the only memory I have from before this morning."

"It is truly a pleasure to meet you, Henry," the skeleton said. "I apologize for not remembering a name to give you in return."

Henry shrugged his shoulders and shook his head. "I've just been calling you 'buddy.'"

"Then you may continue doing so," Buddy responded, nodding his head slightly and extending a skeletal hand.

Henry shook Buddy's hand, then carried on with his account of the events that brought them to the bloodied and scorched courtyard.

CHAPTER 6

Koş brought his sword down hard on the skeleton. Bones splintered in all directions, and the creature crumpled to the ground. Glyphs flashed in his vision, but he didn't have a chance to acknowledge them, only enough time to raise his shield and absorb the attack of another one of the monsters. He didn't see the attacker lurking in a dark corner of the stone building, and it had nearly caught him by surprise.

The creature snapped its boney jaw and clawed with sharp fingers, searching for the flesh behind Koş's shield and armor. It was weak but relentless in its attack. He quickly pinned it to the wall, crushing it with a few heavy bashes from his shield, though the effort left him gasping for breath.

The skeletons just kept coming. Around every corner. In every house. In every single direction he turned. There were hundreds of them. They died easily, usually with one or two well-placed chops from his sword, but he understood how quickly the numbers could overwhelm him and the rest of his team.

His two fellow Acolytes seemed to be enjoying themselves. They would celebrate every kill, keeping a running tally of who could down the most undead. Koş lacked their enthusiasm, but was eager to prove his mettle, if only to ensure the monsters didn't tear him apart.

Their instructor, Master Acolyte Sigurjon, was on a completely different level. Koş had heard stories of the brutality and lethal efficiency of which this man was capable; stories he didn't believe until he saw it with his own eyes.

The man was a mixture of shadow and hurricane. He would appear from seemingly nowhere to unleash a flurry of blows, then disappear back into the nether before his enemies had even hit the ground. He was so fast that Koş's brain couldn't process his movements until well after he had vanished from sight, leaving behind nuggets of wisdom hanging in the air like "elbows in" and "be the darkness," whatever that meant.

Even their instructor's name, "Sigurjon," was a mystery. Koş was sure it was dwarven in origin, but the man's Ikritian accent and long, slender features left little possibility of dwarven ancestry.

With another house cleared, Koş walked into the sandy street to rally with his team. He couldn't remember exactly how many enemies he'd felled, but he was sure it was nearly a dozen. A quick glance at his soul crystal revealed he was close to Tier **4**. A few more skeletons would be enough to push him into the next Tier.

Master Sigurjon stood in the middle of the road with the other two Junior Acolytes, Trix and Kubey, instructing them on proper shield-blocking techniques.

"Smooch, get over here. You need to hear this too. Now, before you block your own vision with your shield, you must be moving into a better position," the instructor began, repositioning Kubey's shield and pushing his body to the side. Koş hated his nickname and thought the general idea of giving Junior Acolytes monikers was unnecessary and overall demeaning.

He didn't enjoy the soldier's lifestyle but knew it was his best chance for a future that would make his family proud. After a few years in the ranks of the Acolytes, he could save up enough money to send himself to the Citadel and finally be able to focus on his education. That was the best a lowly farm boy could hope for, just like his grandfather had nearly fifty years earlier.

"Smooch! Are you paying attention?" Master Sigurjon scolded. "No, of course you're not. Stop daydreaming about books and focus. I'm trying to teach you the art of combat." He cocked his arm back and hurled three daggers from his hand. They spun through the air toward Koş, missing him by mere inches. Koş ducked, even though he knew that was pointless. Master Sigurjon could kill him in an instant if he wanted to.

Koş heard three *thwacks* in quick succession and looked behind him to see a crumpling skeleton that had emerged from the same house he had just left.

"Also, great job clearing that house," he continued sarcastically. Koş stood back up and slowly walked over to the group, failing to hide the embarrassment that turned his face red. He had missed a skeleton in the dwelling, and it could have killed him if his mentor hadn't dropped it.

When it came to soldiering, Koş felt like he was always one step behind. He loathed marching, he was terrible at fighting, and most of all, he hated adventuring through this damn mountain. But if it meant that he could spend the rest of his life poring over the books in Ikrit's Citadel, a few years of working as an Acolyte would be worth it. He may even get the chance to serve under Lord Stavros one day, just like his grandfather did many years ago.

He remembered the stories his grandfather would tell of the Great Lord. Fifty years ago, Lord Stavros had become the successor of Lord Livadi, the legendary Emperor who led the battle against the Necromancer. Even though Lord Livadi couldn't defeat the Necromancer, break the spell, and free the inhabitants of the mountain, he was able to stop the evil of Jallfoss from spilling into the surrounding lands and bring peace to the Ikritian Empire for the remaining fifty years of his life. After that, his nephew, Lord Stavros, assumed his throne and continued the age of prosperity to this very day.

Countless nights Koş had sat in awe by the fireside, listening to his grandfather recount stories of the Great Lord Stavros. His grandfather had joined the ranks of the Acolytes, but because of his exceptional performance on the battlefield, he had been appointed as one of the personal guards of the new Emperor.

Koş's siblings and cousins loved to hear his grandfather's stories revolving around seemingly hopeless battles. The Ikritians were always on the verge of defeat, with no options left. Then Lord Stavros would appear, say something inspirational, cast a powerful spell of destruction, and save the day for the inhabitants of Ikrit. His grandfather would jump from his chair, stomp his feet and smack his hands together to mimic the sounds of swords and magic. Koş and his cousins would squeal with delight every time Lord Stavros and his warriors claimed victory.

He was old enough now to realize those stories were heavily embellished. No human could actually possess that level of power and charisma, but his grandfather spoke of the Emperor with the same admiration until the day he died. It wasn't the stories of battle that showcased that esteem, but rather the thousands of miles his grandfather had traveled on foot and horseback with the Great Lord. Whether it was the muddy swamps, snowy mountain passes, or sweltering deserts, Lord Stavros always knew the best action to take and the right words to get them out of harm's way and smooth things over with the locals of whatever country they were in at the time.

Koş's favorite Lord Stavros story was when hundreds of warriors from the mountain tribe of Gertleg had his grandfather, Lord Stavros, and a dozen other Master Acolytes trapped in a cave on a snowy mountain peak. Freezing to death and on the verge of starvation, Lord Stavros recalled a book he had read on mountain mythology and how that region worshiped mountain trolls. He cast an illusion spell to make half of his men look like the beasts, and then they walked out of the cave and confronted their attackers. Had his trick failed, they would have been killed on the spot, but his spell convinced the Gertlegs that the trolls and his men were friends. The tribe welcomed them into their village, fed them, and gave them shelter. Lord Stavros had to keep the illusion active for two days, and the drain on his magic nearly killed him, but the Gertleg tribe became powerful allies to Ikrit, giving them a safe and efficient trade route through the eastern mountains.

That story convinced Koş that true power could be found in knowledge, and the Ikritian Citadel was the largest source of knowledge in the known world. One day, he would honor the memory of his grandfather by joining the Scholars and maybe even working directly under Lord Stavros. But first, he had to get through this mountain and its creepy, undead inhabitants.

As the four Acolytes made their way to the back of the city, Master Sigurjon demonstrated sword techniques on charging skeletons, then made Kubey, Trix, and Koş imitate his teachings. He'd let them venture into stone dwellings on their own, but Koş felt the instructor was watching him much more closely than the other two. "You must remain vigilant in these caverns. Think of them as a monstrous battlefield. Keep your wits about you and never let your guard down."

"But skeletons are weak," Kubey countered, "I've killed nearly a dozen by myself and haven't even broken a sweat. Why should I be afraid of a creature that has to see you before it can even move? They're dumb and slow, not even worthy of being called monsters."

Master Sigurjon's face broke into a menacing grin. He walked over to the skeleton he had just felled and retrieved his three daggers. "Keep that attitude up, and you'll be dead on your first trip through the dungeon. The skeletons on this level are easily defeated when you're fighting a few, but their numbers can quickly overwhelm you if you're not careful. Smooch would already be dead if I wasn't here." Koş looked down sheepishly at the sand.

Sigurjon continued, "Most of the human skeletons are docile until they see you, but the undead animals and monsters below and above are a different story altogether. They have retained their savage instincts and will hunt you just like their living counterparts in the wild. More importantly, there are unique skeletons even on this level."

"Do they have horns and four arms?" Trix asked excitedly, his eyes wide and his mouth slightly ajar, waiting for the Master Acolyte to continue.

"Not on this level, but I have seen crazier things down below," Master Sigurjon answered. "No, the three unique skeletons on this level are more like wild cards. Each possesses certain qualities that make it unpredictable, and two of them are quite dangerous."

"I can't wait to fight them," Kubey exclaimed, swinging his sword through the air and chopping into the rib cage of the skeleton on the ground. Shards of bone pinged off his metal shin guards. "What makes them so special?"

"I won't pretend to understand the nature of magic. It's much more of an art than an exact science. What I do know is that each creature down here is affected differently by the Necromancer's spell. Some mages will tell you that the way a skeleton behaves has something to do with the clout of its soul. I believe these three skeletons died with an unfulfilled purpose, and they're searching for a way to complete their quest, even after death."

"So how will we know if we see a unique skeleton?" Trix asked.

"The first one is the most obvious but not very dangerous. He can be hard to find, though, because he's always wandering about. You can tell he used to be a mage by the blue fire surrounding his hands as he tries to cast spells at you. Luckily for us, skeletons can't regenerate their Merq, so his spells always fail. He's also attracted to magic items. He'll try to use wands or magic weapons, but as long as you don't give him a Merq crystal, he can't activate anything. He's one of the easiest skeletons to defeat.

"The second unique skeleton is extremely dangerous. He's the last skeleton we'll fight tonight before we make camp, but we'll wait to join with the other three groups of Acolytes before battling him. He's the true definition of a brute, nearly eight feet tall and strong enough to crush through your shield, your helmet, and your soft skull in one single blow."

Kubey shook his head in disbelief. "No way. No skeleton could be that strong."

"He *is* that strong," Master Sigurjon said matter-of-factly. "That's why we've removed all the weapons from this level and stored them in a safe place. As dangerous as he is with his bare hands, if he were wielding a greatsword, even I would approach him with caution. Luckily for us, he guards the ramp to the lower level. He never ventures far from his post, so we always know where he is, and you can retreat if you find he is too much for you to handle."

"And the third?" Koş asked.

Master Sigurjon shot a quick look at Koş as though he had forgotten he was even there. "The third is responsible for more Acolyte deaths than most of the monsters in this mountain," he began, dropping his gaze to the sand floor and tightening his grip on his dagger. "Well over a hundred, if you believe the stories. He's dangerous because he's a predator. Quiet and cunning, he'll stalk Acolytes like a panther, pick them off one at a time, then disappear back into the shadows without a trace."

Kubey sat down and pulled off one of his boots. He dumped out a bit of sand, then reached his hand into the boot's opening to fish out whatever remained. "But Master Sigurjon, that's the same thing you do. I never know where you're going to appear."

A solemn expression took over Sigurjon's usually cocky and jovial countenance. "I have mastered fighting warriors and monsters on the battlefield, but this skeleton doesn't fight like a warrior. He murders without notice and without remorse. It's like a sinister game that he enjoys . . ." His voice trailed off at the end like he was diving into a distant memory. The group stood quietly for just a few seconds, but the silence told the young soldiers that the mountain held true dangers, even on the first level.

The smile returned to Master Sigurjon's face, and he said, "Luckily for us, we've captured the wretch and locked him away so that when we fight him, it's on our terms. We won't encounter him until our second time through the mountain, but Master Tekşan's group should be meeting him shortly."

"Where's that?" Trix enquired.

Master Sigurjon looked toward the center of the underground city. He lifted a finger and pointed to the large round building that towered above the rest. "The coliseum."

CHAPTER 7

Henry continued his account of the day's events as he and Buddy went through the dead soldiers' belongings that hadn't been consumed by the skeletal mage's flames. Buddy decided not to don any of the heavy armor of the younger soldiers, as he thought it might hamper the casting of his spells. He did, however, agree with Henry that wearing the red tunics would provide them with a few valuable seconds of camouflage should they encounter any more humans.

The one tunic that wasn't burnt to a crisp was slightly oversized for Buddy's skeletal frame, but after he secured it with the soldier's leather belt and put on the leather boots, he didn't look too bad. It also helped that he decided to take Henry's bandolier full of magic crystals. It kept the cloth secured to his rib cage, and Henry was sure that Buddy was much more capable of utilizing them to their full potential.

Finally, Buddy pointed to the charred corpse of the warrior that appeared to be the former leader of the troupe. "Can you wield that hammer?" the mage asked. Henry still hadn't gotten comfortable talking to a skull that radiated a human voice, but Buddy seemed relatively unfazed by the exchanges.

Assess

Item: War Maul (Superior)

Description: Weapon (Enchanted). Contains Drift Crystals (Superior). Hardness 10, Structure 30/30

"Maybe," Henry replied as he walked over to the blackened remains. He pushed aside burnt flesh with the toe of his boot and revealed the soot-covered metal handle. He pulled the maul from the dead soldier's grip and knew immediately that he preferred his sword and shield combination. It was massive, nearly forty pounds, with a four-foot handle. Two diamond-shaped Drift Crystals were embedded into either side of the weapon's head, surrounded by runes that Henry didn't recognize. The crystals held miniature lightning storms with tiny arcs of electricity that followed his fingers when touched.

He swung it through the air several times and lifted it above his head. It was cumbersome and threw him off-balance. "No." Henry said, shaking his head. "I may be able to use it to take out a few of the weaker soldiers, but I'm too slow with this to go against a seasoned warrior."

"Shame, powerful magic flows through the weapon. I would hate to abandon something so useful. Here, give it to me and I'll hang onto it until we can put it to use."

Henry asked, "How do you know it's powerful? I can only see its description. *Superior* and *enchanted* don't tell me a whole lot, besides it being better than the Mundane swords that the other three held." Henry had been using the Amulet's Assess Ability on most of the items he'd found while looting the bodies. Most were either Mundane or Uncommon, with the Drift Shards being the only other enchanted items he'd procured.

"I have an Ability called *Magic Sense*. It seems less . . . quantifiable than the divinity provided by the Drift Amulets, but more attuned to the presence of magic. You said that the information provided increased as you learned about an item, so I would guess those words describe its quality and composition; most likely based on comparison to similar items, common knowledge, and the understanding you glean from using it. However, divinity magic is the most unpredictable of all magic, more deceitful than even illusions."

Buddy reached down to the charred corpse and pulled free a chain with a metal pendant. "Like this item. The enchantment is faint, but still detectable." Henry couldn't see anything special about the necklace Buddy held beyond the crispy flesh that still clung to it, so he activated his Drift Amulet's Ability.

Assess

Item: Durmaz Crest

Description: Accessory (Enchanted). Necklace and insignia of a prominent Ikritian family. Damage Resistance +1

"How do you know so much about magic?" Henry asked as Buddy slipped the pendant over his head.

After a long pause, Buddy gave a sharp response, his voice tinged with frustration. "I don't know." Buddy's abrupt cutoff meant the discussion was over. Maybe the mage was embarrassed about his blank memory, but Henry understood how he felt. Henry didn't know how he understood the intricacies of close combat, though his body's instincts knew exactly how to fight, even if his weak skeletal body lagged behind his mind. He wanted to ask Buddy about the Epic and Legendary qualities of his sword but felt that could wait until later.

Henry gave the hammer to Buddy, who hefted it over his

shoulder. He then surveyed the area around them, ensuring they hadn't missed any valuables.

Buddy explored the open area of the plaza, walking over to a metal lamppost that held three small sun globes in separate sconces. He grabbed one of the globes and twisted it, breaking it free with a *snap*. The light in the globe winked out as the skeleton rolled the crystal sphere over in his hands, examining its milky interior and the few inches of crystalline rope that had been connected to the rest of the lamp.

Buddy dropped the globe to the ground as though he'd lost interest and turned back to Henry. He cocked his head slightly and asked, "You believe the answer to our plight lies in the caverns below us, at least according to the memories of the first soldier you killed?"

"Yes," Henry said as he picked up his sword and shield. "I plan to climb to the top of that large building in the middle of the city and see if I can locate a way down." Henry motioned with his head to the building towering above the roofline ahead of them. "I'm going that way, and unless you have more pressing matters, I won't turn down the company."

"I have no evidence that points to a better course of action," Buddy said. "I will join you, for now." Henry internally rejoiced at Buddy's willingness to accompany him. He was grateful to have the capable mage watching his back, but more than anything, he was glad to have someone help him uncover the mysteries of the giant underground city.

Henry and Buddy moved quickly through the narrow streets and alleys weaving around clusters of buildings. While most of the structures were of similar stonework and design, their layout seemed sporadic, almost random. They often found themselves taking shortcuts through buildings as they inched toward the massive structure at the city's center.

Every street and every house contained numerous skeletons. They all stood nearly motionless with their blank stares, swaying ever so slightly as though an imperceptible wind moved through their bones. Henry thought that if the skeletons were distributed evenly throughout the city, there would have to be thousands, if not tens of thousands, in the monstrous cavern. What Henry found curious was the absence of skeletons of children. If these skeletons had been the city's former inhabitants, wouldn't some of them have at least been adolescents?

"What do you think happened here?" Henry asked as the two worked their way through another skeleton-filled building.

"They sold homemade baked goods and earned enough money to support a large family," Buddy replied bluntly.

"What?"

"There are three ovens in the main room on this floor and a storefront with a large display case at the entrance." Buddy pointed to a series of lines on the wall near the back entrance. "There are markings on this wall showing the growth chart of at least four children, the oldest being in their early teens, based on height."

Henry had been too lost in thought to pay much attention to the specifics of each building they walked through. Buddy's situational awareness surprised him. He had assumed the academic had spent his life with his nose in a book and would therefore possess little real-world experience. Henry mentally chastised himself. Once for making an assumption about Buddy that had proven untrue, and a second time for not paying attention in such a dangerous place. At least they had found evidence that children once existed. It made sense, though. Buddy's Perception was **24** while Henry's was only **20**. He made a mental note to ask the mage what the numbers actually meant.

"No, I mean what happened to the whole city," Henry said as they exited the bakery.

Buddy replied, "Again, that is a vague question. If you're asking why the inhabitants of this city are skeletons instead of humans, the answer can be nothing short of war. If you're asking why all the skeletons are animated, I only know that powerful magic must be involved."

"I think you're right," Henry said. "If they had died any other way but war, they would have been buried, not left in what I assume were their homes, but they are still in their houses and out in the streets. That's not how I would defend against an invading force, but it does explain the many homes destroyed by fire and the weird burn marks on the stone."

Buddy said nothing in reply, and Henry took that to mean another discussion had ended. It was probably for the best, as they were almost to the base of the giant building. The street led to a large open space directly in front of their destination.

More storefronts lined three sides of the five-hundred-foot sandy square. Henry thought it might have been used for festivals or as a military parade ground. Now it was littered with the broken remains of tent beams, old horse-drawn carts, wooden barrels, clay pots, and of course, dozens and dozens of silent skeletons. Their destination made up the entire fourth side of the open plaza.

It was indeed an impressive sight, nearly a hundred feet high and five times that wide. A series of stacked arches made of a lighter stone ringed the building. The bottom set of arches was maybe twenty feet tall, but all the subsequent layers were half that size. The dark stone behind the arches making up the bulk of the building was the same red sandstone that comprised most of the other buildings in the city.

"A coliseum," Buddy muttered. "The central node of

commerce and entertainment of any fine city." The two skeletons began picking their way through the rubble toward the monstrous building.

Several other smaller streets led into the plaza at various spots, but there was one larger road that looked like the main thoroughfare that entered from the middle of one of the sides. The coliseum's arcade that was directly across from that street was void of stone and appeared to be the building's main entrance. When the two arrived at the opening, they found massive wooden doors propped open and in surprisingly good shape.

"Boot prints," Henry said, pointing to the sandy path leading through the archway and into a stone tunnel. "The humans use this place regularly." He looked up from the pathway and surveyed the open plaza. "I haven't figured out how long it takes the other skeletons to regenerate, but judging by the lack of smashed ones, it's been a while since they've come through."

"It would be in our interest to hurry, then, should they be due to return." Buddy turned toward the archway and walked into the tunnel. "The sound of battle should alert us to their presence."

Henry nodded in agreement and followed Buddy through the entrance. If he were to stand on Buddy's shoulders, another skeleton's height would still be between him and the tunnel's roof. Its walls were made of a rough gray stone that was much harder than the sandstone of the homes and businesses. About every ten feet, on either side of the tunnel, there were openings. A few had doors, but most led directly into dusty rooms or to smaller, man-sized passageways. The large tunnel brought them directly into the coliseum's interior.

Henry could see from the inside of the structure that it was more of an oval than a circle as they walked out into the sandy pit. Stone walls a bit taller than the roof of the tunnel lined the pit, and there was another similar tunnel on the opposite side from which Henry and Buddy had entered. Besides the two tunnels, sixteen large stone archways were built into the arena's wall, each closed off by a metal portcullis. There was also one single, man-sized door on the narrow left end of the pit. The door and all the archways had stone blocks at their tops carved with various words. Henry read a few of the names on the blocks close enough for him to discern: *Hellhound, Demon, Skull Crusher.*

Stone seating ringed the pit, starting at the top of the arena's wall and extending to the highest part of the coliseum's interior. The stadium had three separate levels: comfortable seats with backs on the first level, then stone slabs on the next two. Nearly a dozen spots throughout the stadium had been reduced to rubble, like giant boulders had fallen from the stone ceiling and smashed into the coliseum. Henry also saw several scorch marks throughout the coliseum's interior like the ones he'd found in the city, only many orders of magnitude larger. Some had even melted through the seating completely, leaving gaping holes ringed with blackened stone. Whatever forces had battled there must have been extremely powerful. Henry was glad to not have been involved in such a fight but found himself wishing he'd been able to witness it.

Henry was surprised none of the walls of the pit or the metal portcullis had been destroyed, but upon further inspection, he found that some of the stonework had been replaced and pieces of the metal structure had been repaired.

This city isn't completely dead, but why would someone take the time to repair the arena's walls and nothing else in the city? More mysteries Henry feared would go unanswered.

Two elegant marble thrones overlooked the pit directly

above the opposite tunnel. Behind them were two rows of stone chairs that likely seated nobility or other people of influence. Strangely, there was one thing missing from the massive coliseum.

"There are no skeletons," Henry said, wondering if Buddy had also noticed the lack of undead.

Buddy returned the glance and shook his head. "Look closer," he replied softly, nodding toward the portcullis nearest them.

Henry stepped toward the opening. He stayed near the edge, careful not to walk too far into the sandy pit. Chips and small gashes dotted the portcullis, but it appeared sturdy and of recent upkeep. Above the arched stone rested a carved block labeled "Fang." Henry peered through the bars but couldn't make out anything in the shadows beyond. He looked over his shoulder to Buddy for assurance, but the mage's gaze was focused on the dark.

Henry took another step closer and looked through the bars again. That was when he saw it. It started as a tiny green swirl of an aura, just slightly larger than an apple. Within a second, it blossomed into a four-foot spinning cloud. The green aura rushed toward the portcullis, and a skeletal claw lashed at Henry's face.

Henry sprang back, narrowly avoiding the slash. He didn't know if he was more surprised by the deep rumble of a growl that accompanied the attack or that the claw belonged to a giant skeletal cat. More surprising was Henry's own reaction. Even while jumping back to avoid the attack, his body responded by countering with a chop of his sword.

The claw and forearm of the beast dropped to the ground in front of him. Its owner reached through the cage with its other arm and swiped at him twice more before retracting it back through the metal bars. It then hobbled back and forth, eyeing him with malicious intent. The cat's skull chomped with incisors long enough to be daggers, threatening to crunch his bones.

The growl from the beast had done more than startle Henry. It had awakened whatever had been dormant in the other cages, and the arena erupted with the sounds of a dozen large, angry creatures.

Henry quickly glanced around the pit to the other openings, raising his sword and shield and preparing for an attack. He saw the swirling auras of the captive beasts and could even make out a few of their skeletal frames. Giant boars sharpened their tusks on the bars, and gorillas pounded their chests and cried out a challenge for battle. Several cages contained other large cats, maybe tigers, lions, or panthers. Henry couldn't tell from their skeletons alone.

"Unlike humans, animals retain their savage nature and have even learned to suppress their auras," Buddy mused, more to himself than Henry. "Interesting."

"Thanks for the warning. You get the first look in the next dark hole," Henry said as the noises from the animals began to quiet down to a few snorts and growls.

"I didn't expect them to react," Buddy replied, seemingly unfazed by the fact that Henry had nearly been mauled. "I can't tell if they're drawn to our auras or if they are simply obeying their bestial instincts. Either way, I am grateful your skill with a sword far exceeds that of your observation."

Henry replied, "Backhanded compliment aside, you are correct. I think my swordsmanship and your magic have stuck with us the same way these animals have maintained their nature." Henry focused on the wounded cat and allowed the Amulet's Ability to display its Status.

Assess

Name: Fang

Type: Skeletal Cougar

Health: Damaged

Vitus: None

Attributes:

    STR: 24

    MOB: 30 (15)

    FOR: 16

    ACU: 4

    PER: 24

    RES: 3

Damage Resistance:

    Physical: -1

        Bludgeoning -2

    Environmental: 2

        Poison: Immune

The cougar was stronger than him, but Henry could see that the damage he'd done to its limb had greatly reduced the animal's Mobility. Losing one of its legs had brought the Attribute down by half. More interesting was the new information about Damage Resistance. Henry assumed the negative numbers meant the creature was less resistant to that specified type of damage, and the positive numbers meant it was more resistant. Without flesh, its bones couldn't withstand as much physical punishment, much less from bludgeoning damage like from a club or mace. *Environmental: 2* likely meant that things like heat and cold affected it less, maybe because it had no flesh to freeze or blood boil.

Henry looked around the arena, searching and listening for

any sign that the animal noises had drawn humans to their location. The only thing that caught his attention was the next cage over from him. It was the only one of the sixteen that didn't contain any animals, but it was still closed.

"*Beast*," Henry said, reading the chiseled stone sign at the top of the archway.

"The humans have locked away all the dangerous creatures of the city," Henry said, "or maybe these animals have been here since whatever happened that killed the inhabitants. This is the only empty one." Henry approached the metal bars but kept a safe distance, not wanting to repeat his last near-miss.

He looked through the lattice, taking his time to scan every inch of the dark enclosure, but saw nothing. "Anything?" Henry asked, turning back to Buddy.

"Yes," Buddy replied.

Henry turned back to the cage and found a skeleton had appeared, almost like it had been conjured from the shadows behind it. He suppressed a cry of alarm as his hand instinctively gripped the hilt of his sheathed sword. He hadn't heard a creak of bone or a rustle of sand that would have alerted him to its presence. He couldn't even see its aura until he took another step forward. It was only a thin strand snaking around the skeleton's bones like a tiny translucent vine.

Assess

Name: Beast
Race: Skeleton
Tier: 1
Health: Full
Magic: None
Attributes:

STR: 8

MOB: 22

FOR: 6

ACU: 0

PER: 18

RES: 0

Damage Resistance:

Physical: -1

Bludgeoning -2

Environmental: 2

Poison: Immune

"Careful," Buddy warned as Henry inched forward, "much is still unknown about the inhabitants of this coliseum."

"This one is different, just like you and me." Henry approached within an arm's length of the bars and asked, "Are you conscious, brother?"

The skeleton didn't reply, but its gaze remained fixed on Henry. "I know what you need," Henry said as he reached into his pouch and fished out one of the remaining Amulets. "This did the trick for Buddy and me." He slowly reached through the bars, ready to pull his arms back should the skeleton mean him harm. He was relieved when no such attack came. The other skeleton didn't move at all as Henry fastened the Amulet around its neck.

It was a small skeleton, more than a head shorter than Henry, and other than the vine-like aura circling its bones, nothing in particular about the skeleton should have caused him unease. However, the menacing way it had appeared out of nowhere and its cold gaze left Henry feeling relieved to step back from the bars.

A noise from outside the arena caught his attention. The

rallying cries of several men and the *thwack, thwack* of their weapons against what Henry could only assume were the skeletons outside echoed down the tunnel. Then a resounding *thump*, like a single beat of a giant drum, reverberated through the ground and into his bones. It was quickly followed by a strong blast of wind carrying sand and debris, shooting into the pit from the mouth of the tunnel. Just as quickly as the noise had started, it faded away. Whatever battle had taken place outside was already over.

Henry turned back just in time to see the skeleton shrink into the darkness and disappear from his view.

"Our new friend can wait," Buddy whispered. "Another group of soldiers approaches, and they have a mage with them. We must hide." Henry didn't argue as the two ran to the far tunnel.

The quick movement of the two skeletons reinvigorated the undead animals in the cages. Growls and snarls filled the arena, drowning out the pad of the skeletons' feet and the creaks of their bones.

CHAPTER 8

enry and Buddy dipped into the shadows of the far tunnel and backed into a stone alcove. There was enough of a lip on the mouth of the passage for them to stay hidden and observe the opposite side of the arena. Henry didn't know if humans were able to see their green auras, but if they could, the skeletons would easily be perceived.

Henry took a few seconds to scan the area around him, hoping to cobble together a plan, either to attack whatever was coming their way or to retreat, should the odds prove overwhelming.

The small alcove served as the entrance to a narrow staircase that went up for ten feet, then took a sharp right turn and continued up, probably leading to the area with the elegant stone chairs. Directly across from them was a series of metal levers sticking out of the wall. There were eighteen levers in total. Two were about as long as his forearm, and the other sixteen were half that size. They were organized in an oval pattern matching the layout of the pit's cages and tunnels. He could only assume each of those levers would operate its corresponding portcullis.

Several other doors and alcoves lined the tunnel's walls, but the far end was blocked off, maybe fifty feet down. One open archway near the far end had a stone block with the word 'Armory' carved above it. It opened to a ramp that sloped down into shadow. If they had to retreat, maybe they could fall back to a weapon-filled room and mount a resistance with whatever they found there. Henry would welcome the time to gather supplies from an armory, but the current situation was unwilling to grant him that luxury.

The animal sounds in the pit rose to a crescendo, and Henry turned to see four soldiers emerge from the tunnel on the far side of the arena. Three of them wore the heavy armor and red tunics of the younger soldiers from before. The fourth didn't seem to be wearing any armor, only a red, hooded robe hanging loosely from his frame.

Their auras filled Henry's vision and clouded his thoughts with anger. He imagined tearing into their flesh with his teeth and pulling the organs from their bloody torsos—anything to snuff out the swirling auras that surrounded their bodies.

Buddy leaned and took a step toward the soldiers. Henry saw the movement from the corner of his eye, and it brought his attention back to their situation. He wanted to race toward the humans and attack them with Buddy, but he had just enough of his senses left to realize that a rage-filled charge would result in their instant deaths.

Henry grabbed Buddy by the nape of his tunic and pulled him back into the alcove before he could take a second step. The two tumbled to the ground, and Henry hoped the animals outside were loud enough to cover up the noise they had made. A glyph flashed and forced its information into his view, but he quickly dismissed the notification.

Status Effect: Enraged

Status Effect Subdued: Enraged Dismissed (RES +1)

He'd gained another point of Resolve from resisting the influence of the red auras, but he'd need more than an extra Attribute point to fight off the four soldiers.

Buddy shook his head as he regained control. "Thank you," Buddy whispered. "I would already be dead if you hadn't stopped me. I couldn't resist such a compelling drive to attack." Henry helped Buddy to his feet, and the two listened for any sign they had given away their position. They heard men's voices but couldn't discern what they were saying.

"We still have the advantage, but I can sense the mage's power. We must proceed carefully. What do you propose, master tactician?"

"We have them outnumbered," Henry said, nodding to the levers on the opposite wall, "but we still need a distraction. Do you have any spells that can hit all of them at once?"

Buddy nodded and pulled two crystals from his bandolier. "These should do the trick. Hopefully I can still aim when I see their auras."

"Take these stairs to the next level but avoid looking at the soldiers until you're ready to attack," Henry said. "Once you hit them, I'll call in the reinforcements and close their exit. Then I'll ambush them right here when they run for cover."

"Good luck, Henry," Buddy whispered. He propped his war hammer against the alcove and bounded up the stone steps. When he reached the first landing, he turned back. "Don't forget that you have healing crystals." Then he vanished around the corner, taking the stairs two at a time.

Henry peered past the dusty stone archway and out to the sandy pit to observe the soldiers and prepare himself for the coming battle. He had to cover his eyes every few seconds as the rage threatened to overtake his senses. The men had made their way to the center of the arena and were now facing each other in a circle. The red mage pointed to the various cages around the exterior, and the three armored men nodded in unison. All three groups he'd encountered so far had the same structure: one stronger, experienced warrior leading a few younger soldiers.

The young men were being trained. Not only were they were using the skeletons to develop battle experience, but the Drift Amulets were allowing them to harvest Soul Essence from Henry's fellow skeletons and increase the soldiers' Tiers.

The realization came as a shock. The skeletons were being killed for sport, and not just once. This had to have been going on for years. How many times had Henry been killed by them before he had awakened? Had he been conscious before, only to lose his memories upon each death? Were they the ones that caused the mass slaughter of the underground city, or were they merely taking advantage of a tragedy?

A new anger welled up from deep within Henry. The feeling was different from the one induced by the aura. It was controlled, seething, vengeful. Everything had been taken from him, even his memories. The closest thing he had to a family was the mass of undead skeletons throughout the city. At that moment, Henry resolved to stop the humans and rescue his kind from their endless death.

The mage in the red robes swiveled abruptly and looked upward. He raised his hands in the air as a ball of lightning exploded just a few feet above him. The purple arcs streaked around an invisible dome surrounding the four men and fizzled away after a few seconds. The attack had begun.

Henry ran across the tunnel's opening and pulled hard on the switch that he thought corresponded to the other tunnel's portcullis. The lever creaked in protest as he forced it down. Then he activated four of the smaller switches, hoping to release some of the caged skeletal animals.

Deep inside the bowels of the arena, he heard the low groans of what he assumed were counterweights straining against ropes, chains, and pulleys. After a few seconds, bars rose into position at the mouth of the opposite tunnel and blocked the only other exit. Some of the cages had also opened, and several skeletal beasts burst from their enclosures and charged at the humans in the middle of the arena.

A giant shard of ice smashed into the invisible dome protecting the soldiers and covered half of it in a thin sheet of frost. Henry hoped the shield would give way before Buddy ran out of crystals and magic so the men would be forced to retreat to his location, but he wasn't that lucky.

The red mage raised open palms toward Henry and Buddy. The sand parted in front of the wizard as two invisible balls of energy launched toward the attacking skeletons, leaving deep trenches in their wake.

Henry didn't have time to move out of the way. He lifted his shield and planted his back foot to brace for the attack. His shield splintered apart, and his left forearm snapped in two as the blast sent him tumbling to the back of the tunnel, finally coming to a stop when he smashed into the stone wall.

His chainmail absorbed the brunt of the blow, and his helmet stopped his skull from being caved in, but he was still severely damaged. Buddy wasn't wearing any armor, so Henry could only hope that he had come up with some other way to defend himself. He had to get back in the fight before the humans were able to rally. More glyphs appeared in his vision, flashing with an urgency he hadn't seen before. He allowed them to display their information.

Status

Health: 8/33
Vitus: 24/24

Status Effects:
  Injury: Broken Arm (Moderate): MOB -5%, STR -10%
  Injury: Broken Ribs (Severe): STR -10%, MOB -5%, FOR -20%
  Injury: Cracked Skull (Moderate): FOR -10%

He reached into his leather pouch with his one good arm and retrieved both red crystals. He squeezed them tightly and let the healing energy flow through his bones. His left arm snapped back into place, as did various other broken bones throughout his body. Henry still found it odd that no physical pain came from his injuries, only a mild pleasant sensation as the magic mended his body back together. A quick glance at his Status showed that he was nearly at full Health, and the Status Effects from the injuries had disappeared.

He leapt to his feet and sprinted back to the levers, flipping the remaining twelve small ones, then ducked behind the lip of the tunnel. His shield and healing crystals were gone, and he knew another hit like the last one would take him out of the fight altogether.

Henry gazed out from the stone archway to see the rest of the animals racing toward the soldiers. A ball of blue flame smashed into the red mage's dome and engulfed the protective shield. When it cleared, the soldiers below had taken enough of the flame that their tunics and hair were scorched. The charging skeletons were just a few seconds away from the soldiers, and

Henry wondered if Buddy's spells had weakened the shield enough for them to get through.

The red mage wasn't going to wait to find out. He lifted his foot into the air and stomped the ground. The same *thump* that Henry had heard earlier echoed through the arena, and a wave of sand shot out from the group of soldiers in all directions. Four wildcats and a gorilla that had almost reached the group were blown apart in a shower of bones. Six other animals—two cats, three bears, and an eight-foot lizard—were all caught up in the wave and sent tumbling backward. Henry ducked into the tunnel, but by the time the wave had reached him, it had lost most of its power, and it rolled to the back wall harmlessly.

The red mage fired another blast in Buddy's direction and then dropped to a knee. Henry saw that he was digging through a pouch on his belt. If he used any magic items or was able to recover his Vitus, the battle would be lost. Henry couldn't wait for them to retreat to his ambush spot; he had to launch his attack now. He sprinted toward the soldiers as fast as his Strength and Mobility would propel him.

The animals had recovered from the blast and were once again on the charge. The men were preparing to defend themselves from the skeletons and hadn't taken notice of Henry yet. He looked to his left and found the wall had been smashed in several spots and was crumbling down. He also saw Buddy standing tall with a blue flame swirling around his wrist. Somehow, the skeletal mage had avoided the red wizard's attacks.

Buddy nodded at Henry, then pulled a crystal from his bandolier. He cocked his arm back and threw it high into the air. Then he raised his fist and launched another blue flame. Henry continued to sprint as he watched the crystal tumble toward the men. The crystal swelled to the size of a melon, then burst apart into thousands of gallons of water.

Buddy's flame impacted the center of the ball of water and exploded into a giant cloud of steam. The soldier's cries and the *thwack* of their swords on bone mixed with the snarls of the animals that had charged into the vapor. Henry couldn't see more than a few feet into the cloud, but Buddy's distraction had given him all he needed to take out the magic user and finish off the other soldiers.

The steam had expanded to nearly fifty feet wide but was dissipating quickly. Henry only had a few moments to strike before the warriors realized he was there, so he dove into the cloud, searching for his target. The moist air obscured his vision, but he could easily make out the auras. Three green auras and two red ones tumbled through the mist on his right. They were killing each other. That would make things easier for him later.

The red aura he sought churned just ten feet to his left. He saw the outline of the man's robes, but the mage was facing Henry. He lifted an arm and unleashed a blast of energy directly at the charging skeleton. Again, Henry didn't have time to dodge the attack.

He focused his Resolve. Magic spread through his bones just as the blast struck him. He staggered, barely holding his ground. Instead of being crushed to dust, his Vitus took the brunt of the impact and drained at an alarming rate. The ball of energy rushed past him just as his Vitus dropped to zero, and he tumbled backward through the mist, landing flat on his back. He tried to pull himself to his feet but couldn't lift his torso. An invisible force held him to the ground, and he couldn't move.

A shape emerged from steam. The mage had dropped his

hood, revealing a shaved head and dark eyes. Tattoos covered every square inch of his bare skin with swirls and geometric patterns. His lips curled into a snarl, revealing jagged teeth. Smeared blood ran from a gash over his left eyebrow.

"What manner of evil are you?" the red mage spat.

Henry struggled to free himself as the pressure from the invisible magic increased and snapped his bones like they were twigs. His Strength was useless against the spell and all he could do was watch his Health tick down, point by point.

"I will kill you and every skeleton in here a thousand times over." The mage lifted an open hand and curled his fingers. The pressure on Henry increased, his bones crunching under the strain. "I will pulverize you all until nothing remains of your pitiful—" The mage's words stopped mid-sentence, and his snarl dropped into a blank expression. The blade of a sword pierced through his eye, covered in bits of brain and skull. The mage dropped to his knees and slumped into the sand.

A skeleton stood in what remained of the mist, holding Henry's sword. The sounds of fighting had stopped, and the pressure on Henry's body released.

"Skeletons and men, two things I can do without," a soft feminine voice said. Henry's savior switched the grip of the sword in her hand and stepped menacingly toward him.

Henry posted on his left arm to stand and fend off the attack, but a bone in his shoulder snapped, and he dropped back to the ground. He raised his other arm in defense as a streak of blue flame flashed between him and the female skeleton.

"You're next, mage. Wait your turn," she said to Buddy who stood over the bodies of the other soldiers with blue flame broiling in his palm.

"A moment of self-reflection may change your intent,"

Buddy remarked politely while maintaining his threatening posture.

The skeleton lowered her sword and turned her head. Then she looked down and began to study herself.

After a moment, she dropped Henry's xiphos to the ground, turned, and walked away. Buddy lowered his arm and rushed to Henry's side, helping him to his feet.

"Thanks," Henry said, checking himself for other broken bones. "I don't think I could have fended her off."

Buddy grabbed the chainmail around Henry's neck and hoisted him to his feet. "Be grateful she stopped. That was the last of my magic."

CHAPTER 9

"**S**mooch! Get your ass back to Kubey and Trix and form up. Are you trying to get yourself killed?" Master Sigurjon grabbed Koş by his armor plates and shoved him to the center of the street where his fellow Acolytes stood back-to-back. Koş had gotten overwhelmed by the number of skeletons attacking them and lost awareness of his proximity to the others. Before he realized it, he was surrounded. Once again, Master Sigurjon had to save him by killing a handful of the monsters with a single spinning attack.

Koş was exhausted. His muscles burned, and a mixture of sweat and blood obscured his vision. Every attack he delivered was weaker than the last. How many more skeletons could there possibly be to fight in this damned city?

Kubey and Trix had dispatched all but one of their opponents. Their last adversary charged directly at Kubey and leapt into the air. Kubey caught the skeleton with his shield. A dim purple radiance emitted from his body and then flowed into his shield. A blast of light exploded toward the skeleton, sending bones flying in all directions.

Master Sigurjon let out a hearty laugh and then clasped

Kubey on the shoulder. "Nice defense. I can tell you've got some skill as an evoker, but your battle tactics still need work. You used the Ability on your last enemy. You should have either used it earlier when you were surrounded or not used it at all to save your Merq. But still, great execution."

Trix spun around to the sound of the explosion. "What happened? Did Kubey get an Ability? Damnit, I wanted to get one first."

Master Sigurjon smiled and shook his head. "You don't *get* an Ability. They're derived from natural talent and strengthened through the Soul Essence of your fallen enemies. You and Kubey are both well into Tier 4," he said, pointing to Trix's soul crystal, "but Smooch still has about three more skeletons to go before he catches you." He turned to Koş and pointed to his belt pouch. "You're bleeding. Use a healing crystal so you have enough stamina to make it to the ramp."

Koş protested, gasping for breath, "If I can just kill a few more I'll gain a Tier and get healed that way."

"Never count on gaining a Tier to get yourself out of danger. Many a brave Acolyte has tried to weather the horrors of Jallfoss only to die a few kills short of the next Tier with a pouch full of healing crystals. Now, stop arguing with me and heal yourself." Koş reluctantly grabbed one of the red crystals from his belt. He squeezed it and let the healing energy flow through his body. He felt the gash on his head close and the fatigue in his muscles fade away.

Even though his grandfather had told him countless stories involving magic, he'd never experienced its effects. Healing crystals and Drift Amulets were amazing devices, and he entertained the idea of becoming one of the Scholars that taught Junior Acolytes how to use their magic.

The idea of one's body having Attributes wasn't hard to

grasp, but the fact that Drift Amulets could siphon Essence from dead enemies to improve those Attributes had been hard to believe until Koş experienced it for himself.

The Attributes of Acolytes were several times those of normal people, allowing them to perform ridiculous physical feats or cast unbelievable spells with little effort. Those six Attributes were divided into body and mind. The body Attributes were easier to understand: Strength and Mobility were rather straightforward, determining the damage an Acolyte could deal with a sword and the ease of dodging an enemy's attack. Fortitude controlled how much damage one could take before suffering serious injury or death.

The mind Attributes weren't nearly as apparent. Acumen was the measure of strength of the mind: directly related to the amount of Merq available and the number of Abilities a person could possess. Koş hoped to discover an Ability soon so he could understand what that meant.

Perception was a bit more nebulous. A high Perception made learning Abilities easier and also made them simpler to modify and adapt. Koş had only gained two points in Perception, but details of the world around him had started to catch his attention. Burned wood and melted stone seemed out of place, where before he would have ignored such trivial things. A skeleton's limping gait indicated weakness and allowed him to attack a vulnerability that would have otherwise gone unnoticed.

Resolve was the final Attribute. It affected Merq regeneration and also protected against mind effects. Master Sigurjon assured them that enemies capable of affecting their minds only resided in the caverns far below, but Koş wanted several more Tiers under his belt before he had to face such an adversary. He had no idea why Lord Livadi had chosen those six Attributes long ago when creating the Drift Amulets, but Koş didn't feel he was qualified to question the most powerful man in Ikritian history. He brough up his Status to review his progress.

Status

Name: Koş Vasilios
Race: Human
Tier: 4
Health: 28/36
Magic: 27/27
Attributes:
    STR: 14
    MOB: 12
    FOR: 12
    ACU: 9
    PER: 10
    RES: 8

Koş's Attributes had increased significantly with the three Tiers he'd gained. Killing skeletons became easier, but Master Sigurjon seemed to know just how long to wait before rescuing him from their onslaught, so the battles were still hard. Koş wondered how high the Master Acolyte's Attributes were to allow him to effortlessly cut down any number of enemies. He'd tried to Assess the instructor, but it had failed every time.

Kubey and Trix compared their Drift Amulets, trying to figure out who was closest to the next Tier. Trix scrunched his eyebrows and looked at Sigurjon. "Your Amulet is under your cloak, so we can't see it. What Tier are you? Are you the strongest instructor in the city right now, sir?"

Master Sigurjon crossed his arms over his chest and scowled, pretending to be angry. "A rather forward question for a Junior Acolyte." A smirk betrayed his serious facade. "But no.

I'm close but not the strongest. If you must know, I'm at Tier **28**, about four years the junior of Master Jacoby who is at **34**."

"What about Master Tekşan with his invisible force magic, or Master Allito with his **45** Strength points and lightning hammer? They're really strong too." Trix flexed his arms and swung his sword through multiple poses.

"The Force Mage and the Maul of Durmaz are amazing warriors who have turned the tide of battle in favor of Ikrit more than once, but they only recently transferred back to the Bastion as Master Instructors. Their experience is nothing to scoff at. However, they have defeated far fewer humans on the battlefield than the number of skeletons we've fought down here." He motioned to the smashed bones on the ground around them. "I don't believe either of them has reached Tier **20**, but that doesn't mean they aren't accomplished Acolytes."

A cacophony of howls, grunts, and snarls interrupted their conversation. Trix and Kubey turned toward the coliseum. They raised their shields and stood shoulder to shoulder. Koş remained in place with his shield lowered and sword sheathed until Kubey whispered harshly, "Smooch. Smooch!" Koş lowered his head and joined the formation when he realized the other two Junior Acolytes and Master Sigurjon were staring at him.

"What is that? Skeletons don't make those noises." Trix kept his shield raised.

Master Sigurjon didn't seem the least bit bothered by the sounds. "Just like the gladiators of Jallfoss from millennia past, entering the arena to thunderous applause." The clamor slowly faded. "*Human* skeletons don't make those noises. There are about a dozen large cats, bears, gorillas, and even a giant salamander that died in their cages a hundred years ago. They still have the character of savage beasts and will attack Acolyte and skeleton alike without regard. Master Tekşan's crew is about to learn what it's like to fight a skeletal lion."

"Should we help?" Kubey asked.

"Yeah, they're getting kills while we're standing around." Trix pouted, drawing his weapon and looking to his instructor for the indication that they would be allowed to take on more robust skeletons. Koş, however, hoped that Master Sigurjon wouldn't make them fight undead animals. He was having enough trouble with human skeletons.

"No, we're clearing a path for them so they can go directly to the ramp without facing much resistance. We'll meet them there in about an hour." A loud *thump* echoed through the city. Master Sigurjon gave a confused look in the coliseum's direction. "He doesn't usually activate *that* spell inside the arena. His group must be struggling," he muttered to himself. He shrugged and started walking toward their destination. "Come, children. They'll be right behind us. We've got another hundred skeletons to fell, and I don't want to listen to Master Tekşan complain if he has to do our work."

Trix and Kubey fell in step behind their instructor with Koş close on their heels. The cries of the animals began again, followed by another deep *thump*. Then everything became silent.

Master Sigurjon ordered the three Acolytes into a loose V formation with Koş at the front so he could catch up to the Tier of the other two. "All right, ladies. Lead the way. We don't stop until we reach the edge of the city."

Koş readied his sword as the skeletons along their route took notice and began their assault. "Just keep fighting," Koş told himself. "One step at a time."

CHAPTER 10

Henry balanced himself on unsteady legs and then looked up to see the female skeleton walking into the opening of one of the cages. "Wait—" he shouted behind her.

"I would caution you to give her space," Buddy interrupted Henry's cry. "She nearly killed you upon her awakening. As did I, just a few hours ago. Give her a moment to process." After a pause, Buddy continued. "I believe she's experiencing the same amnesia as we are. If that is so, we're the only ones that can give her the answers her memory won't."

Henry nodded in agreement. Buddy was right; waking up in this world was a significant emotional event. She'd return when she was ready.

I've got my own self to worry about, he thought, acknowledging a series of glyphs flashing in his vision and studying the information they provided. He'd learned another Ability and gained a few more Attribute points, but he hadn't even wounded one of the soldiers during the battle, so he hadn't gained a Tier or any Soul Essence.

FOR +2

PER +1

Ability Discovered: Harden I. Reinforce the physical structure of your body. Damage Resistance (All) +1. +1 temporary Health point per 3 Vitus spent

Buddy rummaged through the soldiers' leather packs until he found another healing crystal and tossed it to Henry. "I assumed that last torrent from the mage would have ended you, considering how close you were to a spell that powerful. I'm impressed that your tunic is the only thing destroyed."

Henry caught the red crystal in his one working arm and activated its healing powers. His bones mended back together with a few quick snaps. "I can't cast spells like you, but I'm somehow able to use magic to increase my speed and defenses. Thrust and Harden are the names of the Abilities. They're more reflexes than anything else. That's the only way I could have endured the brunt of his attack."

Buddy made his way over to the tattooed mage and started to strip off the man's equipment. "What shall we do with all these animals? They might be able to take out a few more humans for us."

"Maybe, but they'll also attack us and the other skeletons. I don't think it's worth letting them roam free." Henry ripped off what remained of his red tunic and tossed it to the ground before going through the rest of the soldier's equipment. The only items he found of use were a replacement for his wooden shield and three more healing crystals. He'd hoped to find more, as he'd gone through three of the recovery items in the last battle, but any healing crystals were better than none.

"I agree. Putting them back in the cages will keep you busy

while I study this." Buddy held up a metal-covered book inscribed with strange runes. Henry couldn't get a good look at the hefty tome, and it didn't make sense to him that someone would lug around something like that on a battlefield. Buddy sat on the ground, crossed his legs, and opened the book in his lap.

"And that would be . . . ?" Henry inquired.

"His spell book, of course. Now, leave me alone while I educate myself on all the knowledge he's acquired." Buddy dropped his head to the book and began thumbing through the pages.

Henry surveyed the animal skeletons and dead humans scattered around the arena floor. It would take him a while to move all the arena's inhabitants back to their cages, but if he hurried, he would be able to explore the arena a bit before Buddy finished reading.

After a few trips carrying bones back and forth to the cages, Henry found it was easiest to load them on a tunic he'd stripped off one of the soldiers so he could drag them instead.

"What are you idiots doing?" The woman's voice startled him. Henry looked up from his task to see the female skeleton standing a few feet away. He hadn't noticed her emerge from the darkness of the cage. "I asked you a question." Her voice was raspy and haunting, like a midnight breeze snaking through the branches of a willow tree. Henry also detected a significant amount of annoyance and impatience.

Henry pointed to the skeletal mage on the ground. "Buddy is studying, and I'm putting these animals back in their cages before they regenerate and attack the other skeletons."

"What other skeletons?" If she'd had skin on her face, Henry imagined she would be furrowing her eyebrows.

"There are thousands of other skeletons in this underground

city. As far as I know, we're the only three that are conscious." She crossed her arms over her chest and waited for Henry to continue. "I'm Henry. You probably don't remember your name, but do you have something you'd like me to call you?"

She looked back to her cage and thought for a moment. "It says 'Beast' on the stone above that hole I just walked into. You can call me that until I come up with something better."

"Nice to meet you, Beast." Henry extended a skeletal hand in a greeting. She looked at his boney fingers for a moment, then reluctantly shook them. "I don't have many answers, but I woke up just like you a few hours ago, killing humans." He motioned to the bodies on the ground. "I could use some help to make this job go faster. And while we work, I'll tell you everything I can."

"Fine." Beast picked up a few bones and tossed them onto the cloak. "Let's hear it."

Henry talked while the two skeletons dragged piles of bones across the arena floor. He recounted the last few hours and all the insights he and Buddy had gleaned from the human warriors and their dying memories. He finished with his revelation that the humans were killing the skeletons over and over again and that he had resolved to rescue his fellow undead from the cruel cycle.

The two dropped their last batch of animal bones in a cage at the far edge of the arena. Beast examined the spikes of the portcullis jutting from the top lip of the cage's entrance. "The red mage's final words to you certainly back up that assumption, and I can tell you that the last thought in his mind was the intent to crush you and every last skeleton in the city."

"Pleasant fellow. I liked him better after you aerated his skull," Henry replied as the two exited the cage.

Beast nodded in agreement, then pointed to the only

doorway in the entire wall of the arena. "What do you think that is?" Located at the apogee of the oval pit, the double doors mirrored the shape of the cages, but they were about half the size. Iron bands held together heavy wooden planks, and six-inch metal spikes protruded from each door in three vertical rows. Intricate letters were carved into the stone above the door. They read, "Gladiator Supreme."

"Let's check it out." Henry walked over to the fortified doors and ran his fingers along their surface. The wood was solid with no indication of rot. It probably could have held up to several blows from the war maul Buddy had been carrying around. A large iron hoop made up the handle of each door. Henry grabbed one of them and pulled. To his surprise, the heavy door was well-balanced on its hinges and swung open easily.

A small landing led to a stone ramp that sloped down into the darkness. A carved wooden handle in the shape of a lion's head protruded from the wall at Henry's shoulder height. He'd been lucky with the switches of the arena so far, so he decided to give it a try. As with the others, Henry heard the groaning of mechanisms inside the wall. Slats in the arched roof of the walkway opened to reveal small glass globes illuminating the ramp. He wondered if they used the same magic as the ones lighting the cavern from above.

The ramp sloped gradually for about thirty feet to a square landing with another door on the far side. Beast walked past Henry and made her way down. "Oh good, I'd forgotten my torch."

Henry followed her, examining the stonework as he passed. Now that the globes lit the path, light splashed against mosaics across the ceiling depicting battles between humans and monsters. Brilliant stones of all colors reflected the radiance from the globes, even though it must have been decades since they'd been cleaned and polished.

At the bottom landing Beast pushed open another banded iron door. The next room was dark, but she located another switch on the wall, and in a few seconds, the room lit up. Henry followed Beast into the most elegant and luxurious room he'd found so far in his few short hours of life. Even after years of neglect, the abode still radiated opulence. The room was a thirty-foot square with a domed roof and a large sun globe at its center. Around the globe swirled another intricate mosaic, showing a battle between a sapphire-armored knight and an onyx, evil-looking monster with black horns and armored skin. The knight stabbed his sword into the monster's neck as it spewed fire made of rubies.

Silk pillows with tassels adorned the plush furniture. Beautifully carved wooden tables held silver chalices and ceramic bowls holding food rotted beyond recognition. There was another iron door opposite their entrance, flanked by various silk crests that Henry recognized, but his memories turned to fog when he tried to recall how he knew them. Pegs and hooks stuck out from the third wall holding a complete set of leather armor and a round metal shield. Despite a thick layer of dust, the armor was in perfect condition. Bronze rivets held together overlapping leather bands to give the joints maximum flexibility. Leather buckles and straps connected the pauldrons and the tassets to the torso. A set of tall leather boots stood on the floor just below. Their shin guards went high enough to cover the knee but left a few inches of space between them and the bottom of the tassets. The quality of materials would allow significant resistance to damage, and Henry could tell the armor was designed to enable the wearer full mobility.

Assess

Item: Gladiator Supreme Armor (Superior)

Description: Advanced combat armor for gladiators. (Physical Resistance 2, Environmental Resistance 1, MOB +1). Hardness 10, Structure 50/50

He pulled one of the bracers off its peg and examined it closely. It was light but hard as steel. Even the thread of the stitching was woven with thin metal strands to give it extra resilience. After a good oiling the armor would be like new.

Henry replaced the bracer and surveyed the rest of the dwelling. Even though the room's opulence took Henry by surprise, it was the fourth wall that drew his awe. Hundreds, maybe even a few thousand bronze plaques, three inches tall and twice that wide, were hammered into the wall with metal rivets. There was only a two-foot space at the bottom of the wall that wasn't filled. Each plaque had a name and a series of numbers stamped onto it. The numbers went in sequence from the top left to top right, then continued to the next row below.

Beast ran her fingers across the plaques. "These must be the Gladiators Supreme, and the numbers must be dates. Look, some of them are only a single year, but this one covers a period of over forty years." She pointed to a plaque that read, "Kellin Bloodbeard, 3561-3604."

Henry climbed on a table to read the oldest nameplate. "Gerard Degonhart, 852-860. If the numbers are dates, then that's almost three thousand years between them. What does the newest one say? That should be close to our current year."

Beast knelt down to the bottom right plaque and read, "William H. Talisker, 4285." She quickly scanned the bottom few rows. "Half of the plaques from the last three hundred years have the last name Talisker. A warrior dynasty that ended with this one."

Henry jumped down from the table and walked over to the wall with the pegs. "Well, Gladiator Supreme William H. Talisker, I don't think you're using this fine set of armor right now, so I'm going to take it off your hands."

Beast seemed intent on studying every single nameplate. "The armor is of Superior quality, and you damage easily. Put it on. Then we'll return to the wizard."

Henry let out a quick laugh and began stripping off his gear. Beast was right. His bare bones were fragile compared to something covered in muscle and skin. He'd nearly been killed twice in the last battle, and they only had a few healing crystals left. There was no way to tell what kinds of enemies they would face when they ventured below.

Henry pulled the leather torso armor over his chainmail and secured it tightly. If he had been human, the leather wouldn't have allowed the chainmail underneath, but now it clung snugly to his bones. The chain would also protect the open spots on his arms and pelvis from damage. The boots and bracers still needed to be stuffed with cloth, but they would serve him better than the ones from the soldiers.

Henry took a quick look at the chainmail, realizing he hadn't taken the time to identify it.

Assess

Item: Acolyte Chainmail (Superior)

Description: Armor (Enchanted). Damaged chainmail woven with flow shards (Superior). Hardness +7 vs. non-magical weapons. Physical Resistance 2 (Slashing +1), MOB -1). Hardness 8, Structure 45/50

The chainmail was damaged and canceled out the Mobility advantage of the leather armor, but after nearly dying in the last battle, Henry wanted all the protection he could get.

The last piece of armor, the round metal shield, was about two feet in diameter. Its face was etched with the open maw of a dragon, and the edges had a metal plate secured with rivets to give it extra strength. It was a bit smaller than the three-sided, heavy wooden shield Henry had just collected, but it was far sturdier. The leather straps and grip were strong enough to allow the shield to be used for attacking as well as defending.

There was no helmet with the armor, so Henry donned the round skullcap he already had. It was of much lower quality than the rest of his ensemble, but it would still protect him. His gear secure, Henry drew his sword and took a few practice swings in the middle of the room. The armor was strong but light and flexible. Henry almost had his full range of motion and a significantly higher degree of protection at the cost of only a small amount of his speed.

"If you're finished, let's be on our way. I haven't found anything else useful in this place, and I'm eager to see what the mage has learned." While Henry was dressing, Beast had finished examining the wall plaques and had gone through the rest of the drawers and dressers in the room. She'd found a gray hooded cloak that hung a bit loose on her fleshless shoulders. Henry thought it would provide her with some concealment in the shadows of the city.

Even though the cloak covered a petite frame and slight stature, the female skeleton radiated a vigor intertwined with an inkling of unpredictability. Henry and Buddy would need her strength if they hoped to find answers at the bottom of this cavern.

CHAPTER 11

enry followed Beast out of the gladiator's room and back up the ramp, pulling the lion's-head switches and returning the room and ramp to darkness behind him. Buddy had gathered his gear and walked toward them. "I see you've found some useful equipment to go with your fighting style."

Henry met the skeletal mage at the center of the arena and lifted his arms to show off his new attire. "This may stop me from going through healing crystals like a drunk through wine. Did you find anything useful in your book?"

"I have collected information of some significance from the mage's tome, but I will need many days of studying to discern some of the finer details. For now, I can confirm your belief that the humans are using us to bolster their Attributes."

"How so?" Beast took a step toward Buddy. Henry noted that when she walked, she glided across the ground instead of plodding along like the other skeletons. Her movements avoided drawing attention, and Henry thought she would be hard to notice in a crowd if he wasn't looking right at her. She stopped just a few feet from Buddy. She wasn't close enough to cause the mage to step back, but just close enough to give the hint of a threat.

Buddy didn't respond to the uncomfortable proximity. Instead, he opened the heavy metal book before him and flipped through the pages. "The red mage only wrote about magic, so I haven't learned what happened to us or the city. However, I do think I know what the soldiers were doing. The caverns below contain flow crystals that act as conduits for magical energy. They venture below to retrieve the crystals and bring them back to someone the red mage called "Lord Stavros," who is apparently their ruler. This Lord Stavros is able to refine the purest crystals into the Amulets that have brought us back. He can also use them to make powerful arms and armor, like Henry's xiphos or the lightning maul. Lesser crystals can be used to house single-use spells. Sometimes casting the spell will destroy the crystal, but if not, it can be reused. The tome doesn't tell me how to do this, but we should keep any spent crystals, and maybe I'll learn to recharge them."

"What does that have to do with them attacking us?" Beast asked impatiently, crossing her arms over her chest.

"I'm getting to that," Buddy replied, reflecting her annoyance. "The red mage also calls his leader, "Stavros the Protector." He's primarily an abjurationist, but he is also a skilled transmuter. That allowed him to cast a spell on these crystals that creates a connection between two beings when engaged in battle. When one dies, it transfers a portion of that being's Essence to the bearer, fortifying that combatant's power in a tiered system. That explains the numbers on our Amulets."

Henry shook his head. "I don't know what some of those words mean, but it sounds like they're trying to make themselves stronger by killing us."

Buddy looked up from the tome. "Yes, Henry. Each Tier

strengthens the bearer, physically and mentally, in the form of Attributes and physical and mental clout—Health and Vitus, if you will—but the red mage calls it "Merq." It also allows them to manipulate the magic that flows through them more effectively. In essence, increased skills and Abilities. That's what you just showcased, Henry. You've learned the Ability to absorb damage through your Vitus to protect your health. These Abilities should scale based on your Tier and Attributes. As you saw, your low Tier only lets you resist so much damage before draining you of Vitus completely.

Henry held up his Amulet and examined it closely. He hadn't killed any humans in the previous battle, but the **4** was over half-filled. "So, the more humans we kill, the stronger we'll become. That's reassuring, but it doesn't tell us what turned us into skeletons in the first place or how to fix it."

Buddy closed the book and held it at his side. "No, and I don't believe these soldiers had any clue either. Lord Stavros may have some answers, but I doubt we'll come across him anytime soon. In my opinion, our best option is to continue following your plan, Henry. Maybe in the caverns below, we'll uncover answers. At the very least, we should find the strength to fend off the humans." Buddy then looked down at the cloaked skeleton. "Will you be joining us, Miss Beast?"

Beast said nothing but continued to glare up at the mage. After a lingering moment of uncomfortable silence, Henry decided to interrupt the staring contest. "I agree with Buddy. We should search for answers in the caverns below. You've already been a great help, and we'd be happy to have you come with us."

Beast and Buddy both turned their glares at Henry as if to tell him to butt out. After a few seconds, Beast uncrossed her arms and took a step back from Buddy. "Whatever is down there, I doubt you two would survive without me. In return for waking me up, I might as well continue to save your lives."

"That settles it," Henry replied, relieved to have her strength aiding him and Buddy, "but before we climb to the top of the coliseum and scout the city, there's one more place I want to explore. There's a room labeled "Armory" in that tunnel." Henry pointed to where he had found the controls that opened the cages. "Maybe it will have something useful."

The two other skeletons agreed. After another quick rifle through the soldiers' gear, the three made their way to the armory. Buddy now had two extra pouches around his waist, plus a leather holster that carried the metal-covered book on his right hip. He also wore a few rings and bracelets looted from the red mage.

The archway labeled "Armory" had the same layout as the Gladiator Supreme's chamber but without any of the opulence. The switch that opened the light slats was just plain uncarved wood, and the walls and ceilings they revealed were hewn stone.

Henry pointed to the light globes in the ceiling, proud to show Buddy his discovery. "Are these the same type of magic lights on the ceiling of this cavern?"

"I sense no magic in either these small globes or the large ones above. They're probably dwarven engineering, of which I care little." Buddy and Beast walked past Henry to the double doors at the bottom of the ramp.

"How do you know about dwarven engineering?" Henry asked.

Buddy stopped with a hand on one of the doors. "I . . . don't know." After a pause, Buddy pushed open the door and then looked back up to Henry. "But I do know that I don't like it. Now, if you have no further questions, may we continue?"

Henry followed the two into the dark room. He ran his

hands over the walls near the entrance until he located another wooden switch. He activated the dwarven lights and waited for the slats to open and illuminate the armory.

The dim light revealed a long room with a high, arched ceiling filled with piles and piles of every type of weapon and armor Henry knew existed. The heaps of arms and armor lacked any sense of organization, and only a narrow trail snaked its way to the back of the room.

Henry pulled a rusted short sword from the pile nearest him and examined it.

Assess

Item: Short Sword (Mundane)
Description: Weapon, rusted sword from Ammerthall Coliseum Armory. Hardness 5, Structure 8/20

"Ammerthall," Henry read aloud, wondering if that was the name of the city they were in. Since his Assess had reached Tier II, it had started providing more useful information. He'd discussed the skill with Buddy, and they had determined that Hardness was an Attribute of an item relating to how much punishment it could endure before starting to weaken, taking points away from its Structure. From the weapons and armor he'd come across, better quality roughly translated to higher Hardness, Structure, and associated effects. Henry looked at the magical sword sheathed at his waist, wondering if he could gain additional insight from its expanded description.

Assess

Item: Akşam Xiphos (Epic)
Description: Weapon (Enchanted). Ikritian sword crafted with an extremely rare flow crystal (Legendary). Hardness 30, 100/100

Ability: Drain V. Absorbs 20 Vitus/Second. RES determines transfer rate to wielder

Quality definitely *has an effect*, Henry thought.

He was impressed by his sword's aspects, but even more by its Drain Ability. He sheathed the xiphos and chucked the rusted sword back into the heaping pile of decaying weaponry. "They must have cleared out the entire city. I wonder if there's anything useful in all this junk," he mused, loud enough for Buddy to hear.

Buddy tugged on a leather travel pack stuck under a mound of swords until it ripped in half. Broken glass bottles, metal instruments, and stone blocks tumbled out. "Skeletons are more dangerous with weapons. I assume the soldiers gain the same Essence from an unarmed foe that they would from an armed one. A smart tactic, but I find their lack of organization distasteful. It will take me a bit to scan this room for magic."

Henry knelt down to the spilled contents of the pack and picked up a few of the items. "Leather oil, sharpening stone, some blacksmithing tools, a quill and some parchment, even a set of lockpicks. Buddy, you've already found a treasure. This will keep our gear in good working order. Do you mind if I take any of this?"

"I will keep the quill and parchment. You may have the rest."

Henry separated the useful items from junk and piled them near the door. "Thanks. I'll have a look around. Let me know if there's anything special you need."

Beast had disappeared behind one of the mounds, but she shouted a response to Henry's request. "Light leather armor, maybe just some pauldrons and bracers. Some good boots and a leather belt, plus a few daggers and some throwing knives. I also need a bow with an extra string and a few dozen arrows."

"Anything else?"

"Yes. Some rope and a torch. They probably don't have those globes everywhere below. Also, I'll take that lockpick set, and let me know if you find a potion that turns skeletons into humans."

Henry chuckled as he dug through another heap, careful not to bring it crashing down on his head. "Will do. You'll be the first to know."

The three made their way to the rear wall of the armory and then dug through the piles again on their way back to the entrance. Most of the equipment was rusted or rotted beyond use. The gladiator's armor he took from the opulent room and his magic sword was better than anything he found in the armory. Still, Henry managed to uncover a set of four javelins in good condition and a heavy bronze helmet with a gorget and a split face shield. There was no visor, and the eye openings left him a decent field of view, but he had to scavenge leather straps from a few other pieces to make it fit. Henry knew that if he were to fight a skeleton he would target an unprotected neck, so he was happy the helmet he pieced together would protect his own vulnerability. Finally, he found a medium-sized travel pack that could hold his non-battle gear. He strapped the javelins together and secured them on his back.

Beast met Henry at the armory's entrance, looking ready to battle humans and explore the caverns below. She still had her gray cloak, but underneath she wore light leather studded armor covering her torso and legs. She also wore black leather bracers reinforced with thin metal cables and matching boots. Henry couldn't see everything under her cloak, but he had watched her arm herself with two short swords and any number of knives and daggers. She had a leather satchel crossing from one shoulder and sitting on her hip, and a quiver full of arrows on the opposite hip. In her left hand, she held a sturdy, curved short bow with sharp points sticking out from the front. The shape of the bow flowed from end to end like tongues of a flame, but it was pure black. Henry couldn't tell if it was wood or metal, but it was easily one of the highest-quality items they had found in the armory.

Assess

Name: Beast

Race: Skeleton

Tier: 4

Health: Full

Magic: Full

Attributes:

    STR: 10

    MOB: 32

    FOR: 8

    ACU: 14

    PER: 20

    RES: 7

Damage Resistance:

    Physical: 2

        Slashing +1

        Bludgeoning -1

    Environmental: 2

        Poison: Immune

Item: Elven Short Bow (Superior)

Description: High-quality short bow meant for use in close

combat (+20% damage to enemies within 30 feet). Hardness 10, Structure 40/40

Her Attributes had grown considerably from the Tier increases, though most of her gear was of Uncommon quality, except for her short bow, which was comparable to his Gladiator Supreme armor. Henry motioned to her bow. "That looks like a fine weapon, but wouldn't a longbow pack more punch?"

Beast shook her head. "Yes, and it would have a much longer range, but this is more deadly up close. I can also move better without worrying about it getting broken."

Before Henry could respond, a loud crash echoed through the armory. He drew his sword, and Beast nocked an arrow. Buddy walked out from behind a still-tumbling mass of weapons, completely unfazed by the noise he made. Buddy had traded his red tunic for dark-blue robes that looked like an overcoat with long, wide sleeves and black trim. It was made from a heavy but soft material and of such a quality that it should have come from a noble's home instead of a dumping ground for weapons.

A thick leather belt secured the robes around his waist, and he had found a pair of calf-length leather boots to protect his feet. He wore his bandolier filled with spent magic crystals, along with several other leather straps crossing his chest and upper legs, holding pouches of various sizes. The metal tome still rested on his right hip, but on his left, he had tied three round metal bucklers on top of each other.

"Fancy duds, but what are you going to do with three shields?" Henry asked, pointing to the bucklers.

"A technique I took from the red mage. Hopefully, it will be useful." Buddy tucked a dagger into a sheath on his belt and hefted a leather pack onto his shoulders. "I would have preferred light leather armor over robes, but it's the only item containing magic in this entire armory. It will amplify my Vitus and give me a bit of protection from projectiles."

Beast cocked her head and crossed her arms over her chest. "How do you know this room is void of magical items?"

"In addition to evocation, I have an affinity for divination. I'm not skilled enough to scry distant locations or discern the future, but I can detect the flow and magnitude of magical forces through items and casters. Now, if we're done with the small talk, let's get moving." Buddy took a final glance around the armory, then made his way to the exit.

"I don't understand all the magic terms. Is that good or bad?" Henry stuffed the last few items into his pack, then picked up his shield.

Buddy continued to walk out of the exit and up the ramp. "Neither. It's merely an assessment of my capabilities. I'll give you instruction in magic at a more convenient time."

Beast and Henry followed the mage out of the armory, through the tunnel, and into the alcove with the stairs that led to the stadium seats. Buddy picked up the lightning maul and hefted it over his shoulder. The mage seemed intent on lugging around the heavy weapon. Henry wasn't sure if Buddy thought it might be useful or if he simply intended to collect every magic item he came across.

The three made their way quietly up the steep incline to the top of the coliseum. The last row of arches at the apex was only for show, allowing them to scan the city. Henry peered over the edge and gulped—or he would have if he'd had a throat and muscles. The only thing between them and a hundred-foot drop was a crumbling wooden railing.

"It's more impressive than I thought it would be," Beast

admitted, surveying the back half of the city. The fifty or so monstrous stone pillars holding up the cavern's ceiling blocked some of their view, but they were still able to get a good layout of the underground city. The city's roads swirled in a counter-clockwise pattern between houses, buildings, and courtyards, like water flowing down a drain. One main road, three times the size of the others, curved from the back edge of the city to a large open space at the bottom of a two-mile ramp. The ramp had to be over a hundred feet wide and followed the back wall of the cavern on a shallow slope into an opening to the next level. Buildings obstructed their view of anything below the incline, though there was enough space between them and the back wall that it looked like another ramp led down to a lower level.

Hundreds of skeletons filled the streets below them. Green auras were splattered across the city, and one in particular drew Henry's attention. A thirty-foot green blaze swirled in place at the base of the ramp. He was surprised he could see an aura so far away, but his attention didn't stay on that aura for very long. About a mile away on the main road leading to the back of the city, four red auras were smashing their way through a street full of skeletons. Henry turned his head to avoid the accompanying sensation, then checked to ensure Beast and Buddy were averting their eyes as well. The rage effect was much easier to resist than it had been, likely due to the distance and his increased Resolve.

Beast turned her back and started walking down the stone bleachers. "Let's get moving. They're already too far ahead."

Henry followed her down the steep decline. "Do you think we can catch them? They're a mile away."

"They have to battle their way through skeletons, whereas we can walk freely. Also, I want to see what manner of creature owns such a massive aura."

CHAPTER 12

Henry, Beast, and Buddy exited the arena from the main tunnel and made their way to the back side of the coliseum toward the ramp. Dozens of skeletons lay smashed on the ground, and a few bones had already begun the process of reforming.

"That wizard must have blasted them all with a single spell." Henry noted the patterns in the sand that resembled the ones left in the arena. "Can you use that type of magic?"

Buddy cast him an annoyed glance. "There are no *types* of magic, only different ways to channel it."

Henry had gathered that Buddy wasn't much of a conversationalist, but he was curious to find any way that magic could help them to revive the city's skeletons, so he pressed the mage. "What does that have to do with the abolutioner and the transmufalist you mentioned earlier?"

Buddy let out a long sigh but reluctantly took out the metal tome as he walked. He opened the book to a page with a circle diagram divided into different sections and showed it to Henry. "You mean *abjurationist* and *transmuter*, but that's not important. There are no steadfast rules when it comes to magic. As I told you earlier, the forces of magic flow through all corners of the universe. It can be bent, molded, transformed, anything you can imagine.

"Every being can interact with the magic that flows through this world, but each of us has the propensity to do so in different ways. Those we call mages have a talent for this interaction. From the writings in his book, the red mage seemed obsessed with categorizing magic into different schools."

"But you just said there are no types." Henry tried to follow the mage's explanation while simultaneously scanning for threats in the streets and buildings around them.

"Correct. This is where he and I disagree," Buddy replied, speaking to Henry as though he were lecturing a hall full of students. "He was concerned with classifying magic, but I believe it is more accurate to describe magic as one single force, like an ocean or a lake, and to sort the *users* of magic, not the magic itself, based on how they interact with it. For example, regarding the users of a body of water, there are fishermen, sailors, swimmers, brewers, and many others. Then the fishermen can be broken down into those who fish from the shore and those who fish from boats. Travelers and merchants also use ships, but in a different way than fishermen."

"I guess that makes sense," Henry said.

"In the same way, the red mage and I are both evokers in that we control the forces of the world. I am an elementalist who specializes in the various forces of nature. However, he was a telekineticist, as he projected his will into a tangible force to interact with the world without touching it himself."

"So, you *can* replicate his talents?" Beast pointed to a diagram in the book of a man casting a spell. Henry hadn't realized she was between them until she interjected.

Buddy snapped the book shut and returned it to his holster.

"I can replicate most spells with enough research and practice, but yes, his type of magic suits me. I should be able to copy aspects of it with relative ease." He patted the three bucklers strapped to his belt. "Enough talk for now. We're approaching the location where we last saw the humans."

With three skeletons carrying full battle gear, Henry was confident in their ability to put up a fight, but that was no reason to accept unnecessary risk. "The last ambush worked in our favor. However, we'll need a strategy going into every battle to conserve our resources and assure victory."

"What do you recommend?" Buddy inquired.

"They followed the main road all the way to the ramp." Henry motioned to the bones strewn along their route. "Let's take an alley and see if we can observe them before we attack." Beast and Buddy followed him into a narrow passage between two stone houses and a side street winding toward their destination.

Beast perked up as they neared the wall of the city. "Listen. There's fighting at the bottom of the ramp."

"Remember to hide your eyes when you feel the rage taking over." Henry led the way past the rubble and between buildings. The clash of weapons and the men's shouts grew louder the closer they got to the cavern's edge. The alley opened into a sandy plaza about two hundred feet across with a single stone monolith in the middle standing twice as tall as Henry. Shops and derelict merchant booths lined the far wall but stopped before the beginning of the hundred-foot-wide ramp leading toward the cavern's ceiling. A grouping of several buildings across the plaza had been reduced to rubble, reminiscent of the damage from the coliseum.

Henry glanced around the stone edge of a building. Even though the four red auras demanded his attention, he couldn't overlook the swirling tempest of jade centered on the largest skeleton he'd ever seen.

It had to be over eight feet tall with shoulders as broad as a doorframe, and it was doing a fine job holding its ground against the attacking humans. The three junior warriors with platemail and red tunics surrounded the monster skeleton. They stabbed and slashed with their swords, but their assault had little effect. The skeleton shrugged off their attacks while smashing heavy fists into the ground. The brute should have struck down the younger soldiers, but just before an attack landed, a red flash would pull the soldiers out of range.

The man in a red cloak who rescued the other three at the last moment was obviously their leader. He moved faster than Henry thought possible. He wasn't attacking the skeleton, but he would zip behind it, point to a part of its body while saying something to the other soldiers, then dodge away an instant before being pummeled by the giant.

Henry turned back to his companions and relayed what he had seen. "Buddy, give Beast your hammer. I have a plan."

—

"Yeah, he's a giant, but he's still just a skeleton." Kubey puffed up his chest and brandished his sword. "Why can't we just kill him, sir?"

"Patience, young Acolyte. We must follow the curriculum." Master Sigurjon motioned with his hand for Kubey to lower his sword. "The other three groups are late, but we have a few minutes before we can engage the ramp's guardian on our own." Koş prayed the others would arrive soon. He was close enough to the huge skeleton to use Assess, but he instantly regretted it.

Assess

Name: Ammerthall Guardian
Race: Skeleton
Tier: 1
Health: Full
Merq: None
Attributes:
    STR: 65
    MOB: 12
    FOR: 32
    ACU: 0
    PER: 13
    RES: 0

His jaw dropped when he saw the guardian's monstrous Strength. He had no idea an Attribute could even go that high, and he had zero urge to fight the strongest skeleton in the city alone. He was fine with sharing the Soul Essence with all the other groups. The Scholars from the Citadel taught that Attributes would receive a bump after reaching **25**, then a huge increase after **50**. They called them *Threshold*, and they were supposed to mark points that surpassed mortal limitations. With his own Strength slightly above **10**, he couldn't imagine how powerful a being with a **65** Strength would be. Koş doubted he could withstand even a single blow from such an enemy.

Frustrated, Koş sat with his back against the stone wall of a single-story house. The glyph showing his *Exhaustion* Status Effect had just faded and he'd finally caught his breath. He had finally made it to Tier **4** a few hundred yards from the plaza, but shortly after his body had rejuvenated from the gain, three hidden skeletons caught him with a surprise attack. He had to use his last healing crystal to close the wounds on his face after he fended them off.

He must have been looking glum, because Trix plopped down beside him and offered a stringy piece of jerky. "Smooch, I know this isn't your thing, but Kubey and I have your back."

Koş accepted the jerky even though he wasn't hungry. A bit of food might help him relax, and he appreciated the company. "Thanks. I'm trying not to hold the team back, but this is harder than I expected. When my grandfather spoke about his adventures with Lord Stavros, he never talked about the sand in his boots or his aching muscles or his heavy armor. He definitely never talked about fighting a giant skeleton with a Strength of **65**!"

"What *did* he talk about?" Trix took a bite of his jerky and washed it down with a swig from his waterskin.

"In most of his stories, they were surrounded by some kind of goblin horde, or cornered by a basilisk, or sailing through a hurricane. Just when it seemed hopeless, someone, usually Lord Stavros, would do something heroic, and they'd claim victory. Then they would drink and dance and sing songs commemorating their triumph."

Trix swallowed hard to force down the last bit of chewy meat. "So, you're telling me your grandfather remembered the good and bad experiences with his friends and not how often he had to dump sand out of his boots?"

Koş wasn't quite sure how to respond, so he lowered his head and stared at the sand between his feet while Trix continued. "Kubey and I are your friends, and we're here on an adventure. Who knows, maybe Master Sigurjon is our Lord Stavros. How's that different from what your grandfather did?"

Koş hadn't looked at his situation from that perspective. His friends were counting on his help. "Thanks, Trix. This is hard, but it's something I'll tell my grandchildren about in fifty years."

"Just don't tell them about the time you tried to kiss an instructor." Trix grinned and snorted through his nose.

Koş pushed his friend over as Trix covered his mouth to keep his laughing quiet. "First of all, I didn't try to kiss an instructor. I ate a bitter piece of schmeckenroot, and it made my lips pucker. How was I supposed to know Master Tekşan would walk around the corner at the same time? Nicknames are stupid. Now everyone will call me *Smooch* until I get promoted." Koş pretended to be angry, but he was glad Trix was on his team. Maybe this really was how his grandfather's adventures started out.

Trix got to his feet and helped Koş up. "Unless there's a second-of-all to go with your denial, you should probably draw your sword. It looks like Master Sigurjon and Kubey are about ready."

The instructor waved Koş and Trix over to issue his orders. "The others haven't arrived. I'm not well-equipped to fight this brute, but I'd rather not be here after dark. We're going to take him down so we can get camp ready for the night. Once we walk into the open, he's going to attack. Take turns drawing his attention while the others strike. Stay outside his range because if he lands a solid hit, a healing crystal might not be enough to bring you back."

The three young Acolytes nodded and followed Master Sigurjon into the sandy expanse. They had barely entered the plaza before the giant skeleton noticed them. The monstrous undead attacked like a charging bull while the three soldiers spread out their formation. Master Sigurjon hadn't lied when he described their opponent's brawn. He towered over the three Acolytes and attacked with a speed that shouldn't have been possible for a creature of his size.

The skeleton assaulted relentlessly as the Acolytes' strikes glanced off his thick bones. They didn't have a chance to deliver a clear shot, and if Master Sigurjon hadn't been there to help them dodge half of the attacks, they would have been crushed within a few minutes.

Battling the skeleton required all Koş's attention. He couldn't keep up with his instructor's movements and didn't notice the javelin flying toward him until Master Sigurjon snatched it out of the air.

"You three must keep this one busy while I attend to our guests." The Master Acolyte dropped the weapon to the ground and unsheathed two daggers with long, curved blades radiating a faint, sickly green light before sprinting toward the two figures that had walked into the plaza. Koş tried to get a glimpse of the newcomers, but he didn't dare take his attention away from his opponent for more than a second.

A glancing blow knocked Koş to the ground. He ducked his shoulder and rolled back to his feet. Trix and Kubey slashed at the skeleton and drew its attention long enough for Koş to recover his guard. His lungs burned, and his arms protested every strike, but he knew Master Sigurjon was fighting on the other side of the plaza and wouldn't be able to keep them from being harmed. With no instructor to protect them, the Junior Acolytes would have to rely on each other to survive this fight.

Trix and Kubey must have sensed the absence of their instructor as well. They turned up the intensity of their attacks, dancing in and out of the skeleton's range and chipping away at its massive bone structure with every blow. Koş joined his comrades, taking turns distracting their opponent and attacking any opening he could reach.

A metal war hammer impacted the ground between Koş and the skeleton, leaving a small crater arcing with deadly fingers of electricity. He jumped back to avoid the weapon as a cloaked figure leapt onto the skeleton's back. The guardian ignored the unannounced passenger and lunged forward at Koş with a massive skeletal fist.

Koş narrowly dodged its attack by deflecting a heavy blow with his shield, and he managed to get a good look at the cloaked person. The hood dropped off the figure's head, revealing a skull. It was another skeleton, and it was tying a Drift Amulet around the guardian's neck.

CHAPTER 13

"He's faster than you, maybe faster than Beast." Buddy prepped a blue fireball in his fist as he and Henry made their way to the center of the plaza. The charging enemy shrunk the distance between them with every powerful stride. He was obviously the leader of the other soldiers and by far the biggest threat.

"If speed is he only weapon, this won't be much of a fight, but I doubt his strengths stop at agility." Henry could tell the man's fighting prowess surpassed the restrictions of his own skeletal body, but that only made him more eager to engage the soldier—eager to test his own limitations. Henry readied his shield and drew his sword, fighting the aura-induced rage from the four men before him. "My javelin should have taken out their weakest soldier. I don't think I'll get a chance for another shot. Let's hope Beast can finish them off."

The soldier covered the ground between them with surprising speed. His aura was dim, much like Beast's, just a few thin strands circling his limbs and torso. Henry quickened his pace, hoping to separate himself from Buddy and draw the soldier's attention while the mage used his magic.

He was no more than ten yards from the soldier when a blue flash zipped by Henry's head. It crackled with heat that would have singed Henry's hair if he'd had any. Henry considered himself lucky to have Buddy on his side.

The man didn't evade. He didn't even change his pace. He just sprinted toward Henry until the fireball was inches from impact. The space around him blurred, and he was instantly three strides closer. Henry raised his shield to block the attack as he thrust hard with his sword. The man dodged by a hair's width, dropping below the blade, and slicing with a green dagger.

Henry admired the counter. His opponent didn't waste any movement or angular momentum with his dodge. He was efficient—and he was deadly. Henry knew the man's attack would land, but He would choose how to absorb it. He channeled his magic through his bones as he dropped his arm to parry the attack with his bracer. The dagger pierced the leather and would have flayed the skin of a living being, but the bones in his forearm held firm.

Henry spun to his left, turning his back to the Acolyte for just a moment to set up a shield bash. He thought for sure that the attack would connect, but the space around the man blurred again, and the shield passed harmlessly through the air. Master Sigurjon was now halfway between him and Buddy, running to attack the mage.

A glyph flashed, and Henry felt a tingle in his right arm, then noticed his Vitus draining slightly. Whatever magic was in that dagger had a lasting effect, and Henry realized that his poison immunity didn't apply to the *magical* sort.

As his Vitus slowly ticked down, he hoped it would absorb the damage long enough for him to defend Buddy.

Status Effect: Poisoned (Magical). -1 Vitus/Second

Item Ability Discovered: Status II (Drift Amulet). Display more advanced information about the user. This Ability scales with use and Tier

Buddy released the strap on his belt holding the three metal bucklers in place. Instead of falling to the ground, they floated in the air and circled around him. Buddy ignited both fists and launched dual blue fireballs at the attacking soldier. Just like before, the space around the man blurred, and he reappeared within melee range. He struck four times in quick succession, and the orbiting bucklers absorbed the blows and kept the mage safe.

Buddy clenched his fists, and his body radiated blue light. A fiery explosion engulfed the surrounding area forcing Henry to raise his shield to weather the heat wave. When the brunt of the surge had passed, Henry lowered his shield. The soldier's cloak was completely burnt. It clung to him with a few singed threads. The man shrugged off the mantle and pulled a healing crystal from his pouch, not breaking eye contact with the mage.

Henry ran in front of Buddy and raised his shield. He was impressed that Buddy had used the first two fireballs to lure the human close before delivering an area blast, but the mage had failed to deliver a lethal attack. The bucklers were melted and deformed on the ground. Buddy's hands flashed with the blue flame once again, but Henry was now familiar with the mage's bluff and knew he had little, if any, Vitus in reserve. Before they could resume their fight, a shout of anger erupted from across the courtyard.

"Grab the hammer, you damn idiot!" Beast clung to the back of the skeleton, trying to guide him toward the lightning maul while firing arrows at the humans. She was having diffi-culty getting the giant to cooperate, but at least she kept the three busy and gave Henry and Buddy time to take care of the group's leader.

Henry turned his attention back to the human before him. The burn marks on the man's face had healed. The man sur-veyed the ongoing battle for a brief moment, then glared at Henry and Buddy. His face twisted into a snarl as he stepped toward the two skeletons. Henry walked forward to restart his battle with the soldier, quickening his pace with every step. They met with a flurry of blows. The sound of metal on metal rang through the plaza, matching the blinding pace of their exchanged attacks.

Henry and the soldier were closely matched. Henry's armor and defenses were superior, but the man's speed outclassed him. He saw the openings and knew what attack was needed, but his bones lacked the Mobility to respond with sufficiently swift action. He waited for the right moment to use his Thrust. The Acolyte hadn't landed any heavy blows, but the knicks from the magic daggers were forcing Henry to divert his Vitus to his Harden Ability. If he wasted his reserves on Thrust and missed, the soldier would quickly whittle him down.

A crunch of bone and metal from the other side of the plaza halted their exchange. The giant skeleton had finally downed one of the younger soldiers. Henry saw the skeleton standing over the crumpled body as its red aura swirled and faded away. The other two Acolytes stood frozen in shock, hor-ror on their faces.

The leader's snarl turned to a frightening combination of rage and desperation. Henry couldn't react fast enough to block. The space around the man blurred, and he appeared just inches away from Henry. The man caught Henry with an elbow to the chin, then blurred again to reappear behind him. The blow stunned Henry just long enough for the man to slice the straps holding the javelins to Henry's back.

He took one and let the other two fall to the ground before launching one at the huge skeleton. Just like with the man's body, the space around the javelin rippled and vanished. An instant later, it popped into being on the other side of the plaza and buried into the giant skeleton. The impact caught the skeleton by surprise, and it roared in anger. It reached behind itself and grabbed Beast off its back, then threw her into the center of the plaza. She didn't have time to right herself in the air, and she bounced along the sand like a stone skipping across the surface of a lake.

She brought herself to her feet and scanned back and forth between the young soldiers and skeleton on her right, and Buddy and Henry's battle on her left. She looked directly at the lead soldier, almost taunting the man, then nocked an arrow. She turned away, dropped to a knee, and pulled back her bowstring, aiming at one of the younger soldiers.

The man let out a desperate cry and charged toward Beast before Henry could attack. He blurred forward three times, each spell covering ten paces in the blink of an eye. He lunged at Beast, aiming a deadly green dagger between her shoulder blades.

"Beast!" Henry shouted, praying she would loose her arrow and turn to face her attacker before it was too late. Instead, she vanished, leaving behind the tiniest puff of green aura. In the same instant, she materialized behind the lunging soldier, still on her knee with her bow drawn, but now the arrow was pointed directly at his back.

She released the string and buried the arrow in his flesh. She quickly hit him with two more arrows, then drew her daggers and attacked.

—

Koş saw the tip of three arrows emerge from Master Sigurjon's chest. The sight of his leader's peril distracted him for an instant, and he dropped his guard. The giant skeleton grabbed the hammer with one hand and lifted the weapon over its head.

"Koş, run!" Kubey pushed Koş out of the way, taking the brunt of the blow himself. He crumpled to the ground in a shower of sparks.

Koş drew himself to his feet. Seeing his comrades slain by the skeleton filled him with dread and panic, but he raised his sword, steadied his Resolve, and prepared to attack the monster.

"No!" Even with three arrows in his back, Master Sigurjon hadn't lost the will to fight. He raised his daggers and issued his final order to Koş. "Find the others. Now!"

Koş hesitated for a second but realized there was no way to win. He gave his instructor one last look, then ducked into the door of a stone house.

Master Sigurjon turned and thrust a dagger at Beast. His attacks hummed through the air, one after another, but each one was slower than the last. Beast parried with ease as Henry flanked the Master Acolyte. Between the two of them, they overpowered the human, but the warrior never ceded, likely hoping to distract the skeletons long enough to give Koş a chance to escape.

Heavy footsteps thudded on the ground. The massive skeleton bounded toward the human with the lightning maul in its grip. Henry and Beast stepped back to avoid a wide swing. The bulk of the hammer landed square in the soldier's chest. He flew through the air, and his aura vanished before he hit the ground. Arcs of electricity circled his body as he bounced along the sand, finally stopping at the base of the stone monolith in the center of the plaza.

A stillness settled over the battlefield. The monstrous skeleton walked between Henry and Beast, holding the lightning maul in one hand as easily as Henry held his xiphos. Henry was taller than average from what he'd seen of the humans and other skeletons, but this one dwarfed him by well over a foot, if not two. His shoulders were as broad as Beast was tall, and his bones were twice as thick as normal. Despite his massive size, he walked across the sand with surprising grace with his slow but deliberate stride.

Beast and Henry followed the skeleton to the dead human, as the huge skeleton left boney footprints in his wake that dwarfed those of Henry's boots. Buddy approached from the opposite side of the plaza holding two of Henry's javelins, and the four skeletons stood at the base of the stone monument. It was carved from dark marble and its edges were rounded from centuries of people running their hands over its surface.

Henry was the first to speak. "I know you have questions. It didn't make sense for us either, but we'll tell you everything we know so you can understand this world."

The skeleton looked down at Henry. Its voice boomed. "What a silly thing to say. I have no need for your explanations, skeleton. I am Emperor Ortegus Oxendine. And you, my faithful minions, have done your small part by assisting me in conquering these foes."

"You know your name?" Buddy asked.

The skeleton scoffed. "Of course, isn't it obvious?" He lifted a skeletal hand and pointed to an inscription on the stone monolith in front of them.

These roads of stone that lead to the worlds above and below
Are dedicated to the Great Emperor Ortegus Oxendine
Father of the lasting peace between Humans and Dwarves
May the nations of Stone and Sky, Fire and Water
Forever prosper under the watchful eye of our Guardian
3012-3098

"This is my kingdom, these are my dedicated ramps, and you are my minions. What else do I need to know?"

Henry hadn't realized that Beast had crept behind him while he read until she whispered in his ear. "The idiot thinks he's an emperor."

Assess

Name: Emperor Ortegus Oxendine
Race: Skeleton
Tier: 4
Health: Full
Vitus: Half
Attributes:
 STR: 68
 MOB: 14
 FOR: 33
 ACU: 10
 PER: 15
 RES: 11

A crash of breaking wood interrupted Beast, drawing the attention of the four skeletons to the opening of the main road leading into the plaza. The escaped Acolyte tripped over a pile of rotting wooden barrels as two other skeletons chased him.

Henry grabbed one of the javelins from Buddy and took a

few long steps to gather his momentum. He sent the weapon into the air, tracing an arc that ended with the Acolyte. The javelin buried into the man's shoulder, making him stumble, but he regained his balance and continued his escape. The road curved, and he vanished from sight behind a row of stone houses with the two mindless skeletons still in pursuit.

Henry felt confident that if the youth didn't bleed to death from the wound, the hundreds of skeletons nearby would finish him off.

More importantly, he needed the giant skeleton on his side if he wanted the best chance of rescuing the others.

"Emperor Oxendine, the inhabitants of your kingdom have been turned into skeletons. We are adventuring to the caverns below to find a way to save them. Surely a great warrior like yourself would assist us with saving your loyal subjects from this cruel fate." Beast gave Henry a look of irritation. If she'd had eyes, she would have rolled them.

The skeleton clasped Henry and Beast by their shoulders, tilted his head back, and bellowed out a laugh. His deep voice echoed through the cavern. "How could I deny such an earnest request? Very well, let us venture below and strike fear into the hearts of our enemies." Beast pushed the massive hand off her shoulder as the skeleton continued talking. "As we're alone, my minions, you may call me Ox."

Buddy handed the last spear to Henry as he spoke to the newest member of their group. "Before we continue below to find answers, let's bring you to your royal armory. I have a feeling we'll encounter things more dangerous than humans, and you'll need to be dressed appropriately."

CHAPTER 14

"**P**ush, you lousy smacks!" Eudora shouted at the recruits locked in their match of endurance and muscle. Their shields ground against each other as they struggled to gain footing in the rocky soil. The hot sun directly overhead made sweat pour from the men's heads and congeal the dirt below them into a mucky sludge. Their heavy boots skidded through the mud, leaving divots deep enough to plant spumera beans, but neither was willing to give an inch. They sought no prize in victory, save bragging rights, but that was enough motivation for them to push their exhausted bodies to their limits.

It was a simple competition but an important one for prospective Acolytes to grasp. The recruits' numbers had been whittled down from over a hundred a few months ago to less than twenty now that they were nearing the end of their training. Eudora expected five or six more would drop out before the final challenge in a few weeks, based on classes of the past and her assessment of the current group's willpower. This was the fifth class of soldiers she'd brought through the rigorous recruit training program since she'd transferred to the Bastion almost two years earlier. As their instructor, it was her job to guide the best recruits to become Acolytes and send the unworthy ones back to the front lines of the infantry.

Eudora was one of the few women who had made it through Acolyte training, and only one of two that had ever been brought back to teach young Acolytes. The other was twenty years her senior, Commander Lanthe, the current leader of Ikrit's Eastern Army, who at the moment was smashing the remnants of Varanasi's army into submission. Eudora had idolized the woman since she was a little girl, working with her mother peddling vegetables in the market. Commander Lanthe, a newly minted Master Acolyte at the time, had just returned from a victory and marched through the streets of Ikrit with the men she commanded at her side.

Ikrit was a generous city, as far as allowing the poor the prospect of upward mobility. "Luck is the crossroad of opportunity and preparation," her mother would always say. However, Eudora never believed her mother's words because nearly every spare copper they made in the market went to the drinking habits of her father and uncles. Her father was lazy and abusive, and Eudora feared a future being married to man just like him. That belief was shattered the day she laid eyes on General Lanthe.

What was it like to command men? Eudora wondered to herself on that day. She'd had a rough life, but she left the market and the unsavory world in which she'd grown up to join the military. After a year in the infantry and numerous accolades from her superiors, she'd been given the opportunity to attempt to join the ranks of the Acolytes.

Eudora had been on the verge of quitting dozens of times over four months of training, but the memory of her hero that day in the market inspired her to see it through to the end. Years later, after she had proven herself on the fields of battle, she had been brought back to teach the new recruits, or "smacks," as she referred to them.

In her present group of smacks, three girls had started the class, and now only one had made it this far. The girl had earned the moniker "Lash" when one of the other recruits had tried to steal a roll from her dinner rations after a long march. Lash seductively took off the man's belt, then proceeded to beat him with it until he was a blubbering mess crying on the floor. It may have been a small overreaction on her part, but that was the last time any of the men had tried to push her around.

Eudora couldn't help internally rooting for the girl but refused to go easy on her. Eudora wanted Lash to succeed and be an inspiration for other girls, and that was why the Senior Acolyte was toughest on her. If she wanted to survive the trials of the mountain and earn her stripes in the military, she would have to outperform her male counterparts at every turn. Lash lacked the power to win in the current competition of brawn, but that wasn't the point of this challenge.

Early that morning, Eudora had woken the trainees with the usual threat of denying them breakfast if they didn't hurry. Of course they would eat, if only a rushed breakfast, but they would never be able to move fast enough to avoid her wrath. They hurriedly made their beds, dressed, and cleaned their barracks in the panicked fashion of the mornings they had grown accustomed to. Eudora's shouts had become their sunrise rooster, albeit an angry, loud, and violent rooster.

This morning was different for the soldiers. After breakfast, she marched them through the stone corridors of the Bastion and took them to the armory. She suited them up with chainmail and heavy kite shields, then marched them for miles through the rolling hills of the surrounding forest and farmland. The students grunted under the weight of the chain armor, but few complained. *Just wait*, Eudora thought as she smiled to herself, *this is the easy part of their day.*

When she felt they were sufficiently exhausted from the march, she led them to a small dirt meadow. She drew a circle in the dirt with the heel of her boot, roughly twice the diameter of a man's height, then issued her instructions. Two Acolytes would stand in the middle of the circle, press their shields together, and try to push the other out of the ring. The winner would get to rest. The loser would hold their shield over their head until the end of the next match.

A ring of trainees stood outside the circle, nursing minor wounds but still cheering on the final two soldiers struggling in the middle. Red and Chef were both from Ikrit's prosperous farmland, and thus they had the weight and power to push the others out of the ring and make their way to the final round. Red's moniker was obvious. His red hair, freckles, and flush red skin made him stand out in a crowd even more than his massive height and broad shoulders. Chef, who was every bit as large as Red, had earned his nickname one evening during dinner when he called the vegetable stew he was eating *bland*, and asked Eudora if there was any salt. Chef spent the next two hours cleaning the entire kitchen until every last pot, pan, and utensil was spotless.

The men's muscles strained, and the clang of their metal shields echoed through the surrounding forest. The competition may have seemed like a silly game, but it was intended to be another vital stepping stone in the Acolyte training program. Only the recruits who proved themselves would earn the right to wear one of the rare Drift Amulets.

The Bastion was formally known as the Command Brigade and was founded under the premise of training Ikrit's elite soldiers known as Acolytes. Those soldiers would go on to develop unstoppable fighting techniques and magical powers through their trials in the undead mountain of Jallfoss before bringing that strength to the battlefields abroad.

Chef winced as his thigh began to cramp. He tried to reposition his stance, but the momentary lapse in attention was all Red needed to gain the advantage. He lowered his body and pushed hard with his shoulder, throwing Chef even further off-balance. His heels caught in the dirt, and the match was over. The youth toppled over backward and skidded outside the circle.

Red raised his shield and bellowed a victory cry as the recruits outside the circle cheered. Eudora smiled, but not for their celebration. She had a surprise in store for them.

Red walked over to Chef and extended his hand to help the man back to his feet. They stood at ease on the edge of the circle, talking loudly about shield techniques. "If my leg hadn't cramped, I would have beat you easily." Chef massaged his leg, pretending it was more hurt than it really was.

"Next time, I'll use all my Strength." Red smirked and turned back to the center of the circle before a voice from outside the group grabbed his attention as though someone had seized him by the scruff.

"What do we have here?" a man's voice boomed as he strode calmly from the tree row. The recruits snapped to attention, and a few whispered the name: *Cirilo.*

If the recruits had met the man anywhere else in the world without knowing him, they wouldn't have been intimidated. He was of average height and build, with short black hair that would have been curly if he'd let it grow. He had dark, sun-tempered skin and deep-brown eyes that made him look sad and concerned, not dangerous. But the recruits knew better. He was Cirilo Galanis, Commander of the Bastion and one of the most powerful men in all of Ikrit.

He wore no armor and carried no weapons. The large white shield with the sword and scroll of the Bastion was emblazoned on his red tunic. Its fringe showed his rank of Commander, one thick white line above a single thin one. His demeanor was that of a man out for a midday stroll, but this encounter was no accident.

They had only interacted with the man a few times—those being formal occasions. Cirilo walked toward them with a tranquil stride that did nothing to cover his overwhelming presence.

The Commander was one of the Acolytes that accompanied Lord Stavros on his adventures. He was a master swordsman, and some even said that in a battle without magic, he would hold the advantage over the Great Lord. Every soldier knew the story of the time he beat a frost wyvern to death with its own tail, though most considered the account an exaggeration.

Cirilo surveyed the recruits with a look of mild interest, like he was perusing the wares of a market vendor. His gaze settled on the instructor as he addressed Eudora, "I heard the cheers. Is there cause for celebration?"

"They seem to think so, Commander," Eudora replied, slightly lowering her head in a respectful bow, "their merriment would lead one to believe they've conquered the Varanasi on their own, but it was only a simple test of Strength."

"A test of Strength?" Cirilo raised his eyebrows. "That sounds interesting. May I join?"

Eudora nodded and gestured toward the makeshift arena.

Commander Cirilo turned to the anxious recruits, tension hanging uncomfortably in the air. "Which of you is the champion of this test?"

Heads turned to Red as he shyly lifted a hand. "Me, Commander."

Cirilo picked up one of the kite shields off the ground like the thirty-pound chunk of metal was little more than a dinner plate and strapped it to his arm. "Show me." He walked to the center of the dirt circle and raised his eyebrows at Red.

"Don't keep the Commander waiting, smack!" Eudora shouted as Red snapped out of his daze and rushed to the circle. He cautiously approached the Commander and lifted his shield.

"Whenever you're ready, recruit," Cirilo said softly.

Red lowered his shoulder and pushed off the drying mud. He drove his shield forward and rammed the Commander with every point of Strength he had. His bones jarred, and his teeth ground against each other as his head impacted his shield. His body stopped like he had run straight into the stones of the Bastion's fortress wall. There was no budge, not even the slightest give to the Commander's shield. Red struggled, forced, bashed, anything he could do, but the man gave no indication he was even fighting back. Cirilo's calm expression never left his face.

Red was a few inches taller and many pounds heavier than the Commander, so he should have been able to force the man around at least, but his efforts couldn't even get a reaction.

"Whenever you're ready, recruit," Cirilo said again.

It was insane. How could a man be this strong? Red took two steps back, gritted his teeth, and then propelled himself forward.

When Red's vision cleared, he was staring up at the sky. Lash, Chef, and several other recruits loomed over him. "He's alive," Lash said to the others. They helped him back to his feet as he cleared the fuzz from his head. He remembered the impact, but as he looked around, he was ten feet outside the ring. How had he gotten so far away?

Cirilo still stood in the center of the circle holding his shield in front of his torso. "Next," he said, calmly but forcefully. The recruits didn't know what to do.

"Smacks! Your Commander said *next!*" Eudora's voice rang with a force and volume that shook the recruits into action. "Lash. You're up!"

One by one, the recruits approached Cirilo, and one by one, they were flung from the circle after their attempts to best the Commander proved fruitless. He beat them all. Then he beat them again without showing so much as a hint of exertion. No recruit received an injury beyond minor—cuts, scrapes, and more than a few bruises—though Cirilo made sure he pushed each soldier as close to their limits as he could without breaking them.

The recruits lay scattered around the makeshift arena. Some were covered in dirt, some spotted with their own blood. "I don't see a single one with any potential," Cirilo said to Eudora as he dropped the shield. "Would it be a better use of our time to send them back to the infantry?"

Waves of fear spread over the defeated recruits. Eudora hid a smile, but on the outside, she feigned disappointment. "I expected better of them. We'll train harder, Commander."

Cirilo gave Eudora a slight nod, then turned and walked back into the forest without another word.

When the Commander had disappeared from her view, Eudora addressed the recruits. "For many of you, that was your first direct interaction with the Commander. That's the sad thing about first impressions—you only get one. Now the Commander will forever remember you as a disappointment.

"Gear up. We're taking the long way home," Eudora

commanded. The sun was still high. They had plenty of time to march before dinner, then a few rounds of light sword training before bed.

Just before sunrise, Eudora crept into the barracks. The recruits slept soundly, each taking the opportunity for much-needed rest after the grueling day. The day's heat had retreated, and a chill filled the drafty room. Ten beds lined each side of the long chamber. Enough recruits had dropped out of the class that they had been consolidated into a single stone room.

This morning, there was one more empty bed than the day before. One recruit had fallen out of the formation during the previous afternoon's march. He would be returned to the infantry and integrated back into their ranks. There was no shame in failing to become an Acolyte, only a deeper understanding of what it took to earn a Drift Amulet.

They'd rested enough. It was time to start the day. "Wake up, you lazy smacks! Move, move!" she shouted. The quiet room erupted into chaos. Sheets and clothes were flung in the air, and groggy recruits flailed in their confusion.

Eudora continued to shout until the beds were made and two lines of dressed recruits stood in front of their individual trunks.

After breakfast, Eudora marched the group to the armory. Looks of apprehension spread across their faces as she instructed them to don their chainmail and kite shields. Their looks changed to trepidation when the subsequent march took them along the path from the previous day.

They entered the same meadow, and Eudora dug a circle in the dirt with her heel. The recruits approached this day's competition with much less enthusiasm than they had the day before. Those that lost the competition held their shields over their heads with quaking arms and prayed for the next match to end quickly.

Red and Chef met once again in the final match. Chef was the victor, but he won the competition without a cheer from the other recruits. Red congratulated Chef as they caught their breath. Unfortunately for them, the celebration was short-lived. Dread filled their eyes as Cirilo's voice shot through the muggy air around them.

"Are any of them ready to become Acolytes, Senior Eudora?" the Commander asked in his gruff voice.

She glanced at the fearful group. "Not unless they've learned anything from yesterday."

Cirilo picked up a shield and made his way to the center of the circle where Red and Chef stood. "We'll see."

The Commander went through the recruits three times each that afternoon, then returned to the forest, exhausted recruits scattered in his wake.

On the third and fourth days she woke them and took them to the armory, the smart ones began to catch on. "Senior Eudora, may I ask a question?" Lash stood at the head of their formation, ready for another day's march. Eudora nodded, allowing the recruit to question her.

"I saw his Drift Amulet."

"That wasn't a question, smack," Eudora replied.

"**44**," Lash said, ignoring Eudora's quip, "I've never heard of anyone with a Tier that high. How can anyone hope to beat someone that powerful?"

"How many days do we have to keep doing this?" Chef complained from the position behind Lash.

"Until you beat him," Eudora replied, matter-of-factly, "or until you wash out. Whichever comes first."

CHAPTER 15

Flames swirled around Henry. Their red-and-yellow blaze overpowered his vision, and he struggled to breathe through the black smoke. The smell of burnt flesh forced its way into his nostrils. He held up a hand and watched his skin, muscle, and tendons disintegrate, leaving behind boney, skeletal fingers. "Henry!" The woman's voice echoed through his head and drowned out the pain from the fire. He reached through the inferno, trying to locate the woman, but he couldn't determine the origin of her voice.

Henry woke from his nightmare, disoriented and trying to make sense of his surroundings. Slowly, the present moment came into focus. He was in the bottom room of a small dwelling in the underground city, sitting on a stone floor with his back against a wall. Across from him were an open door and window, their wooden coverings struggling to hang on rusted hinges after decades of neglect. Ox sat below the window, asleep with his head cocked to the side. His chest rose and fell as he slept. Even though he didn't have lungs to expand his chest, his bones mimicked the movements of a living human.

Heavy platemail covered most of Ox's body, and he wore

an iron helmet with metal ram's horns curling on the sides. They had returned to the armory the previous night as the sun globes in the cavern ceiling faded, leaving just enough illumination for them to make their way through the haunted streets. It took a few hours, but Henry and Beast pieced together armor, gauntlets, bracers, and boots with leather straps they cannibalized from other armor sets until they had an amalgamation of plate, scale, and chainmail that fit Ox's massive frame. Buddy collected three metal bucklers to replace the ones that had been destroyed in the fight, then elected to study the pages of his metal tome while Henry and Beast garbed Ox.

Glyphs continued to assaulted Henry's awareness, but he had been on edge since the battle's conclusion, not allowing himself to relax and review their information. A dull pain formed in his head, and after a few hours, it had grown to an excruciating migraine. Daggers pierced his mind until his focus began to blur. When the pain became unbearable, he asked Buddy if the magical poison from the soldier's daggers could still be affecting him.

"I sense no trace of the weapon's magic remaining in you. Did you gain a Tier in the last battle?"

"I'm not sure." Henry rubbed his temples, trying to relieve the pressure, but it didn't help. "I've been too busy trying to fight this headache to check."

"That answers my question. You did gain a Tier, but you've been holding back the flood of Soul Essence. I'm surprised you're even conscious at this point." Buddy grabbed Henry's leather armor and guided him to the ground with all the gentleness of a bedside orc.

"So, you're saying the Amulet is giving me a magic headache?" Henry asked, settling in the sand.

"No, I'm saying your own stubbornness is preventing you

from advancing. Now, relax your mind and address the glyphs you've been neglecting."

Henry did as the mage instructed. He knew Buddy was right. He'd likely been holding off the Tier, but something about being told what to do by a piece of jewelry had made him resist its influence. Henry took a deep breath, diving into his consciousness. He had a day's worth of memories, but once he pushed past those he sank into the thick nothingness of his blank mind. Moving through the fog hadn't gotten easier. If anything, the swirling mass had become more unyielding, pressing harder against him the more he tried to move forward.

Henry willed himself past his empty mind, breaking into his core. He winced at the intensity of blue and white light and saw that the small storm cloud at the center of his being had grown several times over. The puffy white cumulus had turned dark and looked ready to burst with rain. Angry arcs of lightning spat from the cloud, filling the space with explosions of brilliant energy. The cloud spun and billowed, threatening to burst from the overload of absorbed Essence.

Buddy was right, and Henry saw the strain in his core from holding back the Tier. Henry relaxed his mind and allowed the release. A rush of Essence erupted from the cloud, diffusing across his mind and body. Balls of lightning violently struck the edges of his core space, but they didn't damage him. Instead, a deep peace echoed through his body as the cloud shrank back down to a peaceful storm.

Power flooded through his bones, strengthening him and mending the last few points of damage. The piercing headache receded as though it had never existed, and Henry returned his awareness to the underground city. He opened his eyes and checked his Status, finally acknowledging the flashing glyphs.

Status

Human Killed, Soul Essence Claimed, +1 Tier:
STR +1, MOB +2, FOR +2, ACU +1, PER +1, RES +3

Ability Discovered: Harden II. Further reinforce the physical struc-
  ture of your body. +1 Temporary Health per 2 Vitus. Damage
  Resistance (All) +1. Max Health +5

Name: Henry
Race: Skeleton
Tier: 5
Health: 47/47
Magic: 26/26
Attributes:
  STR: 16
  MOB: 20
  FOR: 14
  ACU: 13
  PER: 14
  RES: 19
Damage Resistances:
  Physical: 4
    Bludgeoning -1
    Slashing +1
  Environmental: 3
    Poison: Immune

Status Effects:
  Soul Anchor: +2 Health/Hour
  Skeletal Body: STR -20%, FOR -20%, Physical Resistance -1
    (Bludgeoning -1), Environmental +1, Poison: Immune

Ability: Harden II - Damage Resistance (All) +1

Ability: Harden II - Max Health +5

Item: Gladiator Supreme Armor - Physical Resistance +2, Environmental Resistance +1, MOB +1

Item: Acolyte Chain - Physical Resistance +2 (Slashing +1), MOB -1

Henry was certainly getting stronger, not only by siphoning Soul Essence, but also by pushing his Attributes and Abilities. Pressing the boundaries of his capabilities was what allowed him to progress. The danger, he feared, was exceeding those limits during battle.

After clearing his mind, the rest of the evening went smoothly. When the sun globes dimmed, they'd found a small dwelling near the start of the ramps and settled in for the night.

Buddy sat against the wall to Henry's left, having just noticed that Henry was awake. "We grow fatigued, we sleep, and we dream. We blur the lines between the living and the dead. Our emperor even snores." He motioned his head to Ox, still exhaling heavy, slow breaths in his peaceful slumber.

Buddy tapped a finger against the temple of his skull. "Have you uncovered any more clues in your dreams?"

Henry tried to recall the details, but like before, the harder he focused, the more they slipped away. "No, just a bit more vivid than last time. You?"

"Only flashes, but they faded from memory as soon as I woke."

"Where's Beast?" Henry asked, taking a quick inventory of his gear. Beast had helped him sew up a few of the slices in his leather armor, and they had gotten it back in good working order.

"After spending hours with Ox's abrasive attitude and

a night in this room with him snoring, she left to get some fresh air." The dim light outside was slowly brightening. Buddy picked up a tiny rock from the floor and tossed it at Ox. It bounced off his iron helmet with a loud *ping*.

Ox snorted, lifted his head, and looked around the room. "Ah, what a disappointment to wake up with only my minions. I dreamt I was surrounded by beautiful women feeding me meats, olives, and beer." Despite the hundred pounds of armor on his bones, he effortlessly rose to his feet, though the ceiling was too low to allow him to stand at full height. He stretched his arms straight to either side. Bones creaked and popped as he rolled his shoulders, his fingers nearly touching opposite walls simultaneously with his impressive wingspan. "So, we sleep, but do we eat? And what does a skeleton eat for breakfast?"

"I don't believe we can eat. Some sort of magic provides the energy for us to move. I do feel a craving for a morning çuwabee tea, but I don't know if that's hunger or a forgotten habit." Buddy pulled the straps of his travel pack over his shoulders and exited through the open doorway with Henry and Ox close behind. The sun globes on the cavern's roof were slowly illuminated with each passing minute, providing them enough light to make out the dual ramps.

The ramp going up followed a smooth, gradual curve through a large hole in the cavern's ceiling. The light from above was brighter than in their cavern, and Henry could make out buildings of a lighter color than the sandstone surrounding him. The second ramp twisted down and to the left after a half mile. It was darker down below, but sun globes lit the path every few feet.

Henry was taking in the details of the lower ramp when the entire cavern shifted to a light-reddish hue. It took him a few seconds to realize that it wasn't the cavern's light, but that Ox had walked far enough away that Henry was no longer inside his expansive green aura. He had spent so many hours near Ox that he had gotten used to the tint.

Ox sauntered over to the monolith in the plaza's center, swinging the war hammer like a child playing with a stick. After reading the inscription one more time, he cast a glance at Henry and Buddy. "Where is the grumpy one? I'm ready to regain my flesh so I can enjoy wine and breakfast with my women."

"Waiting for *your highness* to rouse himself." Beast made no attempt to hide her sarcasm. She stepped out from a doorway a few houses down from where the other three had been sleeping.

"I would prefer *Guardian Emperor Lord Oxendine*, but that may be too much for a minion to remember," Ox retorted, undaunted by her quip. Beast crossed her arms and cast Ox an angry gaze, but he either didn't notice or chose not to. "Harvey, how do you know that the cure for our ailment lies at the bottom of this ramp?"

"It's Henry, and I don't know for sure, but the first human I killed was convinced that something related to this curse is far below. That's why the humans come into this cave: to search for the treasures under our feet. The power they gain from killing us is just a perk."

"Then why are we wasting time? I've got better things to do than enjoy the company of you three." Beast unsheathed the two magical green daggers she'd taken from the Acolyte's corpse and stormed toward the lower ramp.

"Slow yourself, grumpy minion. How will I protect you if you're too far ahead?" Ox caught up to her with a few long strides. Henry and Buddy followed close behind until they came to a strange device.

Two waist-high pillars at the top of a ramp held a suspended metal wheel between them. Underneath the wheel was a hole just a bit larger than the chain that came out and draped over the metal cog. The chain followed a stone track down the middle of the ramp. As the ramp curved its way down, a series of smaller, sideways wheels kept the chain roughly in the center.

Henry rattled the chain and pulled it in either direction, but it wouldn't budge. "What do you think this is for?"

Buddy started down the ramp without examining the apparatus. "Primitive dwarven machinery. If they would use magic, they wouldn't have to create such ugly devices to do their heavy lifting." Henry wondered if there was some natural conflict between users of magic and those of machines, but he decided it wasn't the appropriate time to broach the subject.

The four skeletons followed the ramp for about a mile as it slowly curved. Small sun globes lined the sides of the path just often enough to light their way down. The pad of their feet echoed off the stone walls, and Henry realized why the floor of the cavern above them was sand. It effectively absorbed the reverberations. Otherwise, the city would have been unbearably noisy.

They didn't have far to travel after the first curve. The path leveled off gradually at the entrance of a long, narrow cavern. The chain wrapped around a second dwarven wheel at the start of the landing. The sun globes in the ceiling were smaller than in the first chamber, but still provided ample light for them to make out the details of a small city.

One broad, sandy road led from the landing to another tunnel on the opposite side of the cavern, about a mile away. Piles of stone blocks and metal ingots lined the main path in various degrees of organization. Stone buildings stretched behind the piles to the edge of the cavern's walls for a few hundred feet.

Dozens of metal carriages were dispersed along the road and throughout the piles of materials. The carriages had low platforms that sat on stone rollers, each with a seat on one side of the platform surrounded by levers, wheels, and gears. Some of the carriages held different stones and ingots.

Giant metal beams spanned the width of the road every hundred feet. Dwarven machines that looked like fat beetles clung to the bottom of the beams. Each machine had a metal claw resembling a crab's pincer hanging below it by a series of metal cables. The beams were high enough that Henry would have to stand on Ox's shoulders and reach with his sword just to touch them. The beetle-machine on the nearest beam held a stone block in its claw that easily weighed several tons. The claw and its block were suspended just a few feet above one of the flat carriages.

A layer of rust covered most of the exposed metal, showcasing the many years the machines had sat in idle neglect. The beams, cables, and devices reminded Henry of the bones of the undead skeletons in this cavern above, quietly decaying over the years. Both sat in patient silence, waiting to be brought back to life before time destroyed them forever. Hopefully, the time to restore this world hadn't already passed.

The population of the city, like the one above, consisted of hundreds of skeletons of varying shapes and sizes, each with its own unique green aura. Henry stopped in front of one particular skeleton that drew his attention. It was almost two feet shorter than him but nearly as wide at the shoulders. Its arms hung just above its knees, and its bones were far too thick to be a child's. "I've seen a few skeletons like this one before, but there are more in this cavern than the last."

Ox was examining a metal bar he had picked up from a stack of ingots. He sat it back down and joined Henry inspecting the skeleton. "That one is a dwarf. You can tell by the thick bones and wide shoulders." He pointed to a few more along the road. "That one has the same thickness in its bones, but is two feet taller, so it's an orc. That frail, short one isn't a human child. It's a middle-aged elf, probably four hundred years old, just like the grumpy minion."

"It's 'Beast,' and I am not grumpy." Beast had stopped a bit further down the road to examine a carriage, but she was still close enough to hear their conversation.

Henry tapped on the dwarf's skull. "Without their skin, it's hard for me to tell the difference between them. I had assumed that they were all human. I didn't realize there were so many different races in these cities.

"Elves and orcs are easy to confuse with humans. And the dwarves look like wide children," Ox responded.

Henry held up his hands to his face and turned them back and forth. "What race am I?"

Ox laughed. "You and Barney are both humans."

Their conversation attracted Buddy, and he joined them in front of the dwarven skeleton. "And you, Lord Oxendine?" He cast a glance at Beast, who was pretending not to pay attention to them but had shown visible irritation every time he and Henry referred to Ox with reverence. "You're far too big even to be an orc, with bones too human to be an ogre, and how are you so well-versed in anatomy?"

Ox clasped Henry and Buddy on their shoulders. "Emperors must have a vast array of knowledge to impart on their subjects. I can't expect the lower classes to educate themselves, so I must be able to bless you with my wisdom." Beast turned up her palms and shook her head. Henry enjoyed the banter, so he let Ox continue. "Regarding my impressive physique, I am probably a cloud giant. I must have descended from the mountain peaks to rule over my subjects in their time of need."

Ox continued talking about his possible lineage as the four made their way to the far end of the cavern. Buddy got close to Henry and said in a voice just quiet enough that Ox couldn't hear, "He's not a cloud giant, and he's still a bit short to be a Gigas and far too quick of speech. I would say half-Jotun, were we to gamble on his origin."

As they made their way along the road, they passed hundreds of ingots and stone piles, consisting of everything from sandstone to marble, iron to copper. The quality of most of the ore and ingots was Uncommon, but some of the ingots had been smelted into steel, and the Drift Amulet labeled them as Superior. Still, without a forge and the skills to use it, the ingots were useless to them no matter how high-quality they were.

Ox continued to educate them on the anatomy of the various skeletons, and Buddy occasionally remarked about ugly dwarven machinery.

A wheel and chain sat at the entrance to the far tunnel, and another ramp led further into the depths. This ramp had fewer sun globes, but there was still enough light for them to navigate down.

Some of the globes were dimmer than the others. When Henry got a bit closer, he found that they were covered in layers of thick spiderwebs. He pushed the webs back with the tip of his sword, and the surrounding wall sprang to life with dozens of tiny green auras. Spiders the size of Ox's hand skittered away from the light. Henry didn't know if they were dangerous, but he moved back to the center of the tunnel nonetheless.

The tunnel was primarily straight with a very gradual decline. It was long enough that it would have required a large amount of energy to move all the stone blocks and ingots such a distance. They came across a few dwarven carriages linked to the chain in the middle of the tunnel. Each carriage was loaded with more cut stones or metal ingots and covered in thick dust and spiderwebs.

There was one tunnel length where the webs completely obscured the sun globes, and layers of thick webs obstructed their path. A few blasts of Buddy's blue flame sent hundreds of spiders scattering and cleared their way. Henry was relieved he didn't have to cut through the mass with his sword.

They eventually came to the entrance of another cavern, even larger than the one from which the four skeletons had awoken. Despite the immensity of the cavern, only four colossal pillars held up the roof, each a thousand feet across. An undisturbed black lake made up nearly the entire cavern, except for a small piece of dry land a few hundred feet wide that wrapped around half of the outside of the lake.

There were no sun globes in the ceiling. Instead, small ones sat in lampposts lining the few streets and casting a haunting glow on the various buildings. The lights made the city look like the sliver of a crescent moon, almost entirely obscured by shadow. However, the dim light intermixed with the green auras of hundreds of silent skeletons and blanketed the city in an unnatural radiance.

The globes cast just enough illumination that Henry could see the far end of the cavern's ceiling sloping down gradually until it met with the lake. Hundred-foot stalactites clung to the roof of the cavern, releasing tiny drops of water every few seconds. The drops echoed through the massive cavern and disrupted the smooth surface with a series of minuscule ripples.

Dozens of dwarven machines lined the edges of the lake. Some of the machines sat in the water, just off the shore. They had huge pipes that went into the water and various cogs and sprockets on their sides. Further inland on the rocky shore, tall square metal buildings rusted in silence between piles of ore and ingots. Each building had several metal pipes coming from its top and sides and going into the ground. Henry thought the buildings might have been used for smelting, but he had no idea how they would have worked.

Just like the last city, the main road had several suspension beams holding the dwarven beetles, but each beetle had metal spikes suspended from its cables in addition to its claw. Some of those spikes were embedded into cracks in large stone blocks and looked like they were used to break down large stones into smaller ones before the metal carriages could transport them up the ramp.

Buddy flipped through his metal tome. "The red mage didn't have much to say about the layout and uses of these underground cities, but this place must have been a middle ground for stonecutting and ore smelting. I want to say the green auras make the globes on the street posts look like will-o-wisps in the swamp, but I don't remember ever being in a swamp."

Several roads curved through the outpost and led to a few small tunnels on the far edge of the cavern. Most of the buildings were hewn from a smooth black stone marbled with veins of white rock. The marbling reminded Henry of the webs they had just cut through in the previous tunnel.

The buildings were small and unremarkable, but one structure caught their attention. It was a long, two-story structure with several windows along both floors. The building had its own set of sun globes directing light to a stone mosaic on its front. The mosaic was an assortment of different green, orange, and white stones that spelled out the words "The Jolly Squid." The bottom half of the mosaic formed a scene of a giant sea creature attacking a boat and pulling its crew underwater.

Ox saw the building and immediately made his way toward it. "Perfect timing. Let's see what they've got on tap." His loud voice boomed through the city and caused several drops to release from the stalactites and drip into the water. Henry thought he heard a splash at the far edge of the lake, but it was too dark and too far away for him to make out anything. It was probably a fish, but with the echoes from Ox's voice still bouncing around the cave walls, he couldn't tell.

Henry, Buddy, and Beast followed Ox to the building, weaving their way through several carriages and stationary skeletons. A wooden overhang on the outside of the building had long fallen and lay broken in front of the main entrance. Ox had to duck to get through the opening. He bumped his head but continued as though he hadn't noticed. The inside of the building was in surprisingly good shape. More sun globes sat in sconces on the wall, casting shadows through the room. Wooden tables and chairs filled most of the space, along with five skeletons and a few rats that fled when Ox entered. Faded paintings, dusty instruments, and all sorts of eclectic items decorated the walls.

A long wooden bar spanned most of the left side of the room. Years of elbows resting on its top had worn deep grooves into the wood. Several mirrors hung on the wall behind the bar, and there were a few shelves holding bottles of different sizes that contained a brown liquid. One skeleton stood behind the bar, patiently waiting for the next customer but unable to provide any service.

Ox sat on a stool and addressed the bartender. The wooden stool underneath the huge skeleton creaked in protest but held steady. "What respectable bartender doesn't greet his customers? Especially when the patron is your Emperor." Buddy took a seat next to Ox, and Henry walked behind the bar. Beast made her way to an overturned table and examined a few papers scattered on the floor.

Henry squeezed past the undead bartender, but as he did, he faced one of the mirrors. He didn't know what he expected to see, but the ghastly skeletal face staring at him from under an iron helmet wasn't it. The shadows from the dim light showed black eye sockets and a menacing grin that he didn't recognize. After a moment, he noticed that Buddy and Ox were also transfixed by their own visages. None of them wanted to admit that they might never get back their bodies or even reclaim their faded memories. There was no way to guarantee that their mission would be successful or that any of them would even survive. Henry was grateful that the other three had chosen to join him and accept that risk instead of taking their own path.

Henry didn't remember his past, but he did know that heavy moments called for heavy alcohol. "I think this bartender has been out of practice so long that he's forgotten his manners. What can I get you, gentlemen?"

"Whiskey," Ox said without hesitation, taking his gaze away from the mirror.

Buddy gave him a subtle nod that served as his order for one of the same.

"And for the lady?" Henry asked.

Beast was looking at a faded portrait on the wall. "None for me," she responded without looking up.

"Nonsense, you can't kill humans without whiskey. Bartender, four rounds of your most expensive draught. On me." Ox slapped the top of the bar with his oversized hand, rattling the glasses on the shelves underneath.

Henry cleaned the dirt out of four tumblers with a rag he found. He lined them up and filled them to the top with the brown liquid from a bottle that had already been opened. The label had long faded, and part of it flaked off the glass.

Assess

Item: Sharinji Single Malt Whiskey (Superior)
Description: Consumable. Famous dwarven whiskey made from grain and mushrooms. Aged for 45 years in charred Ikritian grossoak barrels. ACU -1, PER -1, RES +2

Ox lifted his glass and proposed a toast: "To heat; not the kind that ignites and burns down houses, but to the kind that excites and slides down blouses."

"To heat!" Buddy and Henry replied in unison. Henry opened his jaw and poured the liquid down his throat. It splashed down the neckhole in his armor, hit his spine, and puddled on the floor. The three looked at each other and laughed. They put their glasses back on the bar top, and Henry filled another round.

Buddy wiped a few drips from his chin and pointed to a framed map on the wall. "With the many tunnels leading away from this location, I wasn't sure which one we should take. Based on this, I think we have an answer."

A sheet of glass covered the map, preserving the pigments. It depicted the outline of the lake, the pillars, and the crescent-shaped city. In the middle of the lake, it had a picture of a squid rising out of the water, and below it, written in calligraphy, were the words "Lake Husavik." Tunnels branched out from all the entrances. The one from which they came read, "To Hershwald and Ammerthall." Most of the other tunnels had dwarven names like "Skutarbrekka," "Lundarvik," and "Olafsfass," and branched off into separate mining towns or smaller outposts. The tunnel on the furthest edge of the city from where they entered led to several large caverns and continued past the edge of the map. This tunnel had the label, "To Hjardharfell and the Dwarven Underdeep."

Henry tapped a finger on the whiskey bottle as he examined the map. "At least now we know what tunnel to follow. It looks like the far one will lead us to the deepest parts. Our next stop is Hjardharfell."

Beast approached the bar and sat down on a stool to the right. Ox picked up one of the glasses of whiskey and sat it in front of her, splashing a few drops of the contents onto the bar. She shook her head and pushed the shot back in line with the other four. "While you three were jabbering, I found something of interest." She held up a yellowed sheet of heavy paper. The ink had long faded, but they could still make out the indentations of the words.

To all citizens, visitors, and friends of Jallfoss
Your Empress, Lady Destria, invites you to join her and her sister, Lady
Estreya
Along with their distinguished guest, Lord Livadi of Ikrit
On the fourth day of Moon Harvest, 4285, at the Ammerthall
Coliseum
As we continue our oldest tradition
The naming of the newest Gladiator Supreme
In the closing ceremony of the annual Arena Games
May the grace, kindness, and wisdom of our Beloved Empress continue
to inspire us all

Beast pointed to the date. "4285, the same year as the last plaque in the chamber from the coliseum. These flyers must have been sent throughout this place, which is most likely Jallfoss."

Ox examined the yellowed paper closely. "I wonder which one of those Ladies was my wife. Maybe both? Hopefully, our journey can revive my lost queen." He raised his glass. "Very well, the next toast shall be to the love we shared. To the Emperor's arms, may they always be open, and to the Empress's legs, may they never close."

The toast made Henry laugh. Buddy just shook his head, and Henry and Ox both sent another shot of whiskey down their boney maws and onto the wooden floor.

Beast didn't follow suit. Instead, she folded the paper and set it on the bar. She examined herself in the mirror for a moment before saying, "I don't think we're the heroes of whatever is happening."

"What do you mean?" Henry asked, cleaning streams of whiskey from the front of his armor and refilling the three empty glasses.

"I mean . . . we're monsters, and the only thing we've done so far is murder humans." She stopped looking in the mirror and turned to Henry, Buddy, and Ox. "We have no recollections of our past, so who knows what terrible things we've done to deserve our fates? That's assuming we even have a past at all, and we're not just soulless demons created from some twisted, dark magic. Even if I was just a victim of whatever happened here, how do I know I won't end up making things worse?"

Henry held up Beast's full glass of whiskey and looked at her through the dark refraction. "The fact that you question your own nature, our origin, and the goal of our mission means you've got enough good in you to carry the faith of all the skeletons in these caverns." Henry slid the glass of whiskey down the bar. "I, for one, am grateful to have you with us."

She caught the sliding glass just inches before it careened

off the edge of the bar. She examined the brown liquid, circling it around in the glass a few times. She let out a long sigh, and reluctantly, raised her drink in the air. "To the bones of my enemies, may they crumble to dust. To the bones of the men who love me . . ." She dropped her head so as not to make eye contact with the other three as she finished her toast. ". . . may they always be hard."

"To the bones!" Henry, Buddy, and Ox shouted their approval as the four skeletons sent a final round splashing down their fleshless gullets and onto the floor.

CHAPTER 16

Koş couldn't bring himself to put the heavy armor back on. He was in no shape to fight skeletons, so defense mattered less to him than evading their hordes. He was too low on energy to imagine trekking even a few more feet with iron plates weighing him down like a stone sinking to the bottom of a lake.

The previous night he had been able to outrun a group of the undead, even while wearing his armor, before he found refuge in a house that Kubey and Trix had already cleared. That morning, however, the fatigue from blood loss and lack of sleep made him question his endurance. He'd bandaged his wound as best he could with strips from his red tunic and used the rest as a makeshift pillow, but the stone floor provided little comfort.

He wouldn't have been able to sleep much, even in a regular bed, with the visions of Kubey and Trix being crushed by the giant skeleton repeating in his head. His friends were dead. So was his leader. He had left Master Sigurjon to die. "No," he whispered. Master Sigurjon sacrificed himself so that Koş could warn the Bastion. There were sentient skeletons on the first level that had ambushed and killed his group and probably the other three as well. He had to get justice for the atrocity, even if it meant dragging Lord Stavros himself into the underground city.

His heavy platemail had prevented the spear from going all the way though him. However, the damage it had done was more than he could fix without magic. He'd managed to stop the bleeding, reducing the Status Effect from Severe to Minor, but every movement threatened to reopen the wound. He had no healing crystals and had no Abilities that would let him rejuvenate himself, even though his Drift Amulet showed full Merq. The hole in his torso had dropped his Strength and Mobility significantly, and the blood loss had brought his Fortitude and Resolve down by a quarter.

Status Effects:

    Injury: Puncture Wound (Moderate): STR -10%, MOB -10%

    Injury: Bleeding (Minor): FOR -25%, RES, -25%, -1 Health/Hour

The skeletons could see in the dark just as easily as they could during the day, so he had chosen to hide for the night. He followed the path of slain skeletons that he, Kubey, Trix, and Master Sigurjon had beaten the previous day until he drew the attention of a group of the monsters, and they chased him to his current hiding spot.

Now, the light from the sun globes filled the cavern and gave him the first glimpse of just how perilous his situation was. The horde he had successfully evaded filled the street. He peeked out the back door. The alley looked clear, but a wrong turn would put him face-to-face with any number of enemies, and he didn't have much fight left in him.

He lowered himself to the stone floor and leaned against

the wall. The pressure on his back made him wince as he collected his composure. "Think, Koş," he said. "There must be a way out of this mountain." He saw the broken remains of a ladder on the ground, and right above it was a hole leading to the roof. The slightest glimmer of hope presented itself. "If I can't take the low road, maybe the high one is open." The roof was just above arm's reach, so he would need something to climb, and the wooden rafters and ceiling looked stable enough to support him. The other problem was that the hole in the roof was right in front of the door and in clear view of the skeletons in the street. They would attack as soon as he walked in front of the doorway.

There were only a few pieces of broken furniture in the dwelling, and he didn't trust that they would hold his weight. His only option was to pull himself up and get to the roof before the skeletons could reach him. Koş was getting weaker by the hour, but after months of Acolyte training and with a few Tiers from the Drift Amulet adding to his Strength and Mobility, he was confident he could make it.

He discarded most of his gear except for his sword and drank the last bit of water from his pouch. He didn't need anything weighing him down if he wanted to make it out of this city alive. He brought himself up and braced his back heel against the wall and took a deep breath. *Now or never.*

Koş pushed from a crouch and launched across the small room, hoping to pick up enough momentum for the jump. He only had space for a few steps before he leapt in the air and planted his foot on the far stone wall. His hands caught a wooden rafter and he pulled hard to lift himself up. He felt the wound in his chest reopen, and he also heard the creak of bones and the pad of skeletal feet on sand running toward him.

He had gotten his elbows onto the next level, but his legs still dangled below. Inch by inch, he scrambled to the roof, pushing against the wall with his feet. The clink of bones from the undead horde filled his ears. He struggled enough to get his torso through and lifted one knee past the hole when he felt a skeletal hand wrap around his ankle. He looked below to see the skull chomping at his calf. He kicked hard, trying to free himself from the skeleton as more of the undead poured into the room. Koş stomped on the skeleton's face until its grip finally broke loose. Several more skeletal arms and clacking jaws lunged at him, but he pulled his foot through the hole and rolled onto the rooftop, gasping for air, and wincing in pain.

As soon as he was out of their sight, the skeletal swarm stopped their chase and went silent. He lay on his back, pressing his hand on the wound in his chest to stop further blood loss. He dropped his head against the wooden rooftop and stared at the cavern's ceiling. The sun globes were getting brighter by the minute, lighting up the red walls and pillars.

Koş slowly rolled to his chest and brought himself to all fours. He lifted his head but immediately dropped it when he heard the rustle of bones in the vicinity. He knew every time the undead saw him above the roofline they would rush. He lifted his head just enough to survey the surrounding area. The nearest exit was about a mile away, but luckily, most of the dwellings were single-story and within jumping distance.

He pulled his Drift Amulet from his bloodstained shirt and saw that his Health was still about the same as when he had woken up, though none of his Status Effects had gotten worse. He looked around one last time, then plotted a course to the exit.

Koş pushed off again with enough steps to get him to the stone ledge. He planted his foot and leapt to the next rooftop.

Bones rustled while he was in the air, but he hit the wooden platform and dropped back to a crouch.

Koş repeated the process of jumping to the next rooftop, alerting nearby skeletons, then crawling to the other side of the roof, but he soon found that it was more efficient to keep running and jumping. He would highlight himself for longer and attract constant attention, but each skeleton would eventually lose sight of him beyond the roof line.

His chest heaved from the effort, and his breath gurgled. He had to stop and rest several times to cough up blood. Every time he leapt and every time he landed, arcs of pain shot through his body.

He pressed on, inching closer to the exit. The tunnel grew larger as his energy dwindled. Just a few buildings from the cavern's edge, his boot connected with an exposed wooden beam, and he felt the structure sink in. Rafters gave way, collapsing a portion of the roof into the dwelling below.

Koş tumbled through the air and landed hard on his shoulder. Rubble from the crumbling ceiling crashed down all around him. When everything had settled, he pushed a few pieces of broken timber off his body and wiped the dust from his face. He looked around the room and tried to take a deep breath to calm his nerves, but it caught in his throat, and he coughed and spat blood. Glyphs began to flash, and pain welled in his shoulder opposite the javelin wound, but they were the least of his worries.

The rubble around him shifted. A man who had been caught beneath the falling roof pushed himself from the wreckage. Then two more stood up. It was Master Jacoby, with Skid and Flash. He was safe, and now that he'd found another group of Acolytes, he could bring them back to fight the skeletons that had killed Master Sigurjon, Kubey, and Trix.

Koş's excitement didn't last long. All their armor had been stripped, and they were covered in blood. The three men focused their attention on Koş. That was when he noticed their pale skin and glazed-over eyes. They had been killed in this room and were now part of the undead legion.

The three dead Acolytes lunged at Koş. Low moans came from their throats like howling wind through a mountain pass. Their movements were sporadic, jerky, and they stumbled over the fallen timbers. Koş remembered from his lessons that for the first week after a human was killed and then awoken as an undead, their movements were slow due to rigor mortis. After that, they acted like the rest of the skeletons as their flesh slowly decayed.

Between the soulless Acolytes, a skeleton had clawed its way from beneath the rubble. Koş tried to scramble to his feet, but his shoulder injury from the fall through the roof kept him from propping himself up on his arm as the skeleton charged. He unsheathed his sword and slashed at the skeleton in one smooth motion. He caught the creature at the knees, and it dropped to the ground. It kept crawling toward him with its arms, chomping with its jaw, and reaching for him with skeletal fingers. Koş brought his sword down with a heavy chop and smashed its skull.

The skeleton stopped moving, but now the zombies were on top of him. Koş scrambled to his feet as the Acolytes surrounded him. He kicked Flash in the chest, and the dead warrior tumbled backward, but Master Jacoby and Skid forced him back and pinned him against the wall.

Skid's milky eyes and face were covered in dried blood. Koş lodged the edge of his sword in Skid's mouth, and the ghoul clamped down hard. Its teeth cracked on the metal.

He pushed Skid hard with his left hand and let go of the

sword with his right, turning just in time to stop Master Jacoby's attack with his forearm. The former Acolyte bit into his flesh and tore through the muscle. Koş released a scream and shoved hard, pushing Jacoby to the side.

Koş now had a clear shot to the door, but Jacoby bit harder. Koş felt his knuckles shatter as he punched his attacker in the face and wrenched until he tore his arm free from the bite, leaving behind a chunk of meat.

He picked his way through the room, stumbling on the fallen timbers. Flash had sat up, but Koş planted a boot in his face and sent him back to the floor.

He stumbled out of the doorway, holding his forearm to slow the bleeding. He was only a short distance from the cavern's exit, but there were two skeletons at the mouth of the tunnel. They looked at him and immediately attacked, running with outstretched arms.

Koş bolted straight at them. Just a single stride from impact, he lowered his body for a forward roll. He tumbled on the shoulder, and as the skeletons reached for him, he felt the bones slip out of socket.

The skeletons didn't have the Mobility to stop their charge in time to grab him, and Koş rolled to his feet and sprinted into the dark tunnel, not looking back. Glyphs cried out for his attention, and he brought up their information along with parts of his Status, hoping the injuries he'd received would not prove fatal.

Health: 18/39

Status Effects

    Injury: Puncture Wound (Moderate): STR -10%, MOB -10%

    Injury: Bleeding (Minor): FOR -25%, RES, -25%, -1 Health/Hour

Injury: Dislocated Shoulder (Moderate): STR -20%, MOB -20%
Injury: Forearm Bite (Severe): STR -15%, MOB -10%
Injury: Broken Finger x3 (Minor): STR -5%, MOB -5%

His feet padded on the sandy floor of the tunnel. The wound from the javelin had fully reopened, and the blood in his lungs was making it harder to breathe. He'd hurt his left shoulder falling through the roof, and rolling between the skeletons completely dislocated it. The bite on his right forearm had taken enough muscle and nerves away that he couldn't open or close his right hand. Despite all the injuries, he was still alive, and he'd made it out of the undead city.

The two skeletons still chased him, and the grinding of their bones echoed off the wall until he rounded a curve and went past their vision. Then, all he heard were the sounds of his own faltering footsteps and raspy breath. Gargled words came out of his mouth in slow gasps. "Just keep fighting. One step at a time."

CHAPTER 17

The path in front of Henry narrowed slowly until only enough space remained for the four skeletons to walk side by side. The road was now just a thin sliver of dry land between the cave wall and the rocky lake shore. It had become too narrow for any houses or dwarven machines about a quarter mile back, and only a flat stone road lay ahead of them. One last sun globe sat in a sconce along the wall between them and the dark tunnel leading out of the cavern.

The Lake Husavik sat in perfect stillness, minus the occasional drops from the stalactites. Tiny ripples quietly distorted the reflection from the dim lights of the city behind them. Beast slowed her pace and stepped onto the rocky pebbles of the narrow shore, taking one last look before descending into the tunnel. She knelt and examined the rocks below the lake's calm surface. The water was crystal clear, allowing a perfect view of the smooth blue and gray stones below the surface. The land sloped gently below the water's surface for twice the width of the road. Then it dropped steeply into blackness.

The other three stopped to give her time to examine the shore. Ox adjusted a shoulder strap on his pack, and it let out a muffled clink. He had taken two whiskey bottles from the pub, both of much higher quality than the one they had opened and drank, and stuffed them safely in his leather pack. Buddy had also found a diamond-shaped vial with a cork stopper in the top that held a black, viscous liquid. Back in the Jolly Squid, he had opened the jar and dipped his finger in it, finding that the liquid stuck to his white bone and stained it black. He kept the vial, hoping to use it to write his own notes in the metal tome.

Henry scanned the dark expanse when he noticed a ripple spread through the water without an accompanying water droplet from above. He looked toward the darkness beyond the sunken ledge and saw a shadowy form emerge from the depths. Ox, Buddy, and Beast saw the figure at the same time, but the attack came before they could respond.

A white flash shot from the obscurity like an arrow launching from a bow, but it was larger than a lance. It burst from the water, aimed directly at Beast, impacting her just before she vanished into a puff of green aura. The lance shot a few feet past where Beast had been, stopped in midair, and was just as quickly sucked back into the water. Though the bulbous appendage attacked and retreated with blinding speed, Henry's Perception caught clawlike hooks on its end nearly the size of his fingers.

By the time the arms retracted, the entire shore where Beast had stood roiled as more flailing tentacles lashed out at the skeletons. The squid's main body stayed hidden in the murky water, but its tentacles towered over Henry, reaching high into the darkness of the cavern's ceiling. Each had two rows of red-and-black suckers with talon-like claws in the middle. A black hooked beak opened wide enough that Henry's whole head could have fit inside and let out a menacing hiss. The monster's aura stayed close to its body and shimmered through various chromatic greens. Henry activated the Drift Amulet's Ability while drawing his sword and avoiding thrashing tentacles.

Assess

Type: Mammoth Squid

Health: Full

Vitus: Full

Attributes:

  STR: 28

  MOB: 35

  FOR: 21

  ACU: 6

  PER: 24

  RES: 4

Resistances:

  Physical: 2

    Slashing -1

  Environmental: 1

    Fire -2

    Lightning -2

    Cold +2

Lore: Far less jolly than depicted by the local pub, the Mammoth Squid of Lake Husavik have not been harvested for a century and have grown to the gargantuan size of their distant ancestors

Item Ability Discovered: Assess III (Drift Amulet). Display more advanced information about items and beings. Expanded details and hidden knowledge are now available. This Ability scales with use and Tier

Henry and Ox dodged the tentacles, but the squid had them

backed up nearly to the cavern walls. Another green puff of aura appeared above the squid's head as Beast materialized and sank two daggers into the creature. The monster released a high-pitched screech and flailed its arms. One tentacle wrapped around Beast's torso, plucked her off its head, and smashed her to the ground before she could react. Henry heard the crunch of bone as she crumpled on the rocks. The arm curled and brought the limp skeleton toward its open beak.

Henry rushed forward. Two tentacles whipped at his head, but he dove on his shield and let his momentum carry him skidding across the surface of the water just below the thrashing arms. He drew his sword and sliced a tentacle, releasing a spray of black blood, stopping just between Beast and the chomping maw.

He rose to his feet, waist-deep in the churning lake, and rammed his shield into the beak. The sharp tip scraped against the metal of Henry's armament, and every time the beak snapped, a loud crack echoed through the cavern. Henry dug in his feet and pressed hard against the monster. The giant squid hadn't been able to close its jaw around the shield, but Henry knew if he gave it just a few inches of space it could grab the edge of the metal kite and rip it from his arm.

STR +1

MOB +1

Glyphs flashed, telling Henry he'd earned a point in both Strength and Mobility, and the distraction was enough to make him miss the monster's appendages snaking toward him.

Tentacles snaked around Henry's legs and arms. They were unbelievably strong and threatened to tear him apart. He directed the flow of magic through his body, and his bones held together, but his Vitus drained quickly. He slashed with his sword, slicing deep into the squid's flesh. However, the magic his weapon absorbed from the squid wasn't enough to recharge his Vitus.

Two blue flashes impacted the side of the squid to Henry's right. The creature shrieked again, and the tentacles loosened around Henry's legs but didn't let go. He heard the sizzle of the squid's flesh as more fireballs impacted its sides. Then he heard the heavy splashes of Ox's boots wading into the deeper water toward the monster's submerged body. Dazzling sparks of electricity lit the entire cavern as Ox brought the heavy hammer down on the squid's head right between its two black eyes.

Lightning arced from the squid's tentacles and coursed through Henry's bones. Sensation overwhelmed his mind as his bones locked in place and his vision went black. A deafening hum filled his ears, and jolting pain wracked his body. The smell of burning flesh assaulted his nose. His muscles seized from the shock, threatening to pull themselves from his bones under the force of their contractions.

He pushed past the pain and blind senses, forcing his body to strike where he remembered the squid to be. He thrust with his blade, and the jolts from lightning instantly stopped, replaced by a blast of intense heat. Wind and sand blasted the skin on his face and searing brightness forced its way through his eyelids.

Henry covered his face with his hands and struggled to open his eyes against the onslaught of bright light and blowing sand. His sword was gone from his hand, and the sound of water was replaced by the howl of a terrible squall. He struggled to locate the attacking squid, but he couldn't see anything past the bright light pouring through the gaps in his fingers . . . his flesh-covered fingers.

I have skin!

Where Henry expected only bone, tissue and muscle covered his hands and arms. His eyes adjusted quickly to the light, and he squinted to keep them protected from the relentless sandy deluge. His sword and shield were gone, as was the rest of his equipment. Instead, a thin brown tunic made from light fabric and matching pants snapped in the wind, barely covering his pale skin and well-muscled body.

He had nothing on his feet but corded sandals. Henry flexed his toes, marveling at the way the muscles and ligaments worked together to make them flutter. Another blast of sand and heat made him wince. He tried to turn his body away, but it came from all directions, assaulting him despite his efforts to avoid it.

"Buddy! Ox! Beast!" he shouted, but only the roaring desert answered him. High overhead, the sun's intensity penetrated the blowing particles in the air and radiated him with a heat so intense he felt his skin starting to burn.

He spun, searching in every direction for some type of cover, but all he saw through the blowing dust were rolling dunes fading from view within a few hundred feet.

He strained his eyes and opened his ears, hoping for any indication of the right direction to go, but even the sun was directly overhead, offering no relief to his accosted senses.

Anything is better than staying here. He started to take a step forward, but a shadow rushed over him. He almost missed it while shielding his eyes, but it blocked out the sun for a fraction of a second. The huge shadow disappeared into the blowing sand behind him. Henry looked toward the sky, but whatever had made the shadow was obscured behind the sandstorm.

That direction is either the best or worst place to go. One way to find out. Henry started walking toward where the shadow had traveled.

The sun didn't seem to move in the sky, and he felt like he walked for hours. He pressed over hundreds of sand dunes, each the same as all the previous. His skin burned from the sun and the wind, and his dry throat screamed for water.

The shadow hadn't returned. Heat exhaustion dulled his senses. It was hard to be thankful for the return of his skin when the elements were causing him such pain, but he had to keep going. The other three skeletons were fighting the lake monster, and he needed to get back to help them.

They were his only companions . . . had they been a dream . . . and this desert the true reality? It sure felt real, much more real than being a fleshless monster on an adventure with other skeletons. The mountain seemed so far away from this endless desert. Henry reached into his memory, hoping for something to anchor him to what was real. The blank fog of his mind left no room for memories of a previous existence, almost palpable in its nothingness. Then a piercing cry broke through the murk.

"Henry!" The woman's scream tore through the desert, drowning out the wind and frightening him with its intensity. He jumped and his foot caught on something, sending him tumbling down the dune and face-planting in the sand.

Henry recognized the voice from his dreams, but it was the first time the woman's cry had come from outside his own mind. He spit sand from his mouth and wiped it from his face. It was fine and mixed with his sweat, further aggravating his windblown skin. He looked around, hoping to see something, someone, but only the desert existed before his eyes.

Then a dull pain throbbed in his foot. The big toenail on his left foot had been torn, and blood ran from a deep gash. He ripped a piece of cloth from his tunic and wrapped it around the toe. He secured the strip tightly around his ankle, but stopped when he noticed burn marks on his stomach where the magic from Ox's hammer had struck him. He ran his fingers across the seared skin and winced at the touch. The damage was as tangible as the rock that had sent him tumbling down the dune.

He got back to his feet and climbed back up the hill. He had to use his hands and feet, but when he got to the top, he saw something barely protruding from the sand.

He crawled forward and noticed an arc of static electricity that shimmered from the object and scintillated out into the desert, quickly followed by a second arc, then a third.

As he drew closer, he saw the object was a jagged yellow rock with blue metallic veins. A chunk about the size of his fist stuck out from the sand, but judging by the way it didn't move under his foot, it had to be much bigger. The yellow was almost like a dull gemstone, and up close he saw brown and gold veins paired with the blue ones.

He reached for the stone, and as his fingers touched it a bolt of blue-and-white lightning blasted into his hands. His muscles seized once again, and his vision went black.

CHAPTER 18

Henry felt the shock flow through the tentacles and into his body, searing his bones and paralyzing him. The biggest jolt came not from the effects of Ox's hammer, but from returning to the dark cavern in the middle of a fight with a mammoth squid. He readied his sword for another slice, but the battle was already over. He hadn't even realized he'd activated Harden. The Ability had negated most of the damage, though it had completely exhausted his Vitus.

Ox took a portion of his own attack as well. Lightning shot through the water he was standing in and arced around the various pieces of metal armor, though he didn't seem fazed by the magic.

Fortunately, the electricity dissipated before Henry could sustain any significant damage. The lifeless tentacles unspooled from his legs and slumped with a heavy splash. A thick black liquid oozed from the creature's open beak and spread through the water. It must have been the same liquid as the ink in the vial Buddy had found. Henry felt the emotions of the dead monster lap over his own thoughts like the dark lake that was splashing on the shore. It was hungry and saw the skeletons as a potential meal, but there was something more. The squid had felt threatened by them and had responded with aggression. The feeling wasn't as strong as the red-aura-induced rage that came from the human soldiers, but the similarities were hard to ignore.

Ox splashed his maul in the water to clean off the gooey squid brains. He'd hit the monster hard enough to hemorrhage black innards through its pale, rubbery flesh, and the gore had started to sink below the calm surface. Ox's attention, however, was not on the recent kill, but on the dark lake behind it.

Two more shadows emerged from the rift below the water, and tentacles rose out of the murk. Several more shimmering green auras appeared behind them.

"Time to go," Buddy said, launching two fireballs at the approaching squid. They hit the water and sizzled, halting the squid's approach long enough for Ox and Henry to start running. Beast lay crumpled on the water, but her thin, viny aura still circled her body—she was alive. Ox reached down with one arm, picked her up, and draped her over his shoulder. Henry retrieved the two daggers she had dropped and set off behind the brute.

They sprinted the last few hundred feet as the squid launched their attack. Bulbous lances shot from the water, and Buddy directed his bucklers to intercept, blocking the claws from striking the retreating skeletons.

Henry stopped at the tunnel's entrance and turned to face the water, ready to fend off any squid long enough for Buddy and Ox to get Beast to safety. Three of the creatures wormed themselves onto the shore. The one closest to Henry coiled its tentacles and launched them at Henry. He blocked the attack with his shield, but it pushed him several feet back into the tunnel. As the squid retracted its tentacles, its suckers and claws stuck to his shield and pulled him forward. Henry sliced the appendages. They retracted, covering Henry in a spray of dark blood. The squid didn't advance further as Henry backed down the tunnel past a dwarven wheel and chain.

Ox continued to run with Beast on his shoulder. There were no sun globes, so Buddy created a few floating flames that gave them enough light to see. Buddy blasted heavy cobwebs with blue fireballs. The spiders in this tunnel were enormous, almost two feet wide, and they didn't skitter nearly as far away from the skeletons as the smaller ones had. A few of the larger critters even rose up on their legs and shot webs at the skeletons, but they were quickly dispatched with a mini fireball, a slash of a sword, or a quick hammer smash. With the watery threat behind them, the skeletons slowed their pace and found a moment of respite among hundreds of oversized arachnids, preferring their company to that of the squid.

The tunnel sloped gently, but without any curves or sun globes to judge their distance, Henry lost track of how far they traveled. Buddy's fire cleared the thick layers of webbing and allowed them to stay close to the chain at the center of the ramp.

Henry's mind whirled, and multiple glyphs jockeyed for his attention. He knew they had something to do with the weird vision of the desert—the icons had been screaming at him since he'd returned.

Returned? Awoken?

He wasn't sure, the vision had felt so real. The heat, the blast of wind and sand, and the sear of lightning. Now he was back in his skeletal body where his tactile senses were completely dulled. In a way, the desert had felt both like a dream and yet more real than the underground world before him. With Buddy and Ox clearing the spiders, Henry sent his attention to the glyphs.

Status

Item Ability overruled. Status II and Assess III now subordinate to Haruspex I

Item Ability overruled. Siphon III now subordinate to Consume I

That's new, Henry thought, almost stumbling on a web-covered rock. The display didn't hinder his sight, but it was difficult to focus on both the information and the physical world. Something in the display had changed, however. Where once the numerals looked like they'd been etched in stone, now they looked more natural, like veins in marble or bark on a tree. The words and glyphs still showed him the same information, but for reasons he couldn't explain, it seemed more intuitive, more aligned with the way his mind functioned. *Fine, strange Ability. Have it your way.*

Haruspex

Status Effect: First Path of the Desert. STR -1, MOB -1, Health -1, Fire Resistance -2, Lightning Resistance +2

Ability Granted: Haruspex I. Draw wisdom from the innate knowledge of the world around you. AFI +1, PER +1. Supersedes item Abilities

Ability Granted: Consume I. A lethal blow forms a bond with your enemies. Retain a portion of Soul Essence upon their deaths. MIG +1, RES +1. Supersedes item Abilities

His Status hadn't changed, apart from the new modifiers, but the *Desert Path* Status Effect confirmed his out-of-body experience. Now that Haruspex highlighted the effect, he realized he felt just a bit sluggish. Hopefully the detriments to his Attributes, Health, and Fire Resistance wouldn't hinder him in any upcoming battles. The fact that the vision had affected him so significantly concerned Henry enough that he decided to ask Buddy at the next opportunity.

The Abilities, Haruspex and Consume, were strangely close to those of the Drift Amulet and had apparently meshed with it. Also, Affinity and Might seemed like new Attributes, but when he reviewed his Status, nothing had changed in that regard.

Henry stumbled over another web-hidden stone, bringing his frustration to a boil. He dismissed the notifications with a sigh and tried to clear his mind, hoping the mage would be able to offer some context to his experience. He resigned himself to killing spiders and collecting their minuscule amount of Soul Essence until the opportunity to speak to Buddy arose.

The ramp eventually leveled off at a circular room branching into three separate tunnels. One of the tunnels went up, and the other two sloped down gently. Each had its own dwarven wheel and chain.

Ox stopped in the middle of the room and dropped to a knee. He handed Buddy the lightning maul, then gently lowered Beast from his shoulder to the ground. "Wizard minion, my hammer is out of lightning. Fix it while I attend to her broken body." Buddy took the maul and continued to watch Ox with curiosity.

Beast's elven skeleton looked tiny next to Ox's huge frame. Her skull was cracked, and her chest was caved in beneath her armor. If she had flesh on her bones, she would have been gushing blood and would probably already be dead.

"I have a few healing crystals left," Henry said, reaching into his pouch.

"No need." Ox pressed his palms to Beast's chest. White energy concentrated around his hands and spread over her body, pulsing near her injuries. The crack in her skull mended, and the bones of her torso popped back into place, filling the cavity in her chest.

Henry looked on, clearly amazed. "How are you doing that?"

The magical force from Ox's hands faded. "I'm not sure. When the lightning from the hammer burnt my bones, I was able to focus and heal the damage instantly. I felt like I could do the same for her." They both looked at Buddy, hoping the mage could provide an answer.

Buddy had already pulled out his metal tome and flipped through the pages. "Just like you, Henry, and most other warriors, Lord Oxendine is a transmuter. However, your transmutation focuses on enhancement. You can heighten your attack and defensive skills. Ox, in contrast, is a regenerator, more commonly known as a healer. He can manipulate the body in such a way to facilitate a healing effect. That would explain his vast knowledge of the different races and their bone structures. I assumed you were only a brute, but I was mistaken. You have a gentle side that fits a true Emperor."

Ox cocked his head and let out a deep rumble of laughter. "The mangled bodies of my enemies might not agree with you, Barney."

Henry ran his finger along where the crack in Beast's skull had been. "Buddy, can he bring someone back to life? Would he be able to restore a skeleton's body?"

Buddy shook his head. "No. Not with this type of magic. That would take powerful necromancy. Transmutation can rearrange flesh and bone, but necromancy involves magic of the soul."

"So, necromancy is what brought us back to life?" Henry asked.

"Maybe," Buddy replied. "There are several ways to manipulate a dead body, and this tome offers little insight into our particular situation. Evocation would allow one to manipulate the bones from a distance if the mage were powerful enough. That is most likely not the case, as it would require a massive amount of energy to keep the spell focused. Conjuration, in the form of summoning, could have brought us from some other plane, but the way we were dispersed through the dwellings makes that seem improbable. Necromancy is the most likely culprit, but there would have to be a powerful wizard continually resurrecting the fallen skeletons."

Beast let out a low moan and brought her hand up to her head. "Oh, I feel like my insides have been rearranged."

"Yeah, the squid did a number on you, but Ox put you back together," Henry explained.

Ox lifted his head, reminiscing on the kill. "Indeed. The watery monster's last thought, as I smashed its brains, was having you as a meal."

Beast propped herself up. "I guess I should say thank you."

Ox put a massive hand on her shoulder. "You're welcome, minion. Also, it's fine if you get attached. You've no heart for me to break when I move on to other women."

Beast gave him a spiteful look and pushed the hand off her shoulder.

Henry started to ask Buddy about the desert vision and his new Abilities, but a quiet clicking sound made the four skeletons look up. Buddy summoned three small flames above their heads, revealing a high, web-covered ceiling. A giant spider, three times the size of a draft horse, crawled down the wall. Its aura slowly expanded and flowed around its body in overlapping lines. Its dark-red carapace glinted from Buddy's blue fire and highlighted its long, jagged limbs covered in wiry hairs. Dozens of red eyes all focused on the skeletons below. Two large fangs jutted from muscular quicks and dripped with black venom that Henry had no desire to test against his poison immunity.

Ox reached out a hand toward Buddy, not taking his eyes off the spider. "Benny, I hope you've fixed my hammer."

CHAPTER 19

A bump shook Koş awake. He opened his eyes, and the midday sun and bright blue sky made him squint. He tried to lift his hands to his face, but waves of pain shot through his body, reminding him of his dislocated shoulder and broken hand on one side and his bite would numbing him down to the fingers on the other.

Koş's head pounded as he fought a losing battle against waves of nausea. He tried to lick his lips, but his tongue was dry, and they just cracked and bled.

He knew he was in some sort of moving cart based on the sound of wheels rolling on dirt, the clopping of hooves, and what he could gather from his peripheral vision. He slowly turned his head to the side. He lay on burlap sacks filled with something he couldn't identify, and all the cargo was kept in check by wooden lattice rails on either side. Fields of wheat rolled into the distance, and toward his feet, he saw the Jallfoss mountain range. At least he was headed away from the cursed mountains and in the right direction.

"Hey, you. You're finally awake. I didn't think you'd make it through the night." An older man's voice came from somewhere above him, but he couldn't turn his head any further. From his accent, Koş knew the man was an Ikritian, probably a farmer.

"You're in rough shape, lad. Normally you Acolytes have armor. They must have forgotten to issue yours. Very strange, the Bastion doesn't usually overlook things like that." The man talked fast, and Koş had trouble keeping up with his words.

"Skeletons . . ." Koş managed to rasp, the word catching in his dry throat.

"Yep, mountain is full of the buggers. I'm comin' down from the Nebulari Pass, searching for napunias and snodbells. I gotta be careful travelin' through the ruins on the mountain so I don't end up as one of 'em. Lotsa folks say it's the elves and trolls ya gotta look out for. Not many make it far enough to see what's really goin' on.

"Yeah, most people think I'm crazy for goin' up there every week, but my Pappi taught me a thing or two about using a sword. He was an Acolyte, just like you. Died in those very mountains almost forty years ago. That's how I knew you were an Acolyte. A young one too, judgin' by your rank."

Koş didn't have the energy to follow the farmer's speech. "No, the skeletons are alive . . ." He coughed out more blood than words, and with every heave, the wound in his chest throbbed.

"Ah, lad, this must have been your first time in the mountain. You can kill 'em, but they keep comin' back. I'm surprised they didn't teach you that in your trainin'. Anyways, you just rest up and stay alive. I'll have you back to the Bastion in a few days."

"Water. Please," Koş croaked through parched lips.

"Whoa, Truffle. Whoa, Butternut." The clopping slowed and stopped, and Koş heard the farmer slide off the cart. He walked around into Koş's view. The old man wore a brown felt cap, and his white-peppered hair was pulled back into a neat knot low on his neck. He handed Koş a waterskin, but when Koş tried to lift his arms, he winced in pain and spilled some of it.

"Ah, out of joint." The farmer grabbed Koş's arm and gave it a quick jerk. The joint rolled back into its socket, but Koş didn't expect it, and he let out a sharp yelp. The pain shook him from his daze enough that he could focus on his Status and the several accompanying glyphs.

Health: 9/39

Status Effects:
   Injury: Puncture Wound (Moderate): STR -10%, MOB -10%
   Injury: Shoulder Sprain (Minor): STR -10%, MOB -5%
   Injury: Forearm Bite (Severe): STR -15%, MOB -10%
   Sickness: Infection (Minor): FOR -10%, PER -5%, RES -10%
   Injury: Broken Finger x3 (Minor): STR -5%, MOB -5%

His shoulder was in much better shape and the bleeding had stopped. Perhaps the farmer had managed to stitch him together. His low Health was concerning, but even more so was the infection. Hopefully he could fight it off long enough to get to the Bastion's healers.

"There ya go, good as new. Something Mami taught me years back when me and my brother, Theo, were playin' on the ol' grossoak tree. I fell off the lowest branch. Popped it right out of place. Walked home three miles cryin' my eyes out, and when Mami saw me, she snapped it right back in place. By the way, I'm Yeorgious. Pleased to meet ya."

"Koş . . . my name is Koş," he managed to sputter between gulps. The waterskin had been sitting in the sun, and the liquid was warm, but he didn't care. He savored every drop until he had completely drained it.

Koş laid his head back against the burlap sacks. "Skeletons killed everyone. Not just my group but at least one other. They were smart. They could talk." The world started to spin, and Koş closed his eyes.

"Sorry to hear about your team. That's what happened to my Pappi. His leader got him killed on a fool's venture. Never heard of smart skeletons, though. That must be the fever talkin'. Your wounds are infected, and I'm not much of a medic, so I can't do any more than stop the bleedin'."

Koş tried to talk, but he was too tired. Before sleep overtook him, he heard Yeorgious say, "Don't you worry, young Acolyte. Just stay alive, and I'll handle the rest."

—

"Recharging magical items is not my specialty." Buddy swung the hammer and tossed it back to Ox.

Ox reached out and caught the weapon with one hand, not flinching in the slightest under its weight. He gave a low grunt of disapproval but didn't take his eyes off the spider circling them.

Buddy's hands flashed with blue fire. The spider must have noticed him preparing the magical attack because it lowered its abdomen and shot a wave of webbing at the skeletal mage. Buddy raised his hands to blast the webs, but they hit him first and covered his body, snuffing out the magic and anchoring him to the floor of the cave. The monstrous spider dropped to the ground and clicked its fangs together in anticipation. Its incisors were longer than Beast's daggers, and black drops of venom splattered off with each click.

Ox raised his maul and rushed the spider. Globs of webbing shot from the monster's abdomen, hitting Ox in the chest and covering him in thick strands. The spider was on him in an instant, chomping at his head. Without the leverage to swing his weapon, Ox abandoned the hammer and let it drop behind him. He strained against the webbing to allow himself to grab each of the fangs just inches before they pierced his skull. The spider began wrapping the skeleton with its web, but Ox's grip held strong.

With Ox distracting the spider, Henry didn't waste the opportunity to attack. He crouched low and sent waves of magic through his bones, enhancing his strength and speed.

Thrust

He lunged with the magic sword and blurred across the room, burying the weapon in the spider's abdomen. The spider shrieked and tried to turn its head to bite him, but Ox held the monster's mandibles in place.

Henry wrenched his sword from the spider's body, then jabbed again, cutting into organs and splattering the monster's innards on the stone floor. Beast teleported around the spider and slashed at vulnerable joints so quickly that she almost seemed to be attacking from multiple points simultaneously, leaving tiny puffs of aura and deep wounds in the giant arachnid every time she vanished. The spider recoiled and dropped a bit lower with each cut.

Three flying metal bucklers surrounded by blue flames hit the spider right in the eyes, covering Ox in hot green goo. Buddy had freed himself enough to join the attack, sending a barrage of magic-laced shields that pummeled the monster. The spider sank to the ground under the continued assault.

Eventually, the giant arachnid stopped struggling. Henry heard two loud snaps from the creature's head and saw Ox break off both of its fangs and then stab them through the spider's head. The spider slumped, and a pool of green blood collected under its body from all the wounds. Its hairy legs twitched as its aura faded away.

With the spider's death, Henry felt a swell of energy rush through his bones. His fatigue left, and he felt stronger, more robust, and more aware of his surroundings and body. At the same time, he felt hunger and a little bit of anger. The spider had wanted to eat them, but it had also been threatened by their auras. He lifted his Amulet to his face and gazed into the gem. A transparent **6** indicated that he had gained a Tier and his Health and Vitus showed *Full*, while a glyph confirmed his progress.

Elder Spinner Killed, Soul Essence Claimed, +1 Tier:
STR +2, MOB +2, FOR +1, ACU +1, PER +2, RES +2

Ox pulled at the sticky webbing on his armor. "It would have been easier with a functioning hammer."

"It would have been easier if it wasn't threatened by us and didn't attack in the first place," Beast snapped.

Blue flame radiated from Buddy, burning the last bit of webbing trapping him to the ground. "It would seem that these animals are attacking our auras, but not in the same way we assault the red ones of the humans. They're not consumed by rage. Instead, they are attacking like they would an invader of their territory."

Henry pulled out a dagger and tried to help Ox remove the spider's strands. "I felt the same thing. We share both the enemy's thoughts and Soul Essence when we battle together. If we contribute to the kill, we don't necessarily have to make the lethal blow to benefit from the effect."

"I agree with your theory, Henry, but I can tell something else is on your mind," Buddy said.

The mage's assessment of his demeanor, though accurate, caught him off guard. Without skin, he felt a skeleton's emotions were nearly impossible to detect. Buddy's Perception must have been growing as fast as Henry's Mobility.

"I had a weird experience when we were battling the squid, and I was granted some new Abilities." The other three skeletons listened while Henry described his hours in the desert and the new Abilities and Status Effects, though Ox lost interest halfway through the story and returned to cleaning webs and green ichor from his armor.

"You said *granted* Abilities instead of discovered?" Buddy asked when Henry had finished his account. "As though you'd been given something from a magical item instead of it being internally derived. Even more curious is the detriment of the Status Effect and your new Attributes."

"You shouldn't be concerned about your new Abilities and Attributes. I've had those this whole time," Ox injected, still more concerned with cleaning the sticky spider remains from his armor than listening to Henry's story.

"You mean Haruspex and Consume? What about Might and Affinity?" The revelation was a huge surprise to Henry, but the conversation made him realize that the four hadn't had time to compare their strengths and weaknesses. If they wanted to stay alive . . . mostly alive . . . they would need a better understanding of each other's capabilities.

"Yes, Herbie, I have all of those, plus *Presence*, listed right below my other Attributes."

Henry used Haruspex on the giant skeleton, but it didn't reveal the three Attributes he was talking about. But then, Henry's Status didn't either. Perhaps Ox could provide him with some insight if he'd had a similar experience. "Did you ever have a vision of wandering through a desert?"

"As a great adventurer, I'm sure I've gone on many harrowing adventures. However, whether it be desert, jungle, mountain, or beach, I don't *wander*. I stride with purpose, as the women I leave behind would attest."

Buddy ignored Ox and flipped through his metal tome. After a few moments of searching, he shook his head "I'm sorry, Henry. The red mage left no reference to these happenings."

Once again, Henry was at a loss for an explanation, but he resolved to move forward and uncover the answers to the growing number of mysteries. "I have no idea what all this means, but it seems like we're getting stronger. I'm at Tier **6**. How about everyone else?"

"**6** as well." Beast was at the head of the spider. She cut into the monster's mandibles and pulled out a green, fleshy sack. A viscous black toxin dripped from the organ as she squeezed it into one of her glass vials. She saw Henry watching her and said, "Venom. For my arrows," as though harvesting from a colossal spider was a normal occurrence.

Henry assumed the spinner's venom was natural and he had an urge to test out the poison immunity granted by his Skeletal Body. However, he quickly dismissed the idea as not worth the risk.

When Henry had scraped the last bit of webbing off Ox, he looked down the three tunnels. "If I remember correctly from the map on the wall, this one on the left leads down the furthest."

"You are correct. It's not that I don't trust your memory, but I sketched it down." Buddy snapped his metal tome shut and started walking in the indicated direction.

Henry examined the left tunnel. Buddy's fire illuminated the entrance, and further below he saw splotches of blue and green light. The volume of webbing along the walls receded as the four made their way down the stone tunnel.

The mage had an abundance of Vitus, but it wasn't endless. Preferring not to waste his stores, Buddy slowly lowered the intensity of his fire and eventually extinguished it. By now, the walls were lit up with blue and green streams of light, and they could see almost as clearly as they could with Buddy's fire. Henry looked closely and found that the light was coming from growths of puffy fungus. He touched one, and his finger sunk in. A bit of the fungus stuck to the bone, leaving it glowing blue.

Haruspex

Object: Lumimoss (Common)

Description: Lichen, Cryptogam. Cave moss that uses light to repel insects

"Lichen? Cryptogam?" Henry read the information out loud, not quite sure what the terms meant.

"A lichen is a fungus, usually surrounded by a colony of algae." Ox scraped his fingers along the wall, collecting a handful of the glowing fluff in his hand. He tossed the colorful mound at Beast, but she teleported out of the way, and it smacked into the wall, leaving a splatter of blue-green incandescence.

Beast gave him a look that said, *don't do that again.* Ox wiped his hand on his chest, leaving a smear of color on his armor. He looked around in every direction but back at Beast, acting like he hadn't just thrown the ball of muck at her, and continued his explanation. "Cryptogam means that it reproduces without seeds or flowers."

Ox's affinity for nature and anatomy seemed odd to Henry

at first, but no stranger than his own knack for weapons or Buddy's grasp of magic. Beast seemed beyond proficient with stealth and magic, and she fought with deadly precision, but if she'd gleaned any insight from her skills, she'd kept it to herself.

They followed the chain in the middle of the tunnel for another mile until the floor leveled and opened into another cavern. The new cave was several hundred feet across, with huge stacks of stone and ore and a few dwarven carts. Pathways snaked their way through the heaps and converged on the spot they were entering.

The piles stopped them from seeing to the other end, but they heard hissing and the sound of claws scraping against stone coming from the distance.

They lowered their bodies and quietly made their way around the rubble. The hissing got louder and more frantic. They rounded one massive pile and saw three lizards clawing at the far wall. Including their tails, the creatures were longer than Ox was tall. They had thick, red-brown scales on their backs and their long, clawed hands scraped against the smooth wall. Henry recognized them as the living versions of one of the bone animals from the arena.

They looked like they were trying to climb up to a ledge just above their reach but couldn't quite get a good grip.

"Beak, beak!" They heard a high-pitched squeak coming from the ledge and saw a small animal's furry head and pointed ears looking down at the lizards. The creature picked up a rock the size of its own head and threw it. It smacked one of the lizards on the end of its snout with a painful-sounding *thump*. The lizard opened its mouth wide and let out a hissing snarl. Thick strands of saliva hung between the sharp teeth in its open maw.

It clamored up the back of one of the other lizards, allowing it to reach the ledge with its claws. "Beak, beak, beak!" The furry creature squeaked and smashed a rock onto the clawed fingers, but the lizard had a firm hold and slowly pulled itself up to the ledge.

"I have no reason to hide from such weak creatures." Buddy walked out from behind the stone pile. His left hand lit up with purple sparks of lightning, and his right swirled with white frost. The light from the spells illuminated the cavern, and cracks of electricity echoed off the walls. The three lizards turned to see Buddy's deathly grin as his robes rippled from the force of the magic.

He unleashed the spells and sent the two balls of energy flying at the lizards. They tried to scurry for cover, but the spells impacted them before they had a chance. The ice magic froze them in place, and the lightning shattered them into tiny pieces. Before the last lizard chunk rolled to a stop, Buddy had already opened his metal tome to the page with the sketched map and begun studying the cavern's layout.

Henry walked over to examine the lizards' remains. Small clouds of mist rose from the frozen lumps, and tiny arcs of electricity flitted from piece to piece. The sparks reminded him of the yellow rock in the desert, and he cautiously avoided touching them. Beast joined him near the carnage, standing on her toes to get a better view of the creature on the ledge. Henry tried to use Haruspex to analyze the creature, but he had trouble getting the Ability to lock on to the jumble of fur long enough for it to activate. It resisted for another moment, then gave way to his will.

Haruspex

Type: Trogold
Health: Full
Vitus: Full

Attributes:

> **STR: 3**
>
> **MOB: 18**
>
> **FOR: 5**
>
> **ACU: 12**
>
> **PER: 14**
>
> **RES: 4**

Lore: The trogold is a mystical and solitary creature, feared by vermin and adventurers alike. Its high intelligence leads many scholars to believe it descended from a sentient race, though the theory has never been proven

Haruspex worked almost exactly like the divinity enchantments in his Drift Amulet. The description implied both were operating in tandem, but what that meant was unclear. The Lore feature in the information was interesting, but not very useful. Buddy had a theory that since the human leader, Lord Stavros, was the one to create the Amulets, perhaps the Lore came from knowledge he possessed. If that was true, the further they traveled, the less reliable the information would prove to be.

The claim that the furry creature could cause any level of angst among the warriors Henry had fought was unlikely, but he'd seen many stranger things in the two days of memories available to him.

The animal was backed against the wall so that Henry and Beast could still only see the head with its matted gray fur covering large black eyes. A bushy tail twitched with a combination of agitation and curiosity. It had furry, pointy ears on the top of its head with pink centers and a black, snub nose. Its eyes stayed locked on Buddy with an almost humanoid expression of wonder.

"This way." Buddy motioned to one of the several tunnels leading from the cavern. He closed the tome and started to take a step, but a sound from the tunnel halted him in place. Beast drew her bow, and Ox spun his maul between his hands before taking a firm, double grip. Henry heard the sound too, and it wasn't a pleasant one.

It started as a faint scraping and sliding noise coming from the tunnel, but grew louder with each passing second. It quickly developed into a roar of claws and tails slithering on stone mixed with the hissing sound of many, many lizards. They were close and advancing quickly.

Henry and Ox stepped back before Buddy ignited his hands. Beast quietly summited one of the rubble piles and nocked an arrow. Light from the fungus glinted at the tunnel's far end, reflecting off rapidly approaching lizard scales. Dozens of the animals crowded their way through the narrow space, and from the sound of it, even more were close behind.

Henry looked over his shoulder at Buddy. "That's the way we need to go?"

The mage nodded in response.

"Then we'll have to go through them," Henry said, tightening his grip on his shield's leather straps.

CHAPTER 20

"Red . . . Red, wake up!" Lash tapped a finger on the middle of the sleeping recruit's forehead. Though she was sore and exhausted from the bouts with Commander Cirilo, she hadn't been able to sleep.

Red tried to roll away from his assailant, but Lash pinched the skin on the back of his arm hard enough to elicit a tiny squeal. "What?" the farm boy whispered harshly. "Everything hurts, and now I'm going to be even more tired when the Commander beats me to a pulp again."

Lash had become close with Red over the past few months. Even so, she knew it was asking a lot of their friendship for her to be pinching him in the middle of the night. That was why she'd enlisted help.

"Red. Lash has a plan," Chef whispered, towering behind Lash's athletic frame.

Red rubbed his eyes and tried to focus on the two soldiers. The dim moonlight that came through the stone windows of their barracks provided little assistance.

Lash could be stubborn when she wanted something, and she wasn't about to leave Red alone until he listened to what she had to say. She crossed her arms and cocked her head, indicating she was waiting for his full attention.

"Fine," Red grumbled. "Let's hear it so I can go back to sleep."

"There has to be a way to beat him—" Lash started to say, but Red rolled his eyes, sighed, and started to turn away.

"No, no. Hear me out." Lash pinched his arm again to stop him from going back to sleep. "We've only got a few weeks left before the final test. We're months past the point of being broken down by impossible tasks. There's a way to beat him. We just need to figure it out."

Chef leaned over Lash's shoulder and whispered excitedly, "Yeah, we just have to be stronger than him."

Lash enjoyed being around Chef and Red, but they could be simple at times. They'd lived lives on their farms that definitely hadn't been easy, and Lash didn't look down on them, but they had learned that most of their problems could be solved by simply working harder. Strength was their answer to everything.

Lash didn't have the luxury of just being stronger. She'd grown up in a poor fishing village on the border between Ikrit and Varanasi. Calling it a fishing village wasn't entirely accurate. It had been a battleground between the two warring nations for well over a decade. Lash's parents were killed fighting the Ikritian soldiers they called invaders when Lash was only eight years old. At that young age she didn't understand the war, but she began plotting her revenge nonetheless.

That is, until she met her idol. The woman walked into Lash's village like she had no fear. She wore the red tunic of the feared Acolytes, but Lash quickly realized the only people that needed to be afraid of her were the Ikritian soldiers she was leading. They would snap to attention and scramble to carry out her every order. The woman could have leveled their village. Instead, she had the small band of soldiers bringing food and healing the wounded. Lash refused the bread the woman offered but continued to watch her. As a young girl, she thought it had to be some kind of a trick.

Lash followed the Acolyte from a distance all the way back to Ikrit while the woman slaughtered the Varanasi soldiers one moment and healed a wounded villager the next. She was the perfect balance of violence and kindness, like a lioness protecting her cubs.

The hate Lash felt for her parent's murderers left her as she realized she wanted to become everything this woman was. She cut her hair, worked on her Ikritian accent, and grew into a strong young woman. If she wanted to fully become that woman, she would need to be an Acolyte. She enlisted in the military and spent two years working supply for the same Ikritians that fought the Varanasi, doing well enough to earn a trial with the Acolytes.

She never expected her instructor to be none other than the woman who had visited her village that fateful day: Senior Acolyte Eudora. The instructor hadn't recognized Lash. Why would she after all those years? But now, Lash couldn't fail.

She wouldn't give up. She would die before she quit, before she let down the woman that gave her the strength to aspire to greatness. Red and Chef learned to use their muscles. She would use her brains to become a true Acolyte.

"Listen, you idiots. Tomorrow is the last day the Commander throws us in the dirt." Red and Chef listened intently as Lash explained her plan.

—

Jets of elemental magic surged from Buddy's skeletal finger-tips at the incoming lizard horde. Fire, lightning, ice, and several arrows from Beast impacted the scaled wave. Still, they poured into the open cavern and rushed straight at Henry and Ox undeterred. Henry anticipated the broad, heavy swings of Ox's hammer and timed his attacks and blocks to avoid getting himself hit while also leaving openings for Beast and Buddy to rain down their assault on the monsters. The lizards were easy enough to kill one at a time. However, their sheer numbers threatened to overwhelm the group.

The first few lizards went straight at Ox and Henry, and died instantly. The others soon wised up to the smashing, slashing death circle and funneled into either direction to surround the skeletons. Buddy kept them at bay with waves of magic, culling their numbers just enough to keep the fighters from being overwhelmed. Several of the lizards ran up the mound of stone to get to Beast, but just before they reached her, she vanished. One of the creatures closed its jaw around where she had been and looked confused for a second before it died from an arrow to its head.

Beast reappeared high on Ox's back with a knee on one of his shoulders. Even though the giant was delivering powerful attacks, she was able to keep her balance while launching a barrage of arrows. The extra weight didn't seem to have the slightest effect on Ox's movements. With a Strength now above **70**, Henry suspected Ox could hold much more than the weight of an elven skeleton before being bogged down.

As the last of the lizards piled into the cavern, Henry attacked their bulk with a rapid thrust, using his shield instead of the tip of his sword to plow through their ranks, and leaving a wake of broken lizard bodies behind him. As his enemies' numbers dwindled to a few dozen, Henry allowed flashing glyphs to present their information but kept his focus on the churning mass of scales, teeth, and claws.

Ability Discovered: Bash I. Harness magical energy to power bursts of strength and speed

Synergy Detected, Combining Abilities: Bash I and Thrust I

Ability Discovered: Blitz I. Bolster attacks and defense with massive bursts of strength and speed. STR +2, FOR +2

His bones thrummed with power as he dumped Vitus into his new Ability. It was much more powerful than Thrust, crushing lizard flesh and spraying blood across the open cavern with ease.

"Beak, beak!" In between bashes, Henry managed to look up to the ledge. The fuzzy creature threw rocks at the waves of lizards and hit them with enough accuracy to momentarily cause distractions.

The lizards kept up their attack until a low pounding sound rumbled through the cavern. The lizards halted their assault instantly. They lifted their heads to listen to the sound, then turned and retreated through the other tunnels in the room.

The four skeletons didn't bother attacking the withdrawing lizards as the last few scurried away. They were focused on the rhythmic drumbeat of approaching footsteps quickly growing louder. The hissing and the scraping of claws matched that of the lizards they had just fought, though the intensity indicated that what was coming was much bigger.

They stared down the fungus-lit tunnel as a gigantic reptilian head came into view. It had the same long snakelike snout and red-brown scales as the others, but some of the scales, especially around its neck and head, faded to a light gray.

The monster was every bit of fifty feet long, and its head was twice the size of one of the dwarven carts. The giant lizard struggled to squeeze through the tunnel and let out a loud hiss and charged when it saw them. Stringy globs of saliva flew from its mouth and dripped from its sword-sized teeth. It scraped its back and head against the top of the tunnel, smearing blue and green fungus along its body.

Haruspex

Type: Graybeard Salamander
Health: Full
Vitus: Full
Attributes:
    STR: 83
    MOB: 29
    FOR: 55
    ACU: 8
    PER: 18
    RES: 7
Lore: Few salamanders live long enough to see their scales fade, and those that do tend to grow to tremendous sizes. Scholars believe Graybeard Salamanders have encountered stronger aspects of the Necromancer's curse, allowing for excessive growth and extended lifespan

Henry shook blood and chunks of lizard from his shield. "I hope you all saved your Vitus. This one might be tougher than the little guys."

Buddy ignited his hands with another round of elemental

magic. He sent two simultaneous blasts down the tunnel, and Beast loosed an arrow. Both attacks bounced harmlessly off the charging lizard's scales like flies hitting a pane of glass.

The monster clawed its way out of the tunnel and stood to its full height, nearly touching the top of the cavern, then dove with its head straight at Henry. Its massive jaws chomped at the skeleton over and over, barely missing the dodging skeleton. Henry had to channel Blitz and accelerate his movements just to avoid being crunched, dropping his Vitus well below half.

Ox tried to flank the salamander with Beast still on his back shooting arrows, but the lizard was much faster than any of them expected for a creature of that size. It spun and smacked him with the bulk of its scaley tail. Beast leapt from Ox's shoulders and over the tail as it impacted the larger skeleton directly in the chest. Henry heard bone and metal crunching as the wallop sent Ox bouncing along the ground and into a pile of ore.

Three flaming bucklers circled the lizard's head, not striking but getting its attention long enough that Beast could teleport to Ox. The huge skeleton shook his head and channeled his magic to his broken ribs, grafting them back together instantly. He stood up and tightened his grip on the hammer, preparing for another attack.

"Listen here, you brute," Beast yelled at Ox. "Can you hit that thing hard enough to kill it?"

"If I could get close, then yes. I need to land a clean blow to its head."

Beast jumped back on his shoulders and pointed to a spot on the stone just in front of Ox. "When I tell you to, I want you to smash the ground with all the Strength you have. Understand?"

Ox gave a sideways, questioning glance. "Fine, but I doubt a display of my physical prowess will scare it."

Beast didn't bother to respond. Instead, she waited for an opening. Scorch and frost marks blotted the salamander's scales, and deep gashes from Henry's sword crossed its face, but the wounds were superficial and did little to slow the monster.

"Henry, keep its head still for two seconds!" Beast shouted.

Between slices and rolls, Henry gave her a nod. An instant later, the lizard bit at him again, and this time he didn't dodge. Instead, he jumped straight to the back of the creature's throat, trying to lodge his shield down its windpipe. He braced his feet on the inside of its gums to avoid the jagged teeth. Its tongue was bigger around and longer than Henry. He dropped his sword and wrapped his free arm around the slick organ.

MOB +1

Clearly surprised, the lizard thrashed its head and tried to chomp its teeth together, but Henry had lodged himself in place and even gained a point in Mobility for his efforts.

"Now!" Beast shouted. Ox grabbed the handle of his weapon with both hands and lifted it high above his head. He brought it down hard enough to crater the stone floor, using every point of Strength he had. Beast put both of her hands on Ox's collarbone and focused hard on the lizard's head. As Ox's hammer descended, his aura sucked in toward him, and both he and Beast vanished with a huge puff of green.

Henry heard a sickening thud as the entire lizard shook, and the head of Ox's hammer broke through the roof of its mouth, stopping just a few inches from his own skull.

The scaled beast shuddered and slumped to the ground. The creature's tongue went limp as its head fell to the side. Henry was pinned in its mouth, but Ox pried its jaws open.

"Did you see that, Harry? Another glorious victory for me

and my minions!" Ox grabbed Henry's arm and pulled him free from the maw. Henry was covered with blood and saliva and low on Vitus, but overall unscathed.

"I was a bit distracted, so I missed what happened. I assume I held it still long enough," Henry responded, wiping thick, bloody globs off his armor.

"You did. Long enough for Beast to discover that she can transport more than just herself," Buddy responded. The mage showed little more fatigue and wear from the battle than he would have from a long walk. Fewer direct encounters with an enemy was one of the benefits of his ranged attacks.

Ox yanked on the handle of his maul and wiggled it back and forth for a second before he pulled it free from the lizard's head. "Yes, the grumpy minion is now my favorite. However, you needn't be dismayed. You'll all have a chance to garner my highest favor."

Beast crossed her arms over her chest, "I'm tired. You've got the first watch, *your majesty*." She walked a few feet away and sat down next to one of the lizard's feet. She pulled her hood over her head and leaned back on one of the clawed toes.

"I agree. We all need a chance to recover." Buddy sat down next to Beast and opened his metal tome.

Henry and Ox made a pass around the exterior of the cavern to make sure no more dangers lurked nearby. They grabbed a few broken pieces of wood from the various dwarven carts and joined the other two. Henry piled the wood together and used his knife to chop one of the smaller pieces into tinder. He could have asked Buddy to light the fire, but the mage appeared deeply engrossed in the metal tome. With a few scrapes on his flint, Henry started a small blaze that cast shadows on the cave walls and glinted off the dead lizard's scaly hide.

Henry had just started to nod off when he heard the

faintest sound of padding footsteps. He slowly wrapped boney fingers around the hilt of his sword, but kept his movements to a minimum until he could identify the would-be attacker. Henry knew the other three skeletons were awake and aware of the noise. They had no eyes, no muscles or skin on their faces, but Henry was beginning to gather the subtleties of their expressions from the slight movement of their bones.

The furry creature from the ledge cautiously made its way toward the group. Its body was covered in matted gray hair, which made it hard to see its limbs. It was about knee-high and walked on four feet, but stood on its hind legs when it stopped near rocks or pieces of rubble to examine the skeletons before proceeding. Its long, curved, bushy tail twitched excitedly as it approached, and whenever it stopped, it would clench its hands in little fists as though it struggled between apprehension and curiosity.

Its large, black eyes scanned the fire and the other skeletons, but its attention was primarily focused on Buddy. Its tufted ears perked forward when it approached within a few feet of the mage. It looked up at Buddy, held out a furry hand with long humanlike fingers, and very quietly squeaked, "Beak."

Buddy lifted his head from the metal tome. He slowly and deliberately raised a skeletal finger and pointed at the furry animal. A tiny bolt of lightning shot forward and hit the creature, sending it scurrying away with its hair standing on end.

"That's cruel!" Beast said, giving Buddy a mean look.

Ox nodded his head in agreement. "I think that makes you the grumpy minion now."

"Better grumpy than dead." Buddy held up the metal tome to show a rough drawing of the creature from different angles. "It's called a *trogold*. It's a mildly intelligent but extremely curious creature that has a strange fixation on magic and magical items. Its obsession draws it to magic, oblivious to the detriment of its own safety. The tome says many Acolytes have woken up with a trogold activating a magic item on their person, sometimes killing those sleeping in the vicinity."

So, the Lore is accurate, Henry thought. *I should probably pay more attention to it.*

"That's still cruel, and no reason to hurt such a cute creature," Beast said, searching for the trogold, but it had run behind one of the ore piles.

"Its nature isn't why I chose to scare it off. You don't understand the insult it just gave me."

"Insult?" Henry asked. "I think it realized you were the one that saved it from the first three lizards."

"That's my point. It requested to be my *thrall,*" Buddy answered as if they all should have understood what that was.

"What's a thrall?" Ox asked with what Henry assumed was a smirk.

Buddy sighed and lifted his hands in front of him. Henry noticed that whenever Buddy was lecturing them, he used his hands to talk. "The trogold wants to be magically bound to me, probably because it sees I'm a magic user."

"What?" Beast exclaimed. "It wants to be your pet because you saved it? That's ten times cuter. You *have* to thrall it."

Buddy was sitting with his back against one of the massive claws of the lizard. He had his legs crossed with his metal tome in his lap. "A thrall is not a verb, nor is it a pet. It's a contract for a magical connection and shared power. Certain mages can form such bonds with lowly creatures, also known as familiars."

"Sounds like a pet to me," Henry said, shrugging his shoulders.

"It would be like a human requesting to be the thrall of a dragon. The dragon would have no benefit from entering into a contract with something so comparatively weak. The dragon would just eat the person." While he was explaining, a furry hand gripped the lizard's claw behind Buddy. The trogold lifted itself onto the claw, just outside Buddy's view. It sat down with its legs crossed, placed a round mushroom cap in its lap, and waved its hands in the air, mimicking the mage.

Beast, Henry, and Ox laughed, but Buddy looked around, confused. Then he saw the trogold sitting beside him. It looked back at him as if proud that it could do the same things as Buddy, and confidently squeaked, "Beak."

Buddy erupted with arcs of lightning, but the trogold ducked behind the dead lizard and ran away before Buddy could shock it. The other three skeletons were still laughing hard.

"It won't be so funny when we're blown to pieces from it activating a magic item," Buddy growled at them.

"It's a good thing we're running low . . ." Henry started to say as the sound of claws scraping on stone echoed from the surrounding tunnels. Dozens of black, shadowy creatures with shining red eyes flooded into the cavern.

Beast unsheathed her daggers and pushed herself to her feet. "Break's over, boys."

CHAPTER 21

Senior Eudora noticed a different air about the recruits on the fifth day. There was no complaining. There was no resignation. There was only focus in their eyes.

Red and Chef, who were usually slow and groggy in the mornings, were the first recruits dressed and ready. Eudora still shouted at them, but her threats rolled off like rain off a tortoise. Their jaws were set, their muscles tense.

"Move your ass, worm," Lash barked at one of the recruits taking a bit too long. The girl had leadership potential, even if she wasn't Ikritian. Her Varanasi accent had slipped through a few times in the past months, but Eudora had no reason to question her loyalty. Plenty of soldiers had joined the ranks from far more obscure and questionable origins.

The recruits scarfed down their breakfast and formed a line when they were done. Eudora didn't need to guide them to the armory or on their march through the woods. They moved with intent, and any protest was quickly silenced by a stern look from Lash. The trial had gone on for weeks in her previous classes, but if they could beat the Commander in only five days, it would be the fastest time Eudora had heard of.

When they arrived in the meadow, Red drew a circle in the dirt with the heel of his boot as Eudora had done the previous four days. Chef arranged the group into lines while Lash ordered everyone to drink water.

Organized, Lash looked to the instructor. "Senior Eudora, we're ready to begin."

Eudora gave them the signal to start. "We'll see." The recruits began their competition, displaying just enough struggle so that Eudora wouldn't shout at them. The loser of each match quickly retreated and raised their shield over their head as the next match immediately began.

The final round came down to Red and Chef again. After a brief back-and-forth and a feigned struggle, Red pushed Chef out of the circle. Chef spoke a quiet congratulation to Red—more of a condolence—before he laid his shield in the circle and stepped out. The rest of the recruits scanned the edge of the forest, waiting for their challenger. They didn't have to wait long.

"If I didn't know any better, I'd say you were expecting me. Am I becoming that predictable in my old age?" Commander Cirilo emerged from the edge of the trees as though he were arriving fashionably late for a dinner party. The recruits stood at attention as the Commander approached. A slight breeze wove its way through the forest and moved the branches behind him in synchronized waves like they were blowing in the wake of his presence.

"With your approval, Senior Eudora, I would like to join this competition once again," Cirilo politely requested.

"You are always welcome at our training, Commander."

Cirilo entered the dusty circle across from Red and secured the massive tower shield to his forearm. The eyes of all the recruits were glued to his every movement. "I've spent thousands of hours training and fighting with such a shield on the front lines of the Ikritian Army. My brothers-and sisters-in-arms have stood by my side, repelling the enemies of this realm. I have sworn an oath to protect the nation that I love, and I prove that loyalty today by ensuring the current set of recruits are worthy of becoming Ikrit's chosen protectors long after I'm gone.

"I can feel your energy, recruit. It was disordered these last several days, an unfocused mess without control. Today, your vigor is directed at your task. Show me."

Red didn't wait for a second invitation. The young soldier dug his feet into the loose dirt and exploded forward. If Cirilo had been of the same Tier as Red, the assault would have taken him by surprise. However, their Tiers were miles apart. Cirilo was a mountain, and the young recruit was a pebble. The result was the same as their first encounter. Red slammed into the unmoving mass so hard that his bones shook.

He pushed with all his might, but the Commander didn't budge. He slammed into the unmovable wall over and over. His Resolve faltered, but only for a second before he felt a shoulder plant hard in his lower back.

Lash wrapped an arm around his waist and braced her other hand on Red's shield. An instant later, Chef took the same position on Red's opposite side. Red didn't dare peek over his shield to see the Commander's reaction. If his opponent could use **44** Tiers collected from a Drift Amulet, Red could use the Combined Strength of his fellow soldiers. More recruits joined the assault. Then the Commander's shield moved.

It was only a hair's width of give, but the Commander budged for the first time in five days. "Ready . . . push! Ready . . . push!" Red shouted the cadence, and the others responded with grunts and a consolidated effort. Red was strong, but he wouldn't have been able to hold his ground against Cirilo without Lash and Chef steadying his shield and holding his back. The Commander's shield continued to inch away, but the trial wasn't over.

A gust of hot wind shot through the recruits, blowing sand in their eyes and between the heavy plates of their armor. The ground shook hard enough to send a few of the soldiers tumbling, but they covered their eyes, steadied their footing, and kept moving forward.

—

Cirilo knew the girl—Lash, according to his Amulet's Assess Ability—would be the first to move. Every class of recruits had its leader, and the Commander had been around enough soldiers placed under stress to be able to read body language. When her fellow soldiers began to lose heart, Cirilo watched her expression turn to stone, and she sprinted into the dirt circle to join. The other recruits followed instantly after Lash made the first move.

Good, Cirilo thought, *it's time to turn up the heat and truly test them.* With most of his Attributes past the second Threshold and his Strength nearly to the third, a few dozen Tier **1** soldiers could never move him, but that wasn't the point of this exercise. He purposely yielded just an inch to the recruits, then focused his Vitus into the surrounding landscape.

Calamity

The gale and earthquake caused the recruits to falter individually, but a moment later each would look up, only to see the rest of the group locked together. They would put their heads back down and continue to push harder, moving in step as a single cohesive force.

Cirilo allowed himself to be pushed out more than double the span of the circle before he stopped them. "How much more do you want to win?" He allowed the wind to die down to a simple breeze and the earth to calm.

Lash was the first to look around. "Stop, you idiots. We did it!" The recruits halted their march and looked nervously from Cirilo to Eudora and back to the Commander.

"Recruits," Cirilo said, and gave them a comforting smile. "Join me in the shade." He walked from the hot dirt circle and over to the cool shadows of the forest and sat down on a tree stump, then motioned for them to join him.

Lash moved first, quickly followed by the rest of the recruits as they made their way to the shade and took their seats in the grass. When they had all settled in, Cirilo addressed them. "Can anyone tell me what just happened?"

"We pushed you out of the circle." Chef received a stern look from Lash before adding, "Sir."

Cirilo suppressed a smile at the simple explanation for their victory. "Yes, but how?" the Commander prodded.

The question hung in the air for a moment until Lash responded. "We couldn't beat you on our own, so we had to do it all at once. Your Drift Amulet has too many Tiers. No soldier in the world could beat you alone."

Cirilo knew of a few warriors in the world whose Strength was higher than his own. Only a few, but he wasn't about to let the recruits know that. "I'll tell you this once so that you can learn it through my words instead of harsh lessons in Jallfoss. You will rely far more on your allies than the number of your Tiers.

"But I thought the whole point of being an Acolyte was to collect Tiers, get strong, and kill skeletons?" Chef's babble of an answer was cut short by a jab from Lash's elbow.

"Drift Amulets allow you to gather Soul Essence of your fallen enemies, but those Tiers build on your own vigor as a baseline. That's why Acolyte training is so difficult. A dolt at Tier **20** could be felled by a true warrior without a single Tier," Cirilo explained. "But a few Tiers in the hands of a master who has passed through trials and strengthened their determination? That is something even I would not take lightly.

"What did you decide you needed to beat me? Souls. In the form of your compatriots. The true clout of the Acolytes is our ability to combine our might. The Drift Amulets are useless in the hands of the weak but can add unfathomable power to those who are truly worthy. That's what Drift Amulets give you, the Ability to add the power of other souls in a way that fortifies your own.

"If you hope to gain a few Tiers and conquer the world by yourself, you'll end up like the dead god, Jallfoss." Looks of confusion crossed the recruits' faces as Cirilo continued. "His greed made him collect all the gold in the world, much to the dismay of the other gods he called family. Disgusted by his greed, they left for the stars. Jallfoss couldn't ascend with the world's riches tying him to the ground. He lay in the mud and died. His mind shattered with loneliness, and he turned into the mountain range that bears his name.

"Your fellow Acolytes are all you'll have in that mountain. Your Tiers will mean nothing when you face the horrors below. Learn this lesson now so you don't join the Necromancer's undead."

"Is the curse a punishment for taking up a home inside a dead god?" Chef blurted out. Another sharp elbow from Lash didn't dissuade his curiosity. "Are Jallfoss and the Necromancer still down there?"

"Maybe," Cirilo mused, allowing his eyes to peer at the mountain peaks visible above the tree line, "but we've never made it down far enough to find out."

CHAPTER 22

"Ox, heal Buddy. I'll hold off these last two." Henry blocked a barbed tongue with his shield. The thick plates on the creatures' backs looked like melted knight's armor covering hairless hunting dogs. The monsters had four clawed feet that allowed them to move along the walls and ceilings as fast as they could on the ground. They had no eyes and seemed to smell with their mouths, which folded open into four rows of spikey teeth. From the middle of the ghastly maw, their barbed tongues could launch several feet from their mouths and hit with enough force to break bone.

"I need time to recharge my Vitus before I can heal, but I'll protect him." Ox withdrew to cover Buddy, and Beast hopped down from his shoulders to support Henry. A few of the armored, eyeless monsters had snuck up behind the group and hit the mage hard before the other three skeletons could push them back. All four skeletons were too low on Vitus to rely on their Abilities, forcing them to depend on their Strength and Mobility alone. Unfortunately, the constant fighting provided them little respite to recover either Vitus or Health.

Monsters of every size and shape just kept coming. Giant

mushrooms with whiplike tentacles, swarms of boulder-sized beetles, exploding crystal bugs. They had even found a towering glob of red slime that almost swallowed Henry whole when he examined it a bit too closely. It was no wonder the first human Henry had killed never made it to the bottom.

And now these armor-tongued monstrosities. Henry dropped his sword and shield and focused the last bit of Vitus he had into his arms. The eyeless creatures shot their barbed spears at him. Henry activated Blitz and accelerated his hands to give him enough speed to catch them. He grabbed both tongues mid-shot just before they penetrated his skull. They screeched and lunged backward, digging up gravel as they tried to pull their appendages free. The barbs dug into Henry's hands. He was out of Vitus, so the razor-sharp hooks would tear through his bone any second. "Now!" he shouted to Beast.

She materialized between the two monsters and jammed her daggers into their throats. Her weapons were out of magical charge, but they were still incredibly sharp. She buried the blades to their hilts, and the armor-tongues instantly slumped to the ground.

The constant barrage of monsters had left them out of magic and healing crystals, covered in gore, and low on Health and Vitus. They'd been chased through any number of random tunnels, and the monsters only got stronger the farther down they went. They had fought through so many similar-looking caves and offshoots that they couldn't agree on a way out.

With the last two armor-tongues dead, there was no immediate threat, but Henry didn't know how long that would last. He was definitely having self-doubts about leading the group. Luckily, his companions proved to be ardent warriors.

They all knew their situation was approaching hopeless, but they embraced the onslaught. No, they were living for the thrill of battle.

"Beak, beak," the trogold squeaked from somewhere behind them. The furry critter had been shadowing the group, unwilling to leave Buddy no matter how much the mage resented the creature. It smashed a rock against the corpse of one of the armor-tongues that had attacked Buddy. Much to Buddy's objection, Beast had even named the tiny animal. She'd started calling him Muji, and the trogold had quickly learned to respond to his new sobriquet.

After a few quiet minutes of recharging, Ox had enough Vitus to mend Buddy back together. "Thank you, Ox," Buddy said as Ox lifted him to his feet. They were backed into the dead end of a mining tunnel that looked like the workers had followed a vein for a few hundred yards and then given up. The mage took inventory of his body and cinched his tattered robes to his bones.

"We can fortify ourselves in this position while we catch our breath," Henry said, happy to have a few moments to rest. "I'll take the first watch. As soon as we've recovered, we need to start making our way back up."

The four skeletons looked out to the twisting tunnel ahead of them. Green auras were already starting to swirl around some of the armor-tongue corpses. Buddy kicked one of the mangled bodies, then turned to Henry. "I agree with resting, but not here. We're lost, and . . .

The clash of swords and the battle cries of men rang out behind them. The four skeletons whirled around to see two human soldiers in red tunics battling a score of skeletons, where nothing but a dead end had existed seconds earlier. The red auras of the soldiers blazed, sending waves of anger through

Henry, but something was off. The auras elicited the expected feelings of malice, but they were almost exaggerated.

How had they appeared behind us through solid stone walls? Henry wondered.

Status Effect: Enraged
Status Effect Subdued: Enraged Dismissed

He hadn't seen a red aura since they'd fought the humans in Ammerthall, but now that his Resolve had grown from **14** to **20**, fighting off the mind effects had become easier. Still difficult, but more manageable.

"Don't engage!" Henry ordered. The others fought off the urge to join the fight. They raised their weapons and slowly backed away. The humans and skeletons continued to battle, mixing green and red auras, but neither had the advantage. In fact, neither side seemed to be taking or giving any damage at all.

Just as suddenly as they appeared, the soldiers and skeletons, along with their auras, evaporated into a mist and then faded out of existence. They left no visible sign that a fight had ever occurred.

The four huddled back-to-back. They brandished their weapons and Buddy sent his flaming bucklers orbiting their formation. Fortunately, no attack came.

Instead, a woman's voice echoed off the walls. They couldn't locate its origin, but it sounded cheerful, if a bit raspy, as though the owner had just finished running. It came from every direction at once. "That was unexpected. I've never seen a skeleton, or any creature for that matter, resist joining that fight. You're not Ikritian Acolytes, but you're conscious, so you can't be Jallfoss undead. Who *are* you?"

"We could ask you the same thing," Henry shouted to the disembodied voice. "We mean no harm to anyone that doesn't wish us ill. The human auras are gone, but we can't see yours. Show yourself."

"Ah, so you could see the auras. That at least means you're from here." The woman giggled, but it seemed confident and sincere and not malicious laughter. Her voice converged on a location near where the humans and skeletons had been fighting. A sparkling mist flickered in the air, and a figure instantly appeared where moments before there was nothing at all. Cloth robes covered the woman's body, making it hard to discern much. She was shorter than Beast by a few inches but much broader at the shoulders. The robes hid any other distinguishing shape. A hood covered her face, and thick goggles with a single black lens obscured her eyes. Most notably, she had no aura that Henry could see. Maybe it was small and hidden under her robes. "This way," she said, turning and taking a step toward the back wall.

"Hold on. Who are you? And also, that's a solid wall," Henry said. Just then, the sound of more armor-tongues rang down the tunnel.

"You can stay and fight, but they'll just keep coming. You're loud. Your auras are drawing them near and making them attack. It's up to you." She turned and walked into the stone wall. Instead of smacking into it, she passed right through and disappeared.

The sound of the armor tongues grew louder. At least a dozen now clawed their way closer. "I say we go with her." Beast turned and followed the woman through the wall.

"I don't think we can take much more fighting. I agree with Beast," Buddy said. Henry nodded, and they followed Ox through the stone. Henry didn't even feel the slightest resistance as he passed through. On the other side, the tunnel continued. It was lined with streaks of green and blue fungus, and even a few red and purple globs dotted the tunnel.

The robed woman stood several yards in front of them. She lifted her hands, and a wave of mist rolled through the skeletons. Henry raised his shield instinctively but didn't feel anything as the magic passed over him. What he did notice was a change in the light. There was no longer the green tint of Ox's influence. "There you go," the woman said. "Now they can't see your auras, smell your rot, or hear your footsteps. They might accidentally find their way through the wall, though, so we must leave." She pointed to a shard of clear, jagged crystal in the wall. "Also, don't touch that crystal, or the wall will disappear."

The four skeletons nodded in unison and followed the woman through a series of tunnels and several more fake walls. The faux barriers were so perfectly matched to the rest of the tunnel that Henry had no idea they weren't real until the woman passed through them. The path followed so many twists and forks that they quickly lost any idea of how to get back to where they started. Luckily, the woman knew exactly where she was going.

She eventually stopped before an actual solid wall. She felt around one of the rocks at the bottom until they heard a faint *click*. The wall sunk into the ground, revealing a short path into a small, green room. They followed the woman through the passage, and the boulders lifted back into place behind them.

Henry realized the room they had just entered was much bigger than he first thought. The light-green wall in front of him was actually a massive column that went straight up for several hundred feet. The column emitted a dim greenish-white fluorescence, and it was twice as wide as Ox was tall. There wasn't just one column; there had to be dozens. There were so many that they completely obscured his vision after a short distance.

Haruspex

Object: Grunischwald Mushroom Tree (Mundane)
Description: Fungus. Thought to feed off the inherent magic in flow crystals, these giant mushrooms are the cornerstone of several underground ecosystems

"Welcome to the Grunischwald. The overtoppers have their trees. We have our mushrooms." The woman giggled as she patted one of the massive mushroom trunks.

She removed her hood and took off her goggles. Her dark-red hair was pulled back into tight double braids on each side of her head, with several frizzy hairs poking out in all directions. The goggles had left a ring of red on her freckled face. Her green eyes reflected the light from the mushroom trees, and her full cheeks matched a generous smile.

"You must have been the ones that killed the Graybeard Salamander and thinned out the little ones. Thank you, they've been plaguing our mushroom fields and making it hard to harvest."

"You're a dwarf?" Buddy said, more of an accusation than a question.

"A *Geist*, to be more specific, but, yes, I am a dwarf," she responded with a cheerful grin. Lines crinkled at the edges of her eyes as she gave another laugh. "I'm Torgga Thoroddsstadhur. I'm probably going to get in trouble for bringing you here, but you looked like you needed help. I've never seen cognizant skeletons before, so I want to hear what's going on."

"Beak, beak, beak!" The trogold peeked his head over Buddy's shoulder and chirped at the dwarf. Buddy hadn't noticed that Muji had been hitching a ride on his pack, and he quickly shooed the creature away. Muji clamored up the flesh of a mushroom tree and dodged a tiny lightning bolt from the mage. The lightning struck the mushroom and sent scintillating waves of color flowing over its surface.

Torgga laughed at the spectacle as Buddy collected his composure. "I didn't realize you had a trogold with you. I'll have to keep an eye on that one. Now, back to your story." She raised a questioning eyebrow.

"Thank you for helping us," Beast began. "We're not exactly sure what's going on. The four of us woke up just a few days ago with the help of these." She pulled her Amulet from under her cloak, revealing a half-filled **6**. "We don't have any memories of our past, but these Amulets channel the thoughts and emotions of anything we kill. One of those memories makes us think there are answers somewhere in all these caves." She motioned to herself and her three skeletal companions. "I'm Beast, by the way. The mage is Buddy, and the fighter is Henry. We call the big dumb one Ox."

Torgga smiled and pulled out her own Amulet. It had a mostly filled **13** on the front. "I'm familiar with the Drift Amulets, but I had no idea they could bring the dead back to life." She put the Amulet back under her cloak. "If you're searching for something in the Underdeep, you won't make it very far on your own. The dangers increase drastically the further down you go. I recommend you come with me, and I may be able to convince our Elder to help you."

The skeletons exchanged quick nods and Henry replied, "I don't think we're in any position to turn down assistance."

Torgga spun on here heals and started walking. "Good.

Now, hurry up. I've got a few answers for you, but you're not going to like them."

Despite her stature, Torgga kept up a quick pace as the skeletons followed her down a winding path through the enormous mushrooms. They couldn't tell how big the cavern was with the trees limiting their vision, but it seemed to stretch on indefinitely. Between the large trunks, there were smaller, florescent mushrooms of all colors, shapes, and sizes; fat round ones with white splotches on their red caps, tall skinny-stalked mushrooms with bright-purple caps almost as round as the bigger trees, and hundreds of other types growing on and around each other.

Metallic-blue lizards with smooth skin ran across the mushrooms as they flicked out their long sticky tongues to catch flying insects. Muji chased a few of the lizards, but they would skitter just out of his reach. Without claws, his long fingers had trouble gripping onto the flesh of the mushrooms the same way he used them to climb rocky walls.

The huge amount of brilliantly colored flora that surrounded them fascinated Henry and he used Haruspex on every fungus, insect, and animal he could see. He eyed an odd-shaped mushroom with a purple cap that caught his attention.

Haruspex

Object: Venin Bane Mushroom (Uncommon)

Description: Fungus. Purple-capped mushroom found in the Grunischwald

The information wasn't extremely useful, but a glyph flashed in front of the mushroom's description. He selected it and read.

> **Ability Discovered: Haruspex II. Draw wisdom from the innate knowledge of the world around you. Procure more useful information from higher-Tieritems and beings. AFI +2, PER +2. Supersedes item Abilities**

He dismissed the information, and then the mushroom's description reappeared, more robust than before.

> **Object: Venin Bane Mushroom (Uncommon)**
> **Description: Fungus. Purple-capped mushroom found in the Grunischwald. Contains mild healing properties. Can be boiled to produce a syrup that neutralizes weak toxins and poisons**

His Skeletal Body Status Effect made him immune to poison, so the mushroom itself wasn't useful, but now that his Haruspex Ability had gotten stronger, maybe it would help him find something that *was* useful. He found it strange that the second level of the Ability had been *Discovered* and not *Granted*, but the semantics were less important to him than the effects.

Henry walked beside Torgga as they made their way deeper into the forest. "What can you tell us about this place? Do you know who we are?" he asked.

She looked up at him with a hint of sadness in her eyes. "So, you have no idea what's going on under this mountain?"

Henry shook his head. "I knew we were underground, but I didn't know we were even in a mountain until you just said so. We think the humans are killing us as a form of training, and they're also searching for something in these caves. We kind of . . . killed all of them we've come across so far without having a chance to ask questions. You're the first non-skeleton any of us have talked to."

Torgga picked a few smaller mushrooms growing along the

path and stuffed them into her pouch. "In that case, I'll start from the beginning. You're deep in the mountain nation of Jallfoss. Humans began mining the mountain over four thousand years ago, and most of the other races joined within the first millennium when they discovered the flow crystals. Flow crystals are rare but very useful. Most of them have impurities, so they're only able to transfer light or electricity. Pure flow crystals are highly valued. They can channel and store magic. We once used them to power our golems, store spells, strengthen arms and armor—really anything we could engineer.

"The dwarves, being the most industrious, did most of the actual digging and installed the infrastructure and utilities throughout the entire mountain. Over the years, dozens of wars broke out over everything from mineral rights, to tunnel and cavern locations, to governing control. It wasn't until a thousand years ago that the greatest leader in our history, Lord Ortegus Oxendine, united the entire mountain under the name Jallfoss."

Ox clapped his hands together and let out a cry of excitement, "Put your worries aside, tiny dwarf. My minions and I have returned to bring back the glory of Jallfoss."

Torgga scrunched her eyebrows and gave him a confused look.

Beast crossed her arms and gave Ox an angry stare. "Never mind the dullard. He read an inscription on a monument and decided it applied to him. That's why we call him Ox. He's an idiot. Please continue."

A smile spread across Torgga's face and left tiny wrinkles at the corners of her eyes. Her smile was genuine, but Henry could tell years of hardship had weathered her. "Lord Oxendine was truly a noble man. The Seventh Great Mountain War had just subsided, and there was a tense truce between humans and dwarves. Lord Oxendine was next in line to rule the overtoppers from the mountaintops. Instead, he left the throne to his younger brother and spent twenty years in the lower caverns with us dwarves, learning our customs, working in the mines, and fighting the monsters that always seemed to pop up. He even married a dwarven woman named Selma Gunarrstadhur, who was one of the strongest mages in our history."

"Was it common for humans and dwarves to live together?" Beast asked.

"Not before Lord Oxendine," Torgga answered, "but that slowly changed over the centuries. Humans, dwarves, and elves all had their places through the mountain where they clustered, but most of the city-caves were a mixture of whoever wanted to live there."

How she described it made Henry realize that Jallfoss wasn't just a few mining posts under the range but an entire civilization. He wanted to know more. "So, what happened?"

"Lord Oxendine was content with his life, but the humans didn't want to pay a fair price for what we were mining," she said with a shrug. "Hostilities threatened to break out over control of the flow crystals, so he returned to the overtoppers. Unexpectedly, his brother hated being the Emperor and dealing with the politics of the merchant class. He eagerly ceded power back to his brother."

Torgga picked several more clusters of mushrooms as she continued walking and telling her story. She ate a few and stuffed the others in various pouches in her robes. "Lord Oxendine believed everyone owned the right to their own labor, and he ensured that powerful people couldn't overstep their bounds and impose on the powerless. A few of the richest merchants hated him, but that's why everyone else loved and embraced him. Jallfoss prospered, and he spent the rest of his life smoothing out relations until the dwarves and humans agreed to be ruled under his lineage. There was a lasting peace, until one hundred years ago."

She was silent until Beast prodded her. "Then?"

Torgga shrugged her shoulders a bit. "Then, we discovered the Source Crystal." She sighed and continued, "We had been digging for thousands of years, but one day we came across an open lava cavern with a giant crystal cluster in the center. The crystal was the purest we'd ever found and contained massive amounts of stored magical energy. We were so excited at the prospect of such an amazing find. We experimented with it for several months, developing tools, hooking up flow channels, and enhancing our magic. Then we tapped into it a bit too deep and released something terrible. We called it many things: *the Sorcerer of Death, the Great Corrupter, Harbinger of Silence.* Most just refer to it as *the Necromancer.* Whatever you want to call it doesn't matter. It killed all the miners in the cavern and twisted them into monstrosities." Henry could tell she was holding back tears, and her voice cracked ever so slightly as she continued. "I was just a toddler, no more than twenty years old."

Beast put a hand on Torgga's shoulder. The dwarf looked at the skeletal hand but didn't shy away from the touch. "Thanks for telling us. I know it's hard, but we need to hear it. Maybe there's something we'll be able to do to help," Beast offered.

"Maybe. That's what I'm hoping." Torgga took a deep breath before continuing the story. "At the time, Lady Destria, Lord Oxendine's direct descendent, was preparing to celebrate the annual competition to crown the newest Gladiator Supreme. That was the first year the farming empire of Ikrit had been invited to join the contest. However, the leader of the Ikritians, Lord Livadi, had always been envious of Jallfoss's industrial strength and resources. Somehow, he joined forces with the Necromancer. The undead army attacked during the ceremony and, along with Livadi's fire demons, slaughtered every being in Jallfoss proper. He murdered every innocent family in the upper caverns and mountain tops. He raised the dead and turned them into mindless zombies. Every person that died rose again under his control.

"The only thing that saved us was the brave Empress Destria. She gave her life casting a spell to turn the undead against their master and pushed back the attacking army. That's the spell that makes you attack the red auras. Lady Destria managed to banish the Necromancer back to the Source Crystal and cast Livadi's army out of Jallfoss."

"Fire demons. Maybe that's what I've been dreaming about," Henry thought out loud. He felt like her story had something to do with the visions and the woman's voice in his head. "Where is Lord Livadi now?"

"Dead. He died fifty years ago," the dwarf answered. "Humans don't live very long. Now his nephew, Lord Stavros, uses the mountain to train his Acolytes. He wants to get to the Source Crystal, but he'll never make it that far. Its magic continues to corrupt the creatures below. The closer you get to it, the more powerful the monsters become. We believe the Necromancer is down there, broken, but creating monstrosities to protect himself as he recovers. I wish we had never uncovered that cursed rock. We could never hope to control something that powerful."

They stopped at a stone bridge spanning a tiny babbling stream just a few inches deep. Water gently swirled around smooth river stones, and tiny fish darted between larger pools. Henry saw a flash of color through the ripples as a tiny squid ambushed a small silver fish. He felt a small amount of gratitude that he hadn't suffered the same fate from the squid's larger cousins in Lake Husavik.

Ox sat his hammer on the ground. "Fire demons, undead, necromancers. How did you dwarves survive all this time?" Ox lowered his body to sit on a fat brown mushroom with white stripes, but when he put his weight on its cap, it collapsed underneath him. He fell to the ground in a loud crash of metal and bone, and the mushroom exploded into a puff of brown dust. His body was hollow, so most of the dust rushed through the cavity in his armor, caught under his helmet, and poured out of his eye sockets. He looked like a sooty bone chimney as he scrambled back to his feet, standing tall and looking around like nothing had happened.

Beast and Buddy gave him annoyed looks, but Torgga and Henry burst into laughter. The dwarf sat on the edge of the stone bridge to catch her breath so she could answer Ox's question. "Barely, Lord Oxendine. Our forges have gone cold, and we can't start them with the monsters blocking our equipment. The few golems that are still operating are no longer under our control, and we've been eating nothing but lizard meat, slugs, and mushrooms for decades. As our resources dwindled over the years, we should have been overtaken by the monsters. Luckily, we figured out how to use illusion magic to draw them away from our settlements. That's my job. As a Geist, I trick the Ikritian Acolytes and the monsters." She lifted her palms, and the mist circled around her hands and swirled forward.

It wrapped around one of the mushroom trunks and formed an enormous red dragon with yellow eyes and long teeth. Its dark-green aura filled the area as it stepped forward, splashing water from the creek and shaking the ground. It opened its giant mouth and let out a deafening roar. Muji dropped a lizard he had just caught, jumped up to Buddy's pack, and climbed inside. Ox and Henry instinctively lifted their weapons and stepped in front of Torgga while Beast and Buddy readied their ranged attacks.

"Not to worry, it's all fake." The dwarf closed her hands, and the dragon dissipated back into a mist.

"That's amazing. You must be extremely talented to make something so realistic," Beast said, putting the arrow back in her quiver.

"Yes, you are a powerful mage. I was so convinced it was real, I was ready to take down this whole mushroom forest." Ox lowered his hammer and relaxed his stance.

Buddy had been mostly quiet as they traveled through the forest. He kept his distance but listened intently to everything the dwarf said, occasionally giving her questioning glances. Now that she had displayed her magic, he couldn't resist engaging her. "That's the same magic you used to hide our auras and yours as well. You said it was the Empress's spell, but what I don't understand is why we're able to see the auras at all, and why the red ones drive us into a frenzy."

"Great question," the dwarf said as she smiled at Buddy, "we dwarves can't see the auras, so it took us a long time to figure out what exactly they are and even longer to replicate and then disguise them." She waved her hands in the air while she talked—the same way Buddy did when he explained magic. Henry could tell she was excited to show off her knowledge. "An aura is a representation of life force, or a soul. It reflects aspects of personality and character. Each is unique to its owner. Humans, dwarves, and most other humanoid races can't naturally sense an aura without the aid of divination magic.

"Animals can, however. They've always had the Ability to sense auras and disguise their own. Animals only willfully display their auras as a threat. We believe that's how the Empress was able to turn the undead and the monsters against the Necromancer. Lady Destria was a powerful diviner, so she enhanced the aura perception of all the undead. It had a compounding effect on animals as well, making them much more responsive and agitated when they saw an aura. But the Empress made the aura of anything born outside this cavern red, which drives whatever can sense it insane with rage. Basically, they're responding to a threat from an enemy."

"I didn't think machine-loving dwarves were capable of understanding something as complicated as illusion magic," Buddy said dismissively. Beast smacked his arm, but the mage kept his attention on the dwarf.

Torgga continued with her explanation like she hadn't heard Buddy. "Since you can't hide them, your auras will attract monsters, and they'll continue to attack you until they've snuffed out the threat. I've disguised your emissions, but just because they're hidden doesn't mean you're safe. However, you're no longer at the disadvantage of being seen first, stalked, or attracting the attention of all in the vicinity at once."

She stood up and motioned for the skeletons to follow her. "It took us Geists a long time to master tricking both undead and living creatures with the same illusions. Now we have four other dwarves working nonstop to protect our settlements." They crossed over the bridge and continued down the path. They walked for another hour while Buddy turned the conversation to magic and the intricacies of something called *controlling the flow*, but Henry couldn't follow what they were talking about. Instead, Henry tried to ask about his desert vision and the accompanying Abilities and Attributes, but Torgga was unable to provide further insight.

The path ahead of them widened, and the trunks began to thin. The edge of the forest butted against square plots of black dirt that held rows of white and brown mushrooms. Each plot had its own green shack made of the same material as the trees they had just passed. The simple architecture ran together as though it had been grown instead of built. The plots stretched out for several miles to the far wall of the cavern. Stone roads lined each farm in a perfect grid lit by sun globes every few feet. Some of the farms further away grew strange, spiraled fungi of all different colors, and a few even had large, domed cages made of metal coils. Henry tried to see what was inside the cages, but they were too distant.

The ceiling was much higher than any cavern they'd explored so far. He guessed it was well over a thousand feet, and he wouldn't have even been able to see it if not for the green and blue fungus lining its surface. It was so far away that the streaks blended, making it look like a solid turquoise shell. Hundreds of yellow lights dotted the wall at the far edge of the cavern, contrasting with the green hue from above.

"That's the dwarven capital city of Hjardharfell. It's smaller than some of the human cities, but we live so much longer that we don't breed and expand as fast as the overtoppers. We have a few humans and orcs. No elves, but a good number of gnomes."

Buddy examined the massive cavern and the surrounding farmland. "Are there no pillars supporting the expanse?"

"The pillars don't actually support the caverns. The ones above are hollow and used mostly to pump water and circulate air throughout Jallfoss. Since Lord Livadi's betrayal, we haven't been able to operate our machines. If everyone above were still alive, there'd be no way to support them. Lucky for us dwarves, Hjardharfell is self-sustaining with its springs, mushroom farms, and the Grunischwald making all the oxygen we need."

Ox snorted and cocked his head. "Mushrooms do not

release oxygen. Even in a cavern of this size, dwarves and animals would not do well surrounded by such growths."

"Correct, Lord Oxendine. However, the mushroom canopy is covered in enough algae to compensate. We've been just fine for thousands of years."

Ox nodded and seemed satisfied with the Geist's answer.

Henry looked up and saw that the distant canopy resembled a leafy forest, though he didn't recall ever being around trees. He also hadn't bothered to follow whatever Ox and Torgga had said about mushrooms and oxygen. Instead, he focused on the pillars. "Dwarves can control air and water?" he asked.

"*Could* control air and water, and much more. I don't know how all that engineering nonsense works. I've just stuck to my magic. If you're interested, there are plenty of dwarves and gnomes around here willing to talk you to death on the subject of mechanics, hydro pumps, turbines, and whatever else you want to know about our world. Hopefully you'll make a good first impression, and they'll quickly get used to talking to skeletons instead of running in fear."

Torgga was right about the fear. The dwarves they passed along the way were apprehensive. Those working on the farms stopped what they were doing and watched as the group passed. Dwarven mothers pulled small children inside, and the few people they came across on the stone road would turn down another grid way once they saw the four skeletons. It didn't help that Ox was twice the size of anyone that crossed their path, and the skeletons were mostly covered in blood and gore from their battles. Henry hadn't cared about how dirty he was up to this point. Sanitation wasn't high on a skeleton's priority list, and he had no sense of smell to offend him. Now he wished he'd had a chance to clean up, so he didn't look like a murderous specter.

Luckily, most of the dwarves recognized Torgga. She waved cheerfully and greeted everyone who passed as though she weren't leading a horde of ghouls right to the center of their civilization.

The houses grew denser as they neared the city. The path followed a gentle slope up to the cavern wall, where there were hundreds of lights were built into the rock that Henry saw were windows and balconies.

The bottom of the hill had a smooth stone wall standing taller than most of the houses. A walkway and two turrets topped an open portcullis, and two dwarves sat watch from above. When the group drew near, the watchmen took notice of the unusual cohort. One raised a horn to his lips and blew a long, low note before they hustled down from their post with spears in their hands.

They wore light, bronze platemail, but they had it loosened for comfort, and they were busily tightening it back down. One wore a bronze helmet with horns curving up from the sides; the other had forgotten his. Both dwarves had pudgy cheeks and beards so long they could have tripped over them if they hadn't been careful walking. One appeared to be in charge because he smacked the butt of his spear on the ground and addressed their guide.

"Torgga, what is the meaning of this? You know Thorodd doesn't allow skeletons in Hjardharfell. And how did you get them to follow you?"

Torgga lifted her palms and turned slightly to her left and right, motioning to the skeletons. "Einar, Floks, allow me to introduce Beast, Henry, Ox, and Buddy."

Henry quickly assessed the one named Einar.

Haruspex

Name: Einar Jorrinsson

Race: Dwarf

Tier: 5

Health: Full

Magic: Full

Attributes:

    STR: 22

    MOB: 13

    FOR: 24

    ACU: 10

    PER: 8

    RES: 11

Damage Resistance:

    Physical: 6

        Slashing +2

    Environmental: 2

        Heat +1

        Cold -2

    Magical: -1

Lore: Dwarves are a hearty race known for their high Strength and Fortitude. Their magic and accompanying resistances are relatively low

The dwarven guards acted as if the Geist had just said nonsense until Ox walked forward and proudly stated, "Your great Emperor, Lord Ortegus Oxendine, has returned to free this mountain from its undead curse."

The dwarven guards turned white, and their mouths threatened to drop as low as their beards. They scurried back and readied their spears, visibly shaken.

Torgga walked forward and gestured for them to lower their arms. "Don't worry. They're friends. I'm going in to talk to the Elder. They'll explain everything to you while they wait. Keep an eye on them and be friendly."

Torgga turned to the four skeletons and gave them a big smile and a giggle. "Just wait here while I get permission for you to come in." She walked between the two guards and hustled up a winding, cobblestone road.

The dwarves turned back to the skeletons, their eyes still wide in disbelief.

Ox bent over to address the dwarf without a helmet that Torgga had called Floks. He nearly had to bend parallel to the ground, but he lowered his face to within inches of the dwarf. Ox's platemail was covered in blood and the bits of entrails dangled from the curved horns on his helmet. He opened his jaw and bellowed. "Is that how you acknowledge your returned lord?"

The dwarf's eyes rolled to the back of his head, and he toppled over backward.

"I hope that wasn't the first impression Torgga was referring to," Beast said, taking a seat on the stone road.

Henry sat down beside her. "If he keeps making friends like that, we won't get a chance for a second."

CHAPTER 23

The cool night breeze chilled the sweat on Koş's forehead and made him shiver. He was running a heavy fever and being in the sun all day had nearly cooked him. Now he was cold, even wrapped in the farmer's blanket. With Yeorgious's help, Koş got himself out of the back of the cart and onto the ground. Walking was getting harder, as was breathing, and he would hack up globs of muck every time he inhaled too deep.

He sat on the ground, leaning against the wagon wheel and staring into the fire. He was tired and felt his body wanting to shut down. He took small drinks from the farmer's waterskin, trying not to choke on each painful swallow. He wasn't hungry, but he had a few sips of broth and beans from the cooking pot. Sitting up made breathing a bit easier, with gravity holding down the fluid in his chest.

Koş thought about Master Sigurjon, Kubey, and Trix. He wondered if they were now mindless undead ambling around Jallfoss. He prayed there was some way to save them. His body just had to hold out long enough to get word to Lord Stavros. He'd tried the tell the farmer about the skeletons who'd ambushed him, but the man just didn't seem to get what Koş was saying. Yeorgious treated the youth's stories as nothing more than delusions from a fever dream. Koş couldn't fault the man for thinking so. He was in rough shape and probably looked like he could die at any moment.

Koş brought up his Status, only focusing on his Status Effects and ignoring the Attribute degrades.

Health: 6/39

Status Effects:
> **Injury: Puncture Wound (Moderate)**
> **Sickness: Pneumonia (Moderate)**
> **Injury: Shoulder Sprain (Minor)**
> **Injury: Forearm Bite (Moderate)**
> **Sickness: Infection (Moderate)**
> **Injury: Broken Fingers x3 (Minor)**

The infection was spreading, and every hour he felt worse, but they were within a day of the Bastion and the Acolyte healers. He just had to hold himself together a little longer.

His weary thoughts drifted to Master Jacoby's group. They had already turned into undead and tried to kill him. He touched the bandage on his right arm and winced. It was inflamed and oozing green pus. He could tell it was infected even without the Status Effect.

Yeorgious had pressed the two horses as hard as he dared, but the farmer knew that if either animal died from exhaustion, it was unlikely that there would be any other way to get Koş help in time.

"How are you feeling, lad?" the farmer asked.

"Rough, everything hurts, and my head is swimming," Koş managed in between sips of water.

Yeorgious pointed to his cart. "All I do is pick the herbs. I don't know how to turn 'em into medicine. That's my wife who does that. She would always say, 'Yeorgious, you should pay attention to what I'm sayin' to ya,' or somthin' like that. She's an angry woman, and I don't really listen to her. She's lucky she's got a backside on 'er that could serve as a bookshelf for the heaviest volumes in the Citadel. It's kept me comin' home all these years."

"I appreciate what you're doing," Koş said, thankful for the farmer's help but trying not to focus on the description of his wife. "I never thought I'd have a story of my own to tell. All I ever wanted to do was to serve Lord Stavros."

"I remember a tale about the Great Lord. Took place nearly forty years ago. If your Pappi was one of the Lord's companions, then he was probably there too. Those Acolytes got themselves in a real pickle with the Shargala people in the southern steppes." The farmer tipped back his bowl and slurped the last of his beans. "Those horse people were dangerous, but Stavros always wanted to make friends everywhere he went. Turns out Stavros tried to offer a handshake, which their culture sees as an overt proposition, and he ended up insultin' someone important. Those hoofers chased them into the grasslands. They hid and crawled on their bellies for days. When Stavros finally poked his head up, they'd gotten all the way to the Southern Sea. And, well, we all know what happened there with the women of the southern coast." The old man chuckled. "Now we trade grain for all the fish and whale oil we could ever need. Just goes to show, ya never know how far to venture 'til you're there."

Koş thanked Yeorgious for the story. The Great Lord had been through so many adventures, and at every step, he'd done what was best for the Ikritians. Koş couldn't let down the leader of his nation. He looked up at the stars and gave thanks that he wasn't looking at the sun globes in the ceiling of Ammerthall. "Just keep fighting," he told himself. "One step at a time."

—

Henry had spent the last hour lying on his back, staring at the high cavern ceiling. The longer he looked, the more details from different-colored fungi appeared as specks of light in the turquoise sea. The swirls turned into shapes, then into figures of animals, humanoids, and monsters. He wanted to think it reminded him of the night's starry expanse, but he had no memory of ever being outside the mountain. Maybe he'd never actually seen the sky.

The skeletons hadn't gotten a chance to relax since they'd left the Jolly Squid. Any rest from the few days lost in the caverns had been short and interrupted by attacking cave creatures. Even though he felt tired, Henry couldn't drift off with his mind still racing, so he brought up his Status and attempted to wade through the information.

He'd become familiar enough with the display to understand the difference between glyphs, and Haruspex made navigating it much more intuitive. He'd even learned to expand descriptions that he didn't understand and remove redundant pieces so he could unclutter his view.

The Health and Vitus bars at the top of his vision had been especially useful, allowing him to monitor his Abilities without draining his magic or breaking his body. However, he was still prone to losing himself in the thrill of battle and running out of Vitus in the middle of an attack.

Buddy, Ox, and Beast were leagues ahead of him, and had already mastered their techniques. Or at least they seemed much more proficient than Henry felt, and he knew he couldn't blame it on the Desert Path Status Effect. Its impairments were easily overcome by the gains he'd made. No, there was something else he was missing, and he needed to figure it out soon so he wouldn't let down the other three.

As he organized his display, he noticed the Abilities, Damage Resistances, and Active Effects boxes at the bottom of his view. He selected Abilities and was surprised to see descriptions of not only his skills, but those of the magic items he possessed as well. Haruspex and Consume overlapped with the Drift Amulet Abilities, and even though the Amulet's were of a higher Tier than those granted by his Desert Path, he was content not being forced to rely on the item.

Blitz and Harden were listed just below, and at the bottom sat his sword's Drain Ability. Buddy had told him that the sword was by far the strongest weapon they'd come across according to its Epic and Legendary qualities. The soldier he'd fought at the top of Ox's ramp was much stronger than Henry, and the blade had been the only thing that kept him alive. A few shallow cuts were all it took to keep his Vitus replenished and hold him through the battle. The monsters in the cavern, however, hadn't contained enough magic for the Drain Ability to make much of a difference, resulting in several near deaths . . . near *second* deaths.

The Active Effects box displayed information on Soul Anchor, Skeletal Body, and Desert Path, though it presented little he didn't already know. It didn't list any effects that were no longer in place, like broken bones or the Enraged Effect.

The glyphs frustrated Henry. They had a way of forcing their messages into his view despite his efforts to push them away, but the knowledge they imparted was usually worth the annoyance. Henry dismissed his Status and let his attention meander through the massive cavern.

It seemed to the skeleton that hours had passed since Torgga had left. After Floks woke up, he and Einar recovered their composure quickly. Eventually, they returned to their post, convinced that the skeletons meant them no harm.

Ox slept nearby, with his back against the stone city wall, loudly snoring. A crowd of onlookers began congregating as news of the sentient skeletons spread. Orcish and dwarven men were the first to gather the courage to investigate, but now, even a few women and children had ventured close. Some of the older children examined the skeletons with curiosity but quickly lost interest and started kicking a ball back and forth. One of them punted it a bit too hard, and it bounced toward Beast and rolled to a stop against her side.

The younglings stared intently at the ball, none of them brave enough to retrieve it. Beast picked up the ball in one hand and looked at the dwarven boy who had kicked it. Then she held up her other palm, indicating for the child to do the same. The boy mimicked her, and the toy vanished from Beast's hand and appeared in the child's. He squealed with delight, and it soon turned into a game. The dwarflings took turns rolling or throwing the ball to Beast, and she teleported it back to them. At one point, the ball began to float. They chased it, but it remained just out of their reach.

Henry looked over to Buddy and saw the mage sitting with the metal tome in his lap. He pretended to study the book, but Henry knew he was levitating the toy and playing with the children.

A few moments later, Torgga came skipping down the cobblestone path. A cheerful smile radiated from her freckled visage. Two small gnomes with blue robes and mushroom-shaped hats walked beside her. Henry would have thought they were children, but one of them had a long, white beard. They were half Torgga's height and very narrow at the shoulders. They must have been the gnomes about which the dwarf had spoken.

Torgga beamed with pride as she approached the portcullis. "Everyone with their bones showing, the Elder wants to meet you."

"Finally," Buddy said as he snapped his book closed. "Dwarves build clocks with a surgeon's precision but can't be prudent with their time."

"We can measure a century down to the second, but that won't help get the stench off a skeleton," she fired back. "We'll need to get you bathed and cleaned up before you meet our leader." Torgga motioned to the gnomes beside her. "This is Olafur. He'll take Ox, Buddy, and Henry to the baths. Beast, you'll come with Erla and me."

"Bath? The stench of death will haunt any enemy that survives an encounter with me." Ox had woken up and was gathering his equipment.

"Though I can't smell, I'm sure your stench haunts every living being within a mile. We could all use a scrub." Beast transported the ball to the children one last time, then stood up.

The skeletons followed Torgga through the city gate. Einar and Floks nodded and let them pass but still watched with wary eyes. The men followed the gnome called Olafur to the right, and Erla led Beast and Torgga to the left.

"Thank you for bringing us here, Torgga," Beast said as she walked beside the dwarf. "We wouldn't have lasted much longer in the tunnels."

"You got surprisingly far, considering you're only Tier **6**," Torgga said with another laugh. "But don't thank me yet. I convinced the Elder to give you an audience, though he was skeptical of your story. Hopefully, he'll agree to assist you."

The dwarf and skeleton followed Erla into the city. The gnome didn't say anything as they walked, and she kept up a brisk pace as if she was in a hurry. The buildings they passed were fashioned like the block homes of human cities, but their domed roofs, window shutters, and doors were made of the green flesh of the mushroom trees.

They came to a large two-story building that had a sign carved with dwarven script. Erla pushed open the double doors and ushered them inside. The sound of splashing water echoed from multiple fountains. Beast expected the shop to be furnished with uncomfortable dwarven stone, but the building's lobby was luxuriously adorned. Plush couches and stuffed pillows reminded Beast of the Gladiator Supreme's chamber from the arena. Multicolored mushrooms grew from stone vases, and red and blue fruits sat in large silver bowls. Beautiful silk carpets that changed color depending on the angle of view lined the floors.

"This way, skeleton. We need to get you cleaned before your stench soaks into the furniture." The gnome spoke for the first time. Her voice creaked with age and an accent Beast didn't recognize.

"Yes, no time to waste. I've been polite, but you are rather pungent. It's midday, so there won't be many people in here," Torgga said.

Erla led them to a back room with a tiled floor. There were several stone cubbies, but all were empty. Against the far wall were a few tables in front of a clear space with pipes sticking out of the walls.

"Ladies," Erla said, and motioned to the table. Beast looked at Torgga, confused.

"Take off everything. We'll clean your gear, but we're also going to take your weapons as a precaution before you meet the Elder. I hope you understand."

Beast welcomed the generosity, though she suspected the Elder's charity didn't come without strings. Until she found out what the dwarven leader wanted, she could do little more than accept the kindness.

Even more discomforting than questionable altruism was the idea of being unarmed. However, Beast understood the dwarves' apprehension toward an armed and animated skeleton. She pulled off her pack, cloak, and leather armor and laid them on one of the stone tables. Chunks of lizard hide, spiderwebs, and many other monster pieces and excretions clung to her equipment. She looked at her meager possessions with a sigh. The green tint in her daggers was gone, indicating she had used up all the stored magical charges, and her quiver only had a few arrows left.

Beside her, Torgga did the same. She removed her robes and goggles, then slipped off her undergarments. Beast glanced over at the dwarf. The robes had hidden much of her figure, and the skeleton expected the woman to be pudgy. Instead, she was a solid ball of muscle. Freckled skin clung tightly to powerful thighs that were bigger around than Beast's waist. Her stomach was flat, and Beast could barely see the outline of abdominal muscles. Her arms were thick and toned. Beast knew the **13** on the dwarf's Amulet wasn't just from tricking monsters and humans with her illusions. Each Tier was progressively harder to obtain, and the dwarf next to her was a battle-hardened warrior.

Torgga made eye contact with Beast and gave her a smile.

"I'm filthy after traipsing through the lower caverns and chasing monsters away from Hjardharfell. I'm just thankful I'm a woman and don't have to clean blood and guts out of my beard." She waved her hands in the air, and long red hair sprouted from her face. It hung all the way to the floor and was bushy enough to cover her chest, which was no easy task.

The dwarf twirled, showing off the bristly beard. Beast laughed and took off the last of her gear. "One of many reasons I'm thankful to not be a man."

Torgga padded over to the sunken part of the room with the pipes. Beast followed her into the sloped, stone circle as Erla turned a metal wheel on the wall. Water began spraying out of the pipes and filling the room with steam. Torgga dismissed her beard and stood under the water. "Yes, I needed this. I'd been out in the field for almost a week."

Erla donned a shiny black hooded cloak and grabbed a long scrub brush as she waited for Beast to get in the shower. Beast placed her head underneath one of the heavy streams, and Erla pulled a stool beside her and began scrubbing her bones. It was weird at first, and when Beast looked down to the floor, a red vortex circled around the drain from all the blood and grime washing off her. The hot water rinsed her bones clean, and for a moment, Beast imagined she could feel the warm sensation.

When Erla was satisfied, she handed Beast a towel and ushered her through an arch on the side of the room. Torgga followed her as Beast pushed aside a blue curtain. The chamber was more of a cave than a room. "Isn't it beautiful?" Torgga exclaimed. Several natural stone pools large enough to submerge even Ox lined the room at varying levels. Small waterfalls cascaded between the basins. There were a few dim sun globes, but most of the light came from perfectly manicured fungi on the walls and ceiling. A steaming waterfall poured from an opening in the wall just above the highest pool.

Torgga sat her towel on the ledge of one of the baths and climbed in. "The last hot springs in Jallfoss that aren't infested with monsters."

Beast followed the dwarf and lowered her bones into the water, steam lazily swirling around them.

Both women sat in the spring submerged up to their necks. Not counting the hours surrounded by curious dwarves at the Hjardharfell gates, it was the first chance Beast had to relax since she woke up slicing the throats of human soldiers.

Torgga looked over to Beast with a mischievous smile that the skeleton hadn't seen before. "So, which one of the boys is yours?"

CHAPTER 24

Henry, Buddy, and Ox were not having the same relaxing experience on the other side of the city. An entire contingent of gnomes in their shiny black overcoats had swarmed the skeletons and stripped off their gear before dousing them with bouts of hot water.

Four gnomes clung to Ox's bones. He hadn't resisted much until one of them climbed into his ribcage to scrub him from the inside. Ox did everything he could to control himself, but the brushes tickled. He couldn't stop himself from laughing as he jumped around with the gnomes holding on for dear life while still diligently trying to clean him.

Henry and Buddy had already been scrubbed from skull to toe bones and now waited at the edge of the shower holding their towels and watching the chaos. Henry tried to understand Ox's reaction to the cleaning. "I can't feel any sensation on my bones. Why are the brushes tickling him?"

Olafur stood beside Henry and Buddy, watching the army of cleaning gnomes battle the skeleton. Ox looked like even more of a giant with the tiny militia swarming him. "Never would have guessed the big guy is a healer."

"What does that have to do with anything?" Henry asked.

"I won't pretend to understand necromancy. I know you three can see and hear, that's part of the magic, but you shouldn't be able to feel."

Buddy listened intently to the gnome. "I assume you have an explanation?"

"Maybe. The body has a memory that allows it to rejuvenate itself, but that memory fades with time. That's why you undead can't heal past what your body has already decayed. I should know. I've tried it on several skeletons," the gnome replied.

Olafur stroked his beard as he studied Ox. "But this one is different. Even if his nerves aren't physically there, his healing magic has reached beyond the normal memory of his body. He's probably still oblivious to pain, though."

"You're a healer too, then?" Buddy asked, giving the gnome a curious glance.

Olafur replied, "You could call me that. Gnomes are typically artificers, but I've always had a knack for enchantment. Throw in a little transmutation, and you've got Steam recovery. From there, it's not a far stretch to regeneration."

Henry still couldn't keep all the magic terms straight in his head, so he leaned over to the mage and asked, "Buddy, would you mind translating that for me?"

Buddy lifted his hands, and Henry knew he was about to get another lecture on magic. "*Steam* is the word dwarves use for Vitus, and as I've explained to you several times, enchantment is magic of the mind—though enchantment is also the broad term used to describe items with magical properties. Transmutation is the physical manipulation of objects. You, Henry, use transmutation to enhance and fortify your body. Ox uses it to heal. Our friend, Olafur, claims to have combined mind and healing magic to allow him to regenerate both Vitus and Health. We'll circle back to the term *artificer*."

"So, you use magic to heal . . . magic. That means you basically have unlimited Vitus?" Henry asked excitedly, proud to have made the connection.

"Not at all." Olafur shook his head, still watching the other gnomes scrub the struggling skeleton. "Steam, or Vitus as you call it, is just the way that we quantify mental stamina. As you channel magic, your mind fatigues, so the blue on your Amulet actually represents your mental hardiness, not some pool of magic locked away in you. It's a muscle you can exercise and make stronger, but when you're out of Steam, the magic you channel simply fizzles away instead of materializing into a spell or Ability. Regarding infinite Steam: a bit of magic is always lost in the exchange, so I expend more than I can regenerate. It's really only useful to partially recharge someone else or store in flow crystals for later."

"Ah, those are the blue crystals," Henry said. "You know how to put magic back in them? Can you do that with weapons like Ox's hammer?"

Buddy interjected, "That's where the term *artificer* comes into play. Artificers are adept at handling magical items. They're almost like magic conduits themselves, and some can even take spells from a different mage and route them back into a flow crystal."

"Very good for a skeleton with no memory. You're connecting the dots much faster than most." Olafur looked up at Buddy and gave him an approving nod. "Yes. Although rare, artificers are more common amongst gnomes than other races. Regarding your weapons, however, we'll have to see what the Elder wants us to do."

The gnomes finished scrubbing Ox. They climbed down

from his body and stepped away, looking frazzled. His bones were dull white with the blood and gore cleaned off. Ox looked at Henry, Buddy, and Olafur and said, "I'm not sure what just happened."

"I don't think they are either." Henry pointed to the cleaning gnomes that were taking off their overcoats and grumbling amongst themselves.

"This way, gentlemen." Olafur handed Ox a towel and ushered the skeletons through an archway to the stone pools. They hadn't expected the luxurious, flowing basins of hot water but welcomed the opportunity for a rest.

They had just climbed into a pool when the sound of metal crushing stone erupted from the shower room. "Beak, beak, beak!" Muji cried, and sprang from the archway.

"There was a damn trogold in the pack! It made me drop the hammer," one of the gnomes inside the shower room yelled. "Who the hell keeps a trogold as a pet?"

"Yeah, who does something like that," Ox teased.

Muji sprang from the stone archway leading to the shower room with two gnomes close behind. The trogold was much faster than his pursuers and deftly leaped into the air and splashed into the middle of the pool, spraying water on Olafur and the skeletons. The gnomes gave up the chase with more grumblings and returned to the shower room.

"Beak." Muji popped his head out of the water and chirped as though he hadn't nearly given the gnomes a heart attack. He swam around the pool, paddling with his arms and legs to keep his chin above the water, clearly content and pleased with himself.

Henry smiled as he watched Muji play, then looked around the room. The reflection from the wall fungus sparkled in the cascading water between the pools. Henry directed his attention to the waterfall. "Olafur," he asked, "does this water come from the lake above?"

Drops from Muji's splash had soaked into Olafur's robes, but the gnome didn't seem to mind. "No, this is one of the last natural hot springs. We use it for drinking and bathing. The wastewater goes into the leach fields, and we use it to irrigate. Lake Husavik was mostly used for fishing and to cool the stonecutting machines. I've heard the unfortunate news that within the last few decades, the delicious squid from the lake have gotten a bit out of hand.

"Back when the mountain was full of the living, it was our job the keep water and air circulating. We'd use the lava turbines to force water up through the pillars and provide fresh water for the entire mountain. Then, wastewater would go into one of a dozen leach fields and be cleaned by plants and fungus." The gnome paused to wipe a few drops of water from his beard. "Same with the air. The heat from the lava turbines would blast hot air out of the mountain, but the displacement would then suck cold air from a single inlet at one of the mountain peaks and circulate it through the cities. It took us a few thousand years to perfect, but it *was* a rather impressive system."

"Was?" Henry asked.

"We haven't been able to maintain the turbines for half a century with all the monsters coming from the Underdeep. We still have a few engineers who worked on them, but the machine knowledge of dwarves and gnomes is slowly atrophying."

Henry found it hard to relax in the water with all the talk of machines and monsters. "If we find a way to bring back the inhabitants of Jallfoss, we'll also need to push back the monsters so the dwarves can get the machines running again."

"Leave the crushing of monsters to me." Ox had submerged most of his vast body under the water except the top half of his skull. Even with his jaw underwater, his voice projected clearly.

Muji crawled out of the water and stood on the edge of the stone. He shook his entire body, sending a shower of droplets on the surrounding area. A good amount of dirt had washed away from the trogold's long fur, revealing a white mane around his head and tufts of light gray around his ears and hands.

Buddy scowled at the trogold but directed his annoyance to Olafur. "If more dwarves spent time perfecting magic like Torgga instead of relying on their machines, you might not have found yourself in this predicament."

"You're probably right," the gnome responded. "But with the sun globes and dwarven mining machines, we created a happy life for thousands inside this mountain."

"So, the sun globes *are* machines and not magic?" Henry gave Buddy a nod of affirmation.

"That's correct. We created automatons to work the lava pits and mine stone, metal, and gems, but we were always looking for flow crystals. Most of the crystals we found were impure but still able to channel a considerable amount of light. The great gnome Solufur Alonofnurson discovered how to weave the crystals into a rope that would transport the sun's light over long distances. There are several giant sun globes on the surface that gather light. Then, flow ropes transmit the light. We attach a sun globe at the end and *boom*, instant sunshine. It's much more complicated than that, but you get the idea."

"It sounds to me like the dwarves and gnomes didn't even need the humans," Henry said.

"That's not the case at all. You can only create so much from the rocks in a mountain. Dwarves and gnomes can build amazing machines, but we're not naturally entrepreneurial, and we're more reclusive than the overtoppers. They took the things we produced and traded them with the rest of the world for things we couldn't make here. One of those things was beer."

At the word "beer," Ox surfaced. "You have my attention, Oscar. Tell me all you know about dwarven alcohol."

Olafur obliged with a smile. "Dwarves used to make amazing beer, and gnomes would distill the best spirits in the world, but we can't do it well without grain. Sharinji mushrooms were a key ingredient. However, you must get them extremely hot to separate the starch. Without the forges, it's impossible to make it taste even slightly appetizing. Now, most of our sharinji fields are just used to feed the slugs and lizards."

Olafur clapped his hands together and stood, shaking Muji droplets from his beard. "Sadly, gentlemen, it's time to wrap up the morning."

The three skeletons got out of the pool and went to dry off, but Muji had found his way over to Buddy's towel and curled into a furry wet ball. Buddy glared at the sleeping trogold, then pulled a clean towel off a nearby rack.

Back in the shower room, the gnomes finished scrubbing the muck from the skeleton's gear and armor. They had even repaired some of the broken leather fastenings on Henry and Ox's mail and replaced the blood-soaked clothes they'd used to stuff their boots, bracers, and helmets. Their weapons were missing, as were Henry's shield and Buddy's bucklers.

Ox opened his pack and pulled out one of the bottles of whiskey from the Jolly Squid. He handed it to Olafur and said, "My loyal minions, thank you for your hospitality."

Ox had to bend down so the gnome could reach the gift. Olafur examined the bottle, and when he realized what it was, his face lit up. "Where did you get this? Such a rare vintage. I thought we'd drank the last of it years ago." He ran to the other gnomes and excitedly started talking to them in a language

Henry didn't understand. The contingent of gnomes was still cleaning bits of cave creatures off themselves and the shower floor. They looked grumpy, but when Olafur showed them the bottle, any hint of displeasure left their faces.

The gnomes passed the bottle between themselves, chattering in their harsh tongue. The tiny contingent formed a line in front of the skeletons. They all looked up at Ox and gave him a slight bow. Then Olafur said, "Your generosity is well received, Lord Oxendine."

CHAPTER 25

The last day of travel was the worst yet. Every bump jarred the wound in Koş's chest. He'd lost all movement in his right arm, and his fingertips had gone numb and begun turning a dark greenish-purple. Yeorgious cleaned the bite regularly, but still, infection had taken hold, changing the Status Effect from Moderate to Severe and dropping his Health to nearly zero.

He'd contemplated giving up, hoping that the farmer would pass on his tale, but the sight of the training fields at the Bastion gave him the motivation he needed to hold on a little longer. Potential Acolytes drilled with swords and spears in the open dirt fields. Others climbed over logs and swung on ropes as Senior Instructors yelled orders. The students hadn't yet earned the red tunics of the Junior Acolytes. Koş thought he recognized a few from the classes behind him, but his vision was blurry, and he could only identify them by their movements.

"Easy there, Truffle," Yeorgious spoke as the cart slowed to a stop. Koş knew he was at the stone gates of the Bastion's entrance, and he recognized the voices of the gate guards but didn't have the Strength to turn his head to look at them.

"You know the rules, old man," Koş heard one of the guards say. "All our supplies are contracted. We can't just have every farmer that comes along peddling their goods through the plains."

Yeorgious replied, "I'm here on a different kinda business, lads. I found somethin' that belongs to ya. Might wanna hurry and get him to a doctor. He's in rough shape." Koş heard large wooden doors opening and the shuffle of chainmail as the guard approached the wagon.

The guard walked around the cart and saw the wounded Acolyte in the back. Koş knew his face but couldn't remember his name. "Minoa's second beard!" the man cursed upon seeing Koş's broken body. "That's one of Sigurjon's boys. What the hell happened to you? Where is your instructor?"

"Dead." Koş summoned every point of Strength he had to utter a few words. "At least one other group as well. They've already turned." Koş began coughing uncontrollably, hacking up more blood on his already stained shirt.

"Get him to the healers," the guard ordered another unseen Acolyte. "Fetch Commander Cirilo and a runner. Lord Stavros will want to know about this."

Koş felt the guards gently lift him out of the cart as the world around him faded to black.

—

The gnomes begged Ox, Buddy, and Henry to join them for a round of whiskey, but Henry insisted that it would be wasted on beings without tongues. He didn't let them know they'd already downed a bottle at the Jolly Squid. Now that the gnomes had been given such an unexpected treasure, their annoyance was gone, and they seemed almost sad to watch the skeletons depart.

"There will be many more battles, my minions, so we'll return soon for another scrub," Ox promised as they left. Olafur led them through perfectly organized houses on their way up the hill. There was a bustle about the city as the sun globes' intensity began to brighten, and Henry wasn't sure if it was just normal business or if the inhabitants of Hjardharfell were crowding to see their undead guests. Every window, doorway, and alley had an occupant watching them with an expression ranging from curiosity to hostility.

After a few minutes, they came to an open plaza in front of immense stone doors. The doors were large enough for Ox to walk through without ducking, and they had to weigh several tons each. Interlocking swirls highlighted rough depictions of dwarves, monsters, and machines carved into the stone. The doors didn't have hinges but were instead connected by gears mounted directly into the face of the cave wall.

The plaza floor consisted of large blocks of stone that formed more interlocking circles like the ones on the doors. Beast, Torgga, and Erla had already arrived and stood waiting for them. Beast had her arms crossed and looked impatient, though more relaxed under her clean cloak. "Glad to see you idiots decided to join us."

Torgga gave the three skeletons a knowing smile, but Henry wasn't quite sure of its meaning. She wore a loose green sundress with patterns of white mushrooms that hung just above her knee. Henry was impressed by her muscled physique. The top of her dress was practically straining to contain her.

Ox leaned down between Henry and Buddy and whispered in their earholes, "Now, that, gents, is a real woman. Four feet taller, and she'd be perfect."

Torgga gave her signature giggle, and Henry wasn't sure if she'd heard Ox's comment. "Enough of the rural life and on to Hjardharfell proper. Shall we?" She motioned toward the stone doors. The skeletons followed as she shouted something in a dwarfish tongue.

The doors opened to four guards: two short dwarves in the front and two orcs just a bit taller than Henry in the back. Henry could only tell the back two were orcs because of the front openings of their helmets. The green tint of their skin and their yellow tusks gave away their race. All four carried bronze tower shields and mid-length spears. They were covered from head to toe with heavy bronze armor, shined to perfection.

"This is where we leave you. Until next time, dead guys." Olafur and Erla gave the skeletons another slight bow and walked back into the city.

"Is he ready?" Torgga asked one of the dwarves in the front. Henry assessed the grumpy-looking soldier and could tell the dwarf was doing the same to him.

Haruspex

Name: Craggitt Kollardurransson
Race: Dwarf
Tier: 18
Health: 185
Steam: 92/92
Attributes:
    STR: 35
    MOB: 18
    FOR: 36
    ACU: 20
    PER: 22
    RES: 19

Damage Resistance:

    Physical: 8

        Slashing +2

    Environmental: 3

        Heat +2

        Cold -1

    Magical: 2

Lore: Dwarven Captains are the cornerstone of Hjardharfell's defensive forces. Much stronger and heartier than the average dwarf, they also have fewer weaknesses

"He's ready to talk to them, but I doubt he's ready to see you in a dress like that, Lady Torgga." The guard grumbled. His beard was divided into two large strands and interwoven with bronze clasps.

"After a week in the muck of the Underdeep, there's nothing wrong with dressing like a lady," she replied with a hint of defiance.

The guard gave a judging look to the skeletons, then glanced at Torgga before turning away. "They have Tiers. Never seen a skeleton with Tiers. Just keep them under control so we don't have to." The group followed the two dwarven guards. The orcs waited for them to pass before joining the rear and kept a tight formation as they moved.

"*Lady* Torgga?" Henry asked Beast quietly as they started walking.

"You'll see," she replied.

The central city of Hjardharfell was more of a hive than a settlement. It looked like it had been carved from the inside of a single block of marble. The city wasn't built on a flat surface like the human towns above. Instead, the main cavern opened into a hollow sphere almost half a mile across. Stone ramps and platforms snaked in all directions, splitting off, connecting to others, or leading to exits on the edges of the walls. The ramps wove into a complex, honeycomb shape, supporting small stone buildings throughout the expanse. The walkways and platforms had no railings, but they did have small concave curves to them that guided the inhabitants toward the middle.

Large sun globes hung from chains in the ceiling, and smaller ones sat in lamps lining the platforms or in sconces on the outside of the buildings. Larger ramps had chain setups like the ones from the caverns above. A few of them had carts attached to the chains. None were moving, and they looked like they'd been sitting in place for years. An orc in brown trousers with a hairy chest had a slab of mushroom-wood across the top of one of the carts and used the makeshift table to sell small gray slugs covered in grill marks and a dark-red seasoning.

Hjardharfell wasn't overly crowded, but it was a lively city. Dwarven and orcish women chatted as they carried woven bags full of mushrooms. Gnomes sat in suspended swings, smoking pipes. Patrons walked between open storefronts, purchasing what looked to Henry like chunks of mushrooms and slabs of meat. Buddy asked why anyone would pay for mushrooms when they seemed to be everywhere in the underground caverns. Torgga dove into a long explanation of rarity of certain types of fungus and the effort that went into preparing them. Shop vendors and their patrons stopped their business momentarily as the group passed, their eyes glued to the skeletons. Most gave them curious looks and kept their distance.

The sturdiest ramps directly supported a large spherical structure in the center of the cavern. It looked like a gigantic yolk in the middle of an egg. "This way, stay close," the dwarven guard growled as he walked up the main ramp leading to the center chamber.

From a distance, it looked like a solid sphere, though up close it was speckled with windows and sweeping balconies. They walked up the steep incline to a circular opening on the bottom portion, and the guards ushered them inside.

The first room was several stories high, with curving staircases on either side leading to subsequent levels. Between the staircases, a large hallway led straight through the structure to another opening on the other side. Wooden doors lined the hallway, and a sconce held a sun globe between each. It was the first time Henry had seen wood in Hjardharfell, which meant the material was hard to come by. More interlocking swirls were carved into the walls of the chamber, and the floor was ornately tiled with blue, white, and black marble. Stone tables with vases holding multicolored fungus decorated the tall room and hallway, and large sun globes hung from chains at varying heights, lighting up the different levels of the first chamber.

The guards led them up the spiral staircases to the fourth floor. The level had smaller hallways branching off in different directions, but the main feature of the landing was an archway with carved stone doors. Gears held the doors open, just like the ones at the main entrance to the city.

They followed the guards through the doorway into an expansive, domed room. White stone pillars lined the exterior of the circular chamber, and a singular sun globe hung from the middle of the ceiling, casting shadows on the walls. A smooth slab of marble with beautiful veins of white crystal and black onyx made up the entire floor.

A white stone table sat in the middle of the room. Its sides were carved with more dwarven designs, and around it sat over a dozen elegant wooden chairs.

All the chairs were empty except one on the far side of the table. A dwarf with a white beard sat at the opposite end, ignoring the guards and skeletons that had entered his chamber. On the table and to his right sat a plate of half-eaten food and a dark metal flagon, and on his left sat a bronze short sword beside its scabbard. He wore a thick stone circlet on his bald head with a single black stone in the center. Fine blue robes lined with silver thread hung from his shoulders.

The guards stopped a few steps into the chamber and addressed the dwarf at the table. "Lord Thorodd, your visitors have arrived."

The dwarf didn't look up but instead lifted the flagon and took a long drink. Small streams of dark liquid ran down his beard and dripped on the floor. Wrinkles lined his face, indicating considerable age, but his thick, muscled forearm holding the drink showed no signs of frailty.

Haruspex

Name: Thorodd the Broken
. . . Haruspex Failed

Pain seared into Henry's mind, making him wince and cut off the Ability. Haruspex had never failed before, and Henry felt the other skeletons cringe and wondered if they'd experienced the same.

"Don't be rude." Thorodd's angry voice boomed across the stone room. It was calm, but wielded heavy authority, and no small amount of threat.

He set down the flagon and wiped his chin, still not looking at the skeletons. "I've been drinking this sharinji mushroom garbage since we ran out of beer almost ninety years ago." He stood from his chair, picked up his sword, and used it to point to the table. "Back then, the gnomes and dwarves of Hjardharfell controlled the entire Underdeep, everything from

Husavik to the Source Crystal at the bottom of this mountain range."

Despite the name Haruspex had given him before it failed, the stout dwarf didn't seem *broken* in the slightest. Henry looked at the table where the dwarf pointed. Thousands of precious stones formed an intricate mosaic on the tabletop. It was obviously a map, though it was so detailed that he couldn't make sense of it.

The table was large enough that Ox could have comfortably spread out without hanging off the sides, and the dwarf walked around the edges as he talked. "Then the Betrayal happened. The forges of Hraunfass fell first. Soon after, we lost Skutarbrekka, Lundarvik, and finally, Olafsfass. Now, we've been pushed back to Hjardharfell and a few smaller towns."

As the dwarf pointed to a spot on the map labeled "Hjardharfell," Henry started to make sense of the mosaic. It was a top-down view of the mountain with hundreds of overlapping caverns. Henry saw the central city of Ammerthall where they had woken, then followed it to Hershwald and the squid lake at Husavik.

"We had a thousand years of peace before that bastard Livadi and the Necromancer attacked. I met him once. Livadi, not the Necromancer. Shook his hand, shared a meal and drinks, laughed at his jokes. I wish I could have killed him instead of allowing him to die in a comfortable bed behind the walls of Ikrit." His hand tensed around the hilt of his sword. Veins and muscles swelled in his arm, and finally the dwarf looked up at the skeletons for the first time.

"And now you're here, showing up to the doorstep of Hjardharfell like a bunch of tourists and not some undead abominations." He glared at them. "Did the Necromancer send you? Are you of his evil magic?"

Henry stepped forward between the guards. They moved to stop his advance, but the dwarven leader nodded his head, telling them to allow the skeleton forward. "I wish we could answer your questions, but we simply don't know. It may be evil magic that brought us back, or it may have been dumb luck with these." Henry held up his Amulet. "What I can tell you is that we came here hoping to find a way to lift the curse. I'm Henry." He motioned to himself, then the other three skeletons. "And this is Buddy, Beast, and Ox. We're grateful for your hospitality, and any assistance or information you could offer would help us in our journey."

The dwarf tossed his sword on the table with a loud clang and let out a deep belly laugh. "I'm very skeptical of that account. Fortunately for you, my daughter seems to believe your tale." They turned to look at Torgga, who gave a nervous smile and a giggle.

"I'm Thorodd Skodderrfallson, the oldest one here that can still swing a sword. That makes me the Elder and keeper of your fate. Torgga tells me you were the ones that killed most of the salamanders, even the big one. The lizards have already awoken as undead, but they're easier for our Geists to control that way. More instinct, less thinking. As a show of gratitude, I have decided not to bury your bones under this mountain." Then he raised his eyebrows and added, "Yet."

"Quite the threat from the very dwarves that unleashed the Necromancer on Jallfoss," Buddy spat unexpectedly. "We're like this because of your machines and your greed."

Thorodd's face flushed red, and he slammed his fist on the table. "You know nothing of the hell we've endured this last century. Thousands are dead, and we're losing more of our stronghold every day. I do not need to defend myself from the words of a skeleton. I've lost track of how many of your kind I've killed."

Thorodd snatched his sword from the table and pointed it at the mage while Buddy's eyes flashed with blue fire. The guards turned toward the group and lowered their spears. Torgga gave Buddy a surprised look with a hint of admiration.

Beast teleported behind the orc whose spear was closest to her. One hand clamped around the throat of the guard. She used her other to draw a dagger from a hidden fold of her cloak and pressed it between two plates in his armor. "Easy, now," she said calmly.

Craggitt's arms began to radiate a deep orange glow. The dwarven Captain curled his lips into a snarl and gave Henry a sideways glance that served as more of a threat than any words could.

Ox put his hands on his hips and let out a laugh that echoed off the domed ceiling. "It's been several hours since my last battle, so I am about due for another. Sadly, I don't think this is the right venue." He walked between the two dwarven guards, ignoring their spears, and set his pack on the table. He dug through it and pulled out the second bottle of whiskey from the Jolly Squid.

"I would be in a sour mood, too, if all I had to drink was mushroom beer. A gesture of peace from the great Ortegus Oxendine will cool your temper." Ox towered over Thorodd as he handed the Elder the bottle.

Thorodd gave Ox a suspicious glance as he accepted the gift. "Lord Oxendine has been dead for centuries," he mumbled to himself as he rubbed his thumb over the faded label and squinted his eyes.

"Whiskey!" Thorodd exclaimed, realizing what the glass bottle contained. "Where did you get this?"

"An emperor must be resourceful," Ox said confidently.

Thorodd gave the giant skeleton another curious look, but Torgga walked forward and locked her arm through her father's. She whispered something in this ear, then said out loud, "Surely such a generous gift could come from no other than the Great Lord Oxendine himself."

Thorodd raised his eyebrows. "I understand." A smile worked its way across his lips. Then he turned to Ox. "Very well, Lord Oxendine. Now that we understand each other, let's talk about how you're going to help Hjardharfell. Have a seat."

With the tension in the room abated, Beast let go of the orc's throat, and the guards lowered their spears. Her suspicions about the Elder wanting something were correct. The dwarf didn't seem like one to take "no" for an answer, so Beast hoped his request would be reasonable enough for her and her companions to accept.

Thorodd motioned to the wooden chairs and the skeletons took seats around the table. Gnomes appeared from behind the pillars with plates of food and set them in front of Torgga and Thorodd. "I assume you don't eat, but I do."

He bit into a mushroom, and gravy dripped down his beard. "I have a plan, but not the means. We need to push back the monsters and reclaim the Underdeep. However, that's impossible with our forges extinguished. Our main forges are near the lava fields of Hraunfass, far out of our reach. But we do have some older ones here at Hjardharfell. All we need to start them up is a device the gnomes call a Magma Blaster."

"And you need us to get it for you?" Henry asked. "I assume you know where it is, so why haven't you gotten it yourself?"

Thorodd's eyes bore into Henry, and no one spoke for several uncomfortable moments. Henry held the dwarven Elder's gaze until Thorodd finally spoke. "I'm not willing to sacrifice any more lives of the dwarves it would take to get it." Thorodd snapped a bone from his plate and sucked out the marrow. "I am, however, willing to risk yours. After Livadi's betrayal, our engineers wanted to protect our most precious items from the humans. We should have brought them here. Instead, our former leader decided to store everything at Lundarbrekka and construct a golem to protect our treasures."

Buddy had his metal tome on the table and scribbled notes as Thorodd spoke. "I assume everything worked perfectly with this golem?" the mage asked with palpable sarcasm.

Thorodd continued speaking as though he hadn't heard Buddy. "It was the master creation of the great dwarven engineer Smyrna Skibibidi. Legend says he was the only one to ever meet the Necromancer and survive. Drove the poor dwarf mad. Maybe it was insanity, or maybe he rushed his work. Whatever it was, he accidentally activated the golem before he had installed all the safety mechanisms. It killed its creator and attacked anyone who got close to the main forges. Smyrna was the only one that knew how it worked, and we've been ineffective at getting past the automaton.

"I went there myself, twice. Both times I took a contingent of dwarven warriors, and both times I returned with far too few. I could do nothing against the machine as it devoured the souls of my compatriots."

"What chance do four skeletons have against something that could stop your fighters?" Beast asked.

Thorodd shrugged. "You're already dead. Maybe that will help. Whatever the case, I'm too old and too low on dwarves and equipment to try again. The fires of Hraunfass faded after a period lacking maintenance. The forges allowed us to build our machines but also the weapons and armor needed to fight the monsters in the Underdeep. Dwarven engineering is what made Jallfoss so strong. Our magic is weak, so without our machines, we're just mushroom farmers. With the Magma Blaster we can ignite the older forges here at Hjardharfell and start taking back our holds."

Buddy set down his quill and asked, "How hard is it to make a forge? Can it not be done without this Blaster?"

Thorodd shut his eyes and rallied his patience. "I prefer skeletons that don't ask so many questions," he muttered, then let out a long sigh and looked at Buddy. "There's no coal in the Underdeep, and mushrooms and lizards don't burn hot enough to melt metal. The Blaster will allow us to harness the power of lava from deep within the bowels of the mountain. If you return with the item, I'll make sure you're outfitted with the finest weapons and armor Hjardharfell has to offer."

Thorodd dropped a chunk of meat on the floor as he finished the last few bites on his plate. He reached down to retrieve it, finding the furry trogold already attacking the morsel.

"Beak," the trogold chirped with a mouth full of gravy-covered meat.

"How did a trogold get in here?" Thorodd pushed back his chair and grabbed for his sword. He went to swing at Muji, but the creature had scampered under the chairs and sat on top of Buddy's pack, chewing happily.

Torgga put a hand on her father's arm. "No, that's Muji. He's Buddy's thrall."

"That is no thrall of mine," Buddy snapped. "The creature just follows me around and won't stay out of my gear."

"That sounds like a thrall to me," Thorodd said with a confused look on his face. "Though a trogold is a strange choice for a familiar contract. Your magic must be even weaker than ours."

Buddy gave Thorodd a piercing glare but didn't respond.

Beast fished through one of the pouches on her belt and pulled out a spare Drift Amulet and a bit of leather. "Buddy's magic has proven useful, and Muji is a part of our group." She walked over to the trogold and scratched him gently between the ears before tying the Amulet around his neck. "See?"

Muji examined the gift and looked over to Buddy. "Beak!" He held up the Amulet to show the mage his new possession. Buddy ignored him, but Beast and Torgga cooed over Muji, who beaked happily, enjoying the attention.

Henry was glad Muji had lightened the mood, though he still needed more information on their quest. "Lord Thorodd, what is a Magma Blaster?"

Buddy flipped through the pages of his tome, then held it up for Thorodd and Henry to see. The musty pages held multiple drawings of a strange device, some faded beyond recognition. It had a short cylinder with a hand grip on one end and a metal loop with another grip on the other side. Another drawing showed fire spewing from the end opposite the loop. "Is this what you're talking about?"

Thorodd nodded. "That's it."

Buddy set down the tome and studied the page. "The red mage copied the description from another book. He hadn't seen one himself, but he sought it with great intent. From the account, it sounds quite powerful, yet capable of precision contingent on one's method of employment."

Henry was still having trouble understanding magical conversations. Pushing back the monsters would help the dwarves, but what did that have to do with breaking the curse? "How does that help us with our quest?" he asked the dwarven leader.

"It doesn't," Thorodd replied bluntly. "Restarting our machines will allow the mountain to support the life within, but if you're looking to reverse the Necromancer's affliction, what you care about is a different object the golem guards. When we tapped into the Source Crystal, we needed something to store the immense energy. Smyrna created what he called the Flow Bracers out of the purest flow crystals to hold an insane amount of power."

"What will we be able to do with that power?" Buddy asked.

"Lady Destria was the one who stopped Livadi and the Necromancer from taking Jallfoss," Thorodd replied. "She was the most powerful mage of her time. She gave her life to repel them, and now her spirit clings to existence at the upper spires of the Jallfoss range. The Flow Bracers are the most powerful item this mountain has ever created, and they might be enough to pull her soul from limbo . . . or push her beyond death. It's a gamble, but if you can resurrect her, then maybe she can help break the curse. That seems like a reasonable risk to assume."

"So, we're retrieving two items: the Magma Blaster and the Flow Bracers?" Henry confirmed. The prospect of fighting golems and monsters excited more than frightened him. Plus, the Tiers and equipment he and his friends could gain from the dwarven quest would help them against any humans that ventured into the mountain.

Thorodd finished the last of his meal and slurped down the final drops in his flagon. "You probably won't make it. But we'll spare all the resources we can. Torgga will take you to the armory. It sounds like our best team of artificers is ready to charge your weapons, so you'll need to assist them."

The skeletons conferred amongst themselves, but they quickly agreed that Thorodd's plan was the best course of action they'd come across so far. "All right, Lord Thorodd," Henry said on behalf of his troupe, "we're in."

The dwarf downed the last bit of sharinji juice from his

flagon and pounded it on the table. "Of course you are. Now, take your bones from my chamber and prepare for your journey while I confirm the quality of this whiskey."

CHAPTER 26

Hooves pounded into the hard earth as the mare settled into a smooth gallop. Her rider knew she could keep up the pace for several more hours before they had to stop and rest. Regardless of the content of the message he conveyed, Abderus knew the importance of his mission based solely on the quality of his mount. Cora was the horse's name, and getting the chance to carry a message on her back was the pinnacle for riders in the Bastion. She was the prized horse of the entire kingdom of Ikrit, not just the Acolytes.

Abderus knew Cora was a fantastic horse for much more than her physical prowess. He had felt her mind over many years working with the animal. She had a subtleness about her that most other horses didn't possess. There was calm in her mind, and she had a keen awareness of her surroundings. Cora would trust the intuition of her rider and not lose control, no matter the situation. She was one of a kind.

Even at their speed, the horse glided smoothly over the dirt road. Her mane flowed in the breeze, and a light sheen of sweat glistened off her coat. The mare was the color of pure obsidian, save for the single pink splotch on her nose. It would be several hours of travel, but he had to hurry. He knew the message he had to pass to the Great Lord couldn't wait. As an Acolyte, it wasn't normal for him to be used as a messenger. For Commander Cirilo to hand him the scroll and send him to Lord Stavros meant the information was extremely important.

Abderus had been an Acolyte for several years. After dozens of trips through the lower crypts of Jallfoss, he had just hit Tier **10** and been promoted to Acolyte First Class. His skill with a weapon wasn't the best, and his prospects of advancing much further as an Acolyte seemed unlikely until he'd discovered his pension for enchantment. Specifically, his Ability to work with the minds of animals. Master Jacoby had first noticed his talents and put him to work training horses for the Cavalry Brigade.

He couldn't believe the message when he'd first heard it. Master Jacoby had brought Abderus through the mountain on his first run, and Master Sigurjon had accompanied him on several subsequent adventures. He didn't know Masters Tekşan or Allito all that well, as they had just arrived from the battlefields after pushing back the Varanasi Empire, though their reputations as capable Acolytes preceded them.

Abderus's mind drifted to his days as a Junior Acolyte. He remembered the fear he felt the first time he'd been surrounded by skeletons. The stench of death had filled his nostrils. One of the undead was an Acolyte that had died just a few months prior, and chunks of flesh still clung to his bones as he attacked without mercy. Jacoby had been there to fight back the skeletons just enough to keep him alive but also push him to his absolute limits. It was a terrible experience, but one necessary to harden the minds and bodies of the Ikritian military's future leaders.

The younger soldiers saw the Master Acolytes as idols,

even indestructible gods. Now, according to the boy's account, they were all dead. Koş was the poor Acolyte's name. Abderus hadn't met him personally, and he couldn't imagine the horror the soldier must have witnessed if his story was true. Abderus's mission was to deliver the scroll containing the man's account.

Despite the best efforts of the Great Lord and the Bastion over the years, they hadn't been able to break past the Necromancer's undead. Had the evil sorcerer reemerged and started making stronger, smarter skeletons? Was it the Necromancer himself who killed the Acolytes? Maybe the Acolyte's deaths would be the last straw, and Lord Stavros, with all his might, would finally put an end to the Necromancer's evil. Abderus could only hope.

The city gates of Ikrit rose on the horizon. The sun sunk low in the sky, reflecting off the white walls and forcing the Acolyte to squint. He felt the horse's nearly limitless endurance beneath him, though his own reserves had certainly begun to wane. A nearby alfalfa field was as good a place as any to rest for a few moments and let the horse graze. He pulled back on the reins and eased Cora into a trot, steering her over to feed while he caught his breath. Then they would finish their mission and deliver the horrible news to Lord Stavros.

The morning after their meeting with the dwarven Elder, four skeletons and a trogold followed Torgga from Hjardharfell, through the mushroom trees of the Grunischwald, and into the dwarven Underdeep.

"Beak, beak." Muji bounced around Buddy's feet as the mage plodded along. The trogold's accomplishments the previous night had garnered several rounds of cuddles from Torgga and Beast and a generous portion of grilled lizard meat. Buddy didn't acknowledge the creature, but he had yet to shoot any lightning bolts at him.

"Feels great to have a working hammer. I can't wait to try it out. Thank you for letting us use your Muji," Ox said as he walked beside Buddy.

"For once, I agree with Ox. You sure are amazing, Muji. These ice daggers are exactly what I needed." Beast swiped a boney finger across her blades, leaving a hint of frost on the tip of the bone.

Buddy fumbled with the necklace he'd taken from the maul-wielding Acolyte and pretended not to hear the praise Muji received, though his clenched jaw gave away his sour mood.

Henry laughed as the other skeletons teased Buddy, then focused on the glyphs hovering over Beast and Ox's brandished weapons.

Haruspex

Item: **Durmaz War Maul (Superior)**

Description: **Weapon (Enchanted), Contains Drift Crystals (Superior). Hardness 10, Structure 30/30**

Lore: **This hammer is the traditional weapon of a prominent Ikritian family**

Ability: **Smash. 9/9 charges. +50% force damage. Expending additional charges will release a force nova with a moderate chance to Stun nearby enemies**

Item: **Veiled Brigade Daggers (Superior)**

Description: **Weapon (Enchanted), Contains Drift Crystals (Superior). Hardness 10, Structure 25/25**

Lore: **These daggers are the signature weapons of Acolytes from**

the Veiled Brigade, the branch of the Ikritian military tasked with handling sensitive missions
Ability: Frozen Strike. 22/22 charges. +10% ice damage. High chance to inflict Slow on a damaged enemy

Haruspex gave him an abundance of information, though the divination Ability still confused him. He knew the information it displayed was based on his Acumen, Perception, and the Ability's Tier. Haruspex and Consume came from his desert vision, and the two seemed to overlap with the Drift Amulet's Status, Assess, and Siphon Abilities, effectively making the item useless to him and Ox.

The giant skeleton, who apparently had the same Abilities, seemed uninterested in delving into the mystery. For the time being, Henry chose just to accept that Haruspex worked and appreciate the information it provided.

Tabling his concerns about the strange magic, he wanted to understand how *Muji's* unexpected Ability could help them. "Has the trogold been able to do that this whole time? Are all trogolds artibishops?" he asked.

Buddy summoned the last bit of his patience to respond. "The word you are looking for is "artificer" . . . and I care little about the inherent proficiencies of trogolds."

Henry's memory drifted back to the previous night. After their meeting with Thorodd, Torgga led the skeletons deeper into the dwarven city and into a series of caves that looked more industrial than the rest of Hjardharfell. Ramps with neglected carts and chains branched from the main tunnel into various empty caverns. The group didn't come across any other souls as they made their way. The area looked like it hadn't seen much traffic in years, and the stillness put Henry on edge as he half expected an ambush from armor-tongues or salamanders.

They eventually arrived at a cave that looked like a combination of workshop and armory. It was rather small and sparse compared to the armory at the coliseum in Ammerthall. Stone workbenches lined the walls of the circular room and a round stone table sat in the middle. There were bronze axes and hammers in holders on the wall and a few suits of armor on stands throughout the room. A quick Haruspex revealed none were above Uncommon quality.

Ox's hammer, Beast's daggers, Henry's xiphos, and seven empty flow crystals were arranged on the stone table. The bow, arrows, javelins, and shields sat off to the side on one of the workbenches.

A gnome looked up from his work and wiped a hand across his sweaty brow as Torgga led them in. "Greetings, dead guys. You're not human overtoppers or monstrous underdeepers. That makes you ghoulie inbetweeners," he said with a smile. He wore light-green robes with a thick leather belt and had his white beard tucked into his collar.

Henry didn't know how to respond to the gnome's gibberish, so he tried to give him a cheerful smile. Having momentarily forgotten that his face didn't contain the lips and muscles necessary to display such countenance, he only succeeded in giving the gnome a deathly stare.

"I . . . I can see you're here for business," the gnome continued quickly, suddenly unsure of himself with four animated bone sacks crowding into his workspace. "I'm Gnaz, Assistant Artificer. Please, gather around. It's not much, but it's all we can manage without the ancient forges."

The gnome wore a strange contraption on his head that looked like a metal spider with each leg holding a smaller, multicolored crystal disk. One of the legs with a light-blue crystal was positioned just in front of his left eye. He gripped a strange tool in his hand with a flat crystal disk on one end of a metal handle. The gnome motioned with the tool and the skeletons joined him at the stone table that held their weapons.

Buddy rolled one of the flow crystals over with the tip of his finger. "You said 'Assistant Artificer.' That implies a Master Artificer exists. When can we expect someone proficient?"

"I . . . I doubt he'll make it today. He's a very busy gnome, but you're in good hands. I watched him do this a few years ago." Gnaz stammered, a shaky voice betraying his calm expression.

The skeletons looked at Torgga. The dwarf shrugged and scrunched up her face. "That doesn't surprise me. The old mage works on his own schedule. Don't worry, though. Gnaz has been studying for years. Right, Gnaz?"

The gnome nodded with exaggerated enthusiasm. "Of course, Lady Torgga. I'm the most proficient Assistant Artificer in all Hjardharfell. Now, do you skeletons have any spells you want to load into the hammer and daggers?"

Henry was far from reassured, but he didn't see any harm in putting his trust in Gnaz. "I didn't know there was a choice of spells. The hammer once held lightning, and the daggers used magical poison. Are you able to put different magic in the weapons? What spells do you have?" Henry asked as he picked up his sword and placed it back in the sheath on his belt. From his previous discussions with Buddy, he knew his sword's enchantment didn't deplete with use, so there was no need to recharge its magic.

"*I* don't have any," the gnome responded, matter-of-factly. "We're limited to whatever magic you can produce."

"Henry, please leave any discussions involving magic to me," Buddy scolded.

Henry motioned with his hand and stepped out of the way.

"From my spells, we're limited to lightning, fire, frost, and force," Buddy explained.

"Force for the hammer," Ox said eagerly, "The lightning always shocked me every time I used it."

"Force magic it is," the gnome said, pulling the hammer close to him. "Come here, mage, and give me your hand. By the way, that was a bold move, talking to Thorodd like that. The other gnomes told me what you said to him."

Buddy approached the table. "Why? There were four of us. Even without weapons, he was no threat."

"Don't overestimate your power, mage. Look at your Amulet. You're Tier **6**."

"So?"

"*So?*" The gnome was clearly shocked. "Thorodd is Tier **42**. He would have skewered the lot of you faster than a snidderskod can shake its tail."

Henry took note of Thorodd's alleged prowess, wondering if the Elder's Tier had something to do with the failed Haruspex Ability.

Buddy seemed undaunted. "If you're finished with your assessment, I am ready to begin. What do I do?"

"Give me your hand," the gnome requested a second time. "When I touch the hammer, you can cast your spell. It should travel through me and charge the maul."

Gnaz gripped the mage's boney fingers in one hand, then touched Ox's hammer with the other. "Ready," he said, the word halfway between a question and an instruction.

A wave of force blasted from the maul, sending the weapons, gnome, and skeletons rolling across the room. Armor stands toppled, and weapons fell from the wall. One of Beast's daggers clanged off the wall near Henry's head. Muji tumbled from Buddy's pack and scampered to a safe corner of the room. Henry got back to his feet unharmed, but his legs wobbled, and his skull rang.

Status Effect: Stunned (Minor) MOB -10%, PER -10%

"Is that how it was supposed to work?" Buddy gathered himself to his feet and wiped the dust from his robes.

"So, I've seen it done a few times, but I haven't *actually* accomplished it before. Let's give it one more try. I think I know what I did wrong." Gnaz picked himself off the ground and collected his wits.

They collected the weapons and put only the hammer back on the table, hoping to avoid another deadly blast of flying armaments. This time, when the gnome grabbed Buddy's hand, Muji jumped on the table. The trogold pushed the gnome's hand away and grasped Buddy's fingers. Then he put the skeleton's hand directly on top of the hammer. Muji put both of his tiny hands on top of Buddy's and looked up at the skeleton as if encouraging him to cast the spell again.

"You're putting yourself at the center of the blast, trogold," Buddy warned.

"Beak," Muji chirped in response. The gnomes and skeletons took one step back, then another.

Buddy cast the force spell again, expecting to send the trogold, the hammer, and himself flying across the room. Instead, the metal hummed, and the flow crystal in the hammer flashed and then faded back to clear. Henry noticed the blue Vitus gauge on Muji's Amulet had decreased by a quarter.

"Ah, I see what he did," the gnome said, pulling himself up to the table. "I tried to use myself as a conduit, but the creature opened the flow of magic between you and the hammer directly. Keep doing it to put more charges into it."

Buddy complied, and after three more charges Muji's Vitus had depleted completely.

"Beast, I'm ready for your daggers," Buddy said. "I can't replicate the poison magic, but you've got the choice of lightning, fire, force, or ice."

"I would have preferred magical poison, but ice will do." Beast set her daggers on the table as Ox retrieved his maul. The gnome, having seen the trogold perform the act, successfully loaded frost charges in each of Beast's daggers and then used Ox to charge three flow crystals with healing before depleting his own Vitus.

After the gnome's Vitus—or Steam, as the inhabitants of Hjardharfell referred to it—was gone, he told the skeletons that Thorodd would allow them to take anything in their sparse armory. Beast selected a few quivers full of arrows, and Buddy took three bronze bucklers to replace his broken and melted iron ones.

Torgga and Buddy spent the rest of the night poring over tomes and maps of the Underdeep while Henry, Beast, and Ox tested their gear and Abilities. Buddy wanted to have the most detailed route to their destination possible. He discovered that the mosaic on Thorodd's table was fairly accurate, but it only depicted the major caverns and tunnels. There were hundreds, if not thousands, of miles of passages throughout Jallfoss. It would be several days' journey to get to the protected storeroom at Lundarbrekka, but the path to it was a main road with only a few forks from which to choose. Navigation would be the easy part. Not getting killed by the monsters below would be more of a challenge.

According to Torgga, the monsters near Hjardharfell were mostly larger and more aggressive versions of the mountain's native species: lizards, spiders, bats, and all manner of other mountain denizens. As they got nearer to the Source Crystal, its power corrupted and twisted the creatures into abominations. Some claimed they were tainted remains combined in obscene fashions; others swore that they were otherworldly spirits that had taken physical form. Whatever the case, it would be a challenging journey.

Torgga led the group through the maze of tunnels and illusory walls. Henry and the others quickly became lost, but Buddy had his tome and scribed their path intently. They exited a final illusion to a small landing leading to a steep downward tunnel. At the mouth of the tunnel sat an armor-tongue, one of the sightless monsters that had nearly killed them just a day prior.

"Quiet," Torgga whispered. "It won't be alerted by your auras, and your scent, smell, and sound are somewhat hidden. You can take it out without drawing attention."

As Torgga said, the armor-tongue didn't seem to notice them. Henry drew a javelin from his back and focused on his target. Its defense was tough, but if his aim was true, the javelin would pierce through instead of glancing off.

Henry extended his arm and took a few long steps to gather momentum, then launched the javelin. It flew silently through the air and directly impacted the creature's side, piercing the thick natural armor and killing the monster instantly.

"Nice shot, deadeye! You'll find that without your auras, the creatures are much less hostile, and you're able to sneak up on them," Torgga said.

Henry surveyed the area for signs of other monsters but found none. "No wonder the dwarves have survived so long, and the humans have had so much trouble. With your magic, we might have a chance."

"I only wish I could help you more, but this is where I

leave you." A sad look crossed Torgga's face. "My job is here, keeping the monsters away from Hjardharfell. Before I leave you, though, I had Gnaz help me make these." She held out four silver rings, each with a series of tiny flow crystals set in the metal.

Haruspex

Item: Muffle Ring (Superior)

Description: Accessory (Enchanted). Dwarven ring containing four
    flow crystals (Epic), each with a separate illusion enchantment

Abilities:

    Muffle Aura II. Vitus -1

    Muffle Sound II. Vitus -1

    Muffle Smell I. Vitus -1

    Muffle Sight I. Vitus -1

"Four muffle enchantments powered by your Steam. It should be permanent and give you the advantage you need. Without these, you'd lose the illusions once you were away from me for too long," the dwarf said.

"Thank you, Torgga." Beast put the ring on her finger and admired the jewelry. "We couldn't have gotten this far without you."

"Good luck and hurry back!" She smiled and then said with her familiar giggle, "Goodbye, Buddy. I'm looking forward to our next talk about magic."

Buddy gave her a questioning look. "And I . . . look forward to seeing your progress as a mage."

Torgga waved goodbye to the skeletons as she disappeared through the rock illusion. Buddy awkwardly returned the gesture a few seconds after she had left, displaying a sense of unease that was uncommon for the mage.

"For such a smart minion, you have much to learn." Ox patted Buddy on the shoulder and turned to the open tunnel leading away from Hjardharfell. The others followed him down a fungus-lit path.

—

For two days, they made their way down the gradual decline in the main tunnel. As Torgga had warned them, the monsters had grown in size and complexity, but with the dwarf's rings they were able to avoid any unwanted confrontations and preserve their supplies.

The group found an offshoot from the main tunnel on the third night. A small cave filled with hexagonal pillars of quartz and veins of a purple stone glistened in the light from the fungus. They elected to take a short rest in the middle of the room, and Henry stood the first watch. The cave wasn't small, and the light from the fungus barely illuminated the expanse. There were no other tunnels leading from the room other than where they had entered.

Muji lay curled on a flat stone near Buddy as the mage read from his tome. "The dwarves didn't give us much information about what to expect. I'm interested in what Torgga's magic could do to assist our journey."

"Her magic is what you're interested in?" Ox teased. "Or was it her . . . *assets?*"

Buddy opened his jaws to give Ox a response, but the sound of grinding bones interrupted him.

"Look alive. Someone's coming to play," Henry shouted.

At once, the skeletons spread out. Beast and Buddy took up positions at the rear, and Henry and Ox drew their weapons.

At first, they saw only a spinning green cloud. It looked

like an aura that was fighting itself. Multiple shades of green blended together in a chaotic swirl slowly rolling in their direction.

As the turbulent aura drew nearer, they caught glimpses of the creature within, but Henry couldn't make any sense of the monster. It was a mixture of flowing bones, flesh, and metal. Appendages would emerge from the entity and project forward like legs, propel the monster forward, then merge back with the main body. The skulls from creatures and humanoids alike churned within the mass, occasionally knocking into the myriad arms and armor also encasing whatever the thing truly was. Henry noticed the red cloth of the Acolytes whipping through the mix.

"This is bad!" Buddy cried. "The red mage described it in his tome. He called it an amalgamator. Don't get close or it will absorb you into its body. It's a terrible way to go."

Haruspex

Type: Amalgamator, Abomination

Health: Full, Hardness Variable, Structure 370/412

Vitus: None

Attributes:

    STR: 54

    MOB: Variable

    FOR: Variable

    ACU: 2

    PER: 24

    RES: 0

Damage Resistance: Variable

Lore: Little is known about the abominations from the Dwarven Underdeep, but the amalgamator is a dangerous adversary and best avoided if possible. Some are weak to magic, and their

Attributes can vary greatly between individual amalgamators

Ability Discovered: Haruspex III. Little is hidden from your astute awareness. Powerful divination grants access to all but the most hidden secrets. AFI +5, PER +5 Supersedes item Abilities

The boost to Henry's Perception helped him pick up on the creature's sporadic movements, as though his brain could process faster than the lumbering construct maneuvered. However, even the Tier III Ability had trouble determining if the monster was a creature or an item.

Bones and metal shot from its body and sealed the mouth of the tunnel with a ghastly spiderweb. It separated from the bone web and picked up speed as it approached. Henry searched for a weak point or at least a spot to attack, but it had none. "We're trapped. How do we kill it?"

"Magic." Buddy prepped blue flames in both of his hands. "Lots of it. You can also smash it."

"Then we have a plan." Henry signaled for Ox to step back and Beast to take his position. "Beast, you and I will distract it. Buddy, you do the damage. And Ox . . ."

"What can I do for you?"

"Pick up something heavy and throw it." Henry sprinted left, and Beast teleported to the monster's right. The amalgamator didn't have trouble following them. With so many heads, it could track and attack both skeletons simultaneously. An arm formed from either side of the abomination. The appendages held masses of broken bones and blades. It swung its makeshift arms and launched deadly balls of metal and bone at the two skeletons. Beast had no difficulty teleporting away from the attacks, and Henry could dodge easily enough. The monster flung a mass of bone and armor at Henry. It barely missed the skeleton and smashed into the nearest pillars, cracking them and blasting chunks of quartz all over the cavern.

As Henry and Beast distracted the monster, Buddy and Ox began their assault. The mage led with a blast of each of his four magic types. Weapons and armor melted under the intense heat of the blue flame, while magical lightning and ice shattered charred bone. Buddy's force magic, however, was the most effective. Invisible blasts tore through the amalgamator, ripping apart its churning body and scattering pieces to the far end of the cave.

Ox lifted a massive quartz shard from the pillars the abomination had shattered with its earlier attack. He spun around and then hurled it at the monster. The collision sent the amalgamator reeling, but only for a second.

Henry couldn't tell what the monster used to sense its opponents, but it had enough Perception to determine the most significant threat. It turned and sped toward the mage. Now that a considerable portion of its body had been knocked off by Buddy and Ox's attacks, it was much quicker.

Beast and Henry rushed around its exterior, but its attention was focused on the mage. Henry kicked a lump of sticky armor with his foot. When it didn't react, an idea jumped into his head. "It can only control what it touches! Keep knocking pieces off, and we can whittle it down!"

"Smashing is my specialty," Ox yelled, picking up another huge quartz shard. Buddy used his magic to levitate two boulders, each the size of Ox's, and flung them at the amalgamator. The boulders smashed into the creature and tore significant chunks from its writhing mass.

Now the size of a human and no longer hindered by so much extra weight, the monster rushed directly at Buddy with blazing speed. The mage stood defiantly as the horror plowed into him and enveloped his body. Henry rushed to help, but he was too late. Buddy, now obscured by the broiling objects of the monster's body, stood motionless, completely enveloped. The monster clearly struggled, thrashing at the new skeleton trapped within its bulk, but its attacks failed to penetrate the magical defenses.

Bones exploded in all directions and a force wave spread with a resounding thump. Metal shards clinked across stone and quartz and settled to a stop all over the cavern. Only a single skull sitting on top of a skeletal claw continued to crawl around in disoriented circles. It reminded Henry of an octopus or one of the squid from Husavik. He picked up a rusty sword and impaled the skull, pinning it to the ground. The fingers continued to wriggle, but it was stuck in place.

Buddy stumbled and dropped to a knee. Beast transported to the mage's side and caught him before he completely tumbled.

Henry's Haruspex revealed that Buddy's Health was down quite a bit, and his Vitus was completely empty. The mental fatigue that came with completely draining Vitus could be exhausting and even incapacitating. During one of his previous lectures Buddy had explained to the group that, unlike Health, zero Vitus wasn't the bottom of an experienced mage's magical capabilities. Rather, it marked the point where pressing further could result in long-term or even permanent damage. Buddy's current weakened condition supported that theory.

"Brave strategy, letting it take you," Ox said. "I didn't want to have to smash a minion along with a monster."

"I had a hint from the red mage. He was successful with a similar tactic," Buddy said, slurring his words as Beast helped him to a seated position. After several moments, Buddy recovered his faculties and collected his composure. He took out his metal tome and started reading.

Henry scouted the tunnel to make sure no more enemies were coming to attack, then returned to the group. Ox and Buddy had fallen asleep and Muji was curled on Beast's lap. Henry sat beside the elf. "We'll need to rest until Buddy is fully recovered. I think it's going to get much harder from here."

CHAPTER 27

"We're getting close," Buddy said, referencing the map in his tome. "Just another mile." The variety of monsters had grown rapidly in deadliness and hostility on their fourth day following the main tunnel. They faced two more amalgamators, a handful of mutated cave creatures, and one very unfriendly giant centipede that floated instead of crawled. They were mostly unscathed, though they had been forced to use a few healing crystals. Two shattered upon use, but Ox and Muji recharged the third.

The fights had brought them all into Tier 7, and Henry took advantage of the calm moment to parse through the glyphs and allow the Soul Essence into his core.

Etherpede Killed, Soul Essence Claimed, +1 Tier:
STR +2, MOB +2, FOR +2, ACU +1, PER +1

Strength surpassed first Threshold. Attribute bonus applied (STR +10%)

Modified Strength below first Threshold. Attribute bonus removed

Mobility surpassed first Threshold. Attribute bonus applied (MOB +10%)

Ability Discovered: Consume II. A lethal blow forms a bond with your enemies. Absorb a larger portion of Soul Essence from each kill. Gain a small amount of Health from each kill. MIG +2, RES +2. Supersedes item Abilities

The lightning cloud in Henry's core thrummed with power and flooded invisible channels in his body with magical energy. Buddy had spoken briefly about Attribute Thresholds and the benefits they provided after reaching **25** points, but Henry hadn't given it much thought until that moment. Huge bonuses to his Strength and Mobility pulsated and filled him with innate energy, like a coiled snake waiting to strike.

As quickly as the bonuses came, the Strength increase faded and left him with a weak, deflated sensation. Though his Mobility had received a huge bump, his Skeletal Body Status Effect had kept him below the Strength Threshold. He brought up his Status and reviewed the Effects.

Haruspex

Name: Henry
Race: Human Skeleton
Tier: 7
Health: 60/60
Vitus: 62/66
Attributes:
    STR: 20
    MOB: 29

FOR: 18
ACU: 15
PER: 18
RES: 22

Status Effects:

Soul Anchor: Slowly regenerate all damage, even beyond death. Degradation of the mind can vary and is much more pronounced in sentient beings. This Effect does not stop natural decay. +2 Health/Hour

Skeletal Body: Without flesh and blood, your Strength and Fortitude are greatly reduced. However, your body no longer suffers from many ailments common to living forms. STR -20%, FOR -20%, Damage Resistance: Physical -1 (Bludgeoning -2), Environmental +1, Poison: Immune

Buddy had taught Henry about the numerical bump that came with each Threshold, but the extra **10%** to Mobility felt amazing. He had much more control over his bones, and his movements were smoother and faster. However, he was still far behind Beast and Buddy, who had several of their Attributes well past the first Threshold. Ox had even awoken with his Strength past the second. *No wonder the big guy could lift boulders like they were nothing,* Henry thought.

The Skeletal Body Effect was holding back his own Strength, but with a few more Tiers, he felt he would be able to break past that barrier. As he reviewed his Status, he also noticed the expanded descriptions of Soul Anchor and Skeletal Body. He longed for a body with skin and muscle, and there were many drawbacks to being a skeleton, but he couldn't scoff at some of the benefits that came with the curse. The ability to regenerate and the exemption from many of the downsides of living flesh were perfect for an adventurer. Henry wondered how else he could use the Effects to his advantage.

Lost in thought, Henry found himself lagging behind the other skeletons, but with a few quick steps utilizing his heightened Mobility he caught up. As they continued, the tunnel widened, and the decline flattened out.

"It's getting warmer the further we go down. I can't feel the sensation, but I notice the difference," Beast said as she scanned for hidden danger. With her Perception at **31**, past the first Threshold, she had no trouble picking up small details in the world around her. Humidity formed dew on patches of lumimoss, thicker air added just a bit more resistance to her movements, and even the way her boots scraped against the rocky path gave her immense amounts of information.

Henry slid his fingers across a patch of moss. "Yes, I can sense it too. Do you think that's what caused the lumimoss to alter its hue?" The fungus that provided them light had changed from greens and blues to purples and mostly reds. It cast eerie shadows on the tunnel walls and put the skeletons on high alert.

"That's to be expected, Herbie," Ox said. "You see, the copper-permeable channels in the plasma membranes of the fungus expand when temperatures increase, leaving a higher concentration of iron near the luminescent filaments, causing a spectrum shift—"

A wallop of smashing rock interrupted Ox's explanation. Slow, steady footsteps of something massive echoed around a curve in the tunnel. A deep, cyclical, whirring sound followed. The skeletons clung to the walls and cautiously peered toward the sound.

The red fungus illuminated a humanoid shape lumbering their direction. It was twice Ox's height but had no head, and it was made entirely of dark-gray rock. A dim orange light emanated from an opening in the center of its chest, and gears spun inside its body. The construct gave off a whirring sound like a swarm of agitated bees. In the dim light of the tunnel, the massive golem did not appear to notice the troupe of skeletons.

"That must be one of the golems Thorodd talked about," Henry whispered. "Is it going to attack?"

Buddy studied the golem intently, trying to assess it. "From the dwarves' description, I can't say. It can't reason. It can only respond to certain stimuli."

Haruspex

Type: Stone Golem, Dwarven Construct

Hardness 8, Structure 132/205

Vitus: None

Attributes:

    STR: 85

    MOB: 4

    FOR: 0

    ACU: 0

    PER: 3

    RES: 0

Damage Resistance:

    Physical: 8

        Bludgeoning +4

    Environmental: 10

        Fire +10

    Magical: 4

        Mental: Immune

Lore: Dwarven engineers created stone golems to assist with min-ing operations. They were built with a thin layer of an unknown

dwarven alloy to resist the intense heat of lava flows. Their lack of upkeep can lead to unpredictable behavior

"Unpredictable behavior? I don't like the sound of that," Henry whispered.

"How do we kill it?" Beast asked, readying her daggers.

They spread out and prepped their attack, but the automaton lumbered by, each step shaking the ground. Slow, aimless steps moved the machine forward. Rocky arms tipped with three long, stony fingers swung at its sides.

The golem passed, and the skeletons gathered in its wake. "It should have at least seen Ox's dumb body," Beast said in a hushed voice.

"It probably sensed my tremendous Strength and chose to avoid a fight." Ox's voice was just a bit too loud for Henry's comfort.

Henry studied the tunnel before them and saw many more golems in the path. Some were standing, some were lying in pieces, but they were all inert. He couldn't tell if they'd been destroyed or if they just hadn't been entirely built. Thankful for Torgga's rings obscuring their presence, the skeletons picked their way around the golems. One mostly whole automaton lay on its back like it had just drifted off to sleep. Hammered plates of a thick black metal formed the golem's outer shell and a glyph popped into Henry's view.

Haruspex

Item: Golem Shielding (Epic)

Description: Construct Armor. Forged from a rare ore, this plating is highly resistant to heat and is commonly used in the construction of dwarven golems

Henry ran his fingers along the hard stone armor and touched one of the metal gears in its chest cavity. "Did they grow old and die?" Henry asked.

"Stone and metal don't die of old age, but they can stop functioning if not recharged." Buddy reached inside the golem's chest and tapped his finger on a large flow crystal.

"In that case, Muji shouldn't get close. If he activates one, we have no guarantee it will be docile. The lack of monsters in the area tells us everything we need to know." Beast held the trogold tightly in her arms, but the creature's eyes locked onto every machine they came near.

When everyone had gotten their fill of the golems, Henry rounded up the group and led them further down the curving tunnel. All four skeletons had their weapons ready, waiting for an attack.

After another mile the path opened into a tall vertical shaft with a stone bridge spanning the gap from one side to the other. Sturdy and dwarven-built, the bridge was twenty feet wide with thick stone railings on either side.

Sparse patches of lumimoss clung to the walls and bridge, casting a faint red luster through the shaft. Arches supported the wide stone bridge from below, and two metal carts lay toppled and smashed along the expanse. They were crumpled as though huge stones had fallen from the ceiling and crushed them, but no boulders were nearby. Henry peered over the railing to find the expanse went straight down for several hundred, if not thousands of feet; the distance was too far for him to estimate. At the very bottom of the shaft, a dim red-and-yellow glow shimmered, barely visible to Henry's Perception.

"This must be one of the air shafts that shoots hot air to the surface." Buddy looked up to the top of the shaft where it disappeared into darkness. "As the dwarves said, it's not functioning right now."

"I'm not worried about the air." Beast pointed a finger to the opposite side of the bridge. "But *those* concern me."

Henry gazed across the span and saw several bodies scattered along the stone. Some were human, some were dwarf—they all were pulverized. Metal armor was pounded flat, and weapons lay bent and smashed. The stone underneath them was several feet of solid granite, and it still showed signs of heavy impacts that even Ox couldn't have delivered. Two of the bodies had the red cloaks of the Acolytes, and they still had bits of long-dead flesh hanging from their splintered bones.

"They've been here a long time without regenerating. What's going on?" Beast asked.

"Either their auras never found their bodies after death, or something stripped them away," Buddy answered. "We should hurry. Keep your guard up."

The skeletons followed the stone bridge, creeping around the mangled bodies. On the other side, the bridge led to a circular landing with stone railings. The plaza had two large tunnels forking left and right and a smaller, human-sized opening between the two tunnels.

"The tunnels are big enough for one of the golems. I say we take the small one in the middle," Henry suggested.

"Where's your sense of adventure?" Ox replied, but he seemed completely content with using the smaller doorway.

Rusted metal straps banded the crumbling stone of the center archway, threatening to give at any moment. An opening for what could have been a portcullis lay at the tunnel's threshold, but the portal had been retracted below the floor. Henry found a switch on the side of the wall for the sun globes. When he activated it, the rusted metal broke in his hand. Henry dropped the switch and ducked down to enter a small passageway and creep to the next room.

Another smooth stone arch followed shortly by a larger, rough stone archway opened into a huge circular domed room, nearly a hundred paces wide. It had a similar layout to Thorodd's chamber, with pillars circling the exterior and holding up the ceiling, but only five of the thirty or so columns still stood. One pillar had broken off at waist height near the entrance. Others lay scattered about the room among more smashed bodies. Large cracks in the ceiling led to a hole in the left wall that took up most of the height. Henry peered into the cavity, but it was too dark for him to discern anything.

Metal cages with rusty locks lined the walls between the pillars. Twisted iron formed the bars with a lattice too small for a hand to get through. Most of them had been damaged and were empty, but a few at the opposite end of the room looked intact. Just enough red lumimoss clung to the cracked walls to allow the skeletons to make their way through the rubble.

"There." Buddy pointed to the opposite end. "I sense two sources of magic, both stronger than any we've encountered so far."

They followed the wall most of the way around the right side until they came to an unbroken cage. The cage had metal pegs for holding items, though all were empty except the middle two. They supported a metal tube about the size of Henry's forearm. One end had ridges for a handgrip, and the other had a loop on a hinge. It looked like the loop could be adjusted into several different positions by pushing or pulling it. On one side of the tube were four small flow crystals in a line.

Haruspex

Item: Magma Blaster (Epic)

Description: Magical Device (Enchanted). Dwarven apparatus used to ignite lava forges. Contains flow crystals (Legendary)

Buddy put his hand against the cage and leaned close, studying the device. Muji climbed out of Buddy's pack, stood on the mage's shoulder, then leaned forward with one hand on the cage, mimicking Buddy. "Beak," squeaked the trogold.

"Indeed," Buddy replied.

"There's the Blaster. Now, where are the Bracers?" Henry asked.

Buddy and Muji both gave him a judging glance for interrupting their admiration. Then Buddy pointed to the end of the room opposite their entrance.

The skeletal remains of a dwarf lay against the far wall. The body wore bronze armor and a helmet, though the helmet was caved in on one side. His bracers caught Henry's attention; they didn't match the rest of his ensemble. The armguards were white and from this distance, Henry couldn't make much detail, as it was far too dim in the room.

"I can sense powerful magic emanating from those remains." Buddy raised his hand and ignited a blue flame that hovered in the air in front of him, casting light throughout the room.

The sound of grinding stone pierced the stillness of the cavern, and the four undead turned to where they had entered. An orange glow appeared on the wall a dozen feet off the ground. The stone blocks above the archway started to move. A huge golem, three times the size of any they'd seen before, emerged from the shadows and took a step forward. Buddy's fire illuminated a machine made from jagged chunks of black metal that looked more grown than forged. The whirring of its engine filled the chamber as the internal mechanisms ratcheted into high gear.

"We walked right between its legs. Good thing I didn't stand up, or I would have hit its balls." Ox laughed and hefted a sizable chunk of broken pillar.

The ground shook under the heavy footfalls of the lumbering machine. Smyrna's final creation—the deadly construct that killed its creator and repelled a Tier **44** dwarven Elder—began its assault.

CHAPTER 28

"Lord Stavros, we've routed their final battalion, and their military is in full retreat. We've even managed to capture Basti's Vanguard. Nothing stands in our way. We must lay siege to their capital." Before an intricately carved desk, Commander Alicos delivered his report and stood at attention. Low flames from a marble fireplace to his left lit half his face and cast flickering shadows on the walls of the square room. A grand mantle, inlaid with gold and precious stones, framed the sooty hearth. Such opulence suggested the prestige of the room's owner.

"Chaotically organized" was the only way to describe the collection of paraphernalia from all over the known world that decorated the Great Lord's office: handwoven carpets of the finest quality, strange contraptions with dozens of gears for telling time, magic devices of all sorts, and any number of taxidermied animals. Marble and bronze statues lined the room's walls between wooden bookshelves loaded to overflowing.

The fire roared from a recent addition of another log. It lit a plush armchair and a table stacked with books and teacups.

Like the neglected towers at the mountaintops of Jallfoss, they threatened to collapse at the slightest hint of a breeze.

The Commander waited impatiently. His platemail shone to perfection, though it was crisscrossed with a chaotic hash of scars, dents, and dings from hundreds of enemy weapons. Worn leather straps indicating years of usage held strong through constant upkeep. For all the polish, his armor wasn't for show. Alicos was the Commander of the entire Ikritian military, and he'd earned the respect of every Ikritian soldier with his battle prowess.

His ferocity in combat and harsh management style gave him a reputation as someone who wasn't to be taken lightly. That being said, he wasn't cruel, just pragmatic. He was a brilliant tactician, but Commander Alicos was also a hammer. To him, everything was a nail that could be overcome with enough pounding. In his mind, the border villages of Varanasi were no exception.

The Commander's red tunic was emblazoned with the same large kite shield and sword of the Bastion, but instead of a scroll, a single white rose with a thorny stem crossed opposite the sword, representing the delicate nature of the peace the Ikritian Empire sought to maintain. The fringe of his tunic, one thick line surrounded by two thin ones, was the simple pattern that designated him as the highest-ranking Commander in Ikrit. The only person who had more authority over the Ikritian military forces was the aged man before him.

Lord Stavros sat at the wooden desk with maps and parchments spread out before him. Carved figures placed on the largest map represented different military or civilian locations. Several books were opened to pages of ledgers showing each Brigade's readiness, including logistical, offensive, and defensive capabilities.

The Emperor sat with his elbows on the desk, his fingertips touching as he studied the information in front of him. He ran a calloused hand through his long gray hair, then scratched at the stubble on his chin. Liver spots covered his wrinkled skin, but his blue eyes darted across the map with a sharpness not typical of someone his age. He scowled at the enemy positions, then brushed aside one of the older reports on his desk.

Lord Stavros took a sip of tea that had long gone cold. He knew it made the Commander uncomfortable when he spent a few extra moments formulating a thought. It was good for the impatient Acolyte to be left on edge. Stavros knew the Commander's words were wise, but Alicos didn't have the strategic perspective needed to set the path for the next several millennia of Ikritian prosperity.

"We've destroyed their military," the Emperor began. "It will take them several years to recover. If we lay siege, we'll only create a generation of men set to wage the next war. Recall your armies, save for three Infantry Brigades. Your men have been at war for years, and they need to return to their families to remember what they're protecting. Keep a portion of the supply lines in place and devise a rotation for the infantry to man the areas near the border villages. We need to give aid to the people who have suffered the most."

Alicos balled his hands into fists. "Lord Stavros, I must object. This fight would have been over years ago if they had sided with us. Instead, they supported the Varanasi, supplied them with food and soldiers, and attacked our convoys."

"Of course they did, and they may still side with them in the future. But we're not at war with the border villages. They've been through enough. Let them rebuild, give them supplies, give them a few years of peace without Varanasi or

Ikrit interfering and see how much they like free trade with us," the old man patiently replied.

"If Varanasi gets the Shargala or the Kordoba on their side, we'll be in trouble. They'll regain their strength if we don't take their capital now. We haven't been able to rely on the industrial might of Jallfoss for a century, but the flow crystals our Acolytes bring us and the techniques from Lord Livadi to refine them into weapons and Drift Amulets have given us the edge in battle."

Lord Stavros knew every word from Alicos's mouth came from an unquenchable desire to protect Ikrit, so he let the man continue.

"What's more, the men are passing rumors of a dragon under Varanasi's control. I'm not one to listen to such rumors, but if the Degonharts have returned, we have a major problem."

Stavros knew the Degonharts had returned to Jallfoss long ago but under a different name. Regardless, the Varanasi were too corrupt to seduce either a dragon or one of their human counterparts. That information mattered little, as dragons had been extinct for a thousand years.

Lord Stavros mulled over his Commander's words. "I care little of rumored dragons and more of a war that has taken its toll on the people of both lands. Our Ikritians supported this war and rallied behind us. The people of Varanasi did not do the same for their regime. They were held hostage by a brutal dictator while we flourished. We sacrificed our personal wealth to support the Ikritian farmers while Basti ate cablaronees behind his gates. The people saw his arrogance, and they are moving accordingly. Basti will not be in power much longer. Hopefully, his replacement sees herself as a mortal servant to her population and not as a god."

Stavros flipped through a few pages of the open ledgers.

"However, Commander, I believe your assessment of our capabilities is wrong. Flow crystals are not the strength of our nation. It is the Ikritians themselves. It is the determination of our Acolytes, the productivity of our citizens, and the pride we have in what we've built that have turned Ikrit into the dominating force in the region.

"The nation of Varanasi sought to take that away from us, but the will of our army, and our nation, triumphed. We will not punish the border villages for showing loyalty to a dictator who would have wiped them out had they not complied. They are safe now, and we will work to earn their loyalty until they eagerly add their numbers to our great nation."

A thud against the heavy door of Stavros's chamber interrupted their conversation and a guard burst into the room. "Lord Stavros, apologies for the intrusion, but a rider from the Bastion just arrived. There's been an accident at Jallfoss."

Lord Stavros took another sip of his tea and sat back in his seat. "You have your orders, Commander."

Alicos nodded and left, briefly acknowledging the Acolyte on the way out.

Stavros stood from his desk. "Bring the rider to me immediately."

The man snapped to attention. "Yes, Lord Stavros. He's on his way up as we speak. The Bastion sent him on Cora, so the message must be urgent."

Stavros thanked the soldier and dismissed him, grateful that he no longer had to discuss fictional dragons with Alicos. Normally, he would receive a weekly written report from Commander Cirilo regarding the Bastion's training and readiness, including any accidents or deaths in the mountain. The last time the Bastion had sent their prized mare to deliver a message, a massive horde of gnolls had wandered into the lower plains. Over a thousand of the feral creatures attacked both livestock and farmers, too numerous for a few dozen Acolytes to contain. Alicos dispatched the entire Tenth Infantry Brigade and within a few days had routed the entire horde and scattered the savage monsters past the southern hills. Many lives, mostly civilian, had been lost, but far more would have been killed if the message had been delivered too slow to stop gnolls before they spread.

While Stavros waited, he once again turned his attention to the maps spread on his table. Each distinct location reminded him of a battle or an adventure he'd undertaken with his loyal Acolytes. He chuckled at the thought of the rash man he'd been in his youth, diving headfirst into danger before considering the repercussions.

Then his attention went to the location on the map labeled "Jallfoss." So much death had come from that place. He'd been throwing Acolytes at it for decades, but he was still no closer to breaking past the magic than when he started so many years ago. The forces sleeping in that mountain range were far more dangerous than a few thousand animated skeletons. Only he could fathom the destruction that would befall Ikrit and the rest of the world if those forces were ever released.

The Akşam Xiphos he'd given to Commander Cirilo should have been able to break the curse. Unfortunately, it was only effective at harvesting Vitus, so the Commander of the Bastion had gifted it to one of his Master Acolytes. Stavros would need to double his research until the enchantment became effective.

Two tower guards and a man with an Acolyte tunic entered the room. The man was covered in sweat and exhausted from the long journey.

He lowered his eyes as he addressed his Emperor. Stavros could tell from the rasp in his voice that the man had been riding for hours. "My Lord, I am Acolyte First Class Abderus. I bring an urgent message from Commander Cirilo."

Stavros nodded for the man to continue.

"A single Acolyte has returned from Jallfoss. He's gravely injured and claims that Masters Sigurjon and Jacoby, along with their students, have been killed. He believes Masters Tekşan and Allito have met the same fate."

The man's voice faltered, but he cleared his throat and continued. "What's more, he claims they were ambushed by powerful skeletons that could talk. We don't know if it's a fever dream, but we've already sent riders to Jallfoss to confirm."

"Where is the injured Acolyte? What have the healers done?" Stavros questioned.

"The boy is at the healing ward. The infection has gone into his blood. We're trying to save him, but Commander Cirilo doesn't have much hope. It's been three days since a farmer delivered him to our door. If the young Acolyte is not already dead, I fear he will be soon."

Stavros contemplated the Acolyte's words, but he had no further questions he felt the man could answer. "You have done well, Abderus. I appreciate your dedication to your duty. Rest tonight before your return in the morning."

He finished the last of his tea and addressed the two guards who entered with the Acolyte. "Ready two horses for me. I will depart immediately."

"Yes, Lord Stavros," the guards and Abderus responded in unison before leaving the room.

The journey on horseback would be hard on his body. Conjuration was the one school of magic he had yet to master, so it would take him considerable effort to summon a beast that could deliver him to the Bastion any faster than a horse. He could fly himself, but sustaining the magic at his age over that distance would drain him substantially, and he didn't know how much Vitus he would need when he arrived. No, he decided, a horse was the best available method of travel.

He donned his travel robes and switched into a sturdy pair of riding boots. Behind his desk, he pulled up one of the carpets to reveal the marble floor. He knelt on the hard surface and pressed his palms to the cold stone.

Nullify

Flowstone

The marble liquified and swirled, receding in a wave to reveal a cavity in the floor.

Stavros reached into the shallow hole and pulled out a heavy book with a weathered leather cover. He ran his fingers along the tome's spine, reading the ancient symbols, then quickly strapped it in a pouch on his leather belt.

The magic in Jallfoss was ever-changing but always unforgiving. Had the Acolytes been careless, or had the enemy finally returned? Only the boy could answer that question.

There was no time to waste. Stavros sealed the marble floor and sped from the room.

CHAPTER 29

The wooden shafts of both the arrow and the javelin splintered on impact. Ox's chunk of marble pillar shattered on the golem's rock armor. None of the attacks had any effect.

Buddy's blue fireball hit the machine in the center of its chest and enveloped its torso. The golem paused for a moment as if taking a breath. Then the blue fire turned red and sucked inside the cavity of its chest. The orange glow from its torso pulsated brighter than before as it advanced.

Haruspex

Name: Smyrna's Guardian

Description: Golem, Dwarven Construct

Hardness 14, Structure 450/450

Vitus: None

Attributes: Unknown

Damage Resistance: Unknown

Lore: The famous engineer Smyrna Skibibidi created this golem to protect the dwarven stronghold of Lundarbrekka. Constructed with a thick layer of an unknown dwarven alloy and enchanted

with powerful magic, this golem is extremely hostile to all intruders

The golem was too strong for Henry's Tier III Haruspex to reveal its Attributes and Damage Resistance. That was a bad sign, but Henry continued to scan the construct, hoping his Perception would reveal a weakness. He needed *something*, but he didn't know what.

"We'll need muscle to take this thing down." Ox dashed at the golem with his hammer raised before Henry could issue a protest. He covered the distance between them in a few quick steps and landed a heavy blow just above its hip. Ox activated the force magic in his weapon and slammed the block of steel into the golem's chest. Its armor cracked, but the force wave turned red and instead of projecting out, it distorted and was sucked back into the monster, just like Buddy's fire. The cracks in its exterior quickly sealed shut.

Ox cocked back his hammer to deliver another strike, but the golem lifted an arm across its chest and swatted him with a hefty backhand. The powerful blow caught Ox flush and sent him tumbling. He rolled head over feet and smashed into a dwarven cage. Muji scurried out of the way just in time to avoid being crushed, scrambling into a nearby crack in the room's exterior.

Buddy, Henry, and Beast all stared in disbelief at the skeleton propped against the broken cage. He was out cold with splintered bones sticking from his armor.

Beast opened her jaw and a terrifying scream reverberated from her skull. The sound hit Henry like Buddy's force spell. For once, he was thankful he didn't have organs for fear that her shriek would have burst his eardrums.

Henry couldn't tell if her rage was at the golem or at Ox

for getting dispatched so quickly. She turned and sprinted toward their adversary, teleporting in short increments as she rushed. She moved so rapidly that Henry had trouble following her movements. The golem swung at her, but it couldn't match her speed. She hacked at its legs and spiraled her way up its body, delivering a continuous assault of slashes and leaving behind thick blotches of frost on the golem's back armor. The rough metal creaked and heavy plates ground against each other as the dagger's magic froze the joints below in place.

Her daggers would have flayed the skin from any living being, but they couldn't do much damage to the rock golem's craggy exterior. Still, there was a silver lining. Even if she wasn't hurting it, her daggers had slowed it enough to give Henry and Buddy time to do real damage.

Henry pointed to the chunks of pillar near the mage. "Buddy, same plan as with the amalagator, just no direct magic." Then he ran toward the golem to add to Beast's distraction.

"You mean *amalgamator*," Buddy shouted after him, lifting three chunks of pillar with his magic. "Beast, incoming!" Buddy launched the rocks, and they smashed into the golem, forcing it to stumble backward. Muji crawled out of a hole above the cage that supported Ox's crumpled body and began breaking off loose pieces of the wall and throwing them. He was clearly determined to help the skeletons, even if his attacks could neither reach nor damage the golem.

Henry and Beast distracted the golem as the battle shifted through the room. Their blades were useless, so they didn't bother striking, but their movements were enough to occupy the golem's focus while Buddy attacked. The continuous assault by the pillar chunks was starting to have an effect, and cracks streaked over its armor. The skeletons had the golem corralled to the center of the room. It paused as the orange fire in its chest dimmed and began pulsing.

A second later, the glow faded completely, and Henry thought that it had run out of power. He lowered his shield to get a better look, but the golem's frozen joints turned red, and its chest flared with a blinding white emission. A torrid wave of heat blasted from its body.

Henry couldn't evade the attack. There was nowhere to jump, no cover from the spreading emulsion. Strangely, it wasn't heat that he felt, but fingers of electricity that connected to his legs and ran up his bones and armor. His vision seized shut and his muscles spasmed. The acrid smell of burning flesh filled his nose as Henry willed his body to move in vain.

The blast from the golem wracked his body, but as the effect receded, Henry quickly regained control of his movements. He opened his eyes, preparing to evade or attack, but his adversary and the other skeletons were gone. The dwarven storeroom was now an open expanse of desert.

Sand blasted his body, which was once again protected by nothing more than thin cloth. The sun assaulted his eyes, making him wince and cover them as they adjusted.

Not this again. We're fighting the golem. I have to help!

He looked around and saw nothing but sand dunes. Memories of his previous trip to the otherworldly desert flooded his mind. The yellow stone with blue and gold veins was still there at his feet. He reached down to grab it, expecting to be transported back to the fight, but now . . . nothing happened.

He smacked the stone with his palm, then grabbed the edges and tried to pull it free, but it didn't budge. He even dug his hands into the sand and tried to excavate it. Sweat poured from his brow and dripped onto the stone as he dug. Muscles like corded iron now wrapped his bones, giving a huge edge to his Strength and Fortitude, but his efforts still produced little result. The stone turned into a boulder as he flung away handfuls of the burning desert, giving no indication that he would be able to unearth it.

Most of the stone was a dark yellow and almost looked like opaque glass. Metallic-blue veins snaked across its surface, and there were mineral deposits of brown, gold, and red weaving through the rough, faceted structure.

The searing heat was quickly draining him, and the sweat pouring from his body brought attention to a growing thirst. He'd only exposed a few feet of the stone, and he knew he needed shelter and water . . . preferably sooner than later. Begrudgingly, he picked the direction that he felt he had originally been traveling in and started walking.

Hours passed, and his thirst grew. His skin turned red and blistered as he walked. His eyes strained through the intense brightness, making it harder to pick his way through the blowing landscape.

He pressed forward, willing himself ahead, until a dark shadow rolled over him. He looked up, hoping but also fearing to see whatever had flown over him earlier, but instead, clouds now covered the sun. Henry welcomed the relief, but his skin still burned from the blistering heat. As quickly as the clouds came in, the wind died down to a small breeze and the sand and dust settled back to the desert floor.

Miles of rolling sand dunes surrounded him as far as he could see. An endless sea of desert stretched to every horizon. Thick black clouds had broiled into a massive thunderhead, rapidly spreading across the sky. Beams of sunlight splayed through the cumulous, and the storm's shadow rolled behind him so quickly that the retreating light appeared to flee from the encroaching weather.

Henry marveled at the building tempest, unable to take his gaze from the cloud that grew with an inner strength unmatched by any earthly force. A cool breeze struck his face, and he sucked in a deep breath through his nose, filling his lungs with air that carried a sweet scent—pungent, but in a good way that reminded him of something his foggy mind couldn't quite grasp.

Thunder rumbled deep within the billowing storm, and the clouds lit up with hidden lightning strikes high in the atmosphere. The distant horizon quickly blackened as the cloud's intensity grew, but something below the storm caught Henry's attention. It was far away, but it was definitely a structure of some sort. Though close to the direction he had been walking, he probably would have passed right by it had the dust storm not abated.

Another rumble of thunder, much louder this time, was all the incentive Henry needed to get moving. The heat from the sun had been painful, and Henry was thankful for its departure, but he was sure he didn't want to get caught out in the open during the imminent downpour.

The storm, however, had different plans. A single thick droplet of water smacked into Henry's forehead. It was large enough to run down his face and over his cracked lips. He savored the salty moisture, though it did little to wet his parched throat. He yearned for a drink, and the storm obliged.

What started as a few drops quickly developed into a heavy deluge. The wind picked up again and pelted him with rain drops of the same intensity as that from the sandstorm.

The rain obscured his vision, but occasional lightning strikes lit the stone structure as he moved forward, giving him brief flashes of his destination. As he neared, he saw a natural outcropping of dark gray rock jutting from the desert floor. Spikes of stone protruded from the ground at harsh angles, like the remains of a broken clay pot. The rain came down harder, pelting his face as the wind grew to a furious gale. Henry tried to pick up his speed, but his footing grew more precarious as the rain formed lakes in the troughs between dunes and small waterfalls dumped gallons at a time from the crests.

Lightning struck all around him, roaring in his ears and leaving his eyes nearly blind from the intense flashes, motivating him once more to pick up the pace. At a full run, he fell several times, tumbling hard. The sand was forgiving, even though the water threatened to sweep him away at times. The thick muscles in his arms and legs were much more resilient than his skeletal body, and he even welcomed the pain that came with his flesh.

Gray stone spikes crossed each other like thorns on a jungle vine. He ran past the first few until the sand was replaced with sloping rock. Slick from the heavy rain, the uneven ground caused Henry to stumble several times. He frantically searched for any sort of cover from the fierce elements.

Lightning struck close, roaring in his ears, and revealed the gaping maw of a giant beast. Henry reached for his sword but came up empty before realizing that the monster was nothing more than an outcropping of yellow stone; similar to the one he'd uncovered in the desert sand, but much bigger. The grouping of stones was nearly twenty feet tall, and the natural growth had a large, man-sized cave at the base. Jagged shards of yellow and blue that Henry had originally thought were teeth blocked the cave's entrance, leaving so little space that even a gnome couldn't squeeze through.

Henry was soaked but excited to find shelter. He slowed to

a walk and searched for a way into the cave, but a searing bolt of white-and-blue lightning struck the top of the yellow structure. The yellow rock absorbed the energy, lighting up nearly as bright as the desert sun. Streams of electricity followed through the blue metallic veins before exiting near the mouth of the cave and arcing directly at Henry.

The pain from the lightning was much more intense this time, and a split second before Henry's eyes slammed shut, the cave was illuminated. It was little deeper than it was tall, but Henry could clearly see the shadow of a hunched man huddled in the far corner.

Status Effect:

> **Second Path of the Desert. STR - 3, MOB -3, Max Health -5, Fire Resistance -5, Lightning Resistance +5**

Henry dismissed the notification. His head spun, and searing pain spasmed through his body, though it quickly faded. He felt weak and sluggish but didn't have long to focus on himself. The sound of smashing rock and the roar of the golem's engine quickly reminded him of the ongoing battle. He brought himself up on unsteady legs, noticing scorch marks on his bones and armor, but at last he was back in the fight.

Beast and Buddy continued to fend off the construct, though they had done little more than slight damage to the heavily armored foe. Beast rolled under a wild swipe from the automaton as Buddy caught it in the shoulder with another chunk of broken pillar. The orange fire in the golem's chest dimmed and Henry lifted his shield, preparing for another heat blast, but none came. Instead, he felt a heavy tug on his body as if a wave had just hit him from behind.

Harden

He directed magic to his legs and resisted the pull, though Beast and Buddy were much closer to the construct, and the torrent caught them off guard. The magic sucked the other two skeletons through the air right at the deadly machine. Beast was only a short distance away, and the golem grabbed her with its stony fingers. The construct squeezed, and Henry heard bones snapping. She screamed, and once again, Henry couldn't tell its source, be it pain or anger.

A moment later the golem had Buddy in its grasp. He and Beast struggled in vain to free themselves as their spells failed with loud pops.

The realization hit Henry like a brick to the dome. Not only could the machine absorb spells, but it could also drain Vitus. The cracks in its rocky skin started to close, and Henry knew he had to get his friends out of its grip. *If it killed them, could they return?* He wondered. *Or would they stay dead like the smashed bodies scattered through the golem's home?*

Henry sheathed his sword and tightened his grip on the leather straps of his shield. He couldn't slice the golem, but he could smash it. He directed his Vitus to fortify his bones, then bent his legs and prepared for a rush.

Harden

Blitz

The room blurred as he launched himself at the golem. He leapt and caught the machine directly in its midsection. The force from the shield bash knocked the golem back, forcing it to drop its helpless prey.

Beast lay limp. Buddy struggled to regain his footing. Henry stood between them and knew they needed time to recover. He charged his body for another assault and rammed the golem, sending it stumbling again. He bashed it over and over. It tried to retaliate, but he kept up the continuous attack even as his shield crumbled and his Vitus dropped dangerously low. Every Blitz drained him significantly, but there was still a glimmer of hope. The golem was collapsing under his blows. Finally, its heart dimmed to a dull orange. Henry relented—just for a moment, but the pause was all the machine needed.

By the time Henry saw the blow coming, it was too late to dodge. He could only plant his feet and brace himself. The stone fist hit him with the force of a bull. Though his Vitus absorbed some of the wallop, the strike sent him tumbling through the room. He skidded across the granite floor and smashed into the wall as flashes of light filled his vision—both from the impact and from glyphs.

Status Effect: Stunned (Moderate) MOB -10%, PER -10%

Henry shook his head to clear it and looked up to see Beast pulling herself away from the enemy. The golem raised both of its arms and brought them down hard to crush the elf.

Though the construct had mangled the bones of her torso, Beast kept a grip on her daggers. She rolled to her back and prepared them for a final strike against the automaton, knowing her blades would have little effect. Black metal fists descended with the force of an avalanche. Henry's heart caught in his throat—Ox's hands caught the golem's attack.

The giant skeleton towered over Beast. Ox had blocked the death blow, though the impact sent bone shards flying in all directions. His forearms shattered, his spine bowed, and his leg bones snapped. The only things holding Ox's body together were magic and hope, but that was enough.

Ox spread his healing magic through his body, mending his bones back together. "It's not nice to hit a lady," he yelled, and he pressed with his shoulders, lifting the golem's hands.

The golem forced itself back against the skeleton as its chest glowed brighter. Henry knew it was absorbing Ox's Vitus, and Ox must have felt it too. His yell roared over the hum of the golem's engine as his bones broke and mended in a continuous cycle of agony.

"Henry, your sword." Buddy was trying to pull a healing crystal from his bandolier, but his arms and hands had been crushed.

Why hadn't he thought of that? If the xiphos could steal magic from humans, maybe it could do the same to the golem. The problem, however, was that Henry had too little Vitus for another Blitz. A normal attack was likely to fail, resulting in a crushing death for him as well as Ox and Beast.

Henry needed Vitus, and he needed it fast. He thought back to his conversation with Olafur in the dwarven baths. The gnome had talked about using Vitus to restore that of another. Like Ox and the gnome, Henry was a transmuter. If Ox could turn Vitus into Health, maybe Henry could use the gnome's technique to do the opposite.

Henry focused his magic through his bones. Instead of using it to repair his body, he willed the magic to sap his Health and focus the deficit back to his core. His bones creaked, and he felt ill as he transferred the flow of magic to his mind.

Sacrifice

Ability Discovered: Sacrifice I. Pain comes from the body. Suffering, from the mind. Trade a portion of your Health for a lesser amount of Vitus. Damage Resistance (Mind) +1, Max Vitus +1, +1 Vitus per 3 Health sacrificed

It worked.

Henry had enough Vitus for a single thrust.

Ox was out of healing magic but not out of willpower. He continued his battle cry, holding back the golem's mass with sheer determination. Henry dropped the remains of his shield and drew his sword. He cocked his arm, bent his legs, and shot forward, covering the distance in a flash.

Blitz

Ability Discovered: Bli . . .

Go away!

Henry nearly shouted at the intruding glyph as he dismissed its notification and pressed the attack.

The golem's chest flared bright red after absorbing all of Ox's magic. Henry aimed between two gears, hoping to disrupt as much of its inner workings as possible. His sword screeched against a black, skull-sized flow crystal as it caught in the inner mechanism. Sparks sprayed Henry's face from metal grinding against metal. Fighting against the sheer size of the golem and its inner workings, he held his sword tight as the golem lifted its arms and stumbled.

Giant metal fists pounded Henry. He absorbed the golem's magic and used Harden to fortify his body, but the damage was beyond what he could take, and once again, the monster sent him tumbling. The golem clawed at its chest, though its arms were too long and its fingers too thick to allow it to pluck the sword from its torso.

Two pillar chunks smashed into the golem, sending it reeling and nearly toppling over. Buddy had managed to heal himself and regenerate his magic with the last of his flow crystals, and now he launched an onslaught of rubble at the foe. With every impact, more cracks appeared in the rock armor, and flashes of red and orange erupted from fissures in its black stone skin.

For the moment, the mage held the golem at bay, but the relentless attack forced him to spend Vitus at an incredible rate.

Ox still wasn't moving, and Beast had crawled over to him and was shaking his skull, trying to get a response. Henry didn't bother searching his pack for a healing crystal to give to the giant skeleton—he knew he was out.

Buddy lifted a massive block of stone with his remaining force magic, but the golem had one last trick. Its engine hummed, and a wave of magic blasted from the golem. Buddy's rock crashed to the ground and it pounced, grabbing the mage with both hands. Its chest flickered with Henry's sword still wedged tight. Henry thought the only thing keeping the construct standing was the Vitus it was stealing from the mage.

Using all his magic to avoid being crushed, Buddy couldn't return an attack. He would be drained in a few seconds and dead immediately after that. Henry knew he had to get Ox and Buddy's Vitus recharged, but he had no magic left to get himself close to his sword.

A quick glance at his Health bar revealed he had taken considerable damage, and his fatigue and the weakness of his bones confirmed the punishment from the golem's heavy strikes. Somehow, he was still able to stand. If he converted most of his Health to Vitus, he would be able to attack once and hopefully free Buddy.

On the bright side, the xiphos was stopping the monster from healing, and the cracks in its armor had gotten so severe that pieces of its body were falling off. Could he distract the monster long enough to let the sword drain it completely?

He had to try. If the skeletons failed here, the mountain would return to its endless cycle of death. The dwarves would be overrun by monsters, and the humans would eventually reach the Source Crystal and unleash the Necromancer. Henry couldn't let that happen.

He began pulling Health from his bones, praying to whatever gods could hear him that Buddy could hold out just a bit longer. The tempest in his core swelled with arcane energy as Henry beseeched his body to give him whatever it had left. As his Health trickled down, a shrill chirp pierced through the chamber and halted the spell's ravaging effects.

"Beak!" The trogold's cry echoed over the sounds of battle.

The room went still. The only noise was the unsteady hum of the golem's engine and that of its gears grinding against Henry's xiphos. The golem suspended its drain on Buddy's magic and turned its body to locate the source of the squeak. Muji stood on the broken pillar near the entrance. He bared his teeth, and his fur stood on end. He looked ferocious, determined. The two-foot trogold was ready to fight Smyrna's Guardian.

Muji was carrying something, and it took Henry a second to realize the trogold held the Magma Blaster in its tiny hands. The Blaster wasn't large, roughly the size of Henry's forearm, but the cave creature held it like an archer would a heavy crossbow. He pushed the metal loop forward, clicking it into position. The Blaster glowed a brilliant crimson and discharged a ray of concentrated fire from the end, catching the golem in the middle of its chest. The Blaster's emission sounded like the steady thrum of a hummingbird's wings, only a thousand times louder.

The golem tossed Buddy aside and tried to move clear of the beam, but Henry's xiphos had effectively bled the machine dry of its magical life force and greatly weakened its Mobility. The jet of fire from the Magma Blaster wavered as the trogold fought to steady its force. Muji snarled and clicked the handle forward again. The beam's intensity and volume expanded, and Henry sensed the temperature of the room rising.

The golem held up its arms to block the beam and took a step forward, but it was starting to glow. Muji clicked the loop forward a third time, and a ball of energy traveled along the beam and bored into the construct. The machine halted its advance as fire roared through the cracks in its rock armor.

Muji struggled to hold the device, but he lowered his body and leaned forward, wrapping his fingers around the metal loop for a tighter grip. "BEAK!" the trogold cried as he clicked the lever forward a final time. A spiral of flame shot from the tip of the Magma Blaster and spun around the beam. The blast was too powerful for Muji to hold, and the trogold, along with the Blaster, flew backward and hit the chamber wall.

The tip of the Blaster pointed up and shot the beam through the ceiling before it winked out, but it had done its job. The golem flailed backward with a melted hole in its chest. It toppled over, taking out two of the pillars supporting the room's ceiling. The hilt and pommel of Henry's xiphos fell to the ground, its blade melted by the heat of the Blaster and the golem's engine.

They were alive, but there was no time to celebrate. The Blaster's beam and the toppling of two pillars were enough to bring down the room. The floor shook, and huge chunks of rock fell from the roof.

"The Bracers!" Buddy yelled as he stood on unsteady legs.

Henry leapt over downed pillars and dodged falling rocks. He skidded to a stop next to the armored dwarven skeleton and grabbed the enchanted armor. He pulled with the little Strength remaining in his bones, and both the Bracers and the dwarven bones inside ripped free from the corpse. Then he turned and sprinted to where Beast and Ox were recovering.

Ox was awake but hurting. Beast had one of his arms around her shoulder and was trying to drag the giant out of the hall. Henry grabbed Ox's other arm and helped Beast with a combination of supporting and dragging the huge skeleton. Rocks smashed against the marble floor around them, but, out of options, they pressed forward.

Buddy helped them through the arched doorway, then hobbled as quickly as he could to retrieve the Magma Blaster. Muji lay on the ground near it, unconscious. Buddy stared at the trogold while the hall crashed down around him. The fur around Muji's pink ears was singed black, and his tiny hands were blistered from the Blaster's heat. The mage bent down and claimed the Blaster, then grabbed the trogold by his scruff and ran out of the crumbling storeroom.

CHAPTER 30

"**B**y the time we got him to the healers, the infection had already gone to his blood." Commander Cirilo led Lord Stavros down the halls of the Bastion's healing ward. "We've kept his wounds clean to give him time to talk to you, but there's nothing more we can do for him. The injuries are beyond our capabilities to mend."

Most of the Acolytes hadn't expected Lord Stavros to personally meet the boy. In his old age, the Emperor rarely left the walls of Ikrit. Commander Cirilo, however, knew Lord Stavros would come. He'd been in battle with the Great Lord many times in his younger days and knew how important the happenings in Jallfoss really were. It was so much more than the deadly training ground they used to build their Acolytes.

Commander Cirilo had waited at the Bastion's gates to escort his Emperor to the wounded Acolyte as soon as he arrived. He'd expected the boy to be dead before Lord Stavros had a chance to speak with him, but like a true Acolyte, he held out. Koş could barely form words with the blood in his lungs, so Cirilo relayed his account as they walked.

"Can you confirm his story?" Stavros asked. He and Cirilo

quickly made their way through the main hallway of the stronghold. It wasn't fancy, but it was functional. A single faded carpet ran the length of the hall between stone walls and arches. Along the wall on the left were all the banners of the different Brigades that the Acolytes could be sent to after their initial training. Ceremonial weapons hung on the right.

Two guards opened wooden doors for Stavros and the Commander as they passed. The younger Acolytes had never seen the Great Lord, but they knew who he was immediately. Even in his old age, the man held himself with a powerful sense of authority. The Acolytes gave their Emperor and Commander a slight bow as they walked by. Stavros returned a gentle smile. He was in a hurry, but he made a mental note to return and talk to the younger soldiers. He'd found that a simple conversation and showing concern for the troops went a long way to bolster morale.

"No, we wouldn't have expected them back for a few more days," Commander Cirilo replied. "If he was a deserter, he wouldn't have returned here. I believe him and recommend taking him seriously."

Stavros followed Cirilo into the Bastion's ward. Dozens of beds lined either side of an open bay. The ward was primarily used to treat injured recruits, but it was large enough to serve as a contingency hospital for emergencies in the area. They continued past the bay to a series of private rooms usually reserved for critical or contagious patients and stopped before one of the wooden doors.

"What is his name?" Stavros asked.

"Koş Vasilios," the Commander replied. "His handle is 'Smooch,' but he hates being called that."

Stavros smiled. "I believe I would prefer the Vasilios name as well. He comes from a lineage of heroes."

"May the sun shine on the memories of our lost champions." Cirilo tried to match the Emperor's smile.

"Sadly, Commander, when it comes to the infernal caves of Jallfoss, there is no sun under the mountain."

Commander Cirilo nodded and opened the door. Koş lay on a bed in the middle of the small chamber. He was sitting up, propped on pillows to help him breathe. Two healers stood beside his bed cleaning his wounds and changing bandages. They went to stand when Lord Stavros walked in, but he motioned for them to keep working.

"Koş," Lord Stavros said quietly, assessing the wounded soldier's Status. His Health was all but gone, and the Severe Status Effects threatened to take him at any moment.

The boy's eyes opened weakly, and a smile cracked on his lips. "Lord Stavros, I'm sorry I can't stand for you," he wheezed.

"You have borne the weight of the entire Bastion on your shoulders. I am the one that stands in your honor, my boy." Lord Stavros bowed.

Koş tried to respond, but he coughed instead. The healers wiped drops of blood from his mouth.

Stavros turned to the Commander. "Thank you, Cirilo. You and the healers may leave. I need to speak to him privately." Cirilo bowed and left. The healers collected their gear, and Stavros thanked them for their efforts.

When the door shut, he walked to the side of the bed and sat down next to the wounded Acolyte. "Koş Vasilios," he began, his gaze distant, "I hoped it wasn't true, but the resemblance is unmistakable. You are the grandchild of Risto Vasilios. He and I fought side by side many, many years ago, and he saved my life more times than I have fingers."

The words were a blessing to Koş. Everything his grandfather had told him about Lord Stavros was true.

The Great Lord continued, "He would be very proud of you. I remember him bragging about his first son, Phylo. Was that your father?"

Koş nodded weakly.

"He was so delighted when he told me about his child. What made it even more memorable was that we were fighting a horde of goblins in the east marshes. Between slashes, he told me that his wife had just had a beautiful baby. He retired shortly thereafter, but I was always grateful for both his sword and his loyalty."

Koş fought back tears of pride as the most powerful man in the known world paid tribute to his grandfather. After considerable effort, he rallied the Strength to speak. "Lord Stavros, my grandfather told us so many stories of your adventures. It has always been my dream to study in the Citadel and one day serve you." The strain on him just to quietly whisper was immense, and he had to close his eyes to stop the nausea.

"I could only be so lucky to have one as dedicated as you at my side. You have already done more than should have been asked of you, and I am truly grateful." Lord Stavros stood from his seat and looked down at the boy. He unclasped the leather that secured the spell book to his side. "Now, I must ask one final task of you."

Stavros opened his book and held it in front of him. "I need you to show me the one that did this." The leather creaked from years of nonuse. He flipped through the stiff pages and found what he was looking for. Written in the old language was the spell he needed.

Stavros touched his Drift Amulet beneath his robes, then put his hand on Koş's forehead. He felt the heat from the boy's fever as sweat dripped down his face. Koş didn't have the Strength to open his eyes.

The Emperor read the passage and used his magic to reach deep into Koş's soul. It was weak, but eventually he found what he needed. He pulled on Koş's Essence, using the Amulet to bring it into his own body.

Koş breathed in deeply, and his chest expanded with a hoarse gurgle. Then he slowly exhaled his last breath. His heart stopped beating, and his body turned pale. His skin weathered and aged a decade in an instant, but he was young enough that it would hardly be noticeable to the healers. Stavros felt the youth's vitality flow into his soul, adding years of Fortitude to his bones and muscles, and clearing the fog of age from his mind. His senses sharpened, and the wrinkles on his face smoothed ever so slightly.

The Emperor pulled the last bit of Essence from the Acolyte's body and felt Koş's pride flow into his mind. He had died with a sense of purpose. After hearing Stavros's words, Koş was able to accept his death, knowing he had made a difference for all of Ikrit.

"Show yourself," the Emperor beckoned, and followed the stream of the boy's fading thoughts, but he wasn't after Koş's mind. Stavros searched through the flow to find the skeleton. His mind went to a small dwelling in Ammerthall. He could tell its location by the red sandstone walls, but there was no emotion, no thought. He'd been there before and probably killed that very undead several times over, though Stavros knew it wasn't sentient.

There must be more, he thought as he pushed his mind further. *Where are you?*

"Henry!" The woman's cry echoed through Stavros's head, and he felt desperation. Fire shone before him as tongues of flame licked his skin. The blaze faded, and he felt Henry's mind. The skeleton was thankful for his friends. He was proud of what they had accomplished. And he was determined to get to the Empress and wake all the skeletons in Jallfoss.

The skeleton resisted, and the connection broke, more forcefully than Stavros expected. Though the skeleton would know Stavros's intent, the information he retrieved had made the risk worth it. The young Acolyte's story was true, and the situation was even more dire than he had expected. The skeletons were gaining power and posed a danger to his Acolytes and the entire nation of Ikrit. They had the means and the intent to revive the Celestrial. It would be a disaster.

He pulled in a deep breath and splayed his fingers, savoring the feeling that came from stretching rejuvenated ligaments. He felt stronger, younger, after taking the boy's life. Now it was time to act. He looked at Koş's one last time, then left the room.

Commander Cirilo waited for him in the hallway.

"Promote him to Acolyte First Class and bury him with full honors," Stavros calmly told Commander Cirilo. "The boy is a hero and will be remembered as such."

"I've already begun preparing his commemoration, but if I may, did he give you anything useful?"

Stavros stopped to address the Commander. "Yes, Cirilo, and it is terrible indeed. You were right to notify me. I have a mission for you to undertake personally. The undead have come back to life and are headed to kill the Empress's ghost, which is the only thing holding back the Necromancer. You must stop them at all costs. Gather your team and head out immediately."

"Yes, Lord Stavros," Commander Cirilo said. "We'll depart at once."

CHAPTER 31

With broken bones and dangerously low Health and Vitus, the four skeletons made their way to the quartz pillar cave. Soul Anchor and a Tier increase rejuvenated their bodies, but their minds were still weary from the battle with Smyrna's golem. Ox, however, was in a surprisingly chipper mood.

"If Buddy gets a thrall, I think I should have one too." Ox raised a hand to protect the amalgamator skull that rested on his shoulder plate. His giant palm failed to block the stone that Beast chucked, and the rock plinked off the creature's forehead.

"That's an abomination, not a thrall, and you're an idiot." Beast considered teleporting behind Ox and forcefully removing both skulls from the giant's shoulders, but the battle with the golem had taken a heavy toll on her body. The argument with Ox wasn't helping her recovery.

"Once again, I designate you as the grumpy minion," Ox chided, but Henry sensed the slight waver in his voice. He had taken the most damage from the monstrosity. However, he seemed more content with antagonizing Beast than recuperating. When they had returned to the quartz chamber to make camp, Ox had removed the rusty sword that held the amalgamator's skull to the ground and torn off the hand bones it used for legs. Upon placement on Ox's pauldron, the monster's skull had grafted itself to his mail but was unable to possess either the armor or the brutish skeleton.

"His name is *Gator*. It's Centaur for 'wise one.'" Ox tapped the skull on the forehead as it tried to chomp at his finger. Henry doubted Ox knew any words in Centaur, or if horse-people even existed in the first place.

With a heavy sigh of exasperation, Beast turned back to the small fire and crossed her arms over her chest.

Henry started a blaze from scraps of wood pulled from one of the dwarven carts nearby. It wasn't much, but the meager flames helped calm their racing minds. They had barely escaped the dwarven storeroom in one piece. Somehow, all four members of their group had survived. No, all five.

Muji lay curled in a ball on Buddy's lap. The mage no longer shooed him away. Instead, the mage had actually found water for the trogold and ensured he wasn't hurt.

They hadn't expected the guardian of the storeroom to be immune to magic or for the Blaster to be such a powerful weapon. From Thorodd's description, Henry had assumed it was a pilot light for the forges. He now understood what the item was truly capable of. Though he was gaining power quickly, he still had a lot to learn.

After destroying the automaton, all the skeletons were well into Tier 9. The accompanying recovery from the Tier increase was much needed, as they were out of healing crystals. Even more impressive was Muji's gain. Because the trogold had worn an Amulet when he defeated the golem, he was now at Tier **15**. Henry wondered what else the trogold was capable of.

Henry had tucked the Flow Bracers and the Magma Blaster

safely in his pack. He didn't want Muji to accidentally activate either while nestling in Buddy's rucksack. If the Bracers were as powerful as Thorodd claimed, an accidental activation could be disastrous. Henry didn't have the energy to identify it with Haruspex, let alone address the myriad glyphs that waited impatiently for his attention.

Henry stared into the fire. Red and orange flames flickered over the splintered wood. He remembered the woman's voice calling his name. Looking at the other three skeletons and the trogold, he was thankful they had joined him. Now, they had to make it to the Empress. If they could revive her, there might be a chance to save all of Jallfoss. The feelings of gratitude and determination faded as the world around Henry warped and spiraled.

His mind flowed up from the cave, through solid rock and into the city of Ammerthall. His awareness led him back to the dwelling where he had started, but now he felt only the blank mind of an undead. There were no thoughts or emotions. Henry knew that empty feeling well.

He had become accustomed to the sensation of absorbing another's thoughts through his Drift Amulet, but the fact that no dead body rested at the end of his sword left him unprepared for the new experience. Even more strange, he felt he recognized the mind that was now connected to his. He had already killed this person. Snippets of memories—an imagined version of the Source Crystal—welled up from deep within the undead's subconscious and confirmed Henry's assumption.

His mind spun again. This time he felt himself being pulled out of the mountain. Pride swelled in his mind, along with a sense of accomplishment, then an acceptance of death. It was the Acolyte he'd fought at the top of the ramp. The boy was at peace and had thought about the Ikritian Emperor.

Then he felt the Acolyte's soul leave his body. Instead of the feeling dissipating as he had come to expect from the Soul Essence transfer, a shadow absorbed the soul of the Acolyte. Then the darkness turned its attention to Henry. It enveloped his psyche and surrounded him with a feeling of dread. It probed his thoughts, forcing him to open his mind.

Henry tried to resist. With every last point of his Resolve, Henry fought against the mental onslaught, but it was pointless. He might as well have been throwing rocks at a tidal wave.

The being pried the information from Henry's mind. It read him as easily as a book. Henry could almost hear his own thoughts. *The Flow Bracers can revive the Empress. She was the one that repelled the Necromancer, and she should be able to fix the mountain.*

At the word *Necromancer*, the being bristled. Distracted for a moment, Henry felt its hold on him weaken. He struck back, prying into the shadow's mind. There was anger and sadness, and a deep resounding loneliness. He didn't get much, besides one single word: *Stavros.*

It was the Emperor of Ikrit, and he knew where the skeletons were heading.

The connection broke, and Henry's mind returned to the crystal cave. He reached for his sword out of instinct but found the sheath empty. It had been the most intense, most terrifying experience he could remember. As distinct as the desert visions, but emotionally, far more powerful and ominous. The other three skeletons looked at him, concerned. Even Muji gave him a curious expression.

"Another dream of the woman's voice?" Buddy asked. "I didn't even know you had fallen asleep."

"No." Henry looked for the words to explain what had just happened. "Do you remember the Acolyte that I hit with the spear when we first met Ox?"

"Vaguely," the mage responded.

Henry sighed deeply and tried to calm his nerves. "He just died."

"Then we can assume that time and distance do not affect the Amulet's connection for a kill. Interesting." Buddy scribbled the note in his tome.

Henry paused to collect his thoughts, then said, "No, it wasn't my javelin that killed him. It was Lord Stavros."

Buddy stopped writing and looked at Henry. "What do you mean?"

Henry clenched his fists to stop them from shaking. "The Emperor of Ikrit. He used the boy's death to pry into my mind. Lord Stavros is the Necromancer, and he's coming to stop us from reaching the Empress."

EPILOGUE

What a fitting way to die, battling in the dungeon he had spent his whole life exploring. He regretted not finding his father and grandfather. He would neither make it to the Source Crystal nor destroy the Necromancer and break the curse.

The thought left his head, never to return. Then everything was fog. There had been a moment of rage. Had he fought something? Had something attacked him? It all blurred together, and the harder he focused, the further it drifted from his grasp. A second could have been a year. With no thoughts or sensations to stir him, it didn't matter.

Then the floodgates in his mind opened. Henry, Stavros, Koş—they weren't his memories. An old man had killed a boy. A skeleton wanted to find a ghost. The rush of thought and emotion made little sense.

The world came into focus. He stood in a small room with red sandstone walls, surrounded by wooden debris. There were two men beside him. Green auras emanated from their bodies and flowed around them like fire consuming a tree. He began to speak, but a horrible taste hit his tongue, and he felt something in his mouth.

It was rotting flesh. He spat and choked. The muck hit the floor with a putrid *splat*. The man tried to expel the taste of decay, but it lingered on his tongue.

"Hey! What's going on?" he shouted at the men. "Who are you, and for that matter, who am I?"

No response came from the men. They remained completely still, covered in blood, stripped of their clothes, and staring ahead at nothing with milky, dead eyes.

He turned from the men and cried in shock to find a skeleton standing just a few feet away. He stumbled over the debris and fell to the floor. The skeleton didn't move. Like the two men, it didn't even react. Again, he tried to stand, but his muscles wouldn't support him, and he tumbled onto the dirty floor once again.

Shaking in pain and trying not to vomit, he lay in the rubble. After several minutes the nausea passed. Strange icons pulsated in front of him. He shooed them away and allowed his breathing to steady. As his vision slowly focused, a metal chain hanging from the side of his boot caught his attention. With trembling hands, he pulled a silver Amulet with a blue-and-red crystal from between his broken bootstraps and held it close to his face. A single word was etched into the silver backing.

"Jacoby." He read the inscription out loud. He didn't recognize the name, but since it was on the Amulet in his boot, he assumed it belonged to him.

His gaze left the jewel and settled on the shadowy depths of the skeleton's eyes. Its frozen visage captivated and horrified him. Jacoby turned from the deathly stare and spotted a weapon's hilt amongst the debris. He wrapped his fingers around the metal handle and pulled a rusty sword from the rubble littering the broken dwelling.

Jacoby brandished the weapon and addressed the undead around him. "What curse has befallen me?" he asked the haunted remains. He received no answer from the skeleton and rotting Acolytes.

If you enjoyed this book, please leave a review at your favorite online retailer's website!

Enthusiastic reviews from readers like you are incredibly helpful.

Thank you!

NEF HOUSE PUBLISHING

Discover more awesome fantasy and LitRPG at
www.nefhousepublishing.com